The Dance
Teacher of Paris

THE DANCE TEACHER OF PARIS

SUZANNE FORTIN

embla
books

First published in Great Britain in 2023 by

 **embla books**

Bonnier Books UK Limited
4ᵗʰ Floor, Victoria House, Bloomsbury Square, London, WC1B 4DA
Owned by Bonnier Books
Sveavägen 56, Stockholm, Sweden

A CIP catalogue record for this book is available from the British Library.

ISBN: 9781471415258

This book is typeset using Atomik ePublisher

Embla Books is an imprint of Bonnier Books UK
www.bonnierbooks.co.uk

To my children, Liam, Hayley, Ross and Esther and to my grandchildren, Albie and Elsie

Prologue

Fleur

Fleur sat down in her grandmother's chair, placing the satin ballet shoe on her lap and her hands gently on the armrests. Closing her eyes, she brushed her thumbs across the sun-faded upholstery. Whenever Fleur thought of her grandmother, Lydia, she always pictured her sitting here, in the crook of the bay window, looking out across the green with the sound of the sea lapping at the shoreline just beyond the next row of houses that enjoyed their superior sea-fronted position.

Fleur drew in a deep breath and could detect the faintest trace of Lydia's favourite perfume – one Fleur had bought for her on many a birthday. It was Rive Gauche by Yves Saint Laurent. Lydia had been wearing the 1970s classic for as long as Fleur could remember. It was only in the last few months that Fleur understood the significance behind the name of the fragrance, which referred to the southern side of the river Seine – the Left Bank. But then Fleur hadn't known very much about her grandmother's past until recently, certainly not the time during the war when Lydia was a ten-year-old child living in Paris under the German occupation and attending the school opposite what was now the Musée d'Orsay in the Left Bank district of the city.

Fleur released her breath and opened her eyes, her gaze settling on the Pierre Valois miniature watercolour hanging

1

in the alcove by the fireplace, depicting a ballerina at the barre. Another hidden connection to Lydia's past that had been in plain sight all these years.

Fleur's gaze travelled to the ballet shoe and her heart contracted as it had done ever since she'd found out the story behind it. The fabric was worn from hours of dancing and now delicate from the passing of time. The ribbon was frayed at the edges but still intact. It was a shoe that had graced the boards of the dance studio in Paris; pirouetting, skipping and hopping, rising and falling. It was a shoe that had held so much love and hope over many years. Another connection between past and present. A connection *for* Lydia and *to* Lydia. One Fleur knew she would always cherish, one that made her cry and made her smile, one that made her feel proud.

And, now that Fleur knew everything, it was also one that broke her heart.

Chapter 1

Adele

Paris, May 1942

Adele Basset looked up from the piano, calling out the sequence of steps to her dance class. Today was ballet and whilst her students aged between five and ten years old were probably never going to forge a career out of dancing, their unbridled enthusiasm and obvious delight made up for their lack of technical ability and natural grace.

Today the sun was shining in through the bank of full-length windows that lined the side of the studio, spotlighting the children and bouncing off the mirrored wall. The room could really do with a freshen up. The paint was peeling in one corner and two wooden floorboards needed replacing, having been repaired far too many times. However, paint and wood were scarce after two years of German occupation.

'*Et demi-plié*, knees over toes . . . Rise . . . *Et deuxiéme. Port de bras*, follow your arm to the side.' Adele called out the instructions above the sound of the piano. '*Excellent!* Daniel, *parfait!*' Strictly speaking, it wasn't excellent or perfect, but Adele had always been adamant her after-school dance lessons were not to reach perfection in performance, only perfection in joy.

What more could anyone ask for these children as the war in Europe raged on? The hour after school each day was an escape for them and for her after a long day teaching.

Here at the classes, through the medium of dance, they could be anything and anywhere they wanted. Goodness knows, they deserved the little pleasure and respite the hour brought – they had already witnessed horrors children had no right to see.

Adele rose from her position at the piano, gesturing with her hands for the children to carry on with the steps, just the way her own mother had taught her and her sister, Lucille. Their mother, Marianne, had been the most beautiful and skilled of dancers and trained with the *Ballet de l'Opéra national de Paris* – the Paris Opera Ballet. A career tragically cut short by a motor vehicle accident, and later her life by illness. Adele felt the familiar surge of grief that accompanied any thought of her mother. It had been nearly twelve years since Marianne died, a milestone as she had now been absent from Adele's life longer than she had been physically present. However, taking these classes and passing on the spirit and love for dance somehow made Adele feel closer to her mother and, in some ways, like she was still with her.

Adele smiled at her class. '*Bravo! Allez, tendu.* Remember your arms. Don't let them touch your body. Big circles. That's it, Margot. *Très bien.*'

With her back to the children, Adele joined in, demonstrating the steps for those less assured pupils. They weren't particularly co-ordinated or sharp in their foot placements, but the energy in the room was inspiring. She wasn't sure where they got their energy from and wished she had some of it. Today she felt tired, weary from being in a continual heightened state of anxiety, fearful of stepping out of line with the Germans. They were easy to rile and quick to retaliate. Adele caught sight of her reflection in the mirror. It shocked her to see the weariness on her face and grey circles under her green eyes. Her usually shiny brunette hair looked lacklustre, tied up in a bun, and she could see her collarbones; the ever-tightening supply of rations was doing nothing for her appearance.

The door to the classroom opened and Gérard Basset, her father and schoolmaster, popped his head around the doorway, pushing his spectacles up onto the bridge of his nose. His gaze travelled the room and he smiled an acknowledgement to his daughter. 'I'm leaving now,' he mimed more than spoke so as not to interrupt the class. Adele returned the smile and nodded as her father offered the class a small round of applause before waving a farewell and disappearing back into the corridor.

Forty-five minutes later, Adele brought the class to an end. '*Bravo, mes enfants! Bravo!*' Adele gave a small curtsy to her class, who returned the gesture – a signal that dance class was officially over. As the children gathered excitedly around her, Adele lifted up the lid to the top of the piano and took out a small cloth bag. She put her finger to her lips to hush them.

Ten pairs of eyes looked eagerly up at her as she delved into the bag and brought out a string of apple rings dusted in cinnamon. Adele untied the string and handed out the little treats, watching as the children scoffed them down in seconds, dabbing the tiniest of crumbs from their laps and licking their fingers. They were always hungry these days, and Adele felt compelled to sacrifice some of her own rations to help stave off their hunger pains.

'Now, quickly change out of your shoes,' instructed Adele, once they had finished eating. 'Your mothers will be waiting downstairs for you.' She noticed one girl looking despondently at her shoe as she untied the ankle ribbons. 'What's the matter, Juliette?' Adele crouched down beside the eight-year-old.

'My shoe has a hole in the toe.'

'Oh, let me see.' Adele inspected the shoe. 'Hmm, yes, you've worn the toe right through. You'll have to tell your mother.'

'Maman doesn't know. She can't afford to buy another pair.'

Adele ran her hand gently over Juliette's head and down

her plaited hair. 'Don't worry, *ma petite puce*. I will fix it tonight.' She placed it on top of the piano so she wouldn't forget it later. Juliette's mother had three other children to look after and with her husband in a labour camp in Germany, she had no one to help her so fixing a ballet shoe probably wasn't high on her list of priorities.

She collected in the shoes from those children who weren't fortunate enough to own a pair. Adele and her younger sister, Lucille, had been dancing since they could walk, according to their parents, and over the years had gained a collection of dance shoes that now came into their own and enabled the little ones to participate.

As Adele helped the children change she picked up five-year-old Daniel's outdoor shoe and noticed it was nearly worn through on the sole. It was the same for the other one.

'One moment,' said Adele and nipped out of the classroom, returning a few minutes later with two pieces of stiff paper, once the cover of an exercise book, now repurposed as insoles. 'There, that should get you home.'

She went over to the cupboard and lifted out a basket of jazz shoes, sifting through until she found what she was looking for and handed the right-sized pair to the boy. 'For you.' She pushed a shoe into each pocket of Daniel's coat. 'These used to be mine when I was about your age. Tell your mother they're a gift.'

Once all laces and buckles were fastened, the children lined up along the barre. Adele was just about to lead them out when the door opened abruptly and to her horror, in marched two German soldiers, immediately followed by an officer and a French policeman.

'*Mademoiselle Basset?*' asked the German officer, removing his peaked cap and pushing it under his arm as he referred to his clipboard.

'*Oui,*' replied Adele, trying not to focus on the scar that ran from the German's lower lip and curved its way under his chin, as she placed herself between the officer and the children. She glanced towards the French policeman, who was clearly sweating, which she hoped was from embarrassment and shame. He looked away and Adele felt a small degree of satisfaction for his discomfort as the word 'traitor' rattled around inside her head.

The German officer looked up from his paperwork and paused for a moment before speaking. 'Do not worry, I am just here to gather some information.'

Adele nodded, not convinced she shouldn't worry. She felt the small hand of one of the children slip into hers. The little body huddled up to her leg. It was Daniel. Adele gave his hand a gentle squeeze of reassurance as she looked back at the officer. 'How can I help you?' she ventured.

'I need a list of all the Jewish children in your class. Names. Ages. Addresses.' He looked beyond Adele at the line of frightened faces. Then he swiped a piece of paper from his clipboard and held it out to Adele. 'Complete this form. I shall return for it in twenty-four hours. Do not miss off any names. It will be classed as subversive behaviour, something we will not tolerate. Do you understand?' He flapped the paper.

Adele nodded. '*Oui*.' She took the paper with a feeling of dread in both her heart and stomach. Only yesterday, Manu from the museum next door to the school had told her there were rumours circulating of a round-up of Jewish people. Surely, he didn't mean children too.

'Very good.' The officer looked at the children again as if memorising their faces, then gave a curt nod to Adele before striding from the room.

Adele's knees felt weak and she put out a hand, grasping the barre to steady herself. She took a deep breath and plastered on a smile as she turned to face the children. 'Well done for standing so nicely,' she said. 'Just wait here a moment.'

Adele poked her head out into the corridor to make sure the unwelcomed visitors had left. She could hear their footsteps fading as they went down the stairs. She moved over to the window and watched the figures of the German officer, the two soldiers, and the French policeman leaving the building via the main entrance. A black saloon car was waiting and, once they were inside, it sped away.

Adele heaved a sigh of relief but couldn't get rid of the feeling of violation. She hated the thought of the German soldiers, not to mention the French policeman, inside the school. It was as if their mere presence could infect and pollute the air in the building, settling on the fixtures and fittings, seeping into the floors and ceilings, spreading like bacteria. She shrugged the thought from her mind.

The children were growing restless and, as she turned to face them, she once again ensured she at least looked like there was nothing to worry about. 'Is everyone ready to go home? Your parents are waiting for you.' Adele shepherded her flock of little swans from the classroom and down to the foyer where their mothers were most relieved to see them, except for two parents who seemed to be in the middle of a disagreement.

'It is getting too dangerous to come,' said Juliette's mother. She looked across at Daniel's mother, Madame Charon. 'It's people like you who are making it dangerous.'

Daniel's mother looked up. 'What is that supposed to mean?'

'Jews. You are making it difficult. You should not come here anymore. The Germans would leave us alone then.'

'Ladies, please,' interrupted Adele. 'We should stand together, not fight each other.'

'I was just stating a fact.' Juliette's mother was unrepentant.

'Please, everyone, go home now.' Adele adopted her friendly yet authoritative tone in an attempt to emulate her father. He somehow commanded respect without being confrontational.

It had the desired effect and soon the lobby was empty, much to Adele's relief. She looked at the form in her hand where she was to list the names. The urge to rip it to shreds was great and to avoid temptation, she dumped it on the reception desk. Madame Allard, the school secretary, would find it in the morning. Adele couldn't bring herself to do it.

The entrance door opened, making Adele jump. It was Manu.

'Sorry, I didn't mean to scare you,' he said, closing the door and briefly touching her arm.

'Manu.' She smiled, relieved to see her friend but hoping the small rise in colour to her cheeks went unnoticed. Tonight, his face was etched with concern. 'Is everything all right?' she asked.

'Yes. I was coming to ask you the same question. I saw your visitors.' His dark eyes looked intently at her.

'They want a list of names of our Jewish pupils,' Adele said. Although her father had warned her about speaking out of turn, she knew she could trust Manu. 'I don't know why they are targeting the children.'

Manu let out a sigh and rubbed the back of his neck. 'Maybe checking that no one has been missed from the list. There are rumours some families aren't listing their children. As I've mentioned, there are whispers around town that there will be a round-up of Jews soon. Some are talking about going into hiding or leaving the city before it happens.'

'Where are they taking them?'

'Work camps, apparently, but who knows what they are really going to do.'

'Every day I say I can't believe what is happening to the city I love.' Adele paced from one side of the foyer to the other and back again. 'Did you see the police officer today? They sent him along to make us think it is the French government doing this and not the Germans.'

'I know, but please, Adele, stay calm and do what they say.'

She stopped her pacing. 'I'm not so stupid as to blatantly go against them, but there are other ways.'

'Indeed. But for now, I suggest you comply. What use are you to anyone, let alone the children, if you're arrested?'

Adele knew he was right, but she hated the thought of

being so helpless. 'The parents were arguing this evening. I can't bear all the fear and mistrust that is around us.'

Manu took Adele's hand. 'I know, but you mustn't do anything rash. Now, I have to go. I too have a list to compile.'

Her heart beat a little faster at the touch of his hand holding hers, but she tried to appear nonchalant about it. 'You do?'

'Yes. They want a list of all the artefacts in the museum.'

'They're going to take them?'

Manu nodded. 'Steal them. Steal them from the people of Paris. I know they are not as valuable as your children, but still it fills me with a deep sadness.' He dipped his head and kissed Adele on each cheek. 'Goodnight, Adele. Lock the door behind me.'

'Goodnight, Manu.' She watched Manu leave, disappointed as always that he couldn't stay longer, then she slid the bolts into place before taking the key from the reception desk and turning the lock. She would go home soon. Her sister, Lucille, was preparing a meal for them tonight. Their father had gone to meet her where she worked as a secretary at one of the government buildings in the city, now under the rule of the Germans. Lucille working there concerned Gérard and it put his mind at rest to meet her every evening. Adele wasn't so sure her free-spirited sister totally appreciated this gesture of guardianship.

Back in the dance studio, Adele finished gathering up the ballet shoes into the basket and returned them to the store cupboard. She took a needle and thread from the sewing box and set about darning the toe of Juliette's shoe. The needle sliding through the pink satin, pulling the matching thread through and gradually healing the wound to the footwear. Adele thought of her mother; she thought of her fractured city, the children in her class and the wounds they would all be left to deal with. Like this shoe, they could be repaired but they would forever be scarred.

Chapter 2

Adele

Having finished repairing Juliette's shoe, Adele closed up the school for the evening. Just as she was about to lock the gates, a woman appeared at her side. It was Daniel's mother, alone this time. Her headscarf was tied under her chin and although the evening air was warm, she wore her coat buttoned up and tied at the waist with the belt. She looked agitated and nervous.

'*Madame Charon. Comment ça-va?*' Adele was surprised to see her there. It was most unusual.

'I . . . err . . . I wanted to thank you for the shoes,' began Madame Charon. 'I feel ashamed I cannot provide for my own child.'

'You don't need to thank me,' said Adele. 'I'm glad I could help.'

Madame Charon pressed her lips together, before speaking again. 'And thank you for standing up for me earlier in the foyer.'

'Again, you don't need to thank me. Everyone is scared. People say things they would not normally even think.' Adele turned the key in the gate, assuming the conversation was over, but as she stole another look at the parent, she had the sensation there was something else. 'Is everything all right, madame?' she ventured.

'I need to talk to you,' replied Madame Charon. 'Somewhere private.'

It was the urgency in Madame Charon's voice that made Adele unlock the gate and lead the way back into the school without asking any questions. Once inside, she closed the door and slid the bolts into place. 'What's wrong?'

'Daniel said the German officer asked you for a list of names. Jewish names. Is that right?' Madame Charon gripped one fist in the other as her hands shook involuntarily.

'Yes, that is right. I'm sorry,' replied Adele, feeling guilty even though there was no need. 'I don't want to do it. I really don't.'

Madame Charon nodded, swallowing nervously. 'I'm sure you don't. But you do know what that means, don't you?'

'We don't know anything for certain.' Adele tried to keep hope in her voice, to calm Madame Charon who was becoming increasingly agitated.

'Coward,' snapped Madame Charon. 'You're a coward for not admitting you know exactly what it means. Pretending you don't know so you can wash your hands of it all and excuse yourself from doing nothing to help us or prevent it from happening.'

'I . . . I'm sorry,' Adele stumbled over her words. To be called a coward shocked her. She felt as if she had been physically punched. She wanted to be outraged and refute the accusation, but in her heart of hearts, she knew she couldn't. Madame Charon was right; she was a coward for being so compliant.

'They will take us away. We are not French Jews. We came to France fifteen years ago to make a new life for ourselves. How stupid were we? Everything we had is now lost. Our livelihoods. We cannot trade anymore. They froze our bank accounts last month. Soon I will have just the few coins left in my purse. Only yesterday they gave out a list of professions we're no longer allowed to practise. And now today, they ask for the children's names. Do you not see what is happening in your city?'

Adele took a step back, afraid Madame Charon was going

to try to shake an answer from her. 'I do see. I see it every day. But what can I do? I'm sorry. So very sorry but I must give them the names.'

'Your father is a respected man, a benevolent man who is passionate about his school and his pupils. I have no doubt you have inherited all those honourable traits from your father. My son adores you.' Madame Charon clasped her hands together as if in prayer. 'Please, I beg you, do not put Daniel on that list.'

'I have to,' replied Adele. 'If they check against the census, then they will see.'

'Please, Adele. Just think about it. Please find it in your heart to help me. Help my son.' Tears filled Madame Charon's eyes.

Adele put her arms around the woman, immediately forgetting all that had passed between them. She wanted to offer the mother comfort, to reassure her everything was going to be all right, that there was a solution, but the truth was there were no reassurances to be given.

Madame Charon pulled away. 'I must go. I have left Daniel with a neighbour. I'm sorry for coming. It was wrong of me.'

'No, no it wasn't,' insisted Adele. 'I just don't know how to help, that's all.' She unbolted the main door. 'Please be careful, Madame Charon; be careful who you speak to.'

Madame Charon paused in the doorway. 'If anything happens to me, please try to help Daniel.'

Before Adele could reply, Madame Charon had slipped through the door and out onto the street.

Both visits that afternoon occupied Adele's thoughts as she hurried home. The cream-coloured building rose four floors from ground level, topped with grey leaded dormer windows. Pushing open the communal wooden door, Adele took the steps that spiralled up the centre of the building, until she reached their apartment on the top floor. Her father liked to take the birdcage lift these days as age caught up with him, but Adele liked the challenge of the fifty-two steps.

Lucille and her father were just sitting down at the dining table when she arrived.

'That's good timing,' said Lucille.

Adele greeted her sister and father with a kiss to each cheek and took her seat opposite. 'This looks nice,' she said, picking up her spoon and dipping it into the bowl of soup before her. Potato and carrot – a real treat.

'Do you like it?' Lucille asked, as she watched Adele begin to eat.

'Oh yes, it's very tasty. I can't believe you got carrots. Where did you get them from?' It had been several weeks since they'd had anything other than potatoes as their main staple. The food crisis was getting worse by the day. The Germans were taking at least a third of what anyone could produce, often more, and leaving very little to go around for the rest of the population. It was the main topic of conversation in the street, especially so now that there were long queues forming just to try to get the meagre ration they were entitled to. Often there was less than that available.

Lucille gave an excited smile and her blue eyes sparkled. 'From a friend of mine.'

'A friend?' asked Adele. She could tell her younger sister was dying for her to ask. 'Who is your friend?'

'Someone from work.'

'What's her name?' asked Adele, amused that at twenty years old, Lucille still sometimes acted like she was a young child again.

'They're not a *her*,' said Lucille, as a small blush crept up her neck. 'My friend is a *he*.'

Adele grinned at her sister. 'Ooh. Do tell.' She gave a quick look to their father, who didn't look very impressed. Perhaps he didn't like the thought of his daughter having a boyfriend.

'His name is Peter. Peter Müller.'

It took Adele a moment to grasp what her sister was saying. 'Müller? Isn't that a German name?'

Lucille's expression was one of defiance. 'It is.'

'Tell her the rest,' said Gérard.

'The rest?' Adele looked from sister to father and back to her sister.

'He's an officer in the Wehrmacht,' said Lucille, as she moved her spoon around in the bowl. 'And before you say anything, he's not in the SS, or the Gestapo or anything like that; he's just an officer in the army, doing his job like any other officer in any other army in any other country.'

'But, Lucille, none of that matters. You're in a relationship with a German. You'll be seen as a collaborator.' Adele couldn't hide the shock from her voice, or from her face. What was her little sister thinking of?! She turned to her father. 'Papa, you can't approve of this, surely? Tell her she must end the relationship at once.'

'Adele, stop playing the big sister all the time. You cannot tell me what to do. I am a grown woman and what I do is up to me.'

'Papa . . .' appealed Adele. 'Please, tell her.'

Gérard gave a heavy sigh and, after placing his spoon on the table, he folded his hands together. 'I have told Lucille my feelings on this. I have made it perfectly clear that I do not approve but, as she so rightly points out, she is an adult and it is up to her.'

'This is ridiculous!' Adele couldn't help herself, not after what had occurred at the studio. She loved her father for his liberal and forward-thinking values but surely this was a stretch too far. 'This officer of yours, he's a German soldier. He is the enemy. Can't you see that, Lucille? Don't you care what everyone will say about you? A mattress for *les boches*!'

'Adele, that's enough,' warned her father.

'I'm sorry but it's true.'

'I don't actually care what everyone else says,' countered Lucille. 'All those bitter old women who are just jealous and can't bear to see a young person enjoying life.'

'It's not that,' replied Adele. 'It's more than that.'

'You know, I've always looked up to you, Adele. My big

sister, you may only be four years older than me, but you've nurtured me as if you were my mother. Papa has always taught us acceptance and not to judge others,' said Lucille. 'I can't say I'm not disappointed that you are turning your back on all of those morals and values.'

'How can you say that when the Germans have no morals themselves?' snapped back Adele.

'If you got to know him, you would like him. He didn't want to join the army, he had to. He hasn't chosen this career. He's an engineer by profession,' protested Lucille. 'I thought you would be happy that I am happy. I love Peter. And he loves me.'

Adele's sister was right. When their own mother died, Adele did take on the role of chief carer. It helped her through those dark days to have someone else to carry on for. It was a blow to have that all thrown back at her now. Lucille may be a grown woman, but she was naive. 'You love each other?' said Adele, with a small scoff.

'Yes. Very much so.'

'And how long have you been seeing him?'

'Six weeks.' Lucille remained defiant.

'Did you know about this, Papa?'

Gérard shook his head. 'No, tonight was the first I heard about it.'

'And how do you see this romance playing out?' Adele returned to her sister.

'After the war is over, Peter and I will get married.' Lucille made it sound very simple.

'How old is he?' Adele couldn't bring herself to say his name.

'Thirty-one. And before you say anything, I don't care about the age difference. Neither of us do.'

'Thirty-one? I'm surprised he's still single,' remarked Adele, taking a sip of water.

There was a silence and this time Lucille did not reply. Adele put her glass down. 'He's married, isn't he?' It was just a hunch but judging by her sister's folded arms and refusal to meet her gaze, Adele knew she was right. 'Lucille, he's married, isn't he?' she repeated.

Lucille snapped her head up, anger blazing in her eyes. 'So what if he is? He's unhappy. They don't love each other anymore and, like I said, when the war is over, he's going to divorce her and then we shall be married.'

Adele put her head in her hands, in despair. A silence descended on the room. Finally it was her father who spoke.

'I have to say, I'm not very happy at that news but I do realise these things happen. It is certainly not my choice for you, Lucille, but . . . wait, listen to me . . . but I also respect your decisions. All I ask is that you think about this very carefully before continuing with this relationship. These are not normal times. There is a lot of resentment towards the German army, which is growing and gathering momentum. You must take this into account too.' He paused. 'Plus, you have me and Adele to think about.'

Adele looked up. 'Yes, Papa is right. You can't put us in danger just because you have fallen blindly in love.'

'You're a fine one to talk about being blindly in love,' sniped Lucille. 'At least I act on my feelings, unlike you.'

'What's that supposed to mean?' asked Adele indignantly.

Lucille tutted. 'Manu. You've been in love with him all these years and have waited around in the hope he will see you as a woman, rather than a little sister. You're wasting your life waiting for him. I'm not going to make the same mistake.' Lucille sat straighter and lifted her chin up in that bold way she did when she believed she was right.

Adele felt the sting of her sister's words more acutely than she cared to admit. 'Stop it. You're being ridiculous now.'

Lucille gave a laugh. 'I'm not being ridiculous at all. Don't think I haven't noticed how you grin madly every time you talk about him. You blush like a ripe tomato when he greets you with a kiss, and when he leaves you look like an abandoned puppy. When he turned up last month with his new girlfriend, Edith, you came home and cried like a baby in your room. I heard you through the walls that night.'

'Stop it,' hissed Adele, both stunned and embarrassed by her sister's cruel, yet accurate, words.

'Lucille, that's enough,' warned Gérard.

'Anyway, I don't see how I am putting you in danger,' continued Lucille. 'It's not like you're doing anything wrong. They won't arrest you for abiding by the law.'

Adele thought of Madam Charon and little Daniel. No, she wasn't doing anything wrong, *yet*.

'It's not all about you,' said Adele, her patience wearing thin. How could her sister be so blind to what was happening around her? To what was happening to their people and their streets?

'And it's not all about you either,' retorted Lucille. 'There are lots of benefits anyway. I didn't see you complaining about eating carrots just now. They came from Peter. You can't have double standards.'

'If I'd known, I would not have eaten them – out of principle!' Adele snapped back. 'If I could make myself sick and bring back only the carrots, then I would.'

'And you're supposed to be the mature one.' Lucille rolled her eyes as she took her bowl over to the sink. 'You need to get used to the idea as I've invited Peter for dinner on Friday night.' With that she flounced out of the kitchen.

'Well, I'm not staying for dinner if that's the case!' shouted Adele.

Gérard put a placating hand on his older daughter's arm. 'I don't think that would be a good idea. It will just draw attention to you. It could make things worse.'

Adele let out a frustrated huff as the anger boiled inside her. The last thing she wanted to do was to sit down at the table and share a meal with a German officer, but at the same time, neither did she want to fall under unnecessary scrutiny.

The sound of voices shouting in the street broke Adele's

thoughts. She followed her father over to the window and looked down at the commotion.

A German patrol had stopped and they were questioning a woman and what looked like her teenage son. The woman was backed up against the wall, her basket of food strewn across the ground, while one of the soldiers pointed his gun at her. The other soldier was shouting at the boy, who couldn't have been any older than fourteen or fifteen, Adele estimated. He was clearly frightened and confused.

Without warning the soldier struck the boy in the face with the butt of his rifle. The woman screamed as her son collapsed in a heap on the ground. Adele let out a gasp of horror and grabbed her father's arm. 'Papa! What are they doing? He's just a boy.'

'Don't look,' said her father.

Adele shook her head. She wasn't going to allow the luxury of being able to turn away and not witness the assault. That poor mother couldn't, so why should she have the privilege?

The woman was shouting and went to rush to her son, but the first soldier barred her way, holding his rifle across her chest and pushing back against the wall.

The second soldier was shouting at the boy who was curled up in a ball on the ground. He tried to get to his feet but the soldier kicked him in the stomach.

With that the soldier spat on the boy before calling to his comrade and both climbed back into their vehicle and drove away.

Adele didn't hesitate. She rushed to the kitchen and grabbed a clean cloth and the pan of recently boiled water from the stove, before hurrying downstairs and out onto the street where the woman was now helping her son into a sitting position.

'How is he?' asked Adele, setting the bowl on the side of the pavement next to the boy.

The woman gave Adele a wary look. 'You saw?'

'From my apartment window. I'm so sorry.'

The woman appraised Adele for a moment and nodded. She turned her attention back to her son. 'Lost two teeth.' She swallowed hard and took the bowl from Adele. 'Thank you.'

Adele began to collect up the scattered shopping from across the ground. Her father was out on the street now with some strips of white fabric that looked like a sheet he had ripped up into makeshift bandages.

Between them they cleaned the boy up as best they could and Adele's father wrapped a bandage around the boy's head to help stem the bleeding.

'Can I escort you home?' he said.

'No. You have been kind enough,' replied the woman. She helped her son to his feet, supporting him with one hand and holding her basket in the other. Together they limped away down the street.

'What do you think they did to deserve that?' asked Adele as she and her father walked back up to their apartment.

'Who knows.' Her father sighed. 'They do it for sport.'

'I don't know how they can live with themselves,' said Adele.

She couldn't get the sight of the boy out of her mind for the rest of the evening. How defenceless he was and how his mother was helpless as she was forced to watch.

Anger wasn't strong enough to describe how Adele felt. Rage was a better word. She loathed everything about the occupation but most of all she despised the way her fellow countrymen, women and children were being treated.

As she brushed her hair before climbing into bed, she made a vow that she would do everything she possibly could to fight back against the enemy.

Chapter 3

Fleur

West Sussex, July 2015

Fleur pulled up outside her grandmother's house, Jasmine Cottage, on the Beach Estate in Felpham – a quiet seaside village in West Sussex. Her grandmother, Lydia, had lived in her modest seafront chalet for as long as Fleur could remember. Indeed, Fleur herself had been brought up there as a young child since her own mother's death. Fleur's grandfather had died before she was born, leaving Lydia a widow at a young age, and then when Fleur's mother – Lydia's daughter – had died, grandmother and granddaughter had become each other's rock. They had somehow kept each other afloat as they navigated the stormy seas of grief.

The chalet was almost Swiss-like in its appearance, with a narrow-gabled roof and a small wooden balcony on the first floor overlooking the front garden. Clad with white shiplap boards and a crittall-framed porch that ran the width of the property, it was one of the more old-fashioned houses on the estate but Fleur loved it for its understated beauty.

Although she had moved out into a flat of her own a couple of years ago, she still had her old front door key. Her nan had told her to keep it, insisting Jasmine Cottage would always be a home for her. Fleur let herself in and called out.

'Nan! It's me!'

She went through into the living room, expecting to find

her grandmother in her usual spot overlooking the back garden, but today the chair was empty. On the side table sat a pair of ballet shoes. Fleur recognised these as belonging to Lydia although she hadn't seen them for a long time.

She picked up a shoe. The fabric was faded and delicate, worn through at the toe from many hours of dancing. The block in the toe made the shoe look big and it was hard to imagine Lydia's dainty foot inside. As Fleur replaced the shoe, she noticed a photograph on the table. It was of Lydia when she was perhaps in her late teens, standing at a ballet barre, one foot outstretched, her toes pointing and her arm in an arc at her side. Fleur didn't think she'd seen this before but then she hadn't really seen many photographs of her grandmother in her younger days.

'Nan!' she called out louder, making her way through to the kitchen.

'I'm upstairs!' came her grandmother's voice, her French accent still clear despite her living in England since the early fifties when she arrived as a young and pregnant bride. Fleur found her grandmother in the spare bedroom sitting at the computer.

'Hi, Nan.' Fleur greeted her grandmother with a kiss on each cheek. 'You OK?'

'*Bonjour*, my darling. *Ça-va, bien.*' Lydia still liked to throw French words into her sentences. '*Et toi?* And you?'

'I'm fine,' replied Fleur looking out of the bedroom window at the green, which was the centrepiece of the Beach Estate. Lydia's house was set on one of the four roads surrounding it. One of the roads spurring off Lydia's led to the beach. She sat down in the reading chair and picked up the book resting on the arm. 'Any good?'

'*Pas trop mal.* Not too bad, but I think I've already worked out who the murderer is,' replied Lydia.

'Of course, I've no doubt you have. Mademoiselle Marple,' teased Fleur.

Lydia smiled but it faded on her heart-shaped lips almost

as soon as it appeared. 'Your mother loved all the murder mystery books. Agatha Christie was her favourite author.'

Fleur nodded. 'I know. She always had at least two books on the go at any one time. I remember she always kept one in her handbag.'

Lydia took the book and, resting it in her lap, placed her hand over the cover. 'I can almost feel her presence when I read her books. I know that may sound strange, but it makes me feel closer to her.' She began to flick through the pages. 'Knowing your mother, my daughter, touched these pages with her very own hands, it's almost like I can reach out to her and feel her again.'

Fleur couldn't look at her grandmother. She felt guilty for not experiencing those same feelings. If only her mother hadn't decided to drive into town that day to go to the bloody library because she wanted new books to read. If she hadn't gone, she wouldn't have been in the path of the lorry driver who'd passed out at the wheel and gone through a red light, hitting her mother's car, killing her outright. And all because of a book. As usual, the pain of losing her mother was overwhelmed by the sense of injustice and anger at the life-changing event. Fleur wished she could feel something other than the anger that had stifled her grief but, at the same time, she knew if the anger went then she'd have to deal with the pain – an uncharted territory she had no desire to explore and map.

'Don't be afraid of your emotions,' said Lydia, breaking Fleur's thoughts. 'Try to stop thinking in terms of blame. It was an accident.'

Fleur continued to look down. Of course she knew it was an accident, but if she accepted it couldn't have been avoided, then she'd have to stop being angry, and that fear and anger was her firewall to grief. It wasn't the first time they had spoken about this, but Fleur had noticed Lydia was bringing it up more often in recent months.

'I can only deal with it my way, Nan,' she said apologetically.

'I know, but I worry; it's not healthy.'

'I'm fine, honestly,' said Fleur, finally meeting her grandmother's gaze. She forced a smile and gestured towards the computer. 'What are you up to?'

'Looking at hotels for Paris. Trying to get the best deal,' replied Lydia. Whenever Fleur mentioned to her friends that her grandmother was tech-savvy, did ballet every day, swam in the sea three times a week, had a car but preferred to cycle everywhere, they invariably imagined her a sprightly young grandmother and were surprised to the point of disbelieving when Fleur proudly informed them that Lydia was in her eighties.

'Ah, your annual trip to Paris,' replied Fleur. 'Aren't you staying in the same hotel, as usual?'

'I'm hoping to.' Lydia removed her reading glasses. 'There's something I wanted to ask you.'

Lydia's usually composed facial expression was more troubled. Her eyebrows knitted together and her brow furrowed. For a brief moment, the refinement of her grandmother was outshone by something Fleur didn't witness very often – a sadness. Was that the right way to describe it? A burden seemed too dramatic but, despite Lydia's elegance and grace in everything she did, sometimes there was the tiniest glimmer of a weight she carried around.

'Ask away,' said Fleur, trying to sound light-hearted.

Lydia fiddled with the cuff on her sleeve for a moment and then patted the back of her hair, white now with age and kept in her tidy and trademark French pleat. She rested her hands in the lap of her black skirt. 'As you know, I usually go to Paris on my own every year.'

'Yes,' Fleur replied needlessly. Lydia had indeed travelled to Paris every August to pay her respects to those close to her she'd lost during the war.

'I know I don't like to admit it, but I'm getting on in years and I know I don't have many more left in me.'

'Oh, don't say that, Nan.'

Lydia lifted her hand. 'Much as we don't like saying it,

we cannot deny it. Anyway, that's not the issue. I've been thinking, when I'm gone from this world, which won't be that far off, that part of my life, the time I spent in Paris during the war, will be lost. There will be no living memory.' Lydia shifted in her seat. 'It's been bothering me a lot recently. Too much happened. Too many lives were taken for my story to be forgotten.'

'Nan, as long as a person is remembered and in another's heart, then they cannot die. Isn't that what you always say?'

Lydia gave a small smile. 'Yes. Yes, I do. And it's exactly what I tell myself when I think of your mum.'

Sometimes Fleur forgot that it wasn't just she who had lost a mum but that Lydia had lost a daughter. 'It's a lovely sentiment,' said Fleur, although she acknowledged she didn't quite have the conviction of her words.

'It is and I stand by that,' replied Lydia, 'but you know why it's lovely – it's because we can talk about it and there are lots of people who have equally wonderful memories of your mother. We can access those any time we like. And I know you're not comfortable with the idea but it's there whenever you need it and I'm sure one day you will.'

Fleur wasn't as certain she'd want to but she didn't argue the point. This was about her grandmother's need for comfort. 'And it's not the same for you?'

'Not for what happened during the war. I have no one to talk to about my family, for there is no one else who remembers them.' Lydia pulled a cotton handkerchief from the sleeve of her blouse and dabbed at her eyes.

'Oh, Nan. Please don't upset yourself,' said Fleur, alarmed to see her grandmother reduced to tears.

Lydia took a moment to compose herself. 'I'm all right. What I'm trying to say is, once I'm gone, no one will ever talk about my family or even think about them. It troubles me greatly. I've always thought it best not to talk about the past, but now I think that's wrong.' She took another deep breath. 'I want you to know my story, Fleur. Not so you can talk about me – I'm not that vain – but so what happened to my family and those I lost doesn't die with me.' Lydia patted Fleur's arm. 'And it might help you too.'

'Help me?'

'To allow yourself to talk about your mother.' Fleur went to protest but her grandmother gave a shake of her head. 'I don't want you to get to my age and regret not having spoken about your past, no matter how painful it is. If I can look back and talk about my past, maybe you will realise that you can do the same.'

Part of Fleur wanted to tell her grandmother she didn't need some sort of fixing. That she was happy not to revisit the most painful part of her life. That she didn't believe talking through her grief would make any difference. The fact remained: her mother had died when Fleur was young and that was the past. She'd moved on. She'd had her grandmother and that was all she needed. Yet at the same time, rather ironically, Fleur wanted to soak up every drop of information possible about her grandmother's past so she had a little bit more of Lydia to hold on to in the future. Lydia's early life, until she met and married Fleur's grandfather, was something of a mystery.

'Look, Nan, don't do this for me. Only tell me if you want to. Of course, I'm intrigued. I've always wanted to know more but I've always been respectful of your privacy.' She reached out and took her grandmother's hand in hers. 'I just don't want you to upset yourself.'

'It's not something I can just sit and tell you in a few minutes,' replied Lydia eventually. 'I think it would be too difficult to say it in one go. But what I would like to do is ask you to come to Paris with me. Would you do that?'

Fleur was flummoxed. Had she really heard Lydia right? She wanted Fleur to go with her? To Paris? Lydia had point-blank refused to ever take anyone with her on her trips. She'd always defended her decision by saying it was a journey she had to take alone to honour her family. Too personal to share. But now, Lydia was actually asking Fleur to go. 'Oh,

Nan, I'd love to,' she said at last. 'I'd be absolutely honoured to go.' She flung her arms around her grandmother's neck. 'Thank you. Thank you for asking me.'

'No, thank you. Thank you for saying yes,' whispered Lydia into Fleur's hair. '*Merci, ma petite puce.*' She pulled back. 'Now, I wondered if I could ask another favour?'

Fleur smiled at her grandmother. Going to Paris wasn't exactly a favour. 'Go on, then.'

'Will you come to the cemetery with me? I don't mean drop me off and wait in the car like you usually do. I mean actually come in with me?'

Fleur's automatic response to say no stuck in her throat for some reason. She didn't like visiting her mother's grave; it wasn't a secret. Her grandmother knew Fleur found it too painful, but something made Fleur hesitate and she found herself agreeing to the request.

The churchyard was only a few minutes' drive into the village and Fleur parked in the car park at the rear of St Mary's church. Lydia linked arms with Fleur and they made their way through the wooden kissing gate and along the path before crossing the grass and coming to a stop at the brass plaque marking the spot where her mother's ashes were buried.

Lydia knelt down on the grass and removed a stray leaf that had settled on the plaque. She lifted out the vase and placed last week's flowers on the side, replacing them with the fresh bunch she'd picked from her garden before they'd left.

Fleur stood back and watched her grandmother hold her hands together and offer a silent prayer. Fleur always felt intrusive being here. This was Lydia's time with her own daughter and even though that same person was Fleur's mother, they were grieving in different ways. Their shared grief was different.

It had been twenty years since Fleur's mother had died and her eight-year-old self had few memories to hold on to; they seemed to fade with every passing year.

She looked up at the church spire and wondered what god would deprive a young child of their mother and that same mother from seeing her daughter grow up?

A robin chirped in the tree, distracting Fleur from her thoughts. It hopped down onto a lower branch and then to the grass just beyond the grave, cocking its head to one side as if studying the humans before him.

Lydia looked up at the bird. 'Ah, that's a good sign,' she said. 'It means a loved one has come to visit.' Lydia rose to her feet. 'Thank you for coming with me today.'

'That's OK.'

'I know it upsets you.' She slipped her arm once again into Fleur's.

'I'm not upset,' replied Fleur truthfully as they turned to walk back to the car. Fleur wasn't upset. She didn't want to be upset; being angry was easier. It didn't hurt so much.

Chapter 4

Adele

Paris, May 1942

Adele woke the following morning after the argument with her sister and felt none the happier for a night's sleep. They had barely exchanged another word and this morning, Adele had left early to open up the school in a bid to avoid another confrontation with Lucille. No matter how Adele tried to make the idea of her little sister having a relationship with not just a married man, but also a German officer, sit comfortably with her conscience and her loyalty to France, she could not make it happen. To Adele, her sister had personally betrayed her.

Once she had prepared the classroom and set out the work for that day, Adele's frustrations and hurt had not diminished. With still another forty-five minutes before the first of the pupils would arrive, Adele found herself alone in the dance studio. She took out her basket from the cupboard where her ballet, jazz and tap shoes were kept.

Adele slipped on her tap shoes and tied the laces, before clipping across the wooden floor to the gramophone. She flicked through the vinyl records until she found the one she was looking for – 'The Entertainer'.

Despite the early hour, Adele didn't much care to play it quietly; besides how could she tap in time if she couldn't hear it above the noise. The familiar opening bars played out and Adele took her position on the floor, waiting for

29

the introduction to finish before beginning to dance. It was an upbeat ragtime piece, fast and definitely living up to its name. Adele's feet worked quickly, muscle memory overtaking conscious thought of foot placements and steps. *Shuffle, shuffle, shuffle-hop-step.* She thought of her mother and how she had danced with her and Lucille, patiently and expertly teaching them the steps and techniques, slowly at first, one step at a time, practising and getting faster until they were up to speed with the music. Once they had mastered the routine, they performed it to their father. Adele closed her eyes, immersing herself in the memory. She could see her father standing at the front of the classroom, the look of pride and amusement on his face as his 'three wonders of the world' as he liked to call them, danced their hearts out.

Adele danced twice more to the tune before her hangover of a bad mood lifted. With her hands on her hips, she paced the room, as she caught her breath. As she passed one of the windows overlooking the street, she could see the queues already forming outside the *boulangerie* as the women of Paris hoped to get some bread. As she looked on, a military car pulled up alongside the pavement and a German officer emerged.

From the second floor it was difficult to see his face, but Adele was sure it was the officer who had called yesterday asking for the list of Jewish pupils. He paused and looked up towards the window. Instinctively, Adele ducked back out of sight, her back pressed against the wall. She waited a few seconds before sliding along the wall to the other window and sneaked a look down to the street again.

Another man emerged from the vehicle and Adele was in no doubt who he was. Manu. Her stomach tightened at the sight of the two men talking together and even sharing a joke as they both laughed before Manu extended an arm to the German, allowing him to walk ahead and into the museum. Manu gave a glance up towards the school window, as if he knew Adele was there. This time she didn't duck back.

It bothered Adele that Manu was so at ease in the company of the Germans. She knew he had to work with them as he collated information on the museum artefacts and compiled various lists the Germans demanded, but did he have to like them? It sat uncomfortably with her and reminded Adele that she would have to do the same that evening when Lucille's lover came for supper. She was sure she would choke on her food. The mere thought made her want to vomit.

Adele made her way downstairs to ensure her classroom was ready for the day ahead. She felt sick with guilt at the thought of the list she had left for Madame Allard to compile, and when the children filed in that morning, she wanted to cry with shame at her treachery.

At lunchtime, under the instructions of her father, Adele stayed out of the way, seeking solace in the dance studio, when the French policeman came to collect the list. Even being there, in her favourite space, she couldn't shake the feeling of betrayal. Madame Allard, the school secretary, came and found her.

'Oh, I can't bear it,' sobbed the older woman. 'I feel so responsible. So guilty.'

Adele put her arms around Madame Allard. 'It's not your fault,' she said, feeling every inch as guilty. She thought of Madame Charon, the mother of Daniel, and how she'd begged Adele to help her. Knowing that the list had been handed over was an utter betrayal and Adele hated herself for it.

The door to the dance room opened and Gérard Basset walked in. 'Come now,' he said, as his secretary pulled away from his daughter. 'Don't let the children see you crying.'

Madame Allard retrieved a handkerchief from her pocket and dabbed her eyes before blowing her nose. 'I'm sorry,' she said. 'It's just awful.'

'I know. I know. But we have no choice,' replied Gérard.

Adele sighed inwardly at her father's response. It was true, on the surface, in front of the Germans, they did not have any choice, but secretly, underground, surely they could make different choices? She wished she knew what she could do and how she could make a difference.

'Now, the children are having their lunch,' said Gérard. 'Make sure you eat too.' He ushered Madame Allard out of the room before returning to stand next to Adele. 'I know this hurts you,' he said softly. 'And it hurts me too, but please do not do anything rash. We have Lucille and her companion coming for supper tonight. You must control what you say, for all our sakes.'

Adele nodded. 'I know and that hurts just as much.' She gave her father a small smile before slipping past him and out of the room. 'I'll be outside on playground duty with the children today. I need the fresh air.'

It was a warm afternoon for the end of May, and Adele was looking forward to feeling the summer heat of the sun. It had been a particularly cold winter. The city had been blanketed in thick snow with the coldest temperatures in decades, well below normal until the end of March. There had been numerous power cuts implemented by the Germans to try to save fuel. The whole of Paris had shivered as it tried to keep warm; that, together with the lack of food for the ordinary French citizen, had been a great hardship for so many. The children had come to school cold and hungry. It had been torturous to see and difficult to help them; other than the small portion of food the school was able to provide at lunchtimes, they had little else. Many times, Adele had gone hungry as she tried to share her food amongst the weakest and youngest of the pupils.

To see the children running around now, enjoying the warmer weather, gave her some comfort. The food situation was only getting worse but at least they didn't have to combat the dreadful cold as well.

Eva and Blanche Rashal skipped up to her and she took their hands in hers and joined in with the little song they were singing.

'*Alouette, gentille alouette, Alouette, je te plumerai . . .*'

Soon some of the other children had come over, making a chain with their hands as they skipped around the playground. It was such a sweet and innocent moment, Adele wanted to capture it and bottle it.

As they completed another lap of the playground, she noticed a couple of German soldiers had stopped in the street to watch through the railings. Immediately, Adele felt self-conscious but she didn't want to relay this to the children, and carried on, if a little more guarded. On the next lap of the playground, one of the soldiers called out to her. She didn't know what he said, his French was poor but he repeated it in German and the other soldier laughed out loud. Adele was certain it wasn't something she wanted to hear.

'Now, do try and at least smile,' said Lucille to her sister as she stood in front of the mirror checking her reflection. 'I know you're not happy, but you could at least be happy for me. Or if you can't manage that, just pretend.'

Adele watched her younger sister smooth down the long evening dress over her hips, the black and white fabric contouring her figure. The neckline of the dress was cut to a V in the centre with a white bow, and the back was low and scooped, revealing quite a lot more flesh than Adele thought their father would appreciate. It had been one of their mother's dresses and it fitted Lucille beautifully.

'Don't worry, I promise I will be on my best behaviour,' said Adele, offering her sister a smile.

Lucille raised her eyebrows. 'You've changed your tune. Last night you were spitting feathers at the idea of Peter coming for supper.'

Adele shrugged nonchalantly. 'I don't want to fall out over it. Besides, Papa made me promise not to cause a fuss.'

Lucille turned back to her reflection. 'So, you haven't changed your mind, you're just doing as you're told.'

There was a disparaging note in Lucille's voice, but

Adele chose to ignore it. She had decided to take a different approach with her sister. She knew full well that the more you tried to get Lucille to change her mind, the more she was likely to dig her heels in. What Adele needed to do was use gentle persuasion, make Lucille change her mind without realising she was being manipulated. Adele hated the word *manipulation*, but there was no getting away from it – that's the tactic she was going to employ.

Adele stood up and went to stand next to her sister. 'I do feel a little underdressed compared to you.' Adele had opted for a floral button-up dress with a white rounded collar and white edging to the short-capped sleeves. Rather more modest than Lucille's outfit.

'Nonsense, you look lovely,' said Lucille. 'Besides, Peter is taking me to the theatre afterwards, so I've got to dress up. We're going to *le Théâtre Pigalle*. Don't ask me what we're going to see.'

'I didn't think the theatre was your thing.'

'It's not but Peter likes it. He's very cultured, you know.'

Adele couldn't withhold the scoff from her throat. 'Cultured? I'm not sure I'd use that word to describe the Nazis.'

'He's not a Nazi!' Lucille's eyes blazed with anger as she met her sister's gaze. 'He's a German officer but it doesn't make him a Nazi. He's not in the SS.'

'Does he believe in the Aryan ideology?'

'I wouldn't know. We don't discuss politics.' Lucille stuck her nose up in the air and turned away from her sister. 'He's just doing his job.'

Adele reminded herself she was trying to win over her sister with gentle persuasion rather than outright confrontation. 'Of course,' she forced herself to say, rather more amiably. 'I have to remember, they're not all the same. Peter can't be like some of the others; I know you wouldn't be fooled by that.'

Lucille paused and turned back to her sister. 'Yes, of course I wouldn't. He's shown me nothing but respect and love. I just know he's a good man.' She came over to Adele and took her hands in hers. 'And I really want you to like him. I know you think I'm reckless and self-centred, and maybe I am, but I love Peter very much. I want you to at least like him. Give him a chance.'

Adele's heart contracted at the pleading look in her younger sister's eyes. Lucille wasn't naive but there was a vulnerability, a weak spot, and that was a need to be loved. Adele could pinpoint the moment back to when their mother died. Their world had been fractured and Lucille had felt the loss of their mother acutely, leaving her insecure and wanting to be loved, needing approval. Adele hugged her sister. She couldn't quite bring herself to agree to giving Peter a chance, but neither did she want to argue with Lucille about it anymore.

Adele pulled back. 'Now, we'd better make sure everything is ready for our guest.' She linked her arm through her sister's. 'I can smell the beef cooking away and it's making my stomach rumble. It was very good of Peter to give us the meat and for Madame Allard to offer to cook for us.'

'See, I told you, he's very thoughtful like that and Madame Allard will be able to take some home for her husband,' said Lucille. 'Peter was very happy to hear that.'

Adele couldn't help feeling guilty at accepting the meat and she'd already made up her mind to keep some back to take to the children on Monday. Her conscience wouldn't let her enjoy it when she knew they were starving hungry themselves.

Peter arrived promptly, dressed in uniform, and greeted Gérard and Adele with courtesy and much respect, shaking hands and giving a small bow of the head as he did so.

'Thank you for your kind invitation,' he said to Gérard. 'I've been very much looking forward to making your acquaintance.' He spoke good French with barely any German accent at all.

'Please, come into the living room,' said Adele's father. 'Would you like a drink?'

Peter stood back and gestured for Adele and Lucille to go

first, before following them in, where Gérard poured them all a drink.

'Peter brought us a bottle of wine,' said Lucille, holding up the bottle like a trophy. 'I'll pop it in the dining room.'

'Lucille tells me you and your daughter run the school on rue de Lille.' Peter took the glass tumbler from Gérard.

'That's right. It's just a small school with myself, Adele and four other members of staff,' replied Gérard.

'And you also teach ballet,' continued Peter, turning to Adele.

'Ballet, tap and jazz,' replied Adele, trying to sound at ease, despite the nerves jangling in her stomach. Peter had deep blue eyes and his hair was a dark blonde. He looked younger than his thirty-one years, his complexion clear with only the faintest of creases around his eyes. She glanced at his hand as he lifted the glass to take a sip. No sign of a wedding ring. As she looked up at him, her eyes met his. He'd noticed her looking at his hand. He gave a small raise of the eyebrows but said nothing. Instead asking about their mother.

Adele was grateful when Lucille came back into the room, announcing dinner was ready. Madame Allard paused in the doorway to say goodnight to them, her shopping basket hooked on her arm and Adele was gladdened to know there would be several slices of meat in there. It gave Adele a sense of victory, albeit minuscule.

Dinner went smoothly with polite conversation – a little stilted at first but soon even Adele found herself relaxing. Peter was proving to be very engaging and once or twice Adele had to remind herself of what he represented. It was easy to see how her sister had been charmed by him. Still, Adele wished Peter and her sister would soon leave.

'What time is the theatre?' she asked casually.

Peter checked his watch. 'In one hour. I have a car booked to collect us in twenty minutes.'

'Peter's very organised,' said Lucille reaching over and squeezing the German's hand. 'It's amazing really. He got back from Lyon at lunchtime, had several important meetings back-to-back and still got here on time.'

'Lyon? I have a sister who lives there,' said Gérard.

'You will have to let me know her name and address and I will be sure to visit her when I'm next there,' said Peter. 'I'm organising an exhibition here in Paris next month of some of the finest artwork and sculptures from the city and then later the exhibition is going to travel to Lyon before onward journey to Germany and Hitler himself.' The pride surged through Peter as he spoke, his chest expanding as he sat ramrod straight in his chair. 'It will be one of my finest and greatest honours.'

'Indeed,' replied Gérard, his gaze dropping to his empty plate.

'The city is full of wonderful treasures,' said Adele. 'It will be a shame for them to be lost.'

'Lost? They will not be lost,' countered Peter. 'They will just be in a different place – that is all. Everything now belongs to the Fatherland and you must not think of borders and countries. Mainland Europe now belongs to Germany. We are all one.'

Adele knew better than to argue with a German officer and was aware she could be sailing too close to the wind, but she knew that the artwork and treasures had not only been taken from the museums and galleries across the city, but from the Jewish community too. It was theft as far as she was concerned.

'Peter is just carrying out his orders,' said Lucille, her voice gentle, her mouth a smile, but her eyes issued an undeniable warning to her sister.

'Actually, I would like to extend an invitation to you to accompany your sister to the exhibition and a small party we are holding afterwards to celebrate the event.'

'Adele would love to go,' Lucille gushed before Adele had time to think of an excuse.

'I . . . erm . . .' Adele felt the press of her sister's foot on her toes from under the table. For a second they locked eyes. 'That's very kind. Thank you,' Adele finally managed to say.

'You know who's helping Peter, don't you?' said Lucille.

Adele shook her head. 'No. Who's that?' she asked despite the sinking feeling she wouldn't like the answer.

'It's Manu. Manu Lafon. *Your* Manu.'

'He's not my Manu,' said Adele in an effort to deflect her true feelings at this news. Manu was helping the Germans steal from the city. She had to take a sip of wine to prevent her lip from curling in distaste at the news. 'Manu is very knowledgeable as is Monsieur Braverman. I'm sure they will be a great help to you.'

'Yes. Braverman. He's no longer with the museum,' said Peter.

An uneasy silence fell across the dining table. 'He will be missed,' said Adele. 'I'm sure he would have been a great asset in helping with the exhibition.'

'Yes but even so, he's a Jew. Not that you would know from looking at him.' Peter let out a sigh.

'From looking at him?' Adele forced an uneasy laugh.

'Hmm. Well, it will be easier to identify them now. We have received instructions from Goebbels himself that as of 7 June, all Jews aged six and above must wear a yellow badge or armband, marked with the Star of David, on their outer clothing at all times.'

'An armband!' Adele couldn't hide the incredulity from her voice. 'Why? I don't understand.'

Peter gave her a long hard look before replying. 'You ask lots of questions, mademoiselle.'

'Forgive my daughter,' interrupted Gérard. 'She's a teacher. She has a curious mind. I'm sure she, like myself, is interested to understand the policies.'

Adele watched as her father refilled Peter's glass with wine. Peter took a sip and his face relaxed. 'Of course, it is right to question. That way you can fully understand and appreciate the vision the Führer has for Europe.'

'*Exactement*,' agreed Gérard.

Adele got to her feet. 'If you excuse me, gentlemen, I'll clear the table.'

Peter and her father both rose slightly from their seats as Adele took her leave. She collected the plates and took them out to the kitchen, with Lucille hot on her heels carrying two empty wine glasses.

'You should try being a bit more gracious,' hissed Lucille as she placed the glasses on the worktop.

'Should I? I thought I was,' Adele hissed back.

'Not enough. Being invited to the exhibition and then the party is a real honour. Not many people get invited to such things.' Lucille let out a small sigh. 'It's exciting and even if you don't like it, you could at least pretend to for my sake. Come on, Adele, be happy for me at least.'

'It feels wrong – that's all,' replied Adele. 'Especially when so many people are suffering.'

'It's just the Jews. It's not everyone.'

'Just! Just the Jews. Honestly, Lucille, I can barely believe what I'm hearing.'

'Keep your voice down,' said Lucille, glancing back towards the closed door of the kitchen. 'As I keep saying, Peter is just following orders.'

'Lucille!' It was Peter. 'Time to go.'

Lucille kissed Adele on the cheek. 'He's a good man who treats me well. He makes me happy. What more could I ask for?' With that she whirled out of the room and Adele could hear her giggling in the hallway with Peter as he held her coat for her. Adele looked back as Peter nuzzled the side of her neck, sending Lucille into another fit of giggles before she turned around and wrapped her hands around his shoulders. Peter's gaze met with Adele's as he held her sister tightly and a small smile spread across his mouth.

'Come, Adele,' said her father. 'Say goodnight to our guests.'

Obediently, Adele went out into the hall. 'Have a lovely

evening, Lucille,' she said, kissing her sister. She turned to Peter. 'Nice to have met you.'

Peter took her hand and kissed it. 'My pleasure. I hope to see you again soon.'

As soon as the door was closed, Adele rushed back to the kitchen and ran her hand under the tap, scrubbing it with a piece of cloth. 'Disgusting man,' she muttered to herself.

Her father came over to her and switched off the tap. Taking her hands he dabbed them dry with a towel. 'Now, my dear, you did very well this evening. I know it was hard for you, but you need to be careful.'

'I don't know if I can,' said Adele truthfully.

'It would be foolish of you not to,' replied her father. 'We must do what we can to help those less fortunate than ourselves and if that means using the privileges we have to do that, then so be it.'

'Even if it means befriending the enemy?'

Her father nodded. 'I am not encouraging you to do anything to put your life at risk,' he said. 'But every small act of resistance can have a ripple effect and be part of something much larger. But you have to do so with care.' He put the towel back on the worktop. 'It's easy to hide our true feelings and intentions in plain sight. Where we are not suspected. Where we are trusted. And, of course, we have Lucille to think of.'

'We need to stop her pursuing this relationship,' said Adele. 'It's not right. What will people think?'

'She seems very much in love with him,' said her father. 'You know how headstrong she is. There is no point trying to force her. We have to make her come to the decision herself. That is on top of trying to find small ways to help others.'

'Do you know if Monsieur Braverman is all right?'

'For now he is, but who knows what is going to happen. He may be taken away to one of the labour camps.'

'I can't believe Manu is helping them,' said Adele.

'He has no choice.'

How Adele hated the words 'no choice'. They said them far too frequently. The words summed up the whole awful situation they were in. 'I know,' she said with a sigh.

'However, that doesn't mean he is not trying to help his fellow countrymen in some way.'

Adele looked at her father. 'What do you know, Papa?'

'Nothing. And if I did, I would be wise to keep that knowledge to myself. Not because I don't trust you, but because without the knowledge you are safer.'

Adele knew her father was right but it didn't sit easy with her. She thought of the Rashal girls and their mother, of Madame Charon. Could Adele help them in some small way as her father suggested? How exactly she didn't know, but she was determined to do something.

Chapter 5

Adele

Paris, July 1942

Adele had taken to going into work early the last few weeks. She hadn't been sleeping well, which she put down to the stress of worrying about her sister, the school and more specifically her Jewish pupils. Getting up and keeping herself busy was the best way to cope.

Earlier in the week had been Bastille Day and a national holiday, but it was not celebrated in the occupied parts of France. Adele couldn't help wondering if they would ever be able to mark the day again.

It had been six weeks since her first introduction to Peter Müller, and since then Adele had been forced to suffer his company every Friday evening. Lucille had been intent on making Friday supper a regular occurrence and although at times he was indeed pleasant company, Adele couldn't bring herself to think of him as anything other than the enemy.

She pondered the situation as she walked into school. Lucille was spending an increasing amount of time in his company. Far from showing any signs of fizzling out, the relationship appeared to be stronger than ever, and Peter gave no indication of growing bored with her sister.

It had also been over a month since the Jews had been forced to wear the yellow armbands with the Star of David.

The first day they became official, Adele had gone out into the playground to ring the bell for the start of school.

As the children lined up, Adele had caught her first sight of the awful yellow stars. Her heart had sunk at the fabric symbols sewn onto the sleeves or breast pockets of the children's clothing. Her eyes travelled the line of students, populated with the yellow stars. Her gaze went to that of the parents and the mothers who too wore armbands. Some of the parents looked away. Was it shame? Embarrassment or disdain? Adele wasn't sure. Some looked her right back in the eye and Adele found herself the one feeling embarrassed. She hated the way this visual segregated the pupils and their families.

The children filed in as per usual and Adele followed them in, stopping at reception to put the bell on the shelf by the door before heading up the stairs to her classroom on the first floor.

With their coats now hung on hooks in the hallway, at least in the classroom none of them would have to look at the awful badges. As she approached the door, she was aware of the raised voices of the children – they sounded very boisterous today. As she entered the classroom there was a scuffle of feet, a scraping of chairs as a small group hurried back to their seats. An uneasy silence fell across the room.

'*Bonjour, tout le monde*,' Adele said, pausing in front of the blackboard and trying to gauge the atmosphere. Something was amiss. Her eyes scanned the faces in front of her, most of the children avoiding eye contact and looking down at their desks. Adele's gaze fell on Daniel and Eva, sitting next to each other where the small huddle of children had been. Eva looked frightened and moved her bag onto the top of her desk, while Daniel had his hands on top of his side of the desk.

Adele walked over to the children. 'Can you move your hands away, please?' She asked the boy and then Eva. 'Please put your bag on the floor.'

Reluctantly, but obediently, the children acquiesced. Adele managed to keep the gasp from escaping her lips as she looked at the Star of David scratched into the wooden desk lid. The same crude and hurried image also appeared on Eva's desk. 'Who did this?' She turned and looked around the class. 'I said, who did this?' She walked between the rows of desks.

No one said a word but a small snigger came from behind her. Adele spun around. 'Charles, was that you?' The older boy eyed Adele defiantly but said nothing. Adele walked to the front of the class.

'Jew!' a voice hissed from behind her.

Adele spun around. '*Arretez!* This is not acceptable. I forbid the use of such language anywhere in this school. Do you hear me? I will not tolerate bullying or discrimination of any kind.'

Some of the children visibly shrank into their seats. Adele couldn't remember when she'd last had to raise her voice to the pupils. It wasn't her style and she hated it, but she had to stop this before it went too far. She took a deep breath and addressed the class in a more controlled manner.

'Now, listen carefully,' she began. 'I know there are a lot of things happening in our city. The Germans are bringing in new rules, which we all have to abide by. However, in my classroom, you abide by my rules. We are all equal here and we must respect each other, no matter how we differ. No one of us is better than the others.' She picked up the chalk and in capital letters wrote three words. 'Charles, would you please read the words on the board.'

Charles shifted uncomfortably in his seat. Adele raised her eyebrows, a sign she was waiting for him.

'*Liberté. Égalité. Fraternité,*' he mumbled reluctantly.

'Louder please, Charles.' Adele wasn't going to let him get away with that effort.

Charles repeated the phrase, this time much clearer. 'Thank you, Charles. Now, we must remember this, especially equality.

We are all equal. ALL of us.' Charles put up his hand. 'Yes, Charles.'

'But it's not that anymore is it? My father says it's *Travail. Famille. Patrie.*' Work. Family. Homeland.

Charles was, indeed, right. Pétain and his Vichy government had abandoned the traditional phrase for this new rhetoric, but it wasn't one that Adele condoned. Charles continued. 'He said Pétain changed it. My father says that Pétain is right and we need to protect ourselves from Jews.' He turned his head and looked in the direction of Eva and Daniel.

'Protect from what?' replied Adele but not waiting for a reply at all. 'We are one community. As a nation, we are inclusive and we welcome people from all backgrounds. And, in my classroom especially, we do not single people out for bullying because they are different to us. Do I make myself clear?'

There was a murmuring of '*Oui, madame.*'

Adele took a long look at the children to underline what she had said.

The rest of the morning went smoothly and while the children went out for their morning break, Adele went to the caretaker's room. The school didn't have an actual caretaker anymore. He had left the city to live with his family in Brittany, where they could take care of him and potentially offer him more food, having plenty of land to grow their own fruit and vegetables. Food occupied the thoughts of everyone these days. It was the main topic of conversation, the weather now relegated to much further down the list. Adele went over to the far wall in the caretaker's room where a peg board housed various different maintenance tools. She found the one she was looking for and went back to her classroom.

With a sander in hand, she rubbed at the desktops, obliterating the Stars of David crudely scratched into the surface of the wood. Fortunately, whoever had done it hadn't pressed too hard and the markings were soon gone. There were, of course, fresh patches of wood on the desk lids now, but at least it was better than the vandalism. Once the children had gone home, Adele would stain the wood. There was bound to be something in the caretaker's cupboard she could use. If not, perhaps coffee beans. She was prepared to give up her ration of coffee for the next few weeks if it meant making the desks look better.

The rest of the day passed without incident. The dance class lifted everyone's spirits and she was happy to see Daniel and Eva smiling at the end of the session.

'Well done, *mes enfants*. That was very good,' Adele praised her students. 'Now put your shoes on and line up by the door so I can take you to your parents.'

They traipsed down the hallway and staircase to the reception area where the parents collected their children. Unusually, Madame Charon was not there. Adele checked her watch. It was now twenty minutes since the last child had left. 'Did your mother say she was going to be late?' Adele looked down at the little boy, his face full of concern.

'*Je ne sais pas.*' He rummaged in his pocket and pulled out a piece of paper. 'She said to give you this at the end of the day.'

Adele took the scrap of paper and unfolded the note.

Please take care of my darling boy, Daniel. I have to go away and it is not safe to take him with me. I hope one day to be reunited with him. Tell him how much his mama loves him.

Adele reread the note. Madame Charon was going away? Where? Why? She crouched down beside the boy. 'Did your mama explain what was happening?'

Daniel shook his head. 'No. When is she coming for me?'

Adele ran her hand over the boy's head. 'I'm not sure, but she has asked me to look after you for now. So, we'll go back to my house and have some supper and you can meet Felix, our cat.'

Daniel's eyes lit up. 'I like cats. My grandmother has a cat.'

'Your grandmother? Where is she? Does she live in Paris?' If Adele could locate a grandparent, it would be better for Daniel to stay with a family member, surely.

'She lives in the countryside,' replied Daniel. 'Near the mountains.'

The glimmer of hope Adele felt diminished. The mountains could be down in the south on the Spanish border or to the east bordering Switzerland. Neither an option for her to go to without a travel pass – and to get one of those, she'd need a very good reason. She wasn't sure reuniting a Jewish boy with his family would be considered acceptable. She stood up and left Daniel in the office while she closed up the classrooms.

Her mind went over the letter again. Did it sound like Madame Charon was coming back soon? Perhaps she was trying to visit her mother, the grandmother Daniel spoke of. She couldn't have been arrested as she wouldn't have had time to prepare the note and tell Daniel to pass it on to Adele. It was strange and concerning both at the same time. She couldn't, however, let Daniel know she was worried. She didn't want to pass her fears on to him.

Chapter 6

Adele

Adele and Daniel reached the apartment without any problems. She took him up in the elevator and ushered him into the safety of the house without any of the neighbours spotting her. The last thing she needed was Madame Tebolt from the apartment next door asking questions. Adele had never liked the woman, she was always sneaking a look through her door to see who was coming and going.

Adele just managed to push Daniel in through the doorway as she heard the bolt being slid back on Tebolt's door. Adele pretended not to notice and slipped inside the apartment quickly. She put her finger to her lips so Daniel didn't say anything so close to the door. Madame Tebolt may be in her late seventies but she had the hearing of a listening station.

'Is that you, Adele?' It was her sister calling out from the bedroom down the hallway.

'Yes, it's me.'

Lucille bustled out of the room, as she was fixing an earring in place. 'Now, don't take all night to get ready, Peter is picking us up in an hour . . .' She stopped in her tracks as she saw Daniel who was crouching down making a fuss of Felix the cat. Her eyes widened but before she could say anything, their father came out of the living room.

'Daniel?' He was equally surprised but his face softened into a smile. He looked questioningly at Adele.

'Papa, erm, Daniel is staying with us for the night,' said

Adele, her voice nonchalant, but her eyes over the top of the boy's head spoke a different story to her father.

Gérard appeared to understand the unspoken message and taking a puff on his pipe he extended a hand to the boy who had got to his feet at the sound of his headmaster. 'This is a pleasant surprise. Welcome to my house,' he said to Daniel.

Daniel looked down at the floor and blinked hard. Adele suspected he was near to tears. 'Come into the kitchen, Daniel,' she said taking his hand. 'I'll make you something to eat.'

Since Lucille had been seeing Peter there hadn't been such a shortage of food in the Basset household and, even though Adele hated the idea of being in any way grateful to him, she wasn't about to turn down extra food that she could then take in to school for the children.

She sat Daniel down at the table and ladled some chicken and vegetable soup out into a bowl for him, together with a slice of bread with a thin layer of butter. His little eyes lit up for the first time that evening and he devoured the food.

'Oh, take your time,' said Gérard. 'You'll get indigestion. Take your time and enjoy it.'

Daniel slowed but only slightly. Adele's father tipped his head towards the door and Adele followed him out of the kitchen and into the living room, trailed by Lucille. The late afternoon sun was streaming in through the windows and tiny dust motes floated in the strips of light.

'You know you're not supposed to let the boy stay,' said Lucille before her father had a chance to speak.

Adele bristled at her younger sister's tone. 'I'm fully aware of that, thank you, Lucille; but I'm not going to abandon a child now, am I?' She turned to her father. 'You understand, don't you, Papa?'

Gérard stood with his back to the fireplace and took a moment to draw on his pipe. He tipped it in Lucille's direction. 'Your sister is right. It's just for one night and no one needs to know, do they?' He gave her a long look.

Lucille didn't reply immediately and Adele thought her sister was going to dare argue with their father but, finally, Lucille, sucked in a breath and spoke. 'No. They don't. And they mustn't.' She paced over to the window. 'You mustn't let Madame Tebolt see him. She'll be sure to report you.'

'And if she does, I'm sure Peter could ensure the matter isn't taken any further,' said Adele.

Lucille spun around. 'Funny how you don't mind him now he's bringing food for us and can help us out of a difficult situation.'

Adele sighed and went over to her sister, taking her hands. 'I'm just trying to make the best out of situations I can't control. Now, let's not argue.'

Lucille's shoulders dropped. 'I just want you to like him; that's all. Peter means a lot to me. He makes me happy. He's a good man. I want you to be happy for me.'

Gérard spoke before Adele could. 'If you're happy, then we are too. We are all trying to adjust to the new situation but we mustn't lose sight of the fundamental thing that makes us human: empathy. Not just between us three, but for others out there.' He smiled at his daughters.

Adele could feel the tension release from her sister's hands. 'I'm not inhuman and I do feel for what is happening to the Jews.' She glanced towards the kitchen. 'And, of course, I wouldn't want any harm to come to the little boy. I'm just scared, I suppose. Scared for us and what trouble we could get into.'

'It's just for one night,' reassured Adele. 'You don't even have to mention it to Peter.' Her sister looked up at her in alarm. Adele continued. 'I'm not asking you to lie, just not to say anything. There's no reason why Peter would even ask, so we won't mention it.'

Lucille nodded and there was an uncertainty in her eyes that Adele wasn't often witness to. 'All right. But please find somewhere for him to go tomorrow.'

'I will. I promise.' Adele gave her sister a hug. 'Now, I'd

better get ready for the exhibition.' She forced a smile and hoped she sounded enthusiastic enough. In reality the last place she wanted to go was an event hosted by the Germans.

'Come and help me fix my hair.'

An hour later Adele and Lucille were sitting in a black Citroën car Peter had sent for them. Lucille was snuggled up in a fox fur wrap Peter had left with his driver as a gift. Lucille had been thrilled with it and hadn't stopped admiring it and, every few minutes, stroking it. Adele was having to call upon her acting skills more and more.

One, she hated the thought of some poor animal being hunted for its fur. Two, she hated the thought of who had given Lucille the gift and, three, she hated the fact that Lucille was utterly thrilled with it. To Adele's mind, it was an extravagance that flew in the faces of the families who were only just surviving this war.

Arriving at the exhibition at least meant that Lucille would hand the blasted thing over to the cloakroom attendant.

'I almost wish the exhibition could be over so I could put it on again,' sighed Lucille, as they were shown into the main hall.

Adele took in her surroundings. The room was full mostly of German officers and high-ranking military personnel, as well as a good number of Frenchmen dressed in suits, clearly in the pockets of the enemy. Red Nazi banners bearing the swastika hung around the oval-shaped exhibition hall with a giant flag suspended from the ceiling over the central piece of the exhibition – a marble statue of Mary holding baby Jesus. Adele recognised it from the school visits to the neighbouring museum. A beautiful work of art that had been entrusted into the care of the museum and was now here on display before being shipped off to Germany.

'Ah, Lucille, there you are.' Peter strode across the room and greeted her with a kiss to each side of her cheek. He turned to Adele and gave a lower than necessary bow. Adele felt her sister nudge her arm and, out of reflex rather than desire, Adele held out her hand to Peter. To her surprise, instead of shaking hands, he cupped his fingers under her own and kissed her knuckles. 'So lovely to see you again, Mademoiselle Basset.'

'Hauptmann Müller,' said Adele in acknowledgement, willing herself not to snatch her hand away from him.

Lucille gave a giggle. 'I think it's safe after nearly two months to dispense with formalities, you two. It's Adele and Peter from now on. Isn't that right, sister?'

Adele forced a smile as she withdrew her hand. 'Yes. Of course.'

'Wonderful.' Peter snapped his fingers towards a waiter who was circulating with a silver tray laden with champagne glasses. Without asking his guests, Peter procured two glasses and passed them over to Adele and Lucille.

'Are you not drinking, Haup . . . I mean, Peter?' asked Adele as the waiter moved away.

'No. Not until after the exhibition. Technically, I'm still on duty.' He gave a smile of pride at his abstinence. 'Now, let me show you around. There are some wonderful paintings over on the other side of the room. The Valois collection is my personal favourite. Of course, there's the statue but we'll save the best until last.'

Adele cast her gaze towards the group of paintings Peter had referred to, which appeared to be of the same house portrayed throughout the year.

As she admired the miniature watercolours, she was aware Müller was talking to another officer. She hoped he'd get distracted and wander off, rather than insist on showing her around the exhibition. She wasn't really listening but her ear tuned in to the conversation as she realised he was speaking French.

'There will be thousands of bodies to get rid of,' Müller was saying. 'They can't bury them quick enough apparently, so they're going to start burning them.'

Adele looked out the corner of her eye and saw Müller talking to a French police officer; a high-ranking one if the shiny buttons on his uniform were anything to go by. She looked back at the paintings as Müller continued, all the time trying to control her disbelief and sense of disgust that they could talk with such ease about such an abhorrent act.

'Best thing to do with those Jews. Wipe them off the face of the earth.'

Adele felt sick to her stomach. She wanted to retch. She couldn't bear standing anywhere near Müller as he spewed hatred from this mouth.

She looked around the room and saw Manu talking to a German officer. Manu glanced up and caught Adele's gaze. He smiled and said something to the officer before heading over towards her.

Adele's heart plummeted. She didn't want to speak to Manu. Here he was cosying up with the Germans, laughing and smiling, letting them strip the museum of its finest pieces of work. Müller saw Manu heading over and intercepted him, giving Adele the opportunity to lose herself in the crowd. She only made it as far as the other side of the centrepiece when she came up against a uniformed officer.

'*Pardon*,' she muttered, attempting to sidestep, only for the officer to move the same way. To make matters worse, they both moved in the other direction at the same time.

'*Pardon-moi, mademoiselle*,' said the officer and he gave a small laugh. 'You seem to be in a hurry. It's not that bad in here, surely.'

Adele's mouth dried but as she met the eyes of the officer, she realised he was smiling. 'Oh, err, no. Sorry. I erm . . . it's all very nice. I just wanted some fresh air. Very hot in here this evening.'

Before the officer could reply, Manu was at her side. 'Adele, please, allow me to take you outside. You really shouldn't have come if you're not feeling well. Excuse us, officer.' He placed a guiding hand on the small of Adele's back and cupped her elbow with his other, before whisking her across the room and out through a fire escape door into a small alleyway.

'I'm fine, honestly,' said Adele. 'That wasn't necessary.'

Manu eyed her for a long moment. 'I'm not sure it was the officer you were trying to escape from.'

Adele gazed down at her shoes before looking back at Manu. He was standing close to her. He smelt of citrus. She had an urge to place her hand on his chest but instead clasped her bag with both hands. 'I didn't know you would be here,' she said finally. 'I didn't know you were still working with the Germans.' There was a challenge to her tone, which she made no attempt to subdue.

Manu raised his eyebrows. 'Is that what you think?'

'You looked to be enjoying yourself and, if I'm not mistaken, the central piece of this exhibition has come from your museum.'

'Adele,' said Manu with a sigh. 'I'm not working *with* the Germans. I'm working *for* them because I have no choice. In the same way you're here, not because you want to socialise with them but I guess because you too have no choice. Not if you don't want to make things difficult for you and your father, seeing as your sister is definitely socialising with Herr Müller.'

There was the no-choice expression again. Adele's disappointment and anger towards Manu seeped away. The tension melted from her shoulders. 'You know about Lucille and Müller?'

'It's obvious. Besides, he brought her to the museum one day to show her some of the artefacts.'

It was Adele's turn to raise her eyebrows. 'I had no idea.' She hesitated before she spoke, weighing her words carefully. 'Are you happy to be working for Müller?'

Manu shook his head and let out another sigh, before taking Adele's hand in his. 'I would have thought you knew me well enough not to have to ask but, to put your mind at rest, of course I'm not happy about it.' He cupped the back of her head with his other hand and kissed her on the top of the head. 'I keep on the good side of them; that way I get to hear things.'

Adele breathed in deeply and raised her head to look at Manu. He didn't move away as their gazes locked together. They were just a hair's breadth apart and the desire to move forwards was tantalising. She was sure Manu was just about to move to kiss her when the door to the exhibition hall opened and Lucille burst through into the alleyway.

'Oh, Adele! There you are. Peter said he saw you coming out.' She stopped as she noticed Manu there. 'Oh, sorry. I didn't realise . . .'

Manu had already taken a step away from Adele, who looked at her sister. 'I just needed some fresh air. I felt a bit light-headed, that's all.'

'Probably because you didn't eat,' replied Lucille. 'Giving your food away like that.' She stopped abruptly as if reminding herself she wasn't to mention Daniel.

Adele ignored the quizzical look Manu gave her. 'I'm fine now. I was just going back in.'

'Good. There's a buffet in the other room. We'll get you something to eat.' Lucille slid her arm through Adele's and they went back inside.

As Adele looked back, she saw Manu slip into the room and head straight over to Monsieur Blanc – a local police commander. With serious looks on their faces, the two men exchanged a few words, before Manu was back circulating the room and talking to the Germans.

'Ah, there you are, darling.' It was Peter as he put an arm around Lucille's waist. 'You found your sister, then.'

The rest of the evening passed in a blur. Adele made polite conversation with the other guests, but all the time keeping an eye on Manu and the police commander. It bothered her what Manu might have said to him. Was he suspicious about anything Lucille had said? Neither she nor her sister had mentioned Daniel, but sometimes it wasn't what you said, but what you didn't. She should have thought of an explanation why she had given her food away as Lucille put it. She hadn't given her food away. There was plenty – more than enough for them – she just hadn't felt like eating. Besides, he needed it more. She dreaded to think when he last had a good meal inside him.

'Are you ready to go?' asked Lucille. 'It's been a wonderful night but Peter is exhausted and has asked for the car to wait outside for us.'

'Yes. I'm ready.' Adele couldn't have been more ready if she had tried. What a relief to get away from this awful party. She spotted Manu heading over towards them. He held up his hand, gesturing for her to wait.

'I just wanted to say goodnight,' he said smiling at Adele and her sister.

'It's been a wonderful evening,' said Lucille. 'You must be very proud.'

Manu flicked a glance at Adele before replying to her sister. 'I'm always very proud of these works of art. They are amazing.'

'Why don't you grab your fur,' suggested Adele. 'I won't be long. See you in the foyer.'

'All right. Goodnight, Manu.' Lucille sashayed her way across the room, clearly conscious of the admiring looks she gleaned from most of the men in the room.

'I sometimes wonder how you two can be sisters,' said Manu.

Adele didn't know whether to be offended or not. Did Manu mean he found Lucille attractive – just like every other man in the room or, indeed, anyone who came into contact with Lucille? 'Sweet and sour,' replied Adele.

Manu laughed. 'Not what I was thinking at all. I don't know why you'd say that. How about sweet and sweeter?'

'It's a matter of opinion.'

'Oh, Adele, you are a funny little thing at times,' said Manu. 'You most definitely are sweeter though.'

Adele wasn't quite sure if she wanted to be thought of as sweet or sweeter than her sister. There was an implication of youth and naivety, neither of which applied to her. 'I really should go. Lucille will be waiting.'

At that moment, Peter chose his time to appear at her side. 'Ah, Adele. Are you ready? The car is here.'

'Yes, of course.' She turned to Manu. 'Goodnight.'

Manu leaned forwards and kissed her on each cheek, pausing to whisper, 'I hope the evening hasn't been too difficult. Take care, Adele.'

There was something in the way Manu spoke that made her look back over her shoulder as Peter escorted her to the car, but Manu just stood there watching her leave. Was she reading too much into what he'd said?

As they reached the vehicle, Peter opened the door for her.

Adele offered him what she hoped was a grateful smile. 'Thank you for an enjoyable evening. Goodnight, Peter.'

'I thought I would accompany you,' said the German. 'It is only proper that I ensure you two ladies get home safely. Besides, it would be nice to perhaps see your father and share a nightcap with him.'

Adele's heart thudded with fright at the prospect. A German officer in their apartment when they were hiding a little Jewish boy. 'I rather think my father will have gone to bed,' said Adele. 'Maybe you could come another night. That would be best wouldn't it, Lucille?'

She looked to her sister for moral support and for an awful moment thought Lucille was going to disagree, but then her sister turned to Müller.

'Adele's right. It's late and if Papa has gone to bed, it wouldn't be proper to invite you into the apartment.' She leaned in and stage-whispered, 'You have to excuse my sister; she's very traditional.'

Müller gave a smile of amusement. 'Very well. I don't want to upset your father. All I can say is, I'm glad you're not as traditional.' Lucille and Müller sniggered but Adele didn't care that she was the butt of the joke, just as long as it kept Müller away.

Adele and Lucille sat in silence as the driver sped them through the Paris streets to their home and ensured they were safely in the building before departing.

'Thank you,' said Adele, as soon as they were inside their apartment.

'Just make sure he's gone tomorrow,' said Lucille. 'I can't lie to Peter if he gets suspicious.' She slipped the fox fur from her shoulder and draped it over her arm, before heading down the hallway. 'Goodnight, Adele.'

'Can't or won't?' asked Adele, following her sister. 'Can't or won't lie to a German to save a child?'

Lucille paused and turned to face Adele. 'Don't make me choose.'

Chapter 7

Fleur

Paris, August 2015

The beauty of working as a lab technician at the local university meant that Fleur was able to take time off in August without any problems, allowing her to easily accompany Lydia to Paris. They touched down at Charles de Gaulle mid-morning and were checking into their hotel room on rue de Pont Neuf by lunchtime. Fleur couldn't help marvelling aloud at her grandmother's capacity to accomplish things in the same way someone half her age would.

'I've done this journey so many times, it's like second nature,' replied Lydia. 'Besides, I've experienced far worse ways to travel.'

Fleur wanted to question Lydia on what she meant by that, but the porter had arrived and was taking their bags, ready to escort them to their rooms.

They had single rooms but with adjoining doors. Both of their rooms overlooked the busy Parisian street below with the silver and grey rooftops, domed and triangular, stretched out beyond. Fleur could see the top of the Eiffel Tower poking out above the city landscape, backed by a clear blue sky. The faint wail of a siren could be heard above the low-level noise of traffic but the street the hotel was situated on was remarkably quiet and suburban, with the gentle thrum of life going by.

As they were going to be in the city for two weeks Fleur unpacked and made herself at home. She'd arranged to see Lydia at 1pm when they'd have lunch in the hotel. Lydia had an itinerary sorted out and Fleur was happy to go along with her grandmother's plans. Fleur was excited at the prospect of finding out more about Lydia's life as a child, but she knew she had to be patient. It was a big thing for Lydia to open up, having kept that part of her life well and truly locked away for so many years.

Fleur met Lydia for lunch as arranged. The dining room was as elegant as the rest of the hotel, with its high ceilings, chandeliers, softly draped full-length windows, reproduction furniture that Fleur could imagine Marie Antoinette sitting on. The hotel suited Lydia perfectly and it was no surprise that it was her favourite and one she stayed in each year. The maître d' had even greeted Lydia by name, with Lydia asking after him and his family.

'Do you ever wish you could live back in Paris?' asked Fleur after the waiter had brought their meals. 'You seem so at home here.'

'And I don't in England?' queried Lydia.

'Oh, you do, but I suppose no matter how long you've lived in England, you're always going to be very French.'

Lydia smiled. 'When I'm back here in Paris, I do feel more French, and when I'm in England, I feel more at home there. I suppose I'm like a chameleon. I can fit in with my surroundings.' She paused, looking down at her salad for a moment before back at Fleur. 'When I was a child, in the war, one had to be adaptable. It probably saved my life.'

'How do you mean?' asked Fleur gently, feeling Lydia was on the brink of opening up about her childhood.

Lydia sipped at her water. 'Before the war, I lived a very normal and average life as a young child. I attended school; I went to dance lessons which happened to be taught at the school by my teacher. She was a wonderful dancer, excellent at all the disciplines but particularly so at ballet. It was in her blood. Her mother was a professional ballerina.'

'And that's where you got your love of dancing,' said Fleur.

'Indeed. It was impossible not to be enthused by her. It was infectious. We loved her very much. Even the boys enjoyed dancing.' Lydia smiled at the memory but then her face darkened. 'When the Germans came, things changed. Our world, as we knew it, was never to be the same again.'

'What was it like? Can you tell me?'

Lydia didn't reply and her gaze dropped to the salad in front of her. She pushed the lettuce around her plate for a moment before putting her fork down and looking up at Fleur. 'I hope I can. After all, that's why I asked you to come.' She offered a watered-down version of her usual smile before catching the attention of the waiter and requesting some more water. 'Got to remember to keep the fluid intake up. Have you got a bottle to bring with you when we go out after lunch?'

Fleur knew when her grandmother was changing the subject and resigned herself to the fact that she'd have to be patient in waiting for Lydia's story.

Later that afternoon they took a taxi to rue de Grenelle, stopping outside a small café. 'Up there on the second floor was where I lived when I was a child,' said Lydia. 'That window on the left – that was my bedroom.'

Fleur looked up at the cream-coloured building to the second-floor windows. Each one had a small wrought-iron railing in front of it as was typical of French windows that opened inwards. She felt a connection to her grandmother's past she hadn't experienced before. 'I'm trying to imagine you as a young girl looking out onto the street,' she said.

'We're just a ten-minute walk from my old school,' said Lydia. 'I always like to start my journey here. I like to remember my mother walking me to and from school each day. It's one of my little rituals. You'll have to bear with me.'

'Of course, Nan,' replied Fleur. She'd looked at the route earlier on Google Street View and noted the school was on the same road as the Musée d'Orsay, which had originally been a railway station but long since repurposed after the end of the war. It was a huge, impressive stone building on the banks of the Seine.

'We can have a look around the museum afterwards, if you'd like,' said Lydia.

'That would be nice.'

'There used to be a much smaller museum next door to the school. The curator was a dear friend of the schoolmistress.' They were walking along the road, with Lydia's arm linked into Fleur's. 'I used to walk this way every day to school. During the war there were Germans on the corners of the streets, stopping people for no particular reason, wanting to see their papers. When we had to start wearing the yellow armbands it became worse. We were always being singled out. My mother sometimes used to walk us the long way to and from school, just to avoid as many checkpoints and soldiers as possible.'

'Being here with you today and you talking about it, makes it seem far more real than just reading about the occupation in history books and seeing old film reels,' said Fleur, as she acknowledged the heightened sense of connection she felt with Lydia. 'Thank you for showing me all this, Nan. It means a lot.'

Lydia smiled at her. 'I'm so grateful you came.'

'I'm so grateful you asked me. It's an honour.' Fleur returned the smile and gently squeezed Lydia's arm.

They walked a little further, before Lydia drew them to a stop. 'Here we are. This is the old museum and the building next to it is the school.' They walked alongside the wall with wrought-iron railings embedded in the brickwork. 'These used to be a pale blue.' Lydia ran her hand down one of the railings.

They were black now, thick with many years of paint, chipped in some places, obscuring the details on the finials.

Fleur looked up at the imposing school building towards the leaded rooftop and the small dormer windows running across the top.

She felt Lydia's hand grip her arm a little tighter. 'You OK, Nan?'

Lydia nodded, her gaze fixed on the rooftop. 'Sometimes it only feels like yesterday.' She blinked several times before looking away and indicating to Fleur to carry on along the street. Fleur wasn't sure if it was the breeze in the air making her nan's eyes watery or whether Lydia was holding back tears.

They walked further along the pavement and Fleur looked on towards the gates. She frowned. There was something tied onto the railings. 'What's that?' she asked. 'It's flowers, I think.'

'Really?' Lydia looked up.

They were at the gates now.

'There's a ballet shoe tied to it as well.' Fleur took the shoe in her hand. It was old and worn, the ribbons frayed and the toe darned where it had been scuffed through. 'It must be a child's shoe, it's so small.' Fleur undid the shoe and after inspecting it further, passed it over to Lydia, whose hands shook as she held the small satin ballet slipper. Fleur looked at the flowers tied to the railings.

'There's no card. Not that I can see anyway, unless it's fallen off somewhere.' She looked around on the path and through the bars of the gate in case it had fallen into the playground but couldn't see anything. 'How strange,' she said, as much to herself as to Lydia.

It was only when she turned her attention back to her grandmother that she realised Lydia was ashen-faced as she stared at the shoe. Her lips were moving and her voice so small, Fleur had to strain to hear what was being said.

'*Ce n'est pas vrai. Ça ne peut pas être.*' It's not true. It cannot be.

Chapter 8

Adele

Paris, July 1942

Adele didn't sleep well at all the night before. Her mind just wouldn't settle and instead of taking her off into a restful sleep, it was fuelling her anxiety with dreams of the Gestapo knocking on the door. Several times she had woken with a start at a noise outside, and panic had filled her chest and stomach as she sat perfectly still, waiting for a bang on the door or the sound of boots storming up the staircase, but there was nothing.

It was no more than the usual sounds of Paris at night, with the odd patrol car passing and occasionally the sound of German voices as the soldiers called out to one another on their way home from some nightclub, theatre or cinema they had chosen to spend the evening at. Paris was quite the playground for the Germans and something of a tourist attraction. She hated seeing them posing for pictures beside the Eiffel Tower or the Arc de Triomphe; it made her feel physically sick. How they slept at night knowing what the everyday Parisian had to endure, she didn't know. She would never understand their mentality and for that she was thankful. The day she ever had any understanding of how their twisted minds worked was the day she would kill herself, for she would be no better than them. Bastards.

The anger dominated any idea that she might be able to fall back to sleep and, at four-thirty, she got up from her bed and padded down the hallway to the living room and on into her father's study to check on Daniel. She paused in the dining room and switched on a small table lamp so its light would shine into the study. She could see the little boy fast asleep, cuddling Adele's old teddy bear. Her father must have given it to him last night. Poor thing, he must be so scared, wondering where his mother was.

Adele closed the door and went back to the kitchen where she made herself a coffee and tried to think what she was going to do with Daniel. There was no way he could stay here, not with Peter becoming a more frequent visitor. Then there was her sister. Lucille's parting words the previous evening were not wasted on Adele. Although she found it hard to believe her sister would really choose her German boyfriend over her family, there had been a look in Lucille's eyes that Adele hadn't seen before, something she couldn't quite pin down. Was it sincerity? Determination? A warning? Whatever it was, Adele didn't like it and it troubled her that the unwavering trust she'd always had in her family was now not so stable. She couldn't risk taking the chance and she couldn't put Lucille to the test. Not when Daniel's life was the bargaining chip.

As daylight began to break, Adele went into the study to wake Daniel. She wanted to get him into school as soon as possible, not too early that it would draw attention to them but not so late they would meet all the other children in the playground. She didn't want any of the other parents asking awkward questions about where his mother was.

Adele tapped on the door of her father's study and went in. '*Bonjour*, Daniel,' she said when she found him sitting on the edge of the chaise where her father had made up a little bed for him. 'Did you sleep well?'

Daniel gave a shrug. 'Where is Maman? Is she coming to take me to school?'

Adele gave the child a reassuring smile. 'Not this morning. I'm going to take you to the school when I go in.' She sat down on the edge of the chaise next to him. 'I need some special help today and I wondered if you wouldn't mind. You see, I need someone very grown-up and sensible, someone like you.'

Daniel's eyes widened a fraction. 'What do you need help with?'

'I have to get the registers and take them around to the classrooms. Do you think you'd be able to do that for me?'

Daniel nodded enthusiastically. It was usually the job of one of the older children to hand out the registers, but Adele hoped this would take his mind off his mother, if only for a short time. Once at school, surrounded by others, hopefully it would seem like a normal day and he wouldn't fret.

She took the hairbrush from her pocket that she had brought from her bedroom and handed it to him. 'You need to wash your face, brush your teeth and tidy up your hair.'

Daniel took the brush and ran his finger over the bristles. 'Mama usually does it for me.' There was a small catch in his voice.

'Here, let me do it then,' said Adele. 'Stand up.' Gently she brushed Daniel's hair, easing out the tangles and flattening the sticky-up bits. If only it were this easy to smooth out life.

Breakfast was a quick affair, Adele keen to get out of the house before Lucille got up. Her father came into the kitchen just as Daniel was finishing his porridge.

'*Bonjour*, Adele. Daniel,' greeted Gérard. He gave his daughter a kiss on each side of her face and shook Daniel's hand.

'*Bonjour, monsieur*,' said Daniel, getting to his feet.

'It's all right, you can sit down,' said Gérard. 'You're both up early.'

'We're heading into school before it gets busy,' replied Adele. 'Daniel is going to help me set up the classroom and I've asked him to hand out the registers this morning.'

'Oh, that's a very important job,' said Gérard, looking

solemnly at the child. 'I'm sure you're more than capable of helping Mademoiselle Basset.'

'*Oui. Bien sûr,*' replied Daniel, sitting a little straighter in his chair and puffing his chest out.

'Good. *Trés bien.* Then don't let me hold you up.'

A few minutes later, Adele and Daniel had left the apartment and fortunately managed to avoid bumping into Madame Tebolt from next door. They trotted down the staircase, light on their feet, and were out on the street in less than a minute.

Adele was relieved when they finally reached the school without encountering any soldiers or checkpoints that often appeared randomly overnight without any warning. Once in the safety of the building, Adele took Daniel up to their classroom, and sat him at her desk.

'Now, Daniel, I need to tell you something very important,' she said, crouching down so she was at eye level with him. 'You mustn't tell anyone you stayed at my house last night. I don't approve of secrets as you know, but there are some exceptions to the rule and today is one of them.'

'Why can't I say anything?'

'Because not everyone will be very happy to hear that. They will want to know why and some of your friends may tell their parents and they may tell the Germans.'

'And it's bad the Germans know?'

'Yes. Very bad. They will be very cross. They want everyone to stay in their own houses at night times. I don't want to get into trouble for taking you home. And I don't want Monsieur Basset to get into trouble either.'

'Would I get into trouble?'

'Yes, I think you would.'

'And would my mother?'

Adele nodded. 'She would too. We all would.' She let out a small sigh and offered Daniel a reassuring smile to try to ease the tension in the room. 'Now, how about we hand these books out. I need a copy on every desk and then we can do the registers.'

As Daniel set about putting the textbooks out, Adele began to write some work out on the blackboard and a calmness settled in the room, but no sooner had she finished the second line than the sound of stones pinging against the classroom window brought her to a halt.

It could only be one person – Manu.

Situated on the corner of the school building, Adele's classroom windows overlooked both the main road and the museum where there was a small outdoor space. Manu had a habit of throwing stones up at the window to get her attention.

Adele went over to the window and could see Manu standing below looking up at her. Instead of his usual smile, he wore a serious expression. He signalled to her to come down.

'Wait here in the classroom,' instructed Adele. 'Once you've finished giving out the books, can you make sure all the inkwells are filled and everyone has a pen and piece of paper please?' She didn't often trust her younger students with the ink, especially at the moment with it being in short supply, but she needed to ensure Daniel was occupied.

Adele hurried downstairs but instead of going out the front of the building, she took the side door out into the passageway where a brick wall divided the two premises. She hopped up on the wooden bench that the kitchen staff used to sit on when they took their breaks. Adele looked over the wall and Manu appeared, having used a kitchen stool to be the same height as her. They often chatted like this when no one was about.

'What's wrong?' asked Adele.

'I have something very important to tell you,' said Manu. 'And I'm going to need your help.'

'Of course.' She was flattered he'd asked her and eager to please him.

Manu looked at her intently. 'I wouldn't ask you to do this if it wasn't important.' He placed his hand over hers. 'It could get you into a lot of trouble.'

'Trouble?'

'Yes. It could get you arrested.'

Adele swallowed hard as a few nerves fluttered in her stomach, which she ignored. She'd do whatever it was. This was her chance to follow through with her convictions. To make good on the promises she'd made to herself when she'd seen that poor boy being beaten by that German soldier. 'What do you want me to do?'

'This is serious, Adele. It couldn't get more serious than this. We're talking life or death for innocent families.'

'It's all right. Just tell me what you want me to do.' She squeezed his hand to underline her determination to help. 'I want to help.'

Manu studied her with even more intent and then nodded as if he'd come to a decision. 'I have it on good authority that there is going to be a round-up of Jews tonight. Well, at four o'clock in the morning to be precise.'

'A round-up?!'

'Shh. Yes. They are going to be taken away to the Vélodrome d'Hiver and then transported out to work camps. You need to warn as many of your parents as possible.'

'How do you know?' asked Adele.

'It's not important. You just need to do as I say.' Manu gripped her hand over the top of the fence and then his face softened. 'Adele, how long have you known me?'

'Twelve, thirteen years. I don't know – a long time.'

'And have I ever lied to you in that time?'

She shook her head. 'No.'

'So, why would I do that now? You must trust me. You do, don't you?'

'I do but trust must be mutual. You should trust me also.'

'*D'accord.*' He took both her hands now. 'Last night at the exhibition, when you saw me talking to the French policeman . . . he is the one who warned me.'

'Him? How do you know it's not a trap to catch you out?' The idea that Manu had been manipulated and may be arrested sent a tremor of fear rushing through Adele's veins.

'He's given me certain information before.'

'Information? Are you working for the Resistance?'

'Adele, you are asking too many questions and we haven't got time. The less you know the better. Now, please just tell the Jewish parents.'

'Ah, Manu! There you are!' The voice of Manu's girlfriend, Edith, broke their conversation. 'Oh. Adele, you're there too.'

Manu gave a warning look to Adele before turning to face his girlfriend and jumping down from the stool. 'Edith. *Ça-va?*' He gave her a kiss on the cheek. 'You're early.'

She held up a brown paper bag. 'Croissant. For you. A luxury these days, I know. You can thank me later.' She looked up at Adele who was still at the fence. 'Sorry. Only managed to get one.'

'I can share it with you,' said Manu, waving the bag in the air.

Adele didn't miss Edith's eyebrows shooting so high up her forehead they were in danger of disappearing into her hairline. 'Not for me, thank you. I've already eaten.'

'So, what were you two doing?' asked Edith again.

'I was just congratulating Manu on the exhibition last night,' said Adele quickly before Manu could speak. 'Such a collection of art under one roof.'

'Oh, I didn't realise you went,' said Edith. 'I didn't notice you.'

'It was very busy,' replied Adele. She knew for certain Edith had seen her but had chosen to pretend not to. '*Alors.* I must get my classroom ready.'

It was at that point Daniel decided to appear. 'Mademoiselle Basset. I've finished filling the inkwells. What do you want me to do now?'

Edith looked startled. 'Is that one of your students? They're in early.' She hopped up on the stool and peered over the fence. '*Bonjour.*'

Adele climbed down from her position at the fence. 'Back inside now,' she said, ushering Daniel in before he had time to reply to Edith and be grilled for information.

At the same time, she could hear Manu talking to Edith. 'Come. Let's go inside. I have some coffee beans left from last night. We should eat the croissant and have a drink before I start work.' And then in a louder voice he called over the fence to Adele. '*Bonne journée, Adele. A bientôt!*'

Adele went back into the schoolroom where Daniel was waiting in the kitchen, aware an acute feeling of jealousy had pitched up inside her. Edith had been hanging around Manu for several months now. Adele had hoped nothing would come of it and the relationship would fizzle out, but so far that didn't appear to be happening.

She turned her attention to Daniel. 'Thank you for filling the inkwells,' said Adele. 'Now, let's quickly do the registers and then go out to the playground. The other children will start arriving soon.'

Manu's words kept swirling around in Adele's mind as she stood in the playground. A round-up of the Jews, in the early hours of the morning. She needed to warn as many families as she could without anyone else noticing. She had to trust Manu and, to be honest, if she couldn't trust him, then who could she trust?

Her father came through the gates.

'Is everything all right, Adele?' he asked. 'You looked troubled this morning. Is it Daniel?'

Adele shook her head. Two German soldiers on their patrol walked past the school. Adele tracked them as they made their way along the pavement but they were oblivious to her gaze. Once they were out of sight she turned to her father and, keeping her voice no more than a whisper, relayed to him what Manu had told her.

Gérard's eyes widened a fraction but that was the only visible reaction. '*D'accord*. I have only one Jewish family in my class. I will tell them.'

'There are three families in mine,' replied Adele. 'Do you think Daniel's mother fled because she had heard something?'

'I don't know. I am not sure why she would leave her

child. Unfortunately, I fear the worst.' Gérard's expression was grim. 'Now, we must worry about what we can do and not dwell on something that will make no difference.

Adele's father was as pragmatic as he was caring and she knew he was right.

Five minutes later, Adele was ringing the hand bell to signify the start of the day and for the children to line up in the playground. She could see her friend Jacqueline hurrying through the gates with her two daughters, Eva and Blanche. She scanned the line for the other Jewish child, Thomas. He was near the back and his mother was getting ready to leave the playground.

'Walk quietly into the school,' Adele said in a loud voice, addressing her class. 'You have reading books on your desk. I have written on the blackboard which page you are to begin with. When I come in, I want to hear nothing but the turning of pages. No talking. Do you understand? Good. Off you go. Daniel, lead the way.'

Adele went to call to Thomas's mother, but she had already left. Adele would just have to make sure she told her tonight at picking-up time. 'Jacqueline! Can I have a word, please?'

Her friend gave the girls a wave before approaching Adele. 'Of course. Is everything all right? Is this a word in your capacity as teacher?' Jacqueline was teasing her and Adele smiled at her friend. 'Just one moment.' For the benefit of the other parents, who were gradually filtering out through the school gates, Adele pretended to be casting a watchful eye over the children as they filed into the school. Finally, they were the only ones left in the playground.

'Sorry. I needed to make sure no one could hear what I'm about to say,' said Adele. She could see the concern settle on her friend's face. 'In the early hours of the morning, the Germans are rounding up the Jewish families in the city.'

'What?' Jacqueline let out a gasp.

Adele held her friend's hands in her own. 'Please, Jacqueline, you need to go into hiding somewhere. I don't know where but you need to find a safe house for you and the children.'

'No. This can't be true.' Jacqueline shook her head as if she could rid the notion from her thoughts.

'It is true and you don't have time to question me. My dear friend, Jacqueline, you must trust me.'

'Have you heard this from your Nazi-loving sister?' The venom in Jacqueline's voice bit into Adele's heart and she couldn't hide the shock on her face.

'No. I haven't. It's from a reliable source. Someone I trust very much.'

Tears had gathered in Jacqueline's eyes but she blinked them away. 'They can't just take us from our beds in the middle of the night. I thought it was just the men they wanted for their labour.'

'No. They aren't discriminating based on gender anymore,' insisted Adele. 'I'm sorry to have to tell you, but I couldn't bear for anything to happen to you.'

'But where will I go? I have no family in the city and even if I did, they too would be in danger.'

'Try to find somewhere. Ask at the synagogue. Ask the rabbi. They must be able to help you.'

'I never thought it would come to this,' whispered Jacqueline.

'Neither did I, but you must act fast. When you come back this afternoon to collect the girls, you must behave as normal. Don't give yourself away. Everyone must believe it's just a normal day,' instructed Adele. 'Now, I must go. I have a class to teach.' She hugged her friend fiercely.

'Thank you,' whispered Jacqueline.

Chapter 9

Adele

Adele found it hard to concentrate throughout her classes. She made several mistakes in the maths lesson and another in the spelling test. She was distracted by thoughts of what was going to happen to the Jewish children in her class. How had the world become such a wicked place and how could the German soldiers live with themselves? Surely they had family of their own back in Germany – and yet they could treat other human beings so inhumanely. It was beyond understanding.

She was glad when the end of the day finally came around. Instead of the planned ballet lesson she decided they would tap-dance. As she banged and tapped her feet, she could feel the anger storming through her veins and her feet hammered the wooden floorboards much harder than necessary. The speed increased with each step and she could hear nothing but the stomping of her shoes. She felt she was almost out of control. It wasn't until the door opened and her father shouted out her name that Adele stopped. She was breathless from exertion and when she turned to look at her class, she realised they must have stopped dancing long before her. Some of the younger ones looked terrified.

'What are you doing? I've never heard anything like it in my life,' said her father. 'I thought you must have a herd of elephants up here.' He peered over his glasses at the children. 'No. They are definitely not elephants.'

The children gave a small laugh of relief at the light-heartedness their head teacher had brought to the room.

'I'm sorry.' Adele felt wretched. The last thing she wanted to do was to frighten the children. She hadn't realised quite how much anger she had pent up all day and as with most things in life that troubled her, dancing was a way of dealing with the stresses and strains. It was the only way she knew how to expel that anger and frustration. She turned to the children. 'Sorry, my feet were in a bad temper. Naughty feet.' She smiled at the class. 'Let's try again and this time there will be no stomping from me.'

Her father bade them all a good evening and left quietly once he was assured Adele was composed. She was embarrassed by her own behaviour and especially so in front of the children. She was glad when, by the end of the routine, they looked relaxed and happy, which was the whole purpose of this class. Not for her to show her frustrations.

'*Bravo! Bravo!*' She enthused at the end and clapped her hands in appreciation. 'I think that performance deserves an extra special treat.' Their eyes lit up and quickly the children changed out of their tap shoes.

'What is it today?' asked Juliette, hopping from one foot to another as Adele took the canvas bag from the cupboard.

'What would you say if I told you it was cake?' There were squeals of excitement, gasps of disbelief and cheers of anticipation. Adele was nearly flattened by the children as they excitedly gathered around her. 'Stand in a nice neat line,' she instructed.

She went down the line, handing out the small sponge cakes she had taken from the party the night before. It gave Adele a small sense of victory knowing the very food the Germans stole from the people of France was being used to feed those same people, or at least the children of the city.

The children devoured the cake in seconds, dabbing up the tiniest of crumbs from their clothing. Adele took them down to their parents who as usual were gathered in the reception area.

'We had cake today!' exclaimed Eva as she skipped up to her mother.

Jacqueline looked up at Adele. 'Cake? My that was lucky for you. Did you enjoy it?'

'It was delicious,' said Blanche.

'Can we have cake at home?' Juliette asked her mother.

Madame Ratte raised her eyebrows. 'Cake? How lovely.' Then, to no one in particular: 'It's all right for some who have friends in high places.'

'It was left over from the exhibition last night,' Adele explained.

'Ah, yes. Of course. The party the Germans held in the museum,' said Madame Ratte. 'It must have been nice to eat as much as you like and come home with a full belly and even nicer to bring the leftovers for the children. How very generous of you.' There was no doubt about the contempt in Madame Ratte's voice and Adele couldn't blame her. Why would the woman think any different? All she knew was Adele had gone to the exhibition as a guest of a German officer, one that her sister happened to be in a relationship with. 'Not everything is as it seems,' she said. 'Some things we don't have a choice in.'

Madame Ratte made a scoffing noise in disbelief. 'Come, Juliette, we must get home. Soup again this evening, I'm afraid.'

The jibe was not wasted on Adele and as the other parents filed out, she noticed several of them avoided eye contact with her or didn't say goodbye as they normally would.

Still, it was not the time to feel sorry for herself. She needed to speak to Thomas's mother. 'Madame Kampe! Cecile! Could I have a quick word, please?' Adele noticed Jacqueline loitering near the doorway and guessed she wanted to speak to her before she had to disappear and hide from the Nazis.

'It's all right. I've told Cecile,' said Jacqueline coming over to stand next to the other parent.

'Thank you for warning us,' said Cecile. 'I don't know what I'm going to do. I have family twenty kilometres outside of Paris but no way of getting there. We're going to have to walk.'

'In the pitch-black of the night? How are you going to do that?' asked Jacqueline. 'You will be picked up within hours. We will end up being arrested and held in a detention camp, just like our poor husbands are being held as prisoners of war.'

'I don't know what else to do.' Cecile's face was pale and her eyes glistened with tears.

'What are you going to do, Jacqueline?' asked Adele, her voice almost a whisper.

'I don't know either. It's hopeless. I can cope with what will happen to me, whatever that might be, but I cannot bear the thought of the girls being captured.'

'So you must try to escape,' said Adele. 'As soon as it is dark, start making your way through the city. Use the back streets and alleyways. Hide in the shadows as soon as you see or hear anyone. Just get out of the city.' She looked over at the children who were holding hands in a circle and skipping around singing a song. They were so innocent and happy.

'Where's Daniel's mother?' asked Jacqueline with a frown, as if noticing the boy on his own for the first time.

'I didn't see her this morning, now you mention it,' said Cecile.

Both parents looked at Adele for an answer. For a long moment Adele looked from one woman to the other. Eventually, she spoke. 'I don't know and that's the truth. She didn't return to pick up Daniel after school.'

'Has she been arrested?' asked Cecile, her hand going to her throat.

'I don't think so. She left a note asking me to look after him.' Adele quickly explained how she'd taken Daniel home the night before. 'I thought his mother might turn up this morning or this evening, but no.'

'What are you going to do with him?' asked Jacqueline.

'I'll just have to take him home.' She looked at the women again. 'Unless one of you can take him with you.'

'Oh, Adele, how can we?' Jacqueline shook her head. 'We don't have anywhere to go ourselves. Besides, if we flee, how are we going to manage for food and water? I can barely feed my own children, how would I feed another?'

'It is the same for me,' agreed Cecile. 'An extra mouth will just make things even more difficult.'

Adele rubbed the sides of her temples with her fingertips. 'There must be something we can do.'

'I have been thinking all day and I have not come up with an answer,' said Jacqueline. She let out a long sigh.

'There is one thing,' said Cecile slowly. 'We could leave our children with you.' She grasped Adele's arm. 'At least then, they won't be taken prisoner by the Germans. If it's just me, I can live with that if I know my son is safe.'

'Oh, I don't know . . .' began Adele. Take three more children in. How could she do that? 'I have nowhere for one child, never mind three more.'

'You can't say no,' insisted Cecile. 'Please, I'm begging you. Take Thomas. He will be company for Daniel.'

'Cecile, you don't understand. How will I look after them? Feed them? Where can I hide them?'

'But how can you save one child and send three others to what will probably be their deaths?' Cecile didn't try to stop the tears from falling. 'I'm begging you. Please, save our children.'

'Stop. Let me think.' Adele's heart wanted to break. Cecile was right. How could she turn away three children? She would never be able to live with herself. She looked down at the ground, her hands on her hips, and tried to order her thoughts. There must be a way to help them. She *had* to think of a way. An idea began to form in her mind. She didn't have the answers, not all of them, but maybe, just maybe there was a way. She looked up at the parents. 'Now listen to everything I am about to say.' She glanced over at the children who were now singing to a hand-clapping song, before turning back to the parents.

'I cannot look after four children on my own. It would be impossible to keep them somewhere all day. I couldn't bring them into the classroom because the other children would know they were there and tell their parents. If I look after them, then it has to be a secret and I just cannot do that on my own.'

'Adele, please, you can't turn them away,' implored Jacqueline.

'I'm not going to,' said Adele. 'They can stay but not on their own. You both must stay too. Not just because the children need their mothers but because I cannot live with myself if you give yourselves up. Who knows what will happen, they might torture you when they realise the children aren't with you. No. You both must come as well. Also, it means you can look after Daniel.'

Cecile grasped Adele's arm. 'Oh, I promise you we will look after the boy,' she said. 'Of course we will.'

'How, though? How are you going to hide us?' asked Jacqueline, a little more reserved with her celebrations than Cecile.

'You can hide up in the attic of the school,' said Adele. 'You will have to stay very quiet during the day, so no one knows you are there. I don't know how, but I'll find someone who can help you escape. Hopefully, you will only have to hide there for a few days, just until the round-up has finished and the dust has settled.'

'Thank you, so much,' said Cecile.

'Now, you must go home and get essential things only,' said Adele, the idea shifting into a more solid plan. 'Wear as many clothes as you can. You don't want to draw attention to yourselves by carrying a suitcase with you. Bring only what you can carry without arousing suspicion. Bring any food you have. I will be able to bring some in each day for you but it might not be much. Though it should be enough so you don't starve.'

'I don't know what to say,' said Jacqueline. She hugged her friend. 'You are a good woman, Adele Basset.'

'I know you'd do it for me,' said Adele. 'Now, please hurry. Don't come back at the same time though. Cecile, how long will it take you to go home, get your things and come back?'

'Less than an hour.'

'Good. You come back first. Jacqueline, you come back here in two hours.' Adele's mind was racing and she could hardly keep up with it. 'I'll wait here and be ready to let you in. We must hurry to beat the curfew.'

'Thank you. Thank you,' said Cecile through fresh tears.

Adele let the mothers and children out of the school but kept Daniel with her. 'So, tonight, you get to sleep at the school,' she said to the boy, trying to make it sound like fun. 'And Thomas, Eva and Blanche are coming back and they'll stay too.'

'The whole night?' asked Daniel, his eyes lighting up with excitement.

'Yes, the whole night. Their mothers are also going to stay as I need to go home this evening.' She took his hand and led him up the staircase.

'Where are we going to sleep?'

'At the top of the school is a special room for you all,' explained Adele. 'I'll take you up there now and show you. I bet you've never been up there before. None of the children have. It's right above the dance studio. There's a secret staircase.' She injected enthusiasm into her voice, trying to mask the trepidation swamping her. It was frightening what she was doing – hiding Jewish people from the Germans – but she knew she couldn't leave them at the mercy of the enemy. She wouldn't be able to live with herself.

Adele took Daniel up to the second floor where the dance studio was and walked across to the other side of the room, where next to the blackboard was a walk-in store cupboard.

At the back of the room was another door, which she opened to reveal a narrow wooden staircase spiralling up to the attic room above.

'I always thought that was a cupboard,' said Daniel. He grinned at Adele. 'Is that the way to the attic? I thought it was up the stairs at the end of the hall.'

'Those stairs lead to the main attic but this is the way to a secret attic. Mind how you go, it's very steep.'

At the top of the staircase was another door, which Adele unlocked. It was very dusty in the attic and cobwebs adorned the rafters, draping across the room like a net curtain. Adele pushed them to one side with her hand. 'Yuck. Sticky cobwebs are the worst thing,' she said. There were three dormer windows cut into the roof in total, two for the larger attic and one for this smaller space.

'It's smelly,' announced Daniel as they stepped further into the attic space.

The excitement had already dwindled from his face. The reality was a lot less fun than the thought. 'I know, but it's only for a few nights.'

'Will my mother know where to find me?'

The little boy's face was full of angst and Adele had to remind herself that he was only young and it must be quite frightening for him. 'All your mother has to do is to find me and I will tell her where you are,' said Adele, trying to skirt around an honest answer without telling a complete lie. She gave Daniel a reassuring hug. 'Now, let's see how we can tidy this up ready for when the others come back.'

It wasn't long before Adele had swept the floor and moved some of the boxes to one side, so there was enough room for two adults and four children to sleep. The boxes mostly contained old schoolbooks, some props they used for their theatre and dance shows, together with half a dozen chairs and two desks. A bookcase stood against the wall, full of dusty old reading books. Adele recalled her father saying that this had once been the living quarters for the school caretaker.

Adele remembered him from when she was a child but after his retirement, the new caretaker hadn't lived at the school and the attic room had become forgotten about – unused and not needed.

'That looks much better,' said Adele surveying the space. She checked her watch. 'Now, Daniel, you're to wait here. Promise you won't leave the room. I'm going downstairs to wait for Thomas and his mother.'

'Can we put the light on?' asked Daniel. 'I don't like the dark.'

'Not right now,' said Adele. 'Remember, we don't want anyone to know we're here. Tomorrow I'll get something to put up at the window so you'll be able to light a candle. Stay there, now. I'll be back in a minute.'

Adele made her way down to the main entrance to wait for Cecile. She kept an eye out from her father's office window where she had a clear view of the street. As soon as she heard the faint metal clang of the gate, she went to the front door and opened it. If it wasn't such a serious situation, Adele would have burst out laughing at the sight of Cecile and Thomas waddling in through the doorway. They must have put on every item of clothing they owned.

Cecile pulled off her coat. 'Oh, help me get this thing off! I'm sweating like a pig. It's the middle of summer and I'm dressed up for winter!'

Adele helped tug the clothing off Cecile and then from Thomas. Between them they lugged everything up to the attic room. Daniel was delighted to see the older boy much to Adele's relief. 'He's been asking about his mother,' she whispered to Cecile as they put the clothes to one side and took the blankets from Cecile's shopping basket.

'Poor child. I fear there will be many more like him,' said Cecile.

They worked silently laying out the blankets on the floor, sandwiching some brown paper Adele found in the corner between the two blankets to act as a mattress.

'We can use the clothes as blankets,' said Cecile. 'At least it won't be freezing cold tonight.'

'I'd better go down and wait for Jacqueline,' said Adele.

It wasn't long before Jacqueline and the two girls turned up, in much the same fashion as Cecile and Thomas. All wearing several layers of clothing and carrying bags stuffed with blankets and food.

'My heart is racing,' said Jacqueline as she bundled through the door. 'We had to hide down an alleyway at one point. There were two German soldiers. Fortunately, they were talking so loudly, I heard them from around the corner. But then they stopped and one of them relieved himself by peeing in the alleyway. We were crouched down behind some rubbish.'

'Oh, you were lucky. You poor things. That must have been terrifying.'

'Exactly. How would I have tried to explain what we were doing? I could do with a stiff drink. I don't suppose your father has any whisky stashed away in his office.'

Adele smiled. 'As a matter of fact, there is a bottle of port up in the attic. I found it when I was tidying up earlier.'

'What are we waiting for? Lead on,' said Jacqueline.

'Follow me!' Adele adopted the overly enthusiastic manner of her friend and they trooped up to the top of the school. The girls were equally impressed with the secret staircase as Daniel had been and equally disappointed with the dark attic space. Adele comforted herself with the thought that at least they would be safe tonight. What tomorrow would hold for them, she didn't know but for now, for this moment, they were safe.

Chapter 10

Fleur

Paris, August 2015

'What is it, Nan? What's wrong? Nan?' Fleur gently placed an arm around Lydia's shoulders. The older woman was in shock, disbelief about something, and Fleur had no idea what it could be other than it was something to do with the ballet shoe. She looked around for somewhere for Lydia to sit down, worried that the distress might make her unsteady.

Then a man came out of the café across the road. He put his hand in the air almost like a wave as he made eye contact with Fleur. Then he was striding across the road towards them. '*Comment ça-va?*' he asked as he reached them. He was tall, probably over six feet, well built with his black hair fashioned in cornrows.

'*Ma grand-mère. Elle est . . .*'

'You can speak in English,' offered the man.

'My grandmother has had a bit of a shock,' explained Fleur, grateful she didn't have to call upon her rusty A-level French. Lydia had, of course, tuned Fleur's ear in to the French language from an early age, but she had a long way to go before she could be classed as fluent.

'Would you like to come and sit in the café?' he asked. 'I can get you both a drink. I was just having one myself.'

Lydia looked up at the man, noticing him for the first time. 'Oh, I'm sorry,' she said. 'No. I'm fine . . .' She broke into a stream of French, attempting to convince the stranger she was perfectly OK but as Fleur exchanged a glance with the man, she could see he was thinking the same as her.

'Let's just get a drink anyway, Nan,' encouraged Fleur.

'We don't need to interrupt the gentleman,' protested Lydia.

'I promise, you are not interrupting me,' replied the man. 'I am between meetings.'

Lydia went to object further, but the man gave a warm smile and spoke in French to her. Whatever he said Fleur didn't catch, but it worked and Lydia agreed to the offer of a coffee.

The café's air conditioning was a welcome relief from the warmth of the day. The lunchtime rush was over and they had their pick of seats, choosing a table in the corner of the room. The man ordered them all a coffee, which was promptly brought over by the waiter.

The café was very traditional in style with its dark wooden furniture and red checked tablecloths. A dado rail separated the tongue-and-groove panelling on the lower part of the walls from the cream plaster above. Several old photographs of what Fleur assumed was the local area hung on the wall. The one above their table was a black and white photograph of a man and woman standing in front of an art-deco-styled bar. 'That looks very glamorous,' remarked Fleur. More to fill the silence than anything else.

'A very glamorous era,' said the man. 'But only if you had money. Otherwise, a very poor and difficult time as Europe had just come out of the Great War. *Alors*, let me introduce myself.' He held his hand out towards Fleur. 'Didier Dacourt.'

Fleur shook hands. 'Fleur Anders and this is my grandmother, Lydia Calvin.'

Lydia smiled at Didier and shook hands with him. 'Pleased to meet you. Forgive my granddaughter, she seems to think I've lost the power of speech.'

Didier's grin was broad, revealing a dimple in his cheek just above the sharp precision line of his beard, which highlighted his chiselled cheekbones. Didier was dressed in a dark suit, a white shirt, with no tie and the collar and next button down casually undone. He would certainly grace any Parisian catwalk. He caught Fleur's gaze and she looked away, embarrassed she'd been seen checking him out. There was no denying he didn't just pass the handsome vibe, he was positively beautiful.

'How are you feeling now?' he asked as Lydia took a sip of her coffee.

'Much better,' replied Lydia. She was still holding the shoe in one hand, having refused to let go of it. 'It was a bit of a shock seeing this.'

'You are French and you are English?' he asked.

'Yes. We both live in England,' explained Fleur. 'My grandmother was born in France and lived here in Paris until she met and married my grandfather who is English.' Fleur stopped, realising she was speaking for Lydia again. 'Sorry, I'm sure my grandmother will explain better than me.'

Lydia smiled at Fleur. 'It's all right.' She looked at Didier. 'Yes, I am Paris born and bred as they say, but have spent most of my adult life in England. And you? You're obviously French. Are you Parisian?'

Lydia had always spoken of being Parisian with pride, as if it was a different nation to the rest of France, and Fleur could sense that sentiment in her grandmother now.

'I am, indeed,' replied Didier. 'My father, like yourself, has lived here all his life. My mother moved here from the Ivory Coast in the 1970s. I was born here.'

Lydia smiled and raised her glass of water to the man. 'To a fellow Parisian.'

Didier raised his coffee cup. 'Was it the shoe that upset you?' he asked.

Lydia looked down at the ballet shoe. 'It did take me by surprise.'

'Does it mean something to you?' Didier continued with his questions, which Fleur wasn't entirely comfortable with.

They had barely known him more than a few minutes and he was pressing Lydia for an explanation.

'Do you know anything about it?' she cut in before her grandmother could say anything more.

Didier shook his head. 'No. I do not.' He repositioned himself in his seat. 'What I do know is that the shoe has been there for two weeks now.' He looked over towards the old school. 'The building has been boarded up for several years. There was a legal . . .' he searched for the word '. . . battle, yes, legal battle over the development of the building. It is going to be converted into apartments, I believe.'

'Yes, I heard about that last year,' said Lydia.

Fleur knew she shouldn't be surprised by anything Lydia said or knew. Her grandmother might be in her eighties but she was as sharp as anyone in the prime of their life. She sat back and listened to the two Parisians discuss it further, not wanting to offer any more information than Lydia wanted to give Didier.

As she took a sip of her coffee, Fleur discreetly took a closer look at the man sitting opposite her. She could see his suit was obviously of good quality, expensive, well-tailored but it perhaps wasn't as crisp as a new suit. It had a well-cared-for but well-worn look about it. Not that it mattered; she was still unashamedly taken with his whole appearance and, so far, persona.

She wondered what he did for a living. He had a quiet confidence about him, without being domineering, and there was something else she couldn't quite put her finger on. Maybe a subtle air of authority.

'The same for the building next door,' Didier was saying. 'That is going to be developed at the same time. So much history right there across the street. I think of all those people who have walked through the doors of those buildings, all the history within those walls. It is amazing.'

Fleur wanted to say that Lydia had gone to that school, but she stopped herself, knowing it wasn't her place to share that part of Lydia's life. As it turned out, Lydia was happy to.

'Actually, I was a pupil at the school,' she said, her gaze travelling back across the road.

'You were? Is that why you are here?' asked Didier.

It was funny listening to two French people speak in English and Fleur was grateful for their consideration so she was included in the conversation. 'My grandmother was just telling me about the classrooms and how she would walk to school with her mother,' said Fleur.

'That is lovely that you can share those memories,' said Didier. 'When I was a boy, I was fortunate enough to travel back to the Ivory Coast twice to see my maternal grandmother. I loved all the stories she would tell me about my mother growing up there. She would immerse me in the culture and her cooking was just the best!' He gave the international gesture of good food by kissing the tips of his fingers and flicking his wrist away with a flourish.

'Is your grandmother still alive?' asked Fleur, knowing she was quite lucky amongst her friendship group to have one of her grandparents still around.

For a moment Didier's dark eyes grew a little darker. 'No. Sadly, she passed away when I was twenty but I have lots of very fond memories, which I hope to share with my children one day.'

'Oh, you have children?' Fleur glanced at his left hand and noted the absence of a wedding ring. Not that it was a foolproof marker of someone's relationship status, of course.

Didier gave a laugh. 'No. I mean when I have children, if I have children. It is important, I feel, to share your past with your family. Especially if it is a different past, a diverse past or a special past.'

'Indeed,' said Lydia. 'You're right, it is important and that is why I have brought my granddaughter with me this year.'

Didier raised his eyebrows in question. 'This year?'

'I've been coming every year for the past fifty years,'

explained Lydia. She looked down at the ballet slipper in her hand. 'I like to honour and remember those I have lost.'

Fleur was desperate to ask Lydia about the ballet shoe. She was sure there was something significant about it, especially the way Lydia was holding on to it and the way she had reacted to it, but Fleur didn't want to ask in front of Didier.

'Were you a pupil at the school during the occupation?' asked Didier gently.

'*Oui*. I was.' Lydia took another sip of water. 'It was a frightening time. You see, I am Jewish, so it was particularly difficult. I lost so many people who were dear to me.'

'I can only imagine,' said Didier, his voice still soft, full of empathy and concern. 'But you survived.'

'Yes. I did and every day I have felt a huge sense of guilt because of that.' Lydia didn't speak with any bitterness, just an acceptance.

Fleur was stunned. Lydia had never told her any of this. 'You shouldn't feel guilt, Nan. You were just a young child.'

'Maybe I shouldn't, but I do.' Lydia gazed down at the shoe again.

Fleur could see it was stirring up emotions within Lydia. Fleur lifted her sunglasses onto her head and placed a hand on her grandmother's. 'Has the shoe got something to do with it?' she asked, adopting the same tender tones as Didier.

After what seemed a long moment where Fleur held her breath and exchanged a glance with Didier as they both waited for an answer, Lydia finally replied. 'I'm quite tired. I think I'd like to go back to the hotel now.' She was matter-of-fact as she opened the clasp on her bag and carefully placed the shoe inside before snapping it closed.

Fleur didn't question whether Lydia should be taking the shoe, but whatever the reason for it being left, she had the sensation that the ballet slipper somehow belonged to her. She glanced again at Didier who just gave a discreet nod. He rose from his chair. 'It's been a pleasure to meet you, madame,' he said, giving a faint bow. 'My car is just parked along here. Would you allow me to drive you back to your hotel, rather than try to get a taxi?'

'It's OK, we'll be fine,' said Fleur, suddenly thinking getting into a stranger's car was maybe not their best move, despite how utterly charming he was.

'It's no trouble,' said Didier.

'That would be most kind,' said Lydia before Fleur could think of another objection. 'I just want to use the bathroom first.'

'You can trust me,' said Didier to Fleur, as Lydia disappeared into the depths of the café. 'You can ask the owners. They know me. I come here all the time.'

'It's not that,' said Fleur. It clearly was that, but she didn't quite know how to say it without sounding rude.

Didier fished in the inside pocket of his jacket and pulled a business card from his wallet. He handed it to Fleur. 'That's me.' And then he opened his wallet and pulled out a rather tattered photograph. 'That's me with my parents, when I qualified as a gendarme. Just so you know, I am on the right side of the law.'

Fleur looked at the photograph of a young Didier Dacourt, standing proudly in his blue uniform with his parents either side of him, both of them beaming with absolute pride. It made sense now, that air of authority and confidence she had got from him. She looked at the business card. 'Antiques? You're an antique dealer? That's quite a jump from law enforcement to antiques.' She handed the photograph back and pocketed the business card.

Didier smiled. 'I wanted a quieter life after the police.'

The way he said it, Fleur sensed there was more to the story of why he had switched careers but as the waiter came out to clear the table, the chance to ask was missed.

Didier's phone rang, breaking the conversation. 'Excuse me one moment,' he said, getting up from the table and moving onto the pavement out of earshot. Fleur watched from behind the safety of her sunglasses as he frowned, spoke rapid French and although she couldn't understand him, she could tell he wasn't happy about something. She looked away and busied herself with her phone as he ended his call and returned to the table. 'Apologies,' he said with a tight smile. He glanced over his shoulder back towards the café, his forefinger tapping the table.

'If you need to go, it's OK, we can get a taxi,' said Fleur. 'What? Oh, no. It's fine.'

Fleur wasn't sure it was really fine but she chose not to insist and was grateful when her grandmother emerged. Didier jumped up and briskly escorted them to the car.

The journey back to the hotel didn't take long. Didier hopped out of the car, opening the door for them and offering Lydia his arm to assist her up the steps to the hotel entrance.

'*Merci, beaucoup,*' said Lydia.

'*De rein,*' replied Didier. 'No problem. It was a pleasure to meet you.' He shook hands with them both, which felt oddly formal to Fleur but at the same time very natural. She liked the easy way about him. She was disappointed she wouldn't be seeing him again.

'Take care and thank you,' she called as he got back into his car.

He paused and waved, before climbing in and driving away.

'He was a nice young man,' said Lydia as they entered the lift.

'He was very charming,' agreed Fleur. She heard Lydia give a small laugh but said nothing.

Fleur went into Lydia's room with her to make sure she was settled as Lydia wanted a rest before they had dinner that evening. 'Are you sure you're all right, Nan?' she asked, putting Lydia's shoes neatly under the chair.

'Yes. Too much excitement in one day for me.'

'Excitement?'

'Please, Fleur. I don't want to talk about it right now.'

'I was just worried. You seemed upset about the ballet shoe.'

'Fleur. I said I don't want to talk about it.' Lydia's tone

was firm and she settled her head back on the pillow and closed her eyes.

'Sorry.' Fleur draped the blanket over her grandmother.

Lydia opened her eyes. Her expression was one of kindness. 'I didn't mean to snap at you. I will tell you, just not right now. I need time to think about it. To process it myself.'

'It's all right. I understand.'

Lydia reached out for Fleur's hand. 'The ballet shoe . . . it turns everything I thought upside down.' Tears gathered in Lydia's eyes. 'I don't know if I'm strong enough to confront it, that's all.'

Chapter 11

Adele

Paris, July 1942

After making sure the women and children were settled in the attic of the school, Adele made it back home to the apartment much later than she had hoped, just slipping in through the door a minute after curfew. Her father raised his eyebrows as she came in.

'Is everything all right?' he asked, as she ran herself a glass of water.

'Yes. Nothing to worry about.' She gulped down the water. 'Is Lucille here?'

'Yes! I'm here!' her sister called from the living room. 'And I'm on my own before you ask.'

Adele walked into the room, pausing to give her father a kiss, before sitting down in the armchair on the other side of the coffee table. 'I wasn't going to ask, as a matter of fact.'

Lucille laughed. 'No, but you wanted to.'

'So, where is Peter?' asked Adele. 'I thought you said something about supper with him tonight.'

A look of irritation briefly swept over Lucille's face, so fast Adele might have missed it if she didn't know her sister so well. Lucille's expression was now one of nonchalance. 'He was called away to a meeting.'

'In the evening? Must be important.' Adele thought of

the round-up and her stomach knotted. She had no doubt that's what Peter was actually doing.

'Are you all right?' asked Lucille. 'You look very pale all of a sudden.'

'I'm fine.' Adele smiled at her sister. 'Just a bit tired, that's all.'

'Where's the boy?' asked Lucille, looking around as if for the first time remembering about their guest the previous night.

'He's back with his mother,' replied Adele. 'She picked him up from school this evening after dance class.' She was aware of her father's gaze on her, but she avoided looking his way.

'Oh, that's good. What was her excuse for leaving him with you?'

'I didn't ask.'

'You're too soft,' said Lucille. 'Now you've done it once, she'll expect you to do it again. Peter said a lot of the Jewish women are prostituting themselves. He said they have no shame.'

'Lucille,' warned her father.

'Well, it's true,' Lucille retorted.

'You don't know that,' said Adele. 'It's only what Peter's said. You shouldn't repeat things unless they are fact. Besides, if the women are doing that, then they must be desperate.' She got to her feet. 'Probably trying to get money to feed their children because the Germans have cut off their income and prohibited their husbands and fathers from working. That's if they haven't been deported to a work camp in Germany or captured trying to defend France.'

'They have their reasons for doing that but I don't want to get into an argument with you now about it.' Lucille turned her attention back to her fingernails, which she was painting.

'Nothing can justify what they are doing. Nothing.' Adele wanted to shake some sense into her sister. 'Just be careful you're not blinded by your infatuation for a German officer who supports this Nazi regime.'

'Girls, girls. That's enough,' said Gérard. 'I'll have no more raised voices or arguing in my house. But for the record, the way the Jewish community is being treated is abominable. No woman, whatever the circumstances, should have to resort to prostitution to feed her children. Now, I'll not have this discussed any further this evening. Adele, why don't you go to bed? You do look tired.'

'I'm twenty-five and I'm being sent to bed?' She didn't know whether to be indignant or laugh.

'Night, night. Sweet dreams,' said Lucille.

'Lucille! Enough.' Gérard's voice was stern.

Adele picked up a cushion and threw it at her sister, who let out a yelp as the cushion knocked her hand and the red nail varnish she was holding. 'Adele! Why did you do that? You've made me smudge my nail now.'

'You're lucky you have only that to worry about and not where your next meal is coming from,' snapped Adele.

'Stop it! Papa! Tell her!'

Adele didn't wait for her father to reprimand her. She probably deserved it. Throwing a cushion at her infuriating younger sister wasn't exactly mature, but Lucille could drive her to distraction at times. So caught up in herself, so obsessed with Peter, that she was starting to spout Nazi rhetoric and Adele could not let that go. Adele slammed the bedroom door behind her to underline her anger at her sister and flopped down onto the bed.

Try as she might, she couldn't get to sleep. Her mind kept going back to Jacqueline, Cecile and the children hiding away up in the attic of the schoolroom and to the Jewish families who might not have been warned about the round-up or who didn't have anywhere to go. She wondered about Daniel's mother and where she was and what she was doing. Adele could only hope she'd managed to escape out of the city and was waiting for a safe time to send for her son. And there Lucille was, painting her nails and put out that Peter had cancelled their supper.

Adele must have dozed on and off throughout the night but shortly after four in the morning, she was awoken by the sounds of vehicles tearing down the street, shouts and booted feet running across the pavement. It could only be one thing. The round-up.

She slipped out of bed and crept down the hallway to the living room. Thick blackout curtains hung at the window. Adele hooked a finger behind the fabric and slowly moved it to one side, just enough so she could look out onto the street below.

A truck was parked with its engine running while two soldiers were standing guard outside the apartment building opposite. She could hear muffled shouts and cries. Less than a minute later, a family of four were marched out of the building and ordered into the back of the truck. One of the women dropped her suitcase and stooped to pick it up but a soldier kicked it away from her and, grabbing her arm, heaved her up, before shoving her towards the back of the lorry, shouting something abusive in German as he did so.

Within seconds of the tailgate of the truck being closed, it was tearing off down the road, heading for their next prey, swiftly followed by the two soldiers on their motorbikes. Adele looked at the abandoned suitcase, its contents strewn across the pavement – clothing, underwear, a framed photograph. It seemed wrong to leave it there. Insulting. Condoning.

Without giving it a second thought, Adele took her big coat from the hall cupboard and slipped her arms in, lifting the catch on the door to the apartment, she wedged a shoe in the doorframe to stop it closing behind her. With slippered feet, she pattered down the staircase, across the hallway and out into the street. There was no one about, maybe they were too scared to come out or maybe they didn't care because it wasn't happening to them.

Adele didn't know the family who had been taken, she'd seen the mother a few times and they had nodded in acknowledgement to each other, but they had never struck up a conversation. Their children were teenagers and didn't go to her school. Adele had no idea they were Jewish. She tried to think back to when she last saw them. If it had been since the yellow badge had been brought in, surely she would have noticed then? But, thinking about it, no, she hadn't seen the family. It sat uneasy with her that she hadn't been paying attention. If she'd somehow known, she could have warned them about the round-up. If she had, then maybe they would have been able to escape before being taken from their beds.

Checking there were no more Germans hanging around, Adele nipped across the road and began scooping up the possessions and replacing them in the suitcase. Once it was all collected, she snapped the locks shut. Only one would stay closed, which was probably why it had emptied itself a short while ago. The door to the apartment building was still open and Adele stepped inside. Of course, she had no idea which apartment they lived in but she climbed the stairs thinking that the Germans probably didn't worry about securing the apartment on behalf of the family. On the first floor, she spotted what she was looking for – the door slightly ajar.

Adele cautiously stepped into the apartment. She wasn't sure what she was expecting to find, maybe chaos, upturned furniture, broken crockery or some sign of disturbance but the apartment was neat and tidy. Just how it must have been left when the occupants had gone to bed that night. Such was the efficiency of the Germans in getting the family out, there had obviously been no chance or opportunity for a struggle or a fight.

Something made Adele walk further into the apartment. It could be any Parisian home, anywhere in the city. The dining table was set ready for breakfast. A brass menorah stood on the sideboard, the seven candle holders shimmering in the moonlight coming in through the window.

The two bedrooms were the only place that showed the occupants had left in a hurry. The bed sheets were thrown back haphazardly and a night light had been knocked over in the master bedroom. Adele placed the suitcase on the floor. For some unknown reason, she found herself righting the lamp and making the bed. She felt that with the beds made there was some kind of respect, as if Adele could rid the presence of the Germans ever having been here.

As she left, she made sure the door was locked. If, by some miracle, the family were allowed back, then hopefully their home and belongings would be safe from looters. Much as it pained her to admit, there were opportunists everywhere and in these times of turmoil, they wouldn't hesitate to take advantage of an empty property.

When she went back to her own apartment, Adele was surprised to see her father standing at the living room window. He was in his pyjamas with his flannel dressing gown wrapped around him. He turned and gave her a sad smile, before opening his arms and wrapping Adele in an embrace. 'I was going to come and help you,' said her father.

'I didn't know they were Jewish,' whispered Adele, her face still buried in her father's shoulder. 'If I had, I would have warned them.'

Her father stroked her hair. 'Shh now. You are not to blame and you are not responsible for everyone.'

Adele ensured she arrived early at the school that morning. As she walked through the streets, there was an eerie atmosphere; a sense of unease was spreading across the capital. The round-up had put people's nerves on edge and Adele could sense it in the air.

As she turned a corner, she gave a gasp of horror. Just a few metres in front of her were the bodies of a man and a woman lying face down in the gutter. A priest was standing over them, making the sign of the cross and a small handful of people, who Adele assumed were residents of the street, were standing next to the priest with their heads bowed. One of the bystanders, a woman, was silently crying.

Adele could see the yellow armbands on the dead couple, who – she could only assume – had angered the Germans enough to warrant being executed in the street when the round-up was carried out. She couldn't help wondering if they had died at the hands of Peter. Notwithstanding the fact he was German, there was something about him she didn't trust. She made the sign of the cross as she traversed the road and hurried on her way.

A truck rumbled down the street and passed her. As Adele glanced back over her shoulder, she could see it had stopped alongside the bodies, which were now being heaved up into the back of it. Those poor people, being slaughtered outside their own home and the final dignity of a funeral stripped away from them as they were bundled onto the back of the truck. She didn't know where they would be taken, but she remembered hearing Müller talking to another officer about it at the exhibition. There had been no shame or shock during their discussion, when they spoke of mass graves and incinerations. How there were so many bodies to get rid of they didn't know what to do with them all. Their indifference had shocked Adele then, and it made her want to weep now as the same sense of incredulous disbelief and overwhelming desperation flooded over her once more.

Adele was surprised to see Manu waiting outside the school gates for her. He was leaning against the brick pier, smoking a cigarette whilst reading a newspaper. He pushed himself away as she approached and ground out his cigarette.

'I hope you're not paying any attention to what's in there,' said Adele, nodding towards the newspaper.

Manu rolled his eyes and greeted Adele with a kiss on each cheek. 'Just seeing what lies and propaganda our illustrious government is pushing today.' He folded the newspaper under his arm. 'I need to speak to you. Can we go inside?'

Adele gave a furtive glance around, before unlocking the school and leading the way inside.

Manu shut the door behind him. 'You look tired,' he commented.

'I couldn't sleep properly last night.' She avoided looking at him, and instead busied herself with changing the calendar on the wall.

'Did you manage to warn some of the parents?' he asked.

'Yes. Yes, I did.' Still she fiddled with the calendar. She wanted to tell him they were here in the building but the fewer people who knew, the safer everyone would be. She felt his hands on her shoulders, which made her catch her breath.

Manu reached over and took the wooden date plaques from her, placed them on the desk and turned her around to face him. He tipped her chin up with his forefinger. 'You can trust me, Adele. I promise,' he said as if able to read her mind.

She looked up at him. 'You can trust me too.'

He gave a small nod. 'I know. But I also care about you and by telling you things, it would put you in danger.'

'Then that is my answer as well.' He cared about her? She was sure of that, but probably not in the same way she cared about him.

'I'll make this easy,' he continued. 'I know you have guests here.' He held up a finger to silence anything she was about to say. 'I am glad. It's the right thing but you know you are in serious danger now.'

'I know.' She pulled away from him. 'But what was I to do? They had nowhere to go. No one to help them. I was their only hope.'

'There are people who can help.'

'I'm sure there are but how do you find them?'

'You could have come to me.'

'Yes. I probably could but I didn't have the luxury of time and you were busy with your girlfriend and in case it's escaped your notice, she isn't too fond of me.' Adele stopped, shocked that she had actually voiced those thoughts. 'I'm sorry. I shouldn't have said that.'

'Don't apologise. I'm glad you did. It makes a refreshing change.'

Adele looked at him, confused by the comment. 'What do you mean?'

'You're always careful about saying the right thing,' replied Manu. 'I think because you're so used to being correct in front of the children, sometimes you forget to take your teacher's hat off.'

Adele wasn't sure if she was flattered or offended by the observation. Not knowing how to answer, she deflected the subject away. 'Instead of analysing me, perhaps we should concentrate on trying to help the women and children who are at this moment petrified for their lives.'

'Ah, back to proper and correct teacher.' There was a hint of amusement to Manu's voice.

'It's not funny,' countered Adele. She felt a small blush creeping up her neck.

He leaned in a little closer than necessary and in a whisper said, 'You shouldn't worry about Edith. There's no competition there.'

Adele's heart threw in an extra beat. Typical of Manu to make an ambiguous statement like that. What was she supposed to make of it? But she didn't have time to consider it further as Manu was talking again, as he stepped away from her. 'How many have you got up there?'

'Err . . . Oh, erm . . . Four children and two women,' Adele replied still a little distracted. 'They are in the small attic room where the caretaker used to sleep.'

'Oh, I remember him. Isn't it a bit too obvious though, if the school is searched?'

'No. There's a different staircase to the main part of the attic. The staircase to the little attic is at the back of a cupboard in the dance studio. The caretaker sectioned it off so it was private and he didn't get disturbed every time someone wanted something from the main attic, which is a stock room.'

'Is it visible when you go into the cupboard?'

'Yes. But I thought I'd try to disguise it by putting up some shelves so it looked like a bookcase.'

'And you're good at carpentry?'

Adele gave a shrug. 'I can do more than teach and dance, you know.'

'I'm sure you can.'

Nothing in Manu's voice or face told her if he was teasing her or not. 'You should never underestimate a woman,' she replied aware that she was venturing into flirting territory. She quickly looked away, breaking the moment.

'Let me help you,' said Manu, leaving no doubt that's exactly what he was going to do whether she liked it or not. 'I'll come by later today. I might be able to speak to some contacts about getting your new guests out.'

'How long will it take? To get them out, I mean.'

'I don't know. Everything is very unstable at the moment. Contacts are fluid and changing all the time. The Gestapo are becoming very adept at flushing out the quarry.'

'No one other than you know they are here,' said Adele.

'Make sure it stays that way. I must go now.' He paused at the door. 'Don't even tell your father or your sister. *Especially* not your sister. Understand?'

'Of course.' Adele was affronted Manu was talking to her like she was ten years old and didn't understand the consequences of her actions. 'I don't need things spelled out to me. I'm not a child anymore.'

Manu's gaze met hers. 'I'm fully aware of that.' Then he was gone, leaving Adele staring at the empty space he had just occupied.

Chapter 12

Adele

After Manu left and Adele had managed to put all thoughts of their flirtatious conversation out of her head, she went up to the attic to make sure everyone was safe. The bathrooms were located on the second floor, down the hallway from the dance studio, which was fine for everyone to use during the night when the school was empty but during the day, not so.

'I'm afraid you'll all have to use this bucket,' said Adele. 'I'll put it behind this screen, at least you'll have a bit of privacy that way. Now, remember, you all have to be as quiet as mice during the day. You can't be banging on the floor or moving things around.'

'I'm bored,' said Thomas. 'Can't we go to lessons?'

'That's enough,' said Cecile. 'I've already explained that to you.'

'I've brought up some pencils, paper and schoolbooks,' said Adele. 'You can do some work for me, if you like. I can look at it when I come back up later.'

'Thank you,' said Cecile, taking the things from Adele.

'I think we should try to sleep as much as possible during the day,' said Jacqueline. 'It's the easiest way to stay quiet. We can do all this in the night.'

'Whatever you do, you just have to do it quietly.' Adele smiled at the children in a bid to offer some reassurance.

'Can we still go to the dance class?' asked Eva.

'No. That won't be possible anymore,' said Jacqueline. 'We're not to let anyone know we're here.'

Eva's face fell.

'I tell you what,' said Adele, injecting enthusiasm into her voice. 'How about I come back later, once everyone has gone home, and you can all come down to the dance room and we can do some dancing ourselves – just us. How does that sound?'

'All of us?' asked Eva.

'Yes, if you all want to?'

Eva jumped up and clapped her hands together. 'I would hate not to be able to dance.'

'So would I,' agreed Adele, giving the child a hug. 'It's a way to be free and no one can take that away from us.' She looked at Blanche who so far had not moved from her mother's lap. 'Is everything all right with her? She's not ill, is she?' Adele hadn't thought about that. How would she make sure they got the medication they needed if one of them took ill? Or, even worse, need medical help?

'She's not ill,' reassured Jacqueline. 'She lost her cuddly rabbit on the way here.'

'It's Lulu le Lapin. She has a pink ribbon and a fluffy tail. I like to suck her ear,' said Blanche. 'I want her back. She's my favourite and the only one I was allowed to bring with me.'

Adele crouched down next to the child and stroked her hair. 'I'll see if I can find you something else to cuddle until we can find Lulu le Lapin.' Adele didn't want to say it was unlikely but she hoped it would comfort the child in the meantime. She was sure there were some toys in one of the boxes downstairs. If not, she might be able to make Blanche something out of some clothes she had at home and didn't wear anymore.

After making sure the stowaways were all as comfortable as possible and had everything they needed for the day ahead, Adele went downstairs to greet the rest of the children.

* * *

For the next two days, Adele was on a knife edge as she tried to carry on as normal, knowing any day the guests, as she'd come to refer to them in her mind, in the attic would be discovered or she would fall under suspicion.

The time, though, came far sooner than she expected. It was Friday morning and she had just dismissed the class for morning break when one of the older pupils of the school knocked on her door.

'*Bonjour, Philippe,*' greeted Adele.

'*Bonjour, mademoiselle.* Monsieur Basset has asked that you see him in his office.' There was a trepidation in the twelve-year-old's eyes as he looked away and down at his feet.

'Very well. Thank you, Philippe. Go out for your break now.' The boy scuttled away, leaving Adele more than a little concerned at this summons. It was most unlike her father. If he wanted to speak to her about anything, he would always come to her. To be summoned to his office was very out of character.

As she left her room, Adele met her colleague, Michelle Joffre who taught the middle class. 'Did you get asked to go to your father's office as well?'

'Yes. Do you know what it's about?' Adele asked as they made their way down the stairs.

Michelle shook her head. 'No. But there is a German military vehicle parked outside in the street. I just saw it from my window.'

Adele could feel her heart begin to quicken but she said nothing. On reaching the main reception hallway, Madame Allard's usual sunny disposition was clearly absent. There was a grave look on the receptionist's face. She motioned with her eyes towards the schoolmaster's office and silently mouthed 'Germans' to Adele.

The door was open and Adele could see her father standing at his desk and on the other side, with his back to her, was a German officer.

Both men turned to look as she gave a polite tap on the door. Adele recognised the officer as the one who'd come to take the names of the Jewish children back in May.

The German officer spoke first. '*Ah, Mademoiselle Basset. Bonjour.* Nice to meet you again.' He smiled at her. 'And Madame Joffre. Would you mind coming into the office? I have a few questions.'

'How can I help you?' asked Adele as she stepped into the room.

'Please, would you like to take a seat?' There was no mistaking this suggestion as anything other than an instruction. Adele and Michelle took the seats offered. Gérard Basset and the German officer followed suit. 'So, I was just asking Monsieur Basset about your pupils. Your Jewish pupils.'

Adele kept her gaze on the officer, offering the most unconcerned look she could muster. 'And what about them?'

'As you are probably aware, early this morning, a number of Jewish families were asked to report at the Vélodrome d'Hiver but, according to our records which we have cross-referenced with the information you kindly provided us, there are several missing.' Adele didn't reply and waited for him to continue. There was a slight impatience to his voice. 'So, I am asking you, what Jewish pupils are in your class today. Both your classes?'

'I have none in my class,' replied Michelle.

The officer referred to his list. 'Thomas Kampe?'

'Not in my class.' Michelle fiddled with the wedding ring on her finger.

'Very well, you can leave, Madame Joffre.'

'Thank you, Michelle,' said Gérard.

Michelle exchanged a glance with Adele as she slipped out of the room.

The officer turned to Adele. 'Thomas Kampe? Is he in your class?'

Adele nodded. 'Yes.'

'So where is he today? And what about your other pupils, Eva Rashal, Blanche Rashal and Daniel Charon? Are they in school today?'

'No, they're not and before you ask, no I don't know where they are,' replied Adele. Michelle being questioned first had given her the few moments she needed to compose herself to lie convincingly.

'Did their mothers give any indication that the children would not be in school?'

Adele shook her head. 'None at all. They collected them from school at the end of the day yesterday and I haven't seen them since.' She concentrated on sitting perfectly still, no fidgeting, no shuffling of her feet, no breaking eye contact.

The officer ran his finger along the scar that reached from his lip to under his chin. 'We are also missing a family from your father's class. The Demski family. It seems quite a coincidence that three families from this school are unaccounted for.'

'Perhaps they spoke to one another,' suggested Gérard. 'But they certainly didn't speak to us. Why would they? We would, of course, alert the authorities. As we've already proven, by compiling a list of Jewish children in the first place, we're very willing to cooperate.'

'I sincerely hope you would,' said the officer. He stood abruptly. 'That will be all for today. If you see or hear anything, it is in your best interest to cooperate fully with us.'

Gérard rose to his feet also. 'Of course.'

'I'll see myself out.' With that the German marched from the room, his heels thudding on the wooden floorboards as he went.

'I'd better ring the bell for end of break,' said Adele, wanting to leave the room before her father questioned her. She wasn't so lucky though.

'Just a moment, Adele. I want to speak to you. Please, shut the door.'

Adele walked slowly over to the door, taking a moment

to gather her thoughts. Madame Allard was watching but quickly looked down at the paperwork on her desk. Adele closed the door and returned to the chair. 'What?'

Her father leaned back in his chair and took off his glasses, letting out a sigh as he did so. 'I don't want to ask you if you know where the children and their mothers are, as I don't want you to have to lie to me.'

'I don't want to lie either,' replied Adele.

Her father appeared to be considering his next words carefully. He opened the drawer of his desk and reached in, producing a soft stuffed toy rabbit. 'I found this in the hallway when I came in this morning.'

Adele looked at the soft toy with the pink ribbon around its neck, a fluffy white tail and a chewed ear. It was unmistakably Lulu le Lapin. Her father continued. 'I don't recognise it but if you're tidying up the attic, you might want to take it up with you.'

Adele reached over and picked up the toy. 'Thank you. I think I will.' She got to her feet and pushed the toy into the pocket of her jacket. 'Papa, do you think the Demski family are somewhere safe?'

'I'd like to believe they are,' replied her father. 'Now, you'd better go and ring that bell for the end of break.'

The rest of the day passed quickly and without any further unexpected visits from the occupying force. At the end of the day, once the pupils had all gone home and after the usual dance class, Adele was about to close the door to the school when Manu turned up with a friend. Between them they were carrying a large wooden bookcase.

'Here it is,' said Manu, as if Adele was expecting it. 'Jean-Claude is going to help me get it up the stairs. I'll be able to do the rest on my own. Can you just nip upstairs and make sure there's room for it in the dance studio?'

Adele took the hint and nimbly sprinted up the two flights of stairs and then the hidden staircase, warning the occupants of the attic to stay very still. 'I'll come up as soon as it's safe,' she said before running back down where she met Manu and Jean-Claude at the top of the staircase.

'Where's it going?' asked Jean-Claude.

'Just in this room here,' replied Adele. 'Next to the blackboard, please. Thank you so much.'

'Yes, thank you,' echoed Manu once the bookcase was in position.

They escorted Jean-Claude back downstairs and he went on his way, oblivious to what was happening in the school.

'Thank you,' said Adele as she locked the door.

'Don't thank me yet; you've got to help me get it into position in the storeroom,' replied Manu with a wink, which made Adele just think how incredibly handsome he looked that evening. 'I'm going to attach it to the door itself. It will make it heavier to open and close but that's not a bad thing. I'll leave a few centimetres off the ground but you will need to put some books on it and hide the door handle.'

Before they moved the bookcase, Adele brought the children and women down from the attic. 'We can dance whilst Manu does some work.'

'So it's tap-dancing tonight, then?' said Jacqueline.

'*Bien sûr!*' replied Adele, taking a basket from the cupboard so the children could change into some tap shoes.

Jacqueline and Cecile helped Manu shift the bookcase into position, while Adele began her tap-dance class.

It was the perfect cover and by the time Manu had finished, the children were all exhausted from the rather exuberant dancing. Adele had purposely played loud and fast music on the gramophone to mask the noise of Manu's carpentry even further.

It was another hour before Adele bade her goodnights to the children and their mothers. 'I'll be back early in the morning again,' she promised. She was pleased to see Blanche's mood had lifted since being reunited with her beloved Lulu le Lapin.

Jacqueline had probably been more delighted though. 'Thank goodness for that. I thought I was never going to hear the last of it,' she said. 'Cecile and I are going to try to keep the children awake for as long as possible tonight so they sleep tomorrow during the day. They did start to get a bit restless this afternoon but I think it will be all right.'

She followed Adele over to the door at the top of the secret stairs. 'Do you have any sort of plan for getting us out of here?'

'Not yet,' replied Adele. 'But I'm hoping to have some news very soon.' She hugged Jacqueline tightly, their unspoken anxieties and fears smothered for now. 'As soon as I hear anything, I will let you know.'

Adele left her friend and went down to the bottom of the stairs, heaving the bookcase door closed behind her. She rearranged the books on the shelf to hide the door handle. Manu had done an amazing job. She just hoped he'd be able to help with getting Jacqueline, Cecile and the children to safety now.

'Would you like me to walk you home?' asked Manu as Adele came downstairs.

'I'll be fine. It's out of your way,' replied Adele, although she acknowledged she would love his company. She would be sad to say goodnight to him.

'But it's getting late. I'd sooner you didn't walk home alone.'

'Aren't you meeting Edith?'

'Not tonight.'

Adele gave a shrug, hoping to appear nonchalant about the offer. 'If it will make you feel better, then please do come along.'

Manu gave a small chuckle. 'Thank you for humouring me.'

It was a little chilly but Adele was glad of the cool summer breeze. Just walking alongside Manu this evening felt different. She couldn't quite put her finger on it but she felt closer to him, not just physically but mentally too. They had a shared secret now, something just the two of them knew about, and she couldn't help feeling excited by the idea.

They turned the corner and walked along the road, which was busy that evening, the restaurants and cafés were full of German soldiers enjoying the city nightlife. It was strange to think there was a war going on in Europe as these men drank wine, beer, ate well and were entertained by the local women. Adele had heard that some women had been shipped in from other countries in Europe, some willingly and others not so.

She felt Manu nudge her with his elbow. 'Stop staring,' he muttered under his breath. He put an arm around her shoulder and whispered in her ear. 'You'll just have to act like you're in love with me for a minute.'

Adele felt even hotter. She wouldn't have to pretend. As she glanced in at the restaurant window they were passing, she almost stopped in her tracks. She grabbed Manu's arm.

'Keep walking,' said Manu, without breaking stride.

Adele had to take a second look, just to make sure she wasn't seeing things. She could feel Manu pull her along and with one final look, she quickened her pace to keep up with him.

'What was it?' asked Manu once they were well out of sight of the restaurant.

'It was Peter,' said Adele.

'Peter?'

'Peter Müller. That's Hauptmann Müller to you. My sister's boyfriend.'

'So?'

'So, he was with another woman.'

'And a man cannot have dinner with a woman? Perhaps they were talking business.'

'Not the sort of business that means leaning over the table and kissing each other,' snapped Adele. 'He's supposed to be in love with Lucille. They're supposed to be getting married.'

Chapter 13

Fleur

Paris, August 2015

After settling her grandmother, Fleur's mind kept returning to the shoe and its significance. And then there was Didier, who had come to their aid. What good fortune he had been over the road and how kind of him to offer them a lift back to the hotel. She would have been able to manage it all on her own, but his help had made life a lot easier.

The phone in her hotel room rang unexpectedly and Fleur answered it.

'*Bonjour, Mademoiselle Anders*. Reception, here. I have Monsieur Dacourt on the phone for you. Will you accept the call?'

It took Fleur a moment to compute the information. 'Err, yes. Thank you. *Merci*.' What on earth was Didier Dacourt calling her for?

There were a couple of clicks and then the receptionist informed the callers they were connected before another click as she left the line.

'*Bonjour, Mademoiselle Anders? Fleur?*' came Didier's rich deep voice.

Fleur liked the way he said her name with his French accent – it made her name sound so much more interesting. '*Oui*. Hello.'

'*C'est Didier*. We met this morning. Outside the school.'

Fleur smiled at the long-winded explanation. She knew exactly who he was by just his name. 'Hello, Didier. *Ça-va?*'

He gave a sigh of relief. '*Ça-va bien. Et toi?*'

'*Ça-va.*' Fleur knew she was smiling even broader at their awkward exchange. 'Is everything all right?'

'I hope you do not mind me calling you at the hotel,' he began. 'I have been thinking about you and your grandmother all afternoon. I need to talk to you. I mean, I would like to talk to you.'

'My grandmother is resting at the moment,' explained Fleur. 'The discovery of the ballet shoe has upset her.'

'Yes. I am sorry about that. However, I do not think I have explained myself correctly.' There was a pause and Fleur could hear Didier take a deep breath. She waited for him to continue. 'It would be better if I could speak to you alone.'

Alone? Fleur knocked the thought about in her head. She didn't know Didier and she wouldn't normally agree to meet a stranger on her own but, at the same time, here in Paris felt different. Still, she should be sensibly cautious. 'I'm not sure,' she began.

'Please, it is about your grandmother and the shoe. I need to explain something. I think it would be better if I spoke to you first.'

'OK,' she said slowly. 'When would you want to meet?'

'As soon as you are free.'

Fleur looked towards the closed door to the adjoining apartment. 'I can't come yet. I don't want to leave Nan while she's asleep in case she wakes up and worries where I am.'

'*Bien sûr*. But I do need to speak to you as soon as possible.'

'Could you come to the hotel in the morning? Maybe we could meet in the lounge.' It seemed not only a sensible suggestion but a safe one too. Despite her gut feeling that she could trust Didier, Fleur still erred on the side of caution. At least in a hotel she was surrounded by other people.

'That will be good. Is ten o'clock all right for you?'

'It's perfect.'

'There is just one thing,' said Didier. 'Before you meet me, could you ask your grandmother if either the name Bridget Sutter or the town Geneva mean anything to her.'

'Bridget Sutter? Geneva?'

'Yes. I will explain when I see you.'

Fleur had to wait until that evening to tell Lydia about the phone call with Didier. They were having dinner in a nearby restaurant on the Left Bank, just a few minutes' walk from the hotel.

'I like to come here,' explained Lydia as they settled themselves at their table. 'It's very popular with the Parisians and I love to hear the chatter of French voices around me.'

Once they had ordered and had been served their meal, Fleur brought up the subject of Didier, explaining to Lydia the phone call and his request.

'Bridget Sutter? Geneva?' Lydia repeated after Fleur had finished relaying the conversation she'd had with Didier. 'The name means nothing at all. Not that I can remember, anyway. And Geneva? Well, of course, I've heard of it, but it has no significance. Sorry. Why do you think Didier is asking?'

'He said he'll tell me tomorrow. I think it might be to do with the ballet shoe.'

Lydia looked up at her. 'The shoe? What on earth do you think he means?'

'I've no idea. You never said earlier why the shoe upset you so much,' said Fleur gently. 'Do you feel up to telling me now?'

Lydia rested her cutlery on either side of her plate and took a sip of the wine they'd ordered. 'It made me think of my days at the school, in particular all the children and what happened. It brought back some memories I thought were forgotten. Well not forgotten, but ones I've chosen not to revisit very often.'

'Such as?' Fleur asked, aware she needed to balance her desire to know more and her grandmother's capacity to deal with the emotion those memories would undoubtedly release.

'We were only young but we understood the unspoken fear that filled every waking moment of the lives of the adults around us. We didn't need it spelt out to us, we just understood. And that fear was visceral, relentless and paralysing. Some of us were able to suppress it. Bury it. Leave it behind us, me being one of those. Or so I thought. But that shoe was like a key and it unlocked all those memories. For a short time, it was like experiencing them all over again.'

Fleur's heart went out to Lydia. She couldn't even begin to imagine what Lydia was telling her. How could she? The closest thing to danger she'd ever known was when she was about six years old and had got lost in the supermarket for five minutes. Hardly comparable. 'I don't have to meet Didier, if you'd rather I didn't.'

'I want you to,' said Lydia, her voice strong. 'I want to know what he knows.'

'If you're sure.'

'Very. Just go along and see what he has to say,' replied Lydia, and then added, 'I can chaperone you if you like.' There was a mischievous twinkle in her eye as she spoke.

Fleur laughed. 'It's OK, I'll be fine. And don't worry, I won't let my drink out of my sight.'

Lydia's face grew serious. 'I wasn't thinking that, but now you've got me worried.'

'Honestly, Nan, I was just joking. I'll be careful.'

Lydia looked thoughtful. 'What I'll do, I'll ask Jean-Paul to keep an eye on you.'

'Jean-Paul?'

'Yes, he's the barman. Been at the hotel for several years now. He'll be discreet, don't worry.'

Fleur didn't know whether to laugh or not, at the thought her grandmother was arranging personal protection for her. 'It's not a date. Just a chat.'

'Better safe than sorry. Charming as he is, we have to be careful. I haven't travelled the world on my own and not been streetwise.'

It was true, Lydia had been solo-travelling for years now, since Fleur's grandfather had died. Fleur didn't remember him as he passed away before she was born, but Fleur had grown up thinking for a long time that her grandmother travelling around the world on her own was normal. It wasn't until she was older and exchanged stories with her contemporaries, she realised her grandmother was a little different to her friends' grandparents.

'What made you want to travel so much when you were younger?' asked Fleur.

Lydia didn't answer immediately and when she did, she was somewhat pensive. 'After I was widowed, I felt very alone. I had your mother and then you came along a year later, of course, but I didn't want to be a burden. I was still youngish and I was . . .' She stopped speaking, her gaze dropping to her plate.

'And?' prompted Fleur. She studied Lydia's face and felt her grandmother was on the brink of telling her something. Some sort of secret, something she'd never told Fleur before. 'What was it, Nan?'

'And I felt it was my duty to discover the world. To go to far-off places we'd only read about at school. Countries and cities our teacher told us about. I had the privilege of living and I owed it to all those children who didn't make it out of Paris, who didn't survive the war. I owed it to them to embrace the world, to live and to love. I've tried to make it up to them every day of my life.'

'You shouldn't feel guilty for surviving.'

'I was lucky. I wished for a long time I could swap places.'
'With who?'

Lydia shook her head. 'With any one of them who didn't survive.'

Fleur had never known her grandmother had carried this

burden around with her. She'd heard of survivor's guilt but never in a million years thought her own grandmother was suffering.

Lydia slid her cutlery together and pushed her plate away. 'You mustn't feel guilty either. For not going with your mother the day of the accident.'

It was Fleur's turn to push her plate away. 'I can't help it.' She took a sip of her drink, knowing Lydia was waiting for her to say more. Somehow, it seemed the right moment, as if her own words to Lydia had new meaning to herself. 'I've always thought if I had gone with Mum that day, just got in the car with her, we would have arrived at those traffic lights sooner and we would have missed that lorry.'

'Fleur, you cannot think like that!'

'I do though,' said Fleur before Lydia could continue. 'Or what if I'd said yes but taken my time getting my shoes and coat on? Again, we would not have been crossing those traffic lights at that moment.'

'My poor child,' whispered Lydia. 'All these years and I never knew that's what you thought.'

'Why did she even want to go to the library that day? Why was that book she wanted so important? Basically, it cost Mum her life.'

'For the same reasons you have told me not to feel guilty, you shouldn't either,' said Lydia. 'Neither of us are to blame for what happened. The only difference is, your mother's death was an accident and, therefore, you must accept it. As it is my duty to travel the world and live a full and happy life, to compensate for the past, then it is yours also. Your mother wouldn't want her death to stifle you, to eat you up and cause you bitterness. She was a wonderful woman, who loved life and life loved her right back.'

Fleur gulped as memories she had long since shut away rushed to the fore. 'She did love life – you're right. We were always going on mini adventures: festivals, camping, exploring places. Every day was a surprise.'

'She didn't waste a day. Every day was lived to the full. Not a minute was wasted. After your father finally walked out on you both when you were just four years old, she was even more determined not to waste time. She packed more into her forty-three years than most people pack into a lifetime.'

'I wish I'd had more time with her.' Fleur's voice was scratchy as tears threatened and her chest tightened.

'So do I,' said Lydia. 'So do I.'

The arrival of the waiter to clear their plates broke the moment, and Fleur was glad for the reprieve. She and Lydia both had guilt and it was ironic how they were each trying to advise the other to let go of that guilt, yet seemingly determined to hold on to their own.

'I feel quite hot,' said Lydia. 'Is it hot in here or is it just me?' She picked up her napkin and dabbed at her top lip.

Fleur could see a red flush creeping up her grandmother's neck and her forehead glistening with perspiration. Fleur asked the waiter for the bill, insisting on paying it, before leaving the restaurant. The fact that Lydia didn't argue about paying the bill was a sure sign she wasn't feeling herself. 'Do you want to sit on that bench over there?' she asked as they walked out into the fresh air.

Lydia shook her head. 'Let's walk on for a while.' She linked arms with Fleur and guided them away from the restaurant and over a bridge to the other side of the river.

Fleur realised they were heading in the direction of the school. She said nothing, allowing her grandmother to take the lead. Sure enough, some minutes later they were back on rue de Lille and standing in front of the school gates once more.

Lydia looked up at the building. 'Our teacher used to teach us dance after school. Every day for an hour. We didn't have to attend but we wanted to. It brought light into the darkness of those days. It was what I looked forward to the most. Obviously, being Jewish in Paris during those times was very difficult and dangerous, but dancing could make us forget those things.'

This was something Fleur had never heard her grandmother speak about before. Over the years Fleur had filled in the gaps herself and assumed that her grandmother had somehow survived any of the round-ups either by luck or planning, but she'd never dwelled deeply on the matter. 'That must have been very comforting for you as you would only have been about eight or nine when the war broke out.'

'Our teacher was not only a beautiful dancer but she was brave and courageous. She took us in when it became too dangerous. When they began taking Jewish people from their homes.'

Fleur's eyes widened. 'Took you in?'

Lydia looked at her. 'Yes. We hid in the school attic for a time.'

Fleur immediately thought of the history lessons at school and how Anne Frank and her family had been hidden, how hundreds of Jewish families were given shelter by non-Jews. Her grandmother was part of that history. It was hard to imagine. 'I had no idea,' she said.

Lydia looked back at the building and Fleur listened as she spoke of her time in the attic and the other children – Blanche, Daniel and Thomas. 'It was both our sanctuary and our prison,' she finished.

'Oh, Nan. I don't know what to say,' said Fleur, barely able to take in what she had been told.

Lydia let go of the railings and took a deep breath, composing herself. She looked at Fleur. 'You don't have to say anything. I just need you to know, that's all. As I said to you before we embarked on this trip together, I need to tell my story so it doesn't die with me. I need someone to remember my friends for me.'

The weight of the task Lydia had bestowed upon her wasn't wasted on Fleur, but she was happy to take the burden and carry it.

Chapter 14

Adele

Paris, July 1942

'You're late tonight,' said Lucille as Adele arrived home. She looked up from the book she was reading. 'What's that down your dress?'

Adele looked down and there were dirty marks on her clothes. She brushed them away with her hand. 'Just some dust.'

'Dust?'

'Tidying one of the cupboards.' Adele went through to the kitchen where there was a pot of food warming on the range. She wondered whether she'd be able to smuggle some out to the guests at the school. It wasn't like Jacqueline or Cecile could get food – they couldn't leave the school or use their ration cards. Before she could do anything though, Lucille wandered out into the kitchen.

'Peter is coming for dinner tomorrow evening,' she said.

Adele ladled some of the rabbit stew out into her bowl, avoiding looking at her sister. 'That will be nice.' After spotting Peter in the restaurant with that woman, Adele had been conflicted whether to tell her sister or not. She wished there was some way she could find out more about the woman he was with. Was it his wife or was he simply seeing someone else too? It certainly hadn't looked an innocent encounter. Adele sat down at the kitchen table.

'I'm glad you said that,' Lucille replied, taking the seat opposite her. 'I know you weren't very keen at first, but you have to admit, he is nice, isn't he? Now you're getting to know him better, you can see what he's really like and not just a German in uniform.'

Adele looked up at her sister, whose eyes were pleading for approval – even though Lucille would never admit to it. 'He did seem very gentlemanly the other night,' Adele said, hoping the smile she added appeared warm rather than pitiful. She took a spoonful of the stew. 'So, where has he been the last few days?'

'I'm not sure, to be honest,' admitted Lucille. She fiddled with the salt and pepper pots on the table. 'All I know is it's work. Important meetings. That sort of thing. He can't really say and even if he did, I wouldn't be able to tell you.'

Adele worded her next question as gently as possible. 'He is good to you though, isn't he? I mean, he's kind and considerate?'

Lucille looked startled for a moment. 'Yes! Of course he is. I told you before, we love each other. It's not some silly game or wartime romance. It's serious.'

'And you trust him? Despite his marital situation?'

'Yes. Absolutely. He's only married in name.' Lucille looked offended now and a flicker of anger danced in her eyes. 'He loves me and I love him, so of course we trust each other.'

'Well, then, I'm glad,' said Adele, looking back at her food. 'That's how it should be.'

The following day, Adele was again up early so she could smuggle some food out to the attic. Fortunately, the children still thought it was a great adventure although Daniel seemed a little withdrawn.

'He was upset in the night,' explained Jacqueline, as they waited outside the toilets for the children. 'He wants his mother.'

'What did you say?'

'I just comforted him, told him that his mother loved him and if there was some way she could come back for him she would. But that he would have to be patient.'

Adele touched her friend's arm. 'You're very good.'

Jacqueline shrugged. 'I don't know about that but eventually he drifted off to sleep.'

'I'm going to ask Manu today if there's any news on getting you out of here. You can't stay here indefinitely; it's not healthy.'

'It's a lot healthier than going to one of the camps the Germans want to take us to,' said Jacqueline.

It was an attempt at humour that wasn't lost on Adele. 'I'll do whatever I can to help you all. You do know that, don't you?'

'Of course, my friend. You shouldn't even ask. I would do exactly the same if it was the other way around.'

The children exited from the toilets and they were shepherded back up to the attic room with promises of food.

'What will happen at the weekend?' asked Cecile. 'What will we do for food?'

'Don't worry. I will come back tomorrow,' assured Adele. 'If I'm asked, I will tell them I left my purse at school and am going to fetch it, while stopping on the way to deliver some shopping to one of the parents.'

Cecile nodded. 'Please be careful.'

'It will be nicer at the weekend as you won't be confined to the attic. You can come down to the second floor. Just be careful to make sure the shutters are closed and the curtains stay drawn.'

'Of course.'

'Don't go down to the ground floor though, just in case someone unexpected comes to visit. You need time to be able to hide back up in the attic,' carried on Adele, who had lain awake in bed last night, going through all the possible scenarios in her mind. 'If I'm here and there's danger, I will ring the bell. Hopefully you will hear it and be able to hide.

So, no shoes on. You must have stockings or bare feet, that way no one will hear you.'

'And if they find the hidden staircase?' asked Jacqueline.

'There's no way out from the attic,' said Adele, with a frown. 'But I'm going to ask Manu if there's any way he can create a secret door or a gap you can crawl through into the main attic next door. That way you may be able to hide in there if they've already searched that room.'

'Let's hope it doesn't come to that though,' said Jacqueline.

'Hopefully, you'll be gone in the next few days,' said Adele. 'Somewhere safer.'

She exchanged looks with the two women, acutely aware that none of them were very convinced there would be a happy ending to all this.

Adele didn't see Manu that day, which was disappointing and a little troubling. She hoped everything was all right and he hadn't been detained or caught up in something. That was the constant fear now; if a friend disappeared, the mind always went to the worst-case scenario. As she was leaving the school that evening, she caught sight of one of Manu's colleagues, a junior curator, leaving the museum. She was about to go over and ask him about Manu when to her surprise Peter Müller followed him out onto the street.

Adele stepped back into the shadows of the school gates, pretending to look for something in her purse, while watching the two men. They shared some sort of joke and shook hands before the curator headed off down the road. Müller approached the car that was waiting for him and was just about to get in when he turned and looked in Adele's direction.

Adele glanced down at her purse and then back again, trying to make out she had just noticed her sister's lover. She smiled brightly. 'Oh, hello, Peter,' she called and waved at him.

He came over. 'Good evening, Adele. Is everything all right?' He nodded towards her purse.

'Yes, I was just checking I had my papers with me. I thought for a moment I'd left them inside the school.' She pulled them out and waved them at him. 'There. All safe.'

'I'm glad to hear it. Wouldn't want to lose those.'

'No. Of course not.'

'I'd better go,' said Adele, not wanting to linger outside the school or to be seen talking happily to a German.

For a second he looked uncomfortable as he glanced back at his car. 'I would offer you a lift because, as you know, I am dining with you tonight but I'm afraid I'm heading somewhere else first.'

'Oh, that's all right. I like to walk. It will give me a chance to clear my head after being with the children all day.' Adele wondered what he was trying to hide. Did he have his wife, or whoever he was at the restaurant with, in the car? Surely not. He wouldn't be that bold to come and talk to her.

'Actually,' he said suddenly, checking his watch. 'I do indeed have time to make a detour and take you home. It would be very ungentlemanly of me to let you walk. I will drop you home and then run my errand. You can let Lucille know that I will be a little late.'

'No. Honestly,' she protested but Müller wasn't listening. He took her elbow and guided her over to the car. Despite her suspicions, there was no one else in the vehicle. Müller gave instructions to his driver and the car pulled away.

'The city looks busy tonight,' said Adele, trying to think of something to say to fill the awkward silence, not liking the feeling of being confined in a small space with him.

'Yes. Hitler said that every German should experience Paris at least once in their lifetime. We like the city very much.'

'It's nice that you get to eat out and enjoy shows,' said Adele, aware that the little flame of anger and resentment had ignited itself. 'Do you have a favourite restaurant?' She turned to look at him. She wanted to look for any reaction. Any sign of guilt.

'They are all so wonderful, it's hard to choose.'

'One that you go to often, then? Or the last one you visited?'

Müller cocked his head to one side and studied her. 'I don't recall the name of it,' he said evenly.

Adele held his gaze. Unsure if she was playing a clever game or a very stupid one. 'Have you ever been to the restaurant just around the corner from the school? I've noticed it's popular with the Germans.'

Müller pursed his lips and looked up to the ceiling, as if trying to remember. 'Not that I recall.'

'That's a very nice restaurant,' she replied, smiling sweetly. 'It's funny, when I was walking home last night, I had to do a double take. I thought I saw you in there.'

'And what exactly did you see?'

'Oh, it was an officer with a woman. They looked very comfortable together. I couldn't see properly and I couldn't just stand and stare, but I realised it wasn't you at all.' She gave a self-deprecating laugh.

Müller entertained a tight smile but didn't laugh. 'Really?'

'Oh, look, we're here now,' said Adele, never more grateful when her building came into sight.

Müller stepped out of the car first and held out his hand to help Adele out. However, he held tight when she went to walk away. 'Adele, I just want to assure you that I am very fond of Lucille and I will take good care of her. As her older sister, you must not worry.'

'I'm pleased to know that.' Still he didn't release his grip.

'I'd very much appreciate your support in our relationship. Your sister thinks a lot of your opinion, and your blessing would make her worry less.'

Adele was amazed that Lucille would have spoken to Müller about wanting her approval. 'I will always support my sister and do everything I can to see that she is happy.'

Müller gave her another one of his appraising looks, which made Adele feel decidedly uncomfortable, but he released her hand and gave a nod of his head. 'Thank you, Adele. In return, I can make sure you and your father are not troubled and are well looked after. I will see you shortly.'

As Adele took the stairs up to the apartment, she wasn't quite sure if she'd just made some sort of deal with Müller. He didn't want her causing any problems between him and Lucille and, in return, he'd make sure her and her father's lives were easy. That was the long and short of it. She didn't like the thought of doing deals with the enemy but at the same time, if it meant her father was kept safe and she was too, which would mean she could help the Jewish children and her friends escape, then maybe she should just go along with it.

Lucille was put out that her beloved was going to be a little longer but she seemed appeased by the fact that he had brought Adele home and the two of them were, in her eyes, clearly now friends.

'I did tell you how considerate he was, didn't I?' She swooned, her eyes taking on a glassy, faraway look.

Lucille was most definitely in love with Müller and Adele knew telling her about the sighting in the restaurant was not the way to break these two up. She had a feeling her sister would refuse to believe her.

When Müller arrived an hour later, he was his most charming self and Adele could easily see why Lucille was taken with him. However, she wasn't prepared to allow *herself* to be taken in by him.

'That was a most delicious meal,' Müller was saying, as he dabbed at the corners of his mouth with the linen napkin.

'It's not hard to prepare a satisfying meal when we are supplied with such wonderful food,' gushed Lucille.

Adele went to collect the plates and take them out to the kitchen so she could make coffee but Müller stopped her. 'Please, just a moment, Adele. I have something I want to talk to you about.'

Adele's heart thumped against her chest as her mind raced with all the possibilities. Did he know about the guests in the schoolhouse? Was he going to confess about the woman in the restaurant? Something else, that she didn't know anything about? Manu? She exchanged a glance with her sister who just smiled sweetly and Adele knew whatever it was, Lucille had prior knowledge. She sat back down, as controlled as possible. 'What did you want to talk about?'

'I am to organise another exhibition,' Müller began. 'The exhibition in the museum was such a success, I have been asked to take it to Lyon and to expand on it.' He sat up straighter in his chair. 'There it will be seen by the Führer himself.'

Adele realised he was waiting for her to respond. 'The Führer? Adolf Hitler?' she asked needlessly.

'Indeed,' replied Müller. 'So you can see this is a great honour for me and one I take on with pride. It must be the best exhibition that has ever been laid on. No expense spared.'

'Naturally,' replied Gérard, without expression in his voice. 'Congratulations, Peter.'

'Thank you.' Müller's face radiated pride. 'So, how does this affect you, I can see you thinking? Well, I know from Lucille that you and her both dance beautifully. She has told me all about your mother and what a wonderful dancer she was.'

Adele took another look at Lucille, who was reflecting the pride in her boyfriend's face. For some reason this incited an intensity of anger Adele was experiencing more and more recently. The sound of her mother being mentioned by this German officer was abhorrent. Lucille must be able to read her mind. She shot a warning look Adele's way. Müller appeared oblivious to the unspoken war between the sisters and continued.

'I have already spoken to Lucille and your father,' said Müller. 'They are both happy with a proposal I have.'

Adele shot a glance at her father whose expression was unreadable. 'And what may I ask, is this proposal? Seeing as I'm the last one to know, perhaps you'd care to share it with me.'

'I would like you and Lucille to perform at the reception for the Führer. It would be such an honour for you both, and I know the Führer would be enthralled by such a performance.' Müller smiled at Adele.

'What do you say, Adele?' Lucille asked with obvious enthusiasm. 'It could lead to a promotion for Peter and that would be wonderful for us, you know, thinking ahead to when we are married.'

Bile rose up in Adele's throat. She wanted to splutter it out all over her ridiculously naive and materialistic sister and her pompous, egotistical, two-timing boyfriend.

But she didn't.

'I don't know what to say,' she said instead.

'You say yes. Silly!' Lucille laughed.

'It's up to Adele,' said her father, with a certain amount of caution for which Adele was grateful. At least her father didn't think she should accept without asking any questions.

'Can I think about it?'

'Why do you want to think about it?' exclaimed Lucille. 'I've said yes.'

'Then maybe you would like to perform on your own,' suggested Adele. 'You always danced so beautifully. You could use the opportunity to showcase yourself.' She was appealing to her sister's vanity and she could see Lucille contemplating the idea.

'But I would like both of you to dance,' insisted Müller. He reached over and squeezed Lucille's hand. 'I would of course like you to perform a solo but a duet would feel more of a grand affair.'

It seemed to pacify Lucille's ego and she smiled back at Müller. 'That would be perfect.' She turned back to Adele. 'Say yes, please?'

'As I said, I want to think about it,' insisted Adele. 'It's a long time since I danced in front of anyone other than the children at the school. I'm not sure I have the confidence and I wouldn't want to make a fool of myself, or of Peter for that matter.'

'No, I understand but you will have time to practise,' replied Müller. 'I tell you what, you and Lucille prepare a routine, and next week I'll come to the school and you can perform. For my eyes only. I'll be the judge of whether you're good enough or not.'

Adele looked uneasily around the room, the tension prickly and tight.

'I think we should give Adele a day or two to think it over,' said Gérard.

'Tomorrow. Let me know by tomorrow,' said Müller who probably wanted to argue the point or even demand Adele did what he said but, out of respect for her father, he was not pressing for an immediate answer.

'I'll make that coffee,' said Adele getting up and collecting the plates.

'I'll help you,' said Lucille, who trailed her sister out to the kitchen where she closed the door behind them.

'Adele,' she hissed. 'What do you think you're doing? You have to say yes.'

'Do I? Who says so?'

'It's for the Führer. You can't say no. Peter has already said we will perform at the party. How will that look for him?'

'He's already said we will be there? Well, he shouldn't have. He should have asked first,' Adele responded, her voice rising in volume. 'I don't know why he's so keen for us to dance; he's never even seen us perform. We might completely embarrass him.'

Lucille looked a little self-conscious. 'I actually told him about our dancing. He trusts me.'

'You mean, you boasted and probably made us sound better than we are. Why wouldn't he get a famous dancer there? Why us?'

'I want to do it, if you must know. I persuaded him to

ask us.' Lucille pouted. 'Besides, I don't want some prima ballerina showing up and taking the limelight.'

Adele shook her head in disbelief. 'Now we're getting to the truth. Honestly, Lucille, if he loves you like he says he does, then you should have nothing to feel insecure about. Let him get someone else.'

'No. Peter wants to show me off as much as I do. He wants to impress Hitler, so much so, that we will be allowed to marry.'

'That won't happen. It doesn't happen,' said Adele. 'They won't allow it.'

'Keep your voice down – Peter will hear you.'

Adele rolled her eyes. 'Good. I don't care.'

Lucille grabbed her arm. 'You should care. Remember, Peter can make things very easy for us or very difficult,' replied Lucille. Her gaze dropped to the floor.

'Has he threatened you?' asked Adele.

Lucille twiddled her fingers together. 'No. He hasn't.'

'But he's insinuated something.'

'If this reception is a failure, Peter could get posted somewhere else. Someone will replace Peter and they could make life less . . . comfortable.'

'Is that all you care about?'

'I care about the man I love. If he's posted back to Germany, then I will go too.'

'Honestly, Lucille, you have such fanciful ideas at times. Why would you want to go to Germany? You'll be living on your own, not knowing anyone. And you don't honestly believe they're going to welcome you there with open arms? They won't have any respect for you.'

'That's not the point. The point is, we need to keep Peter happy. If you care about Papa, you'll do that.'

'That sounds very much like blackmail.'

Lucille shrugged. 'If that's what you want to call it, then go ahead. But to me, it's just common sense. You know, sometimes I think I'm the older and more mature out of us two.' Adele stopped herself from snorting at the audacity of the comment.

With her parting words, Lucille went back out into the dining room, leaving Adele to make the coffee alone. As she prepared the drinks, a small idea began to form in her mind. The reception was in Lyon. That was close to the Swiss border. Her mind started hurtling ahead of her, and she had to stop what she was doing to take stock. It was an audacious plan for sure but maybe it could work. She pinched her bottom lip as she tried to line her thoughts up in an orderly fashion. She would need help from Manu, of course. She was sure he would help her.

She needed to speak to him as soon as possible, but there was nothing she could do tonight.

Her sister reappearing in the doorway broke her thoughts. 'Are the drinks nearly ready? Shall I help?'

Adele and Lucille took the drinks into the dining room, Adele taking her seat at the table, while her sister poured from the pot. Adele smiled at Müller. 'About your proposal,' she began. 'The performance, I was wondering . . .' She paused. 'No, it's a silly idea.'

'I'm sure it's not. Please . . .' replied Müller.

'I was thinking if it's for the Führer, it really does need to be special, doesn't it?' Müller nodded his head in agreement, a look of curiosity on his face. Adele continued. 'Wouldn't it be incredibly special if not only were myself and Lucille dancing for him, but the children as well? It would be a show of solidarity. An opportunity for you to show how much the city approves of the Führer, how the next generation support him too. He'd be flattered, I'm sure.'

Müller's eyes lit up like fireworks on the first of January. 'That is a magnificent idea. I can see it now. Are you saying you'll do it?'

Adele nodded. 'If the children can perform too, plus it will make me feel less self-conscious.' She spotted the surprised look on her sister's face. 'And of course Lucille can still have her solo spot. You know, the highlight of the evening.'

'It sounds perfect,' said Müller. 'Wonderful. You know it's the right decision.' He sipped from his cup, looking very smug with himself, as if it was his idea.

Adele smiled politely, ignoring the questioning look from her father. All she had to do now was to convince Manu to help her.

Chapter 15

Adele

The following morning Adele managed to get to the school without being stopped and questioned. She had to ensure it was a fleeting visit to simply make sure they were all right.

'I'm bored,' said Blanche. 'Mama said we could play in the dance room.'

'And you can,' replied Adele, smiling at the young girl. 'You have to be very quiet and stay away from the windows but, yes, you can play in the dance room for a little while today.'

Blanche beamed at her sister. 'Told you so.' To which Eva poked her tongue out at her younger sibling.

'Have you heard anything yet from Manu?' asked Jacqueline.

'Not yet,' replied Adele shaking her head. 'I was going to see if I could speak to him this morning. I have a plan on how to get you all out of here.'

'You do?' whispered Jacqueline, glancing around to make sure the children were occupied.

Cecile moved closer. 'What's this about a plan?'

'I can't say anything yet,' said Adele. 'I need to speak to Manu first. Just be a little more patient, my friends.'

She stayed another thirty minutes with the women and children before deciding it was time to leave. 'I really need to see if Manu is at the museum today. I won't be able to come tomorrow, but you should have enough food to get you through. I'll be back first thing on Monday morning.'

Repeating her instructions again, to all the children this time, that they could play in the dance room as long as they didn't go near the windows and they were not to wear their shoes, Adele left them in search of Manu.

The museum was quite busy, full of Germans on their holidays from the army, wandering around, showing their wives, girlfriends and probably lovers the wondrous collection of art and sculptures.

She couldn't find Manu anywhere and was just about to give up and leave when Edith appeared in front of her. 'Hello, Adele,' she said. 'What a nice surprise.' It was clearly anything but a nice surprise.

'Hello, Edith. I was just looking for Manu.'

'I thought that's probably why you were here.'

Adele looked expectantly at the woman. 'So, is he?' she asked after an awkward pause.

'He's very busy at the moment,' said Edith. 'He's in a meeting with Hauptmann Müller. They are organising another exhibition. An extremely important one.' She drew closer to Adele. 'I don't mean to be rude, as I know how much you care about Manu, but you really shouldn't waste your time on him. He is far too busy to be pestered.'

Adele was startled by this unexpected comment from Edith but refused to let the woman see her surprise. 'I've known Manu for many years; of course, I care about him as I would a sibling.'

Edith raised her eyebrows and gave Adele a sceptical look. 'Like a sibling? Really?'

'Yes. As for the exhibition, I already know about it. Hauptmann Müller is a friend of the family.' Much as Adele hated saying the words, she was delighted to see the look of surprise register on Edith's face. This small sense of victory spurred her on. 'In fact, Peter, sorry I mean Hauptmann Müller, dined with us last night. He and my sister are to be married.' Now that really did make Edith look shocked.

'To be married. I had no idea. Well, I must congratulate

Hauptmann Müller when I next see him.' Her reply was cool and controlled. 'I'm glad we cleared up that misunderstanding about Manu too.'

'Me too. Anyway, I must get back home now.'

'Can I give Manu a message?' asked Edith. 'Is it something to do with the school? I saw you were there early this morning. Is it anything to do with your guests?'

Adele's heart stumbled a moment. How did Edith know about the guests at the school? Surely Manu hadn't told her. She looked blankly at Edith. 'Guests?'

'Yes, the ones up in the attic. Manu had to fix a hole they were getting through. You know the ones he had to come over and sort out the other day. To be honest, I can't bear mice. The thought of them getting through tiny little cracks. Manu said they were at the back of a store cupboard in the dance room.' Edith gave a shiver.

Was she talking about mice or was she talking in code about the women and children? Adele didn't trust her. 'It's not important.'

'If you've got any more vermin up there, you need to get some traps set as soon as possible. As I say, Manu is very busy. I can ask one of the soldiers to come over and have a look for you.'

'No! No, thank you.' Adele tried to keep her tone neutral. 'It's fine. It's nothing to do with the mice. They've all gone, I think.'

'That's good. Wouldn't want word to get out you had an infestation. Might have to have the school closed and fumigated.'

Adele nodded. 'I must go now. *Au revoir*, Edith.'

As Adele hurried down the street, the conversation between her and Edith played over and over in her mind. Edith must know. Was she trying to blackmail her though? Was she warning her off Manu by threatening to send the Gestapo to the school? It didn't bear thinking about and Adele couldn't risk putting Jacqueline, Cecile and the children in danger.

She'd have to back right off from Manu and try to find someone else who could help her.

As she hurried around the corner, she was so lost in thought, she didn't see Manu coming towards her and almost crashed straight into him.

'Ouf! Adele!' Manu caught her by the tops of her arms. He was smiling in that amused way he usually did but, as he looked at her, his face turned serious. 'Is everything all right?'

'Yes. Everything is fine,' replied Adele stiffly.

His eyes narrowed a fraction. 'Are you sure?'

'Yes. I'm in a hurry.' She looked away and then back at him, offering a tight smile. 'Sorry but I really need to go.'

Manu wasn't being easily fooled and, hooking her arm into the crook of his elbow, he took her across the road and into a café on the other side, ordering them both coffee. They sat in silence, Manu studying her, Adele looking out of the window, until the waiter brought the drinks over and left. Manu leaned in towards her. 'Want to tell me what's really going on?'

She shook her head. 'No.'

'Well, I'm a patient man, I can sit here as long as it takes for you to tell me.'

She looked at him now. 'And I'm a very patient woman. You forget, I have to deal with children all day long. I'm pretty sure you'll crack before me, so you might just as well not bother with this . . . this interrogation.'

She went to push her chair back but Manu reached out and held her hand with his. 'Adele, please sit down. I know there's something wrong. I can tell. You forget, I know you. I've known you since you were a child. Please, tell me what's wrong.'

The gentleness of his voice, the way he said please and the intensity of his gaze had Adele pulling her chair back in. All right, if he wanted to know, then she'd tell him. She moved her hand away from his, despite how nice it felt. 'Why did you tell Edith about my guests?'

There was a look of confusion on Manu's face. 'I didn't.' He moved to Adele's side of the table so he was sitting next to her and put an arm around her. 'You will have to pretend to like me for a while, just so we can whisper and not have to broadcast our discussion across the table to anyone who is in listening range.' He dropped a kiss on her head. 'Now, what's all this about?'

Adele's shoulders relaxed involuntarily as she allowed herself to sink a little closer into Manu, into this pretence that made her heart flutter. She relayed the conversation she'd had with Edith, leaving out the part about her liking Manu.

'She said you were very busy and I wasn't to bother you. That she could ask the Germans to close the school and get rid of the infestation. Or words to that effect.' She looked up at Manu to gauge his reaction.

He frowned. 'I have no idea why she would say that. I certainly haven't told her about the women and children. I did say I was there helping you get rid of some mice. I had to say something.'

'It doesn't sound like she believed you.'

'Maybe she is just suspicious about why I spend so much time at the school. Or maybe it's you she thinks I spend too much time with.'

'Do you think that?' asked Adele, not able to meet Manu's gaze.

He held her a little tighter and rubbed the top of her arm with his hand. 'I like spending time with you.'

Adele's heart was hammering and she was sure Manu would be able to feel the vibrations. She still couldn't bring herself to look at him. 'I like spending time with you too,' she said. She took a deep breath and pulled out of the embrace. 'However, I don't think you should help me anymore.'

Manu looked genuinely surprised at the suggestion. 'Why not? I want to. I'm not going to stop just because Edith has got a silly notion in her head.'

'I can't risk the women and children being found. I can't

risk you getting into trouble either,' replied Adele honestly. She squeezed Manu's hand. 'I couldn't live with myself if anything happened to them. Or you.'

'Edith is bluffing,' said Manu. 'If she tells the Gestapo then she knows I too will be arrested. She wouldn't do that. I don't know if she's jealous of our . . . friendship, but I shall do what I can to reassure her.'

'No. You mustn't say anything,' said Adele. 'She will know I've spoken to you. If you think you can trust her, then I trust your judgement on that, but please don't say anything. If you want to help me then you must do it without Edith knowing.'

He put a hand up and stroked Adele' face. 'If that's what you want, but I never thought I'd have to sneak around just to see you.'

'I never thought I'd be hiding my friends in the attic of the school. These are dangerous times, Manu. None of it is a game.'

'I know.'

She thought for a moment he was going to kiss her but he pulled away and swore under his breath. 'It's Edith.'

Adele looked up through the window and saw Edith walking along the path on the other side the road. Adele immediately moved in her seat so she had her back half-turned to the street, shielding Manu from sight. Manu was spying over Adele's shoulder. 'Has she gone?' asked Adele after a few moments.

'Not yet, she's stopped outside a building. She's going in!'

'What?!'

Manu was sitting up straight now, straining to look through the window. 'No, wait. She's coming out. Look, she's walking on down the road.'

'Did she actually go in?'

'I couldn't tell properly but I don't think she could have, otherwise she would have been in there for longer.'

'Perhaps she was just giving a message or delivering one,' said Adele, her heart was racing at the thought.

'Go back to the school,' instructed Manu. 'Tell them to hide up in the little attic and not to make a sound.'

'What are you going to do?' Adele was on her feet and following Manu out of the café.

'I'm going to check out the building and try to catch up with Edith.' He kissed Adele's forehead. 'After you've done that. Go home and wait for me. Do not say a word to anyone.'

And then he was cutting across the street and heading for the building Edith had just visited. Funny how you could pass by a building every day and still not be aware of what went on behind the door. Adele couldn't remember seeing a sign so assumed it was a private residence. She took a look over her shoulder and saw Manu disappear into the premises. She wanted to wait to see how long he took but didn't dare loiter and draw attention to what they were doing. She needed to get back and warn the others.

As she turned the corner to the school, Adele's knees almost buckled underneath her. A German army lorry had stopped outside the school and two soldiers were standing either side of the school gates while a German officer spoke to them. He looked up at Adele. It was the same German officer she had spoken to in her father's office. A French policeman was with him too.

'Ah, Mademoiselle Basset, perfect timing. Come here.' He beckoned her with his hand.

'*Bonjour*,' said Adele as she reached him. To her relief there was amazingly no wobble to her voice.

'As you know, we are missing some children from our list,' he said. 'I want to search the building to make sure they didn't somehow hide in the school.'

'That's not possible,' said Adele. 'I mean, it's not possible that they are hiding. I would know. I personally saw the children go home that evening. They couldn't have stayed at the school.'

'Where do you keep the keys during the day?'

'Hanging up in the office.'

'So, they could have got the keys and unlocked one of the back doors, returned the keys and then sneaked into the school later that evening.'

'No, I would have noticed. I always check the building before I leave. I would have known if the door was unlocked.'

'Did you check the building that night? Every single door and window? Your father's office, for example?'

Adele nodded. 'Yes. Every door and window.'

'Then did you let them in?' There was a glint in his eyes as if he was enjoying this debate with her.

'No. Because there is no one in the school,' said Adele with a determination she hoped translated as annoyance she was being questioned.

'Then, if you are so sure, you won't mind us taking a look?' He nodded at the two guards, who turned and walked through the gates and up to the main doors. 'Mademoiselle, would you care to go ahead and show us the rooms, please? I take it you have keys on you as you must have been on your way here? If not, we can always break the door down.'

'Yes I have keys,' replied Adele. 'I was coming because I'd left my bag there yesterday.' She said a silent thanks at her foresight of leaving a decoy bag in the building just for such an occasion.

Adele unlocked the door and stepped back to allow the soldiers entry into the building. The officer held out his hand for her to go first. As she reached the reception desk, she put her hand to her head. 'Oh, goodness, I feel a bit faint.' Adele made to grab on to the desk but purposely knocked the bell onto the ground. It clattered and made a clanging noise as it hit the floor. Adele stooped to pick it up. 'I hope I haven't broken it.' She gave it a shake back and forth. The bell sounded out loud and clear.

The officer stepped forward and snatched it from her hand, silencing the bell. 'I think it's perfectly fine.' He replaced it on the desk. 'You are feeling unwell, Mademoiselle Basset? Why is that?' He pulled out a chair and sat her down.

'I didn't eat this morning,' she replied.

'Hmm.' He eyed her with a certain amount of disbelief. He turned to the French policeman. 'Fetch her a glass of water.'

Adele could hear the footsteps of the soldiers as they ran around on the first floor, opening and closing doors, checking the classrooms and cupboards. She hoped to God that Jacqueline or Cecile had spotted the Germans outside, heard her ring the school bell and were now safely hiding in the attic.

Chapter 16

Fleur

Paris, August 2015

Fleur gave herself the once-over in the mirror. She had opted for smart casual to meet Didier, a pair of jeans and a floral blouse – after all, it was just a drink in the lounge bar. It wasn't like they were going for lunch. She left her hair loose, hanging just beyond her shoulders, and had applied a small amount of make-up.

'You look very nice,' said Lydia as Fleur went into her room to say goodbye. 'And smell lovely too.'

'I'm not trying to impress anyone,' replied Fleur attempting to sound casual. 'I just like to look smart.'

Lydia raised her eyebrows. 'Is that so?'

'It is, actually.' Fleur felt the heat in her face and called out a goodbye before Lydia could see she was blushing.

Didier was already waiting in the lounge bar when she arrived. He rose to his feet to greet her, his hand outstretched. 'Thank you for meeting me.' He waited for her to sit down in the chair opposite him before resuming his position on the leather sofa. A small table breached the gap between them. Didier gave a nod towards the waiter who came over and took Fleur's order of a sparkling white wine. 'How is your grandmother?' he asked.

'She's all right. We went out for dinner last night and have had a quiet morning so far. She's in her room now.'

The waiter brought Fleur's drink over and she glanced over towards the bar area. The man behind the bar was drying a glass and nodded in Fleur's direction. That must be her bodyguard, Jean-Paul.

'Did you have a chance to ask Lydia if the name Bridget Sutter and Geneva mean anything to her?' asked Didier.

'I did, but before I tell you what she said, can you explain to me what's going on?' Although Fleur had nothing to tell Didier, she was on the back foot and needed to exercise some sort of leverage to find out what he knew. If she told him Lydia didn't recognise the names at all, then he might not bother sharing any information with her.

Didier eyed her speculatively and then as if coming to a decision, sat forwards, his forearms resting on his knees. 'Yesterday, outside the school, it was not an accident that I was there.'

Somehow Fleur wasn't surprised. 'Have you been following us?' It was an unsettling thought and she tried to recall if she'd seen anyone acting suspiciously around her, or if she'd seen Didier before that afternoon.

'No. I have been waiting,' he replied. 'Waiting for Lydia for two weeks now.'

'I don't understand. What do you mean waiting for Lydia? How do you know her? She doesn't know you.' Fleur frowned, trying to make sense of it. She glanced across at the bar and Jean-Paul met her gaze. He gave a questioning look, to which Fleur gave a reassuring nod.

'You know the barman?' asked Didier. 'He is watching over you?'

'Assigned bodyguard, courtesy of my nan,' said Fleur, not even attempting to deny it. 'Can you please explain to me, in full, what's going on?'

'I hope we can help each other,' said Didier. 'As you know, I am an antique dealer with my speciality being art. Paintings. Have you ever heard of the artist Valois, Pierre Valois?'

'I don't think so.'

Didier gave a shrug. 'I suppose there is no reason why you would. He is not one of the famous ones, but his work is becoming more and more collectable. His watercolours are perfection.' Didier's face was alight with enthusiasm as he spoke. 'He died in 1905 and it was after then his work became more sought after. Sadly, that is the case with many artists; they die in poverty and it is only afterwards their work becomes collectable.'

'So, what has this to do with Lydia?' Fleur asked.

'Valois's most famous work was called *Un An au Chalet*. A Year at the Cottage. He painted the same house in Brittany every month for a whole year. He painted in miniature – each painting was just ten by ten centimetres but the detail was exquisite. For a long time, these were on display at the museum next door to the school, but they were stolen by the Nazis during the war. The collection ended up in Germany and has since been returned to the museum. However, records verify that instead of twelve paintings, only seven reached Germany. Over the years, four of the missing five paintings have been mysteriously returned to the museum but there is still one missing. The one called *August*. I have been trying to track this painting down for the past five years, ever since I left the police force.'

'And how is this connected to Lydia? I don't understand.'

'The last painting that was returned to the museum arrived only last year. It was handed in on behalf of Bridget Sutter by her daughter, Marie-Anne. Bridget has lived in Geneva since she was a child. She has, so far, refused to say how she came by the painting.'

'What was her painting of? What month?'

'It was September.'

'Do you think it's significant?'

'I'm not sure.' Didier paused and took a long slug of his drink before signalling the waiter for another one. 'There is only a small report about the return of the painting.' From his bag under the table, Didier brought out a laptop and switched it on. Once he'd found the file he was looking for, he turned the screen towards Fleur, who frowned at the report all in French. 'Oh, sorry. It's easier if I translate,' said Didier.

'My French isn't that great,' she confessed. As he moved around to her side of the table Fleur was aware of their closeness. The fresh apple and minty smell of his aftershave drifted in the air. When he began to read the content, Fleur had to remind herself to concentrate on the words rather than the rich low tones of his voice.

'I have spoken with the curator at the museum who couldn't really tell me anything else. But he did say that when Bridget Sutter came with her daughter to return the painting, she asked about the school next door. She seemed to take quite an interest in it. Asking about its history since the war and what happened to the staff. He said it was strange, as if it meant something personal to her.'

'But he wasn't able to explain or expand?'

'No. He did say that when he told her about the lady who visits the school every year, Bridget Sutter was very interested but he wasn't able to tell her any more as he didn't know himself.'

'The lady who visits the school – he means Nan, doesn't he?' said Fleur.

'That is correct. I tried to contact Bridget Sutter myself but her daughter refused to allow me to talk to her. She's very mindful of her mother's age and frail health,' explained Didier, repositioning himself so he was facing Fleur with one hand resting on the back of the Chesterfield sofa. 'I was at a dead end. The only other lead I had was the lady who comes every year and lays flowers at the school. So, I have been . . .' he searched for the word '. . . staking out the school, waiting for your grandmother.'

Fleur wasn't sure how she felt about essentially being spied on, albeit it unwittingly, but with everything that Didier had told her, it seemed a minor point and something not to linger on. 'Has the ballet shoe on the gate got anything to do with this? It seems too much of a coincidence not to be.'

'I don't know who put that there. It was already there when I began waiting but it seemed significant to Lydia.'

Fleur sat back and took a moment to gather all the information Didier had dropped on her and line it up in some sort of order. 'And you think there is a connection between Bridget Sutter and my nan?'

Didier nodded. 'And the missing painting. I think Lydia is the link.'

Chapter 17

Adele

Paris, July 1942

She could hear the search party clatter up the second staircase to the floor of the dance studio. She sipped her water but her hand shook so she put the glass down.

'You are shaking,' said the officer.

'I really feel quite faint,' stammered Adele. She leaned over and rested her head almost in her lap. Not because she needed the blood to rush to her head, but she needed to hide her nerves.

A shout from one of the soldiers calling the officer made her sit up suddenly. This time she did feel genuinely dizzy. The solider called something in German, which Adele didn't understand.

'Get up,' ordered the officer. 'We need to go upstairs. One of my men has something to show me.'

Adele's stomach lurched in fear and her heart was pounding so hard, she was sure it could be heard. She got to her feet and accompanied the officer up both flights of stairs to the dance room.

The soldiers were standing near the cupboard door. 'We found this,' one of the soldiers said. He bent down and picked up the crust of a piece of bread. 'And this,' continued the soldier, holding Lulu le Lapin up by its ear.

The officer took the bread and broke it, before smelling it.

'Can you explain this?' He looked at Adele with steely eyes.

'Yes. It must have been left last night by one of my pupils. We have dance classes up here every day after school. I sometimes give them bread. One of them must have dropped it.' She walked over and held out her hand for the rabbit, which the soldier gave to her. 'Sometimes the children bring their toys in; they're a safety blanket for them in these dark times.'

'I can understand why a toy might be left behind,' said the officer after a pause. 'But why would they leave food?'

Adele shrugged. 'We were running late last night so I hurried them out of the dance studio.' She hoped she sounded convincing but in a casual, dismissive way.

The officer pursed his lips and looked around the room, his gaze coming to rest on the cupboard door. 'What's in there?'

'It's just a storeroom,' replied Adele, making a conscious effort not to squeeze the toy and betray her nerves. The officer was shrewd and smart; he wouldn't miss the body language. 'It's unlocked if you want to look inside.'

The officer nodded to one of the men, who hurried over and pulled open the door. He stepped inside and reappeared just a few seconds later. Again, Adele couldn't understand what was being said, but the soldier's voice was non urgent and he gave a shrug as he reported to his superior.

The officer walked over and looked inside the cupboard himself but much to Adele's relief didn't start tapping walls or pulling things about. 'Very well. I suggest you make sure you don't leave food lying about,' said the officer. 'You will encourage vermin.'

Adele swallowed hard at the term. Her mind automatically going back to Edith. That was the word she had used. It couldn't be a coincidence, could it? As they were about to leave, the officer stopped in the hallway. He spoke something to his men, who looked blank and shook their heads. 'Is there an attic here, Mademoiselle Basset?'

Fear threatened to engulf Adele again but she knew she had to hold her nerve. 'Yes. Of course. It's just over here.'

She moved around the officer and opened a door revealing a staircase.

Two soldiers scurried past her. Their boots thumped on the wooden steps and Adele hoped the children would remain quiet. They were all so close to each other with just a stud wall separating them.

The soldiers returned a minute later and appeared to be reporting back that nothing had been found.

'Thank you for letting my men search the school,' said the officer, as he indicated to Adele to go downstairs.

Adele didn't reply. What was she supposed to say? It was her pleasure or no problem at all? It was anything but her pleasure. It was heart-racing, fear-inducing terror. She locked the school up behind her as she left, aware the officer was sitting in his car, watching her.

As she came out of the gates, he wound down his window. 'Remember, Mademoiselle Basset, don't leave food around for the vermin.' He nodded a goodbye and said something to his driver. The car pulled away and Adele watched it disappear down the road. She wanted to go back into the school, but she knew it was too risky. All eyes in the street would be on her and what had just happened. Any one of them could see her returning to the school again and report her.

As she walked away, she forced herself not to look up at the attic windows. She wondered where Manu had gone and as she turned the corner, she saw him waiting for her. He fell into step with her.

'Ça-va?'

'I think so,' she replied.

'Just keep walking,' he said needlessly. She wasn't about to stop. All she wanted to do was to get home, flop down on her bed and cry out the range of emotions she'd just had to deal with. 'What did you find out about the building?'

'It's empty,' said Manu. 'I have no idea what Edith was doing in there. There's a caretaker and he said he has been ordered to look after the property and not let anyone in.'

'That sounds very odd. Can you trust Edith?' asked Adele gently. 'I mean, really trust her?'

Manu stopped walking and turned to look at Adele. 'Yes. I can.'

'You must still be careful.'

'I know. I'm not stupid.'

'I know that too. I'm just scared.'

'Don't be. I'll handle this. Now the children and the women. We need to get them out of the school and to safety as soon as possible. I'm meeting with a contact tonight. I may have some news then.'

'I haven't had a chance to tell you, but I have a plan,' said Adele.

'Don't tell me now,' said Manu, guiding her down the road. 'Just in case anyone is watching us. We'll part at the corner of the road. You go home. Tomorrow, meet me at Our Lady of Sorrows Church at ten o'clock mass. I'll be in the back pew on the right-hand side. Make sure you're not followed. If I don't turn up by ten-thirty, something is wrong and you must leave. Understood?'

'Yes. Understood.'

They came to a halt at the corner and Manu kissed her on each cheek before heading off to wherever it was he was going. Adele watched him for a few seconds. His tall figure striding confidently down the road, almost daring anyone to stop and question him. She gave a sigh and then headed back to the apartment.

Adele didn't sleep very well. Her thoughts were constantly on a loop of worrying about what had happened today at the school with both Edith and then the search, worried about the children and their mothers, worried one of them would leave something else to concern the Germans with, worried about Manu and meeting him and worried about what he'd think of her plan.

She arrived at Our Lady of Sorrows just before ten o'clock

mass, as instructed. It was a large church occupying the centre of a square near to the school. Adele joined the congregation and as she entered the church, she looked for Manu but couldn't see him. She was a little early but it didn't stop the butterflies in her stomach. She did as she was told and took her seat at the back of the church on the right-hand side. She didn't want to draw attention to herself by turning around all the time and her stomach was a bundle of nerves.

This was a bad idea. Maybe she had inadvertently put Manu in danger. She shouldn't have agreed to meet him here. The congregation rose and the priest began to make his way down the aisle followed by the choirboys in their white robes carrying a crucifix. It was a wonder the Germans hadn't taken that yet.

The priest took his position at the altar and turned to face the congregation. Speaking in Latin he recited a prayer and made the sign of the cross. Adele did the same along with everyone else in the church. As they all sat down in their seats, Manu slipped in beside Adele. She breathed a sigh of relief. 'I was beginning to get worried.'

'I told you not to worry until ten-thirty. I had to make sure no one was following.'

'I checked like you said,' whispered Adele, keeping her eyes trained on the priest as he began the service.

'I like to double-check,' whispered back Manu.

He picked up the hymn book and Adele wondered how on earth she was going to tell him her plan when they were in the middle of a church service. 'What happens now?' she whispered again.

'Just wait. I'll let you know when we have to go.'

Adele only had to wait another ten minutes until Manu placed his book down and taking her hand, led her out of the church.

The brightness of the daylight was a stark contrast to the darkness of the church interior and Adele squinted as they trotted down the steps. 'Where are we going?'

'You're asking a lot of questions,' said Manu. He didn't let go of her hand as they walked and Adele was more than content for it to remain that way.

They made their way through several more streets, before stopping outside an innocuous-looking apartment building, not dissimilar to the one Adele lived in. Manu opened the door and ushered her in. Instead of going up the staircase, as Adele imagined, they went through the hallway and out into the courtyard beyond. Washing was strung from one balcony to another. Young children played in the courtyard. One of them was pedalling a tricycle around the central water fountain feature. It would have once been a very grand courtyard, but since the arrival of the German forces, maintenance had obviously been lacking as a priority.

A couple of the children called out to Manu. '*Monsieur! Monsieur!*' One of them ran over, where Manu scooped him up into the air before bringing him back down again. '*Ça-va*, Jacques?' he asked. 'I hope you're being good for your *mémé*.' He looked over to a woman, maybe in her seventies, who was sitting outside with a cigarette in one hand and a cup in the other. '*Bonjour, madame!*' he called over.

'*Bonjour, monsieur.*' She smiled at Adele. '*Mademoiselle.*'

Adele smiled back and wondered if she should stop, but Manu was taking her hand again and hurrying her on across the courtyard. 'You all seem to know each other and yet none of you have used your names, except for the little boy's name. Why is that?'

'It's safer that way. No one knows anyone's real name,' said Manu. 'I should have warned you. Do not offer your name. You won't be asked but just don't introduce yourself.'

A little thread of fear snagged in Adele's stomach. Manu was far more involved with pushing back against the Germans than she'd imagined. They took the stone steps up to the first floor and stopped outside the third door along. Manu didn't need to knock; it opened almost immediately.

A woman probably in her mid-forties eyed Manu and then Adele. 'Were you followed?'

'No. This is the friend I told you about.'

The woman opened the door and stepped aside. Adele was grateful Manu was still holding her hand as he took her down a hallway to the back of the apartment and through double doors into a large sitting room. The curtains were pulled closed over the three full-length windows and a layer of cigarette smoke hung in the air. At the far end of the room was a grand piano where a man was hunched over the closed lid. The top of the piano was strewn with wire and what looked like the insides of a clock. The man looked up and acknowledged Manu with a nod. He turned and appraised Adele, offering her the same greeting.

Three other men and another woman sat around a dining table. They too offered a simple bow of the head.

'This is the one who needs the papers for four children and two adults?' asked one of the men. He was older than the rest.

'You're the schoolteacher,' said one of the women.

'That's right,' replied Adele. She guessed they probably knew a lot more about her than they were letting on.

'Apparently you have a plan, Mademoiselle Schoolteacher,' said the older man.

'That's right.' Adele looked to Manu for reassurance. He gave a brief smile of encouragement. Adele quickly went on to explain about how she and her sister had been asked to perform at the art exhibition in Lyon. She could see the eyes of some of the men in the room narrowing. They were suspicious of her and quite rightly so. She carried on regardless – this wasn't about her, this was about saving her friends and the children. 'I thought if the children I am hiding, together with their mothers, could be part of the dance group, then once they have performed at Lyon, they can somehow slip away into the night and cross the border to Switzerland.'

There was a deadly silence in the room for a few seconds before the man burst out laughing. He looked at his comrades.

'Did you hear that? They are going to dance for Hitler and then just slip out and cross the border. Because of course it is so simple to do that.'

Adele looked at Manu and there was a look of annoyance in his eyes, although she wasn't sure if that was directed at her or the other people in the room. 'That's exactly what I think will happen. There are pipe works all around the border,' said Adele referring to the underground network of safe houses and routes out of France. 'People have been smuggled out before. I don't see why it can't be done again. Besides, I'm not seeking your approval or your help in the plan, all I need is the false papers.'

The laughter subsided and the man cleared his throat. He addressed Manu. 'And you approve of this?'

Manu looked at Adele before turning back to the man. 'Of course.' Adele wanted to hug Manu for standing up for her. He'd had no idea what her plan was and yet here he was pretending like he knew and that he approved. 'If this works, we can open up a whole new pipeline.'

The man exchanged looks with the others around the table. 'In that case, you'd better pull up a chair and we will talk about this properly.'

Chapter 18

Fleur

Fleur and Didier had gone over the circumstances several times, but even though Fleur now had a clear idea, she couldn't see how all these little pieces of the puzzle joined up. She still wasn't entirely convinced Lydia had any connection with Bridget Sutter and the missing painting.

'There's an awful lot of assumption and guesswork going on here,' she said to Didier. 'It's hard to see any tangible proof that everything is connected.'

'I know. I appreciate that but until we ask the questions, dig deeper into the past, we won't know for certain.'

'I don't want to upset Nan. I'm not comfortable with interrogating her.' Fleur frowned at the prospect of applying any sort of pressure on her grandmother. 'I could gently ask, but if she doesn't want to talk, then I'm not going to push her.'

'I wouldn't expect you to, but it is very important to me to try to find out what happened to the painting.'

'Nan has never once mentioned a painting. Maybe Bridget Sutter got it dishonestly and that's why she won't say where it came from. Even so, I can't figure out the connection.'

'I would still like to ask your grandmother some questions though,' said Didier.

'We have different agendas. I'd like to think a woman in her eighties is a higher priority than a watercolour.'

'I understand what you are saying,' Didier replied.

They lapsed into a small silence as they each contemplated the puzzle before them. Fleur appreciated that Didier's interest was in finding the missing painting, but she wasn't sure if Lydia really had anything to do with the search. On the other hand, the ballet shoe had certainly stirred some feelings within Lydia, but at the moment she wasn't sharing those memories with Fleur. 'Let me have a think about it all and see if I can broach the subject with my nan,' Fleur said breaking the silence. 'If I'm going to talk to her, I need to do it with care and understanding.'

'*Bien sûr. Absolutement!*' Didier held her gaze. 'Thank you.'

'I have your business card. I'll call you tomorrow, once I've had a chance to talk to her.'

Didier accompanied Fleur to the lift and thanked her again for taking the time to meet him. 'I will look forward to speaking to you tomorrow,' he said as the lift doors opened and Fleur stepped inside. He smiled and gave a small nod of his head as the doors closed. As the elevator travelled up, Fleur was aware she was a little disappointed to be parting company with him.

Once inside her room, she tapped on the adjoining door to where Lydia was sleeping. When there was no answer, she opened the door and peeked inside. Lydia was asleep on her bed with the curtain drawn. The dim light of the bedside lamp cast a soft yellow glow across the space. Fleur listened for the reassuring rhythm of Lydia's breathing. It was then she noticed Lydia was holding something in her hands. The ballet shoe. Fleur stood for a moment, her gaze resting on her sleeping grandmother. She hoped Lydia would be able to talk more about it and unburden herself from whatever weight she'd been carrying around all these years. Lydia deserved some sort of peace at this time of her life.

Closing the door between the rooms, Fleur wandered over to the window and looked out at the Parisian skyline beyond – her grandmother's birthplace and the city where Lydia had endured so much pain.

Fleur had nothing but admiration for the way in which Lydia dealt with her own loss. There was no anger, just a sadness. If anyone had a right to be angry, it was Lydia. She had endured so much in her life. Fleur couldn't help feeling a little embarrassed at her reactions to her own situation, which although tragic, wasn't in the same league as her grandmother's suffering. Fleur suspected the more she learnt of her grandmother's past, the more the gulf between their own experiences of grief would be highlighted.

To distract herself from dwelling on the loss of her mother, Fleur retrieved her iPad from her bag and logged onto the hotel network. She should have done this earlier, she thought as she typed in the website for Didier's antique business.

It was pretty much as she would expect a small antique business website to look, a landing page showing the shop Didier ran, together with some of the items for sale. There was a specific page for art, which wasn't surprising given that Didier had said he specialised in this field, as well as a contacts page and a testimonial page.

Next Fleur typed in Pierre Valois and *Un An au Chalet*. Images of the twelve miniatures appeared on the screen with a small biography of Valois. She went back to the search results and scanned further down. She almost dismissed one of the results, which started with €50,000 *Récompense offerte pour le retour en toute sécurité . . .* She went back to it. Recompense offered for the return in total security, she roughly translated. OK, that was literal, but she knew enough to work out it was talking about a fifty-thousand-euro reward. Fleur clicked the link.

Naturally it was all in French and she was grateful for the translation option offered.

'Wow,' she said out loud as she digested the information. She went through the document again, just to be certain she had it correct. There was a €50,000 reward for the return of the missing painting '*Août*' by Pierre Valois, thought to have been stolen by the Germans during the war. This much Didier had told her, but he hadn't mentioned the vast sum involved. No wonder he was interested in speaking to her grandmother.

The idea that he hadn't been honest annoyed Fleur. She was also irritated with herself for being so gullible and not pressing Didier as to his motives. Now it seemed obvious that he was after the money.

It struck her that the website for his business didn't have any personal information about the owner, i.e. Didier. There was no photograph of him, no 'About' page that gave a small bio or a welcome page, no friendly face of the business to put to potential clients. She clicked back on the website and went to the contact page. Again, no personal information about who to contact, just the business name. The more she thought about it, the stranger it seemed. Fleur picked up the business card he'd given her and flicked it over several times. It wasn't the most luxurious card she'd seen, made with thinner card and probably something anyone could create and print themselves at home.

She had a sinking feeling she was being duped somehow. Back to the iPad and she typed in Didier's name this time.

Scrolling down again, she came to a link that looked promising. A quick click of the translation option revealed a rather eye-opening article.

Apparently, four years ago Didier owned a large and well-established auction house, which was the subject of a burglary and arson. His premises and all the antiques inside that weren't stolen had been destroyed by fire. Although covered by insurance, the insurers had a limit and due to an irregularity, which Fleur couldn't see explained, the insurance company only paid out on half the supposed value. This had left Didier in debt and the company had been closed.

Again, Fleur had to take time to absorb this new information and try to work out what relevance it had to Lydia's visit to Paris, the missing painting and the mystery ballet shoe. She drew a blank. There were lots of fragments of information, but none of them complete enough to show the whole picture or, indeed, several different unconnected pieces. It was as if someone had thrown several boxes of puzzles up in the air and she was trying to sift through them without any clue what the final images should be.

After ending the call, she checked in on Lydia again who was still sleeping. Fleur went over to her grandmother, watching the rise and fall of her chest, the ballet shoe still in her hand. Lydia was now wearing an eye mask and although Fleur couldn't see her grandmother's eyes, she got the distinct feeling she wasn't really asleep. 'Nan, you OK?' she whispered.

'I'm fine,' replied Lydia without moving or attempting to lift the eye mask. 'Just need a little longer resting. The travelling takes it out of me these days.'

'I was just checking.'

'Stop worrying. I'm not about to depart from this world just yet.' She waved a hand in the direction of the door.

Fleur hesitated and, sensing she was still there, Lydia pulled up her eye mask. 'What is it, *ma petite puce?*'

Fleur shuffled awkwardly on her feet. 'I wasn't going to tell you just yet, but I found something out about Didier.'

Lydia pushed herself into a sitting position and took the eye mask off fully. She patted the edge of the bed. 'You should tell me.'

'Well, it turns out it wasn't that much of a coincidence that Didier was outside the school. To cut a long story short, he had been hoping to meet you. He's actually trying to find a missing piece of artwork that there's a big reward for.' Fleur went on to give the abridged and concise summary of her conversation with Didier and what she'd later found out on the internet.

All the time Fleur was explaining, Lydia had listened attentively, not asking any questions, but Fleur could see her sharp brain working away as she assessed everything.

After a long pause, Lydia finally spoke. 'When I invited you on this trip, I thought I had it all clear in my mind what I was going to tell you. Since the appearance of the ballet shoe and Didier and what you've just told me, I'm not sure I even know what the truth is.' She looked down at the shoe in her hand, her thumb stroking the delicate silk fabric.

'Is there anything you feel you can tell me now? Anything that will help us make sense of this?' coaxed Fleur.

She looked at the strained expression on Lydia's face and suddenly she looked her eighty-one years, her skin translucent and paper-thin. She looked like a little sparrow that had flown from its nest too soon.

In that moment, Fleur knew she herself didn't care anymore that she didn't know her grandmother's story. It wasn't about Fleur knowing her heritage. This was only as important as it was to Lydia. 'We can just leave things as they are. I can tell Didier we don't know anything else. He can go back to trying to find the painting himself and we . . . we can just be tourists for the next two weeks as we planned, and we don't have to think about paintings, ballet shoes and the past anymore. Not if you don't want to. It only matters if it matters to you.'

Lydia held the ballet shoe to her chest and closed her eyes for a few seconds before looking at Fleur. 'I stand by what I said to you originally. The truth needs to be told. My story needs to be told so that all the sacrifices will not be forgotten. If this means finding out more truths, then so be it. And I want it to help you too. I want you to be able to accept your past.'

'You don't have to worry about me,' reassured Fleur.

'But I do. I know it's difficult but we both must not bury it. That's using our privilege of being alive. Others who we have loved have been denied that privilege.'

'And are you sure you're up to this, Nan?'

'Yes. Besides, I don't have the luxury of time. I've used most of mine up already. I don't want you to waste yours.' She thumbed the ballet shoe again as if it galvanised her. 'I think Didier can help. It's as if he's been sent by some higher authority to help us.'

Fleur was sceptical about this but she didn't argue with Lydia. 'If you're sure.'

'I'm positive. Talk to him again and then we can work out what to do next.'

Chapter 19

Adele

Paris, July 1942

Adele hadn't stopped smiling to herself since her meeting with Manu's friends – well, maybe not friends but associates at least. She had real hope now that there was a way to get her friends and the children out of France and to safety, with the possibility of making a new escape route. Manu had warned her to keep her hopes realistic and reminded her of the danger.

'It's not a game,' he'd said as Adele had grinned madly at him when they'd left. 'It's real lives and if anyone messes up, then the whole chain could collapse.'

Adele had tried not to be hurt by his words. She hated that he thought she was naive and didn't understand the severity of the situation. It was the way he thought of her as young and inexperienced that bothered her. Maybe Lucille had been right: he only ever thought of her as a younger sister. She also hated herself for overanalysing it so much.

Monday came around quickly and Adele was eager to see her guests at the school. A knot of anxiety had pitched up in her stomach after the search of the building, and she hadn't been able to shift it. She hadn't dare come back yesterday, just in case the building was being watched. She had to behave like she did every Sunday and that didn't include going to her place of work.

She called up to the attic as she ascended the staircase. The smell of bodies and lack of fresh air was strong that morning and Adele was glad she'd managed to smuggle out some soap from home. Peter had bought some luxury toiletries for Lucille, who had shared them with Adele. Much as Adele would have loved to keep the lavender soap and use it herself, she knew it was best used elsewhere. She still had a smaller bar Lucille had given her and she would make do with that for now and hope Lucille didn't quiz her about what she was doing with it.

'Look what I have,' said Adele holding up the bar of soap.

Jacqueline and Cecile were much more impressed with the offering than the children. 'I also have some sweet bread.' This produced a more enthusiastic response from the little ones. 'But only after you've all had a wash.'

'I'll take them,' said Cecile. She shepherded her little flock out of the attic and down to the bathrooms.

'How are you all doing?' asked Adele once they were alone.

'It's hard,' admitted Jacqueline. 'What happened the other day? Fortunately, I'd heard the rumble of the lorry pulling up outside and managed to get the children up here quickly. We were playing in the dance room.'

Adele handed the soft toy that had been found. 'I know. This was left. Along with some bread.'

'Oh, that rabbit! I will have to tie it to her wrist. I'm so sorry.' Jacqueline sighed. 'I didn't realise. It was such a panic. If it happens again, I'll take more care. I promise.'

'Did you hear me ring the bell?'

'Yes, we did, but we were already in the attic by then. I'm not sure if we would have had enough time if we hadn't heard the lorry.'

'At least you managed to keep everyone quiet.'

'It was so frightening. We could hear the soldiers downstairs. We didn't dare move. I was worried just breathing would give us away. And then when they came up to the attic next door.' She closed her eyes momentarily at the thought.

'They were so close. So very close. The children were amazing though. We had practised staying quiet and they are getting used to it, but I was so very scared.' Jacqueline bowed her head and wiped at her face.

'Jacqueline,' said Adele. 'It's all right. Don't cry.' She hugged her friend. 'You're safe now and you might not have to stay here for much longer.'

Jacqueline looked up. 'What do you mean?'

'Lucille and I have been asked to dance at an exhibition Müller, her boyfriend, is holding in Lyon. I wasn't going to do it but then I had an idea.' She held Jacqueline's hands in hers. 'We get false papers for you, Cecile and the children. The children will be part of the dance routine and once it is over, they can disappear. They can escape with you both and cross the border to Switzerland.'

Jacqueline's eyes lit up. 'You make it sound very easy.'

'We are working on the plan. Manu has made contact with people who can help us. You just have to be patient for a little longer.'

'And hope our luck holds out.'

'Yes.' Adele looked earnestly into her friend's eyes. 'We need luck too. Lots of it. But what is the alternative? You can't stay hidden up here forever, especially as the Germans have already searched the place once.'

'What made them do that? Are they suspicious of us?'

Adele hadn't planned on telling Jacqueline about Edith but it felt wrong to withhold the information. 'I'm not sure. Edith, Manu's girlfriend, said something that made me suspicious. I don't trust her. She talked about vermin in the attic and then the German officer used the same words.'

Jacqueline gave a sharp intake of breath but before she could say anything more, Cecile came back with the children. 'Ah, there you all are,' she said, pulling Blanche in for a hug. 'Oh and how nice you all smell now.'

Daniel followed in last, his hair still wet. He looked downcast. 'Hey, Daniel,' said Adele going over to him.

'*Ça-va?*' She took his hand and led him over towards the window. 'Here, sit down and I'll comb your hair for you.' She picked up the comb that was on the side and, kneeling down beside him, began to tidy his thick dark hair. 'Perhaps we can find some fresh clothes for you too. Maybe Thomas has something you could borrow.'

Daniel might smell clean and fresh but body odour and the faint whiff of urine clung to his clothing.

'I don't want Thomas's clothes,' said Daniel, his head bowed.

'But you need to put on something clean to wear,' said Adele.

Daniel shook his head. 'No.'

Adele saw two blobs of tears land on his knees. 'Oh, Daniel. Don't cry. What's the matter?' She pulled the boy onto her lap and held him to her, rocking back and forth as sobs racked his little body. After a few minutes, the crying eased but Daniel clung to Adele. 'Tell me what's wrong,' coaxed Adele. 'Then I can help you.'

'I don't want to wear Thomas's clothes,' he repeated. 'When Mama comes back, she won't know it's me and she'll leave me here again.'

Adele thought her heart might break. She held him tightly and stroked his hair. 'Your mama will always know it's you,' she whispered. 'She could have her eyes closed and she would be able to pick you out in a room full of children. She doesn't need to see you, she will just follow her heart to find you. Every day, you are in her heart and mind. She loves you so much.'

'I want Mama,' Daniel whimpered.

'I know you do, *ma petite puce*. I know.' Adele held Daniel for a long time, offering words of reassurance and comfort. Eventually, he had stopped crying. Adele sat him up. 'Now, how about you only borrow some of Thomas's clothes, just for the night while I wash yours for you. We can do that now and then hang them up to dry. Tomorrow you'll be able to put your own clothes back on.'

Cecile silently slid over some clothes to Adele. Daniel eyed the bundle. 'Just for one day?'

'Just for one day,' replied Adele with a reassuring smile and was relieved when he agreed.

A few minutes later with Daniel in clothes that were too big for him, Adele left him and Thomas playing a game of marbles she had found in the depths of her desk drawer. She stood over the sink in the bathroom downstairs washing Daniel's clothes the best she could with the bar of soap she'd brought from home. Her tears mingled in with the grey soapy water as Daniel's fears replayed in her head. In her heart of hearts she didn't think his mother was coming back for him and she had no idea what was going to become of the little boy.

Footsteps behind her alerted her to someone coming into the bathroom. It was Jacqueline. She put her arms around Adele and rested her head on her shoulder. 'He's all right now. He's playing happily with Thomas.'

Adele wiped her tears away with the back of her hand and pounded the clothes in and out of the water. 'What has become of the world? How can one human be so cruel to another?'

'It is not mankind, just the Germans,' said Jacqueline, moving to lean against the sink. 'It is the minority not the majority.'

'I hate it that you are all suffering in this way. Having to hide to save your lives.' She slapped the wet clothing back down into the water. 'It's inhumane.' The tears had made way for anger and frustration. 'I cannot stand by and passively accept what the Germans are doing.'

Jacqueline placed a hand on Adele's shoulder. 'You're not standing by. You are doing something.'

'But I can do more and I will.' Adele felt a renewed sense of purpose well up inside her and for the first time her fear of the consequences took second place. 'All the time there is a breath left in my body, I will do everything I can to protect you all and get you to safety.'

'And after that?'

'And after you, there will be more. You are just the first of many.'

The rest of the day passed without any incident. Even when Adele was taking the usual dance class, she didn't hear anything from upstairs. They were very good at keeping quiet. Cecile had said they'd all adjusted to the different sleep pattern of being awake during the night and sleeping during the day.

Adele had just finished the class and was handing out dried apple rings to the children when, to her surprise, Lucille bustled her way into the room.

'What are you doing here?' Adele asked, as she packed the shoes into the basket. Lucille hardly ever came to the school.

'I thought we should start on our routine for the exhibition.' Lucille dumped her bag on the piano stool and took out her ballet shoes. 'I really think we should do ballet. It's classical and beautiful.'

'And the dance you're best at,' said Adele with a wry smile.

'Nothing wrong with wanting to show off the discipline I'm actually very good at. Besides, you are too.'

It was true, both Adele and her sister had excelled at ballet. Maybe it was because it was their mother's talent and the love for the dance was in their blood.

'I'm happy with ballet. I just didn't realise you'd want to start now.' She thought of the guests in the attic. They knew not to come out after school until Adele gave them the all clear. She just hoped they would realise someone was here and wouldn't mistake any noise they heard for Adele being alone.

'Let me just put these things away.' She picked up the basket of shoes and rather than put them in the cupboard at the front of the classroom where they were usually kept, she took them into the storeroom and placed them on the bookcase Manu had installed, all the time talking to her sister, in a louder voice than necessary, about what piece of music they should dance to. She hoped Jacqueline or Cecile would hear her and realise she wasn't alone.

'You can tell you've been with children all day,' said Lucille with a laugh. 'You're talking really loudly, like you're trying to be heard over the noise. I'm not deaf, you know!'

'Sorry. Force of habit,' she said, even though she rarely raised her voice in class. 'So, what piece of music?' She sat on the piano stool next to her sister, who shifted up to make room. Adele lifted the lid and began to play the opening bars to the 'Dance of the Sugar Plum Fairy'. 'This is a classic and I'm sure we will soon remember the steps. Unless you want to do this as your solo piece.'

'Stop. Adele! I can't have a proper conversation with you if you're playing.'

Adele took her hands away from the keys and smiled at her sister. 'Sorry. So, what did you have in mind? I'm sure you've thought about it.' As she spoke, she was aware of a brief scuffing noise from the attic. It was momentary and then stopped, thank goodness. Adele quickly rested her hands on the keys and played a few notes to distract her sister.

'I used to dance the Sugar Plum Fairy so much. Yes, it might be nice to dance a solo to that. We also need something we can do together. Maybe something else from *The Nutcracker*.'

Adele didn't really care. Her main purpose of the performance wasn't to impress anyone. She would dance to anything if it meant saving her friends and the children. 'What about 'Waltz of the Flowers'? That's nice and upbeat. A good contrast to the 'Dance of the Sugar Plum Fairy'.'

'Do you think Hitler will like it?' asked Lucille with a frown.

Adele's stomach curled at the thought of doing anything to please Hitler. She couldn't care less one way or the other, but she kept her thoughts to herself.

A creak of the floorboard from above sounded out. This

time there was no mistaking it for anything else. Lucille's gaze shot upwards and then to Adele. 'What was that?'

'Just the floorboards. You know what this old building is like. Probably mice.' Adele started up on the piano keys again but her sister leaned over and took her hands away.

'Listen. There it is again.'

'Honestly, Lucille. It's nothing. Let's start our rehearsals. It's been a long day and I want to get home. I'm very tired.'

'What's going on, Adele?' Lucille closed the piano lid. 'Up there.' She got to her feet and pointed to the ceiling. 'There's something up there. Or someone.'

Adele stood also, her eyes level with her sister's. 'The only thing that might be up there are mice.' She spoke firmly as if talking to one of her children who needed reprimanding about something.

'I don't believe you,' said Lucille softly.

'You need to believe me.'

Lucille looked up at the ceiling and then over to the storeroom door. Adele knew at that moment, her sister had remembered about the secret staircase. 'Don't,' said Adele. 'Lucille, just don't.'

It was too late. Lucille was striding across the floor. She yanked open the door and stepped inside the storeroom. Adele was right behind her. Lucille looked around the small space, her gaze coming to rest on the bookcase covering the door. She walked over to it and stopped. Adele's heart was pounding. She was expecting her sister to try to open it, but she didn't. 'Oh, Adele, please say it's not what I think it is.'

'It's not what you think it is,' replied Adele. 'And if you don't look any further, if you turn around now and walk out of here, you won't have to know.' When her sister didn't reply but remained staring at the bookcase, Adele tried again. 'We can go back out to the dance room and practise our routine. We don't even need to discuss this.'

'And I won't need to say anything?' Lucille turned. 'That's what you mean, isn't it?'

Adele nodded. 'That's exactly what I mean.'

'You're putting me in a very difficult position,' said Lucille.

Adele was amazed at the rather haughty tone her sister had adopted. 'Putting you in a difficult position?' she repeated. 'A difficult position? You have no idea.' Her sister was incredible! Unbelievable. Adele's temper flashed. She grabbed her sister by the arm and bundled her out of the storeroom, slamming the door behind her. 'A difficult position is nothing compared to what some people are going through.' Her voice was a hiss. 'Some people's lives are in danger. Mortal danger. Not just something that's a discomfort or a bit awkward, but real fear for their lives. Do you understand what I'm saying, Lucille? Some people could be murdered, including me. Now that's a difficult position.'

Lucille shrugged her arm away from Adele's grip. 'You're asking me to lie to the man I love,' she retorted.

'No! No, I'm not,' snapped back Adele. 'I'm asking you not to say anything about something you don't know for certain.'

'It's the same thing.'

'It's not. I'm not asking you to lie.' She threw her hands in the air in exasperation. 'I can't even believe we're having this conversation. Think about it, Lucille. Just think about it. You go running off to your German lover, telling him what you think you know. He sends out a search party and one of two things will happen. One, there's nothing to be seen, heard or found or, two, something is discovered. Something so awful that it will have ramifications for me and Papa. And possibly you. Can you live with that? Are you willing to sacrifice your family and other innocent people? Are you really that callous and hard-hearted?'

'And if I don't and let's not mix our words here, dear sister, when your secret is discovered, and believe me it will be, whether I have anything to do with it or not, how do you think that will look for me and for Peter?'

'I don't care about Peter. I care about innocent lives.'

'If you don't care about Peter then you don't care about me.'

'Just listen to yourself. You're talking rubbish.' Adele let out a long sigh. Could her sister really be so selfish? 'Lucille, please . . . please don't betray me. It will be the saddest day of my life. It will break my heart if my own sister does that to me.' She stroked her sister's face. 'If you can't do that for me, then do it for Maman and Papa.'

Lucille looked at her for a long moment. Her eyes shone as tears gathered, but she blinked them away. Adele knew it was the mention of their mother. Lucille raised her chin a fraction. 'Just don't make me lie to Peter.'

'It's only for a few days, that's all.'

Lucille nodded as the unspoken agreement passed between them.

Chapter 20

Fleur

Paris, August 2015

After speaking to her grandmother about Didier, Fleur went back to her room to call him to arrange a meeting. She used the number on his business card and tried the shop first. After several rings a woman answered the phone.

Fleur inwardly sighed, knowing she'd have to use her basic French. Hopefully it would be straightforward. '*Bonjour. Je voudrais parler avec Didier Dacourt, s'il vous plaît.*' She felt quite pleased with herself until the woman rattled off a reply which Fleur didn't quite understand. '*Plus lentement?*' she asked, hoping that was right for asking the woman to speak slower.

'Monsieur Dacourt is not here,' said the woman in proficient English. 'Can I take a message and ask him to call you?'

'Do you know when he will be back?' asked Fleur. She could hear a young child in the background. 'Papa. Papa,' the little voice wailed.

'Sorry, excuse me a moment.'

Fleur could hear the woman put the phone down and attend to the now crying child. Several seconds later, the woman was back on the phone and the crying had downgraded to a few sobs. Fleur guessed the child was now being pacified on the hip of the woman. '*Alors.* Sorry. My son was crying,' explained the woman.

'Don't worry. I have Didier's mobile number. I'll ring that,' said Fleur feeling sorry for the woman having to juggle a phone call and a child.

The woman didn't object and Fleur tried Didier's mobile number, which was also quoted on the business card. It went to voicemail and she left a message asking him to call her.

There was a knock at the connecting door and Lydia appeared in the room, ready to go down for tea. 'I thought we could have a little walk afterwards,' she said. 'I do like an evening stroll and there's somewhere I'd like to take you.'

Lydia wouldn't be drawn on where she wanted to take Fleur who had to stop herself from impatiently scoffing her food. Lydia was in good form initially but as the meal drew to a close, Fleur noticed a dip in her spirits.

'If you're feeling tired, we can just go back to our room,' she suggested. 'It is getting late in the evening.' She glanced out of the window at the lowering sun just beginning to dip behind the rooftops, filling the sky with a warm orange glow.

Lydia shook her head. 'No, this is the right time of day to go.'

Before Fleur could question her grandmother further, her phone pinged with a text message from a Paris number. Fleur opened it.

Didier: *Salut. C'est Didier.* I received your message. When would you like to meet?

Fleur briefly wondered why Didier hadn't phoned, but it was probably better this way seeing as she was in the middle of the restaurant. Logging his number into her phone she then tapped out a message.

Fleur: Would tomorrow afternoon be OK?

She received a reply almost straight away.

Didier: Tomorrow will be good but I am not free until the evening. Perhaps we could talk over a glass of wine.

Fleur read the message a second time.

'What's wrong?' asked Lydia.

'It's Didier. He's suggesting a drink tomorrow evening. He can't make the afternoon apparently.'

'I expect he has to work.'

It was a logical suggestion and Fleur replied, agreeing to meet him. She wasn't sure why the idea pleased her so much but it did.

'Now that's sorted, perhaps we can go for that walk,' said Lydia.

It was a little chillier that evening and Fleur quickly nipped upstairs to fetch her grandmother's jacket and a cardigan for herself.

'You know I won't be coming with you tomorrow when you meet Didier,' said Lydia as they made their way along the street. Lydia appeared to know where she was going and Fleur allowed her to lead.

'You're not! Why?' Fleur had assumed Lydia would want to speak to Didier as well.

'I think if you speak to him first, then relay it to me, that way you can prepare me for any shocks. I am getting on now, *ma petite puce*.'

Fleur looked out of the corner of her eye at her grandmother and wasn't entirely convinced by the explanation. 'It's not a date,' she said just in case there was any misunderstanding.

'I know,' replied Lydia. 'He's more likely to be honest if it's just the two of you.'

Fleur remained unconvinced.

They had been walking for about ten minutes and Fleur was just about to ask Lydia if they should turn back when Lydia spoke. 'Here we are.'

They were at the entrance to a park. It was still light and there looked to be quite a few people enjoying the green space. 'This is nice,' said Fleur as they went through the gates and took the path that essentially cut the park in two. 'Did you come here as a child? Did your mum bring you here?'

Lydia sighed. 'Yes, I did come here when I was young. Only the once though.'

There was a deep sadness to her voice, which alarmed Fleur. 'And you still remember it?'

'*Oui*, I will never forget this park. Something terrible happened here. It changed my life forever.'

'I'm so sorry, Nan,' said Fleur, once again concerned this trip was proving too painful for her grandmother. 'Do you want to go back to the hotel?'

Lydia shook her head vehemently. 'No. I come here to remember what happened, not to hide from it.' Lydia took a deep breath. 'I come because it reminds me of the love I have lost. It reminds me to be happy that I have that memory. To be grateful of what I once had. Being angry only keeps the pain of the evilness alive.'

Fleur couldn't imagine what had happened here but it was clearly important to Lydia. She also couldn't help but admire her grandmother's passion at remembering the love through the pain. 'What happened that night?' she asked softly.

Chapter 21

Adele

Paris, July 1942

Adele and Lucille never mentioned the noises in the attic, even over the next few days when Lucille came to the dance studio and they rehearsed their routines. There was the occasional noise from upstairs, but Lucille didn't even acknowledge it and for that Adele was grateful. She had to remind the children to stay as silent as possible.

'Whenever you hear anyone downstairs, you must be as quiet as little church mice,' she told them.

'But it's boring,' said Daniel.

'I don't like it here,' said Eva. 'I want to go home.'

'Me too,' said Blanche. 'If they hear us, they will let us go home. You can't keep us up here.' With that, she picked up her shoe and started banging the heel onto the floorboards.

'That's enough,' said Adele. 'Stop it.'

Blanche ignored her and carried on smacking the shoe down onto the floor.

'I said, that's enough!' To her horror, instead of stopping, Blanche picked up her other shoe and proceeded to bang both of them onto the floor, ignoring her mother's attempt to stop her. Adele's nerves were already frayed and she marched over to the child, snatching the shoes from her hands. 'I said stop! Now if you can't do as I say, then I'll just take your shoes away from you.'

'Adele, please,' said Jacqueline. 'She's only a child.'

'I don't care. She can't behave like this.'

Blanche glared up at her and then slowly raised her leg and, with a defiant look, thumped her foot down onto the floorboards. She did it again and again. Then started pummelling the floor with both her feet.

'BLANCHE!' Adele heard herself yell above the thumping. She went to grab the child, not really knowing what she was going to do. She just wanted her to stop. 'ENOUGH!' She pulled the child up on her feet.

'Adele!' Jacqueline shouted, placing herself between her child and her friend. Blanche began to cry, her defiance outrun by the fear of her teacher's anger.

Adele stopped and took a moment to calm herself. 'I'm so sorry,' she said. 'It's just all getting to me.'

'You can't take it out on the children,' said Jacqueline. 'They're frightened enough as it is without you making things worse.'

'Forgive me.' She knelt down so she was at Blanche's eye level. 'I'm sorry for getting cross and shouting, but you have to promise not to do that again. It's very important, Blanche. Extremely important. Do you understand?'

The little girl nodded. 'Say sorry,' prompted Jacqueline.

'*Je suis désolé, mademoiselle*,' said Blanche.

Adele forced a smile and stood up. She felt strained and weary with worry about them all being found. She reminded herself that everyone up here must be even more scared than she was and having to hide up here every day was not good for the mind.

Adele hadn't spoken to Manu that week. She'd seen him a few times pass by the school but he was never alone. He was either with Edith or with Müller, probably discussing the exhibition.

It was Sunday morning and both her father and Lucille had gone to mass. Adele had excused herself from attending and although her father raised a concerned eyebrow, he didn't question her. Her belief had waned since the occupation and she found little comfort in the once regular ritual. Today, she wanted time alone and, as always, was drawn to the Cimetière du Père Lachaise, where her mother was buried.

The cemetery was the largest in Paris and the Basset family plot had occupied its position for the past two generations. Adele was familiar with the route along the brick paving, past the monuments and mini chapels, shaded by the mature trees, which softened the austere landscape.

Soon she was at the family grave and, as always when she visited, an overwhelming sense of calm descended on her. She felt close to her mother, not just in the physical sense but also in the emotional sense.

Adele wished she'd been able to bring some flowers. The stone cross bearing her mother's name and that of her paternal grandparents was clean and free of algae. Adele knew her father cleaned the stone on his weekly visits.

'*Bonjour*, Maman,' Adele whispered, kissing her fingers and then touching the stone. She sat down on the kerb that edged the plot. '*Alors*, the Germans are still here. They continue to enjoy the city as if it were a playground for them while the people suffer.' She traced her mother's name with her fingertip. 'I miss you, Maman. I wish you were here. I am trying to be brave.' She wiped a tear from her eye. 'I cannot do nothing for, in my mind, that makes me complicit. I hope I would make you proud.'

'And she would be very proud of you.'

A voice behind her had Adele spinning around. She let out a gasp. 'Manu!' She jumped to her feet. 'What are you doing here?' Adele used the sleeve of her cardigan to wipe any trace of tears from her face.

He stepped forwards and put his arms around her. 'You don't have to be brave all the time,' he said, not answering her question. He kissed the top of her head.

Adele couldn't deny the feeling of comfort and pleasure she derived from being held by Manu, but her mind was trying to make sense of him being there. She pulled away. 'You didn't answer my question.'

For the first time, Manu didn't appear as confident as he always did. He looked a little embarrassed. He gave a shrug. 'I was hoping to see you. I was waiting at the church but I saw your father and sister arrive alone.'

'How did you know I was here?'

He gave a small amused laugh and brushed a strand of hair from her face. 'Because, my dear Adele, I know you come here. Particularly, when you're sad or worried. Don't forget, I've known you for a long time now.'

It made sense. She nodded. 'Why did you want to see me?'

'Do I need a reason?'

'No. I am flattered but I suspect there is a reason.'

'Yes, there is actually,' said Manu. He took her hand and they began to make their way back through the cemetery. 'But first, are you all right? Are you coping?'

'I'm fine.' She didn't want to appear weak or give Manu any reason to doubt her or worry about her. Bigger things were at stake. People's lives depended on her.

'You can talk to me if you ever need to,' he said, still holding her hand.

'I know. Honestly, I am all right.'

'What about your guests?'

'Yes, they are all right too.'

'We need to take them to get their photograph taken by the man who is going to arrange their papers.'

Adele frowned. 'Take them? But how?'

'Over the next two nights. Tell Cecile and Thomas to be ready at ten-thirty,' said Manu. 'Tomorrow night, it will be Jacqueline and her daughters, and I'll take Daniel.'

'I don't like the sound of that,' said Adele. 'Taking them through the streets after curfew.'

'We can't risk taking them in broad daylight. What if

someone who knows them sees them? Or if they are stopped? They won't have any papers. It will be better to risk it when it's dark.'

'Did you find anything out about the building Edith went to?'

'No. But it's not important now.'

Adele wasn't sure if Manu was telling her the whole truth. She had a sensation he was keeping something back from her. 'You know you can tell me things,' she said.

They had reached the gates of the cemetery now. 'I know,' said Manu. 'You don't have to worry about anything, though. Especially not Edith.' He looked up and down the road as they exited. His grip on her hand tightened and Adele felt the tension of his body through his touch.

'What's wrong?'

'Just keep walking,' he said, smiling at her. 'Just look up at me and laugh, like I've just told you something funny.'

Adele did as she was told and put her other hand on his arm. 'How long do you want me to laugh for?'

'Don't overdo it. That's enough.'

Adele did as she was told. From the corner of her eye she saw a black sedan car, with the Nazi flag fluttering on the bonnet. Two men sat in the front of the vehicle, openly watching them. She gulped and had to force herself to look away. 'Gestapo,' she said through a false smile.

'Yes. Here, this way.' They slipped in through a doorway of an apartment behind another couple, who got into the lift.

'*Bonjour*,' said the man.

Manu and Adele returned the greeting but declined the lift. They went straight across the foyer and out through the rear door, which led into a courtyard. Manu hurried Adele along, his pace quickening. Then they were out through another door and onto the street behind the building.

Adele hurried to keep pace with him. 'Are we safe?' she asked, resisting the urge to turn around and look over her shoulder.

'Yes but we need to get home as quickly as possible.'

Manu got Adele back to her apartment in record time and stepped into the foyer for a moment. 'Are you all right?'

Adele nodded. 'I am now.' She was still holding his hand and had no intention of letting go until the last possible moment. 'Do you think they're following us?'

'I don't know. It may be just coincidence but I don't like taking chances.'

'Do you want to come in for a coffee? Wait here a while until it's safe to go home?'

'Thank you but I should go. Edith will wonder where I am.' He leaned in to kiss her but instead of her face, he kissed her lips. A soft, gentle fleeting brush of his mouth against hers, but it made Adele catch her breath all the same. She wanted to return the kiss, but he had pulled away, momentarily holding her gaze, before stepping back completely. 'I should go. Be careful, Adele.' And then he was gone, leaving Adele staring at the oak door.

Adele walked slowly up the steps to the apartment, replaying the last hour or so in her mind. It was a complete morass of emotions and she wasn't quite sure how she'd cope with it all in such a short space of time. And as for that kiss. He'd actually kissed her mouth, and she was sure it had been intentional, not just a mistimed gesture. He had looked at her afterwards, properly looked at her. It must have meant something to him. Surely she wasn't reading too much into it.

Adele set about making a fresh pot of coffee, knowing Lucille and her father would be home soon and within a few minutes Lucille was bustling into the kitchen.

'I'm not going to rehearse this evening,' she said to Adele, lifting the coffee pot and breathing in the rich aroma. 'Peter is taking me to the theatre.'

'That's nice. You haven't seen him much this week, have you?' Adele had secretly been hoping that Peter had finally grown weary of Lucille, especially if he was taking other women out to dinner.

'Yes. I'm looking forward to seeing him. He's been unusually busy recently.' Lucille frowned.

'Is everything all right between you two?'

Lucille hesitated, before answering. 'He's been a little distant, if I'm honest. I know the exhibition is playing on his mind but I get a feeling there's something else. I just wish he'd tell me.'

Adele was surprised at this confession from her sister. Lucille wasn't one for confiding in her about any doubts she might have. Adele posed her next question carefully. 'Do you really think he's just busy with work?'

'Honestly? I'm not sure. I'd like to think so.'

Adele reached out and took her sister's hand. 'And what would you not like to think?'

Lucille's gaze was fixed on the floor. It was uncharacteristic of her to be so honest and wide open with her thoughts and feelings. She gave a shrug. 'I don't want him to become bored with me.'

And there was the doubt that Lucille hid so well. She projected confidence, vitality and a love for life, but it was always a front. Underneath it, she was full of self-doubt, insecurities and the need to be loved. Their mother's death had hit Lucille hard and, being the youngest, she had been cosseted, indulged and protected. Adele was probably the most guilty of all as she tried to step into her mother's shoes but, ultimately, had it done more damage? Adele was reminded of Lucille at ten years old: eyes to the ground, scuffing her foot and biting her bottom lip as anxiety snipped at her heels.

'But if he loves you, then how will he be bored?' questioned Adele. 'And if he is so easily bored, then maybe he doesn't love you enough and maybe you should wait for someone who does.'

Lucille physically jolted at Adele's words. She snapped her head up. The vulnerable Lucille was banished and the resilient, self-assured reinvented Lucille was back. 'You'd love that, wouldn't you?' She said taking a step away. 'If Peter didn't love me enough.'

'I didn't mean to upset you,' said Adele, feeling the opportunity to persuade her sister otherwise slip away. 'I just don't want you walking blindly into a relationship that is going to hurt you. You are worthy of so much more Lucille. You have a joy for life and people gravitate towards you because of that enthusiasm. Remember how when we were young, we used to talk to Maman about all the places in the world we wanted to see. How we would dance our way through Europe and then America. You remember, don't you?'

'Of course I do,' said Lucille. 'I was going to marry a rich American and you were going to marry Manu.'

'I was?'

'Yes. You never said that but you always imagined your husband to be a poet or a writer or something to do with the arts,' said Lucille with a smile. 'I always knew you meant Manu.'

'Don't think you can change the subject by mentioning that,' said Adele. 'This is about you and your future. The war won't last forever and when it's over, Peter will go back to being an engineer and, if you go to Germany with him, you'll be stuck at home all on your own, washing his socks and underpants, shopping and cooking his tea. It will not be the fun and decadent lifestyle you're enjoying here in Paris. Maman always told us to be the most and best we can be and, for you, my darling sister, that is a dazzling star shining bright, not a flickering candle flame in the corner of a room.'

Lucille dropped her gaze for a moment and Adele remained silent. Eventually, Lucille spoke. 'They were just childish dreams. Peter loves me. I love him. He's just very busy with work. And, if I bore him, then I need to up my game and keep my man.' She smiled at her sister. 'Actually, talking to you has helped. It's made things clear in my mind. I mustn't take Peter for granted. I'll make sure he doesn't grow bored with me.' There was a glint of devilish excitement in her eyes. 'Thank you, sister. Now, I must go and get ready. I need to make an extra effort tonight.' She blew Adele a kiss as she left the room.

Adele muttered an expletive under her breath. Her sister was insufferable. Obsessed with Müller. More so now. Just when Adele thought she might be able to get through to Lucille. Agh. She stomped her foot on the floor in frustration.

This instantly reminded her of Blanche and she felt guilt rush through her again for letting her frustrations and anxiety get the better of her. Dear little Blanche, she was just as confused and frightened as everyone and yet being the youngest, probably understood what was happening the least.

The following morning, Adele went up to the attic to explain about the photographs and to make sure Cecile and Thomas would to be ready for Manu later that evening.

'Here's the key for the side entrance,' she said, passing it to Cecile. 'Make sure you lock it behind you and hide the key under the brick, just in case.' She didn't need to say just in case they were caught by the Germans who would then want to know what the key was for, but Cecile understood.

'Don't worry. I won't forget.'

'Manu will do two single knocks on the door, followed by a double knock. Do not open the door to any other knock. If, before you open the door, you hear him calling your name, or saying anything, that will mean danger is imminent. You must run back up and hide.'

'Understood.'

'When you come back, Manu will lock the door behind you and leave the key there for me to collect in the morning.' She hugged Cecile. *'Bonne chance, mon amie.'*

Adele spent a restless evening and night worrying about Cecile. By the time the clock in the living room had chimed midnight, she finally relaxed. She was sure if anything had happened, she would have heard by now. The Gestapo would be banging down the front door.

She hadn't needed to worry. The next morning when she arrived at school, she had spotted Manu across the wall and he had given her a nod, indicating everything had gone to plan.

Now she was in the attic, making sure Daniel was ready. She smoothed down his hair. 'So, you must listen to what Manu tells you,' she said. 'Blanche and Eva will be with you, as well as their mother.' She gave his chin a little tug. 'Don't be sad. You're actually going outside tonight on an adventure.' Her attempts to rouse a smile from the boy were futile. He went and sat down back in the corner where his bed was.

Jacqueline came over to Adele and spoke softly. 'He's even more withdrawn this week. I'm worried about him. He doesn't want to join in with any of the games.'

'He's missing his mother,' said Adele.

'I think he is grieving for her. He maybe doesn't understand what might have happened to her, but he doesn't think she's coming back. He was crying this morning.'

'I just hope that one day his mother will turn up and they will be reunited. It breaks my heart. He has no one. I haven't been able to trace any of his other relatives. I think they must all be either rounded up or in hiding.'

She crossed the room, picked up a book and sat beside Daniel, putting her arm around him. He resisted at first, his body rigid and his gaze fixed on the attic window, but as Adele opened the book and began reading the story of a prince who had lost his crown, he began to relax. Thomas came over and sat the other side of Adele. She ruffled his hair as she continued with the story.

By the time she had finished, the girls were sitting at her feet, all of them glued to the tale Adele was telling. 'And they all lived happily in the castle for the rest of their days,' concluded Adele.

'Can we have another one?' It was Daniel. His voice was small and his sorrowful eyes large as he looked up at Adele.

Even though it was getting late, Adele couldn't refuse. 'Of course. Go and choose one.' Daniel scuttled off while Adele quelled the appeals of the other children to choose a book and promised it would be their turn tomorrow.

When the time came for Jacqueline and the children to wait by the side entrance of the school, Daniel was particularly reluctant. Adele had stayed to try to offer the boy some comfort, but he had barely said a word and had refused to let go of Adele's hand the entire time she was there, huddling up to her whenever she sat down. He gripped on to Adele's hand even more tightly as they made their way down to the door.

They only had to wait a few minutes before there was the knock, knock, knock-knock on the door. Then silence. Adele nodded at Jacqueline and she slipped the key into the lock and opened the door.

Jacqueline and the girls stepped out into the shadows of the evening. It was getting dark now and despite it being July, there was a chill in the air that night. Or was Adele just imagining it? She held out Daniel's hand, to pass him over to Manu, but the child wouldn't let go. Instead he pulled against them, his legs locked straight out in front of him as he refused to move.

'Come on, Daniel,' coaxed Adele. 'Remember what we said. You're going with Blanche and Eva this evening, just to see someone and then Manu is bringing you straight back.' The adults had agreed not to tell the children exactly what they were doing – just in case they were stopped. That way, they couldn't unintentionally blurt out any information.

'I don't want to go with him,' said Daniel. He pulled back harder. 'Leave me alone.'

'Daniel, stop this at once,' said Adele, aware she was having to deal with another child who was frightened and didn't understand what was happening. 'Manu will look after you.'

'No! I don't want to,' the boy repeated, only this time louder.

'Shh!' hissed Manu. 'You're going to have the whole street looking out at us.'

'Daniel, please stop,' said Adele.

'We haven't got time for this,' said Manu.

'Just give me a moment.' She turned Daniel to face her, stroking his hair. 'Listen, Daniel. Sometimes we have to be very brave, even when we don't feel like it. Tonight is one of those nights. You do trust me, don't you?' The boy nodded. 'Then, go with Manu and the girls and Madame Rashal, nice and quietly, and I promise when you come back, I'll be here waiting for you and I'll read you a story. I might even stay the night.'

Daniel's eyes were full of fear and Adele's heart went out to him. He swallowed hard. 'Will you come with me?'

Adele looked up at Manu who gave a shake of his head. 'I can't.'

'Then I'm not going.' He folded his arms to underline his mutiny.

Manu let out an impatient sigh. 'We need to go.'

'Then I'll come with you,' said Adele.

'No. I don't want you coming. It's too dangerous,' protested Manu.

'If it's too dangerous for me, then it's too dangerous for a child to go on their own,' retorted Adele. 'I'm coming whether you like it or not.' She took Daniel's hand and crossed the threshold. This time the little boy didn't protest.

'Very well,' said Manu, clearly not happy at the change in plan. '*Allez.*'

They made their way through the dusky streets of Paris, taking the less-used roads and ducking in and out of the shadows, until twenty minutes later, they arrived outside a bookstore. Manu opened the iron gate at the side of the property, which groaned in protest, and the party of three adults and three children filed through. Manu knocked on the door and it was opened by a little man, balding with wire-rimmed spectacles. He looked over Manu's shoulder and frowned.

'Two women? There was only supposed to be one,' he said unimpressed by the extra visitor.

'She's just chaperoning the boy. He wouldn't come on his own,' said Manu as he sidestepped past the man. He gave a jerk of his head to Adele and the others to follow him in.

'Monsieur,' both Adele and Jacqueline said as they followed on in.

The older man took them through to the back of the bookstore, into a small room that looked like an office. 'Help me move this desk,' he instructed Manu. Together they shifted the heavy oak desk to one side and kicked the rug back out of the way to reveal a trapdoor. 'Come, quickly.'

They followed him down the stone steps into the basement room. The man turned on the lights and the room was illuminated by two bulbs hanging from the ceiling. Adele looked around her. There were two small windows high up which, had they not been covered with black boards, would have looked out onto the path outside. She imagined during the day, the many feet of people passing by could be seen. There was a workbench at the side of the room where an array of photographic equipment was; developing fluids, trays and film were neatly organised. A line was strung above the workbench and several photographs were hanging from little pegs. They were mostly landscapes and tourist attractions of the city.

'I'm a photographer as well as a bookkeeper,' said the man, watching Adele. 'It's a good cover in case the Germans ever decide to poke around.'

In the centre of the room was a pine table with more photographic equipment and a small printing machine. The man went over to the other side of the wall and opened a cupboard. He then removed the back of the cupboard, revealing the exposed brickwork of the basement wall. She watched intrigued as he then took out several bricks, revealing a hole in the wall where a box was hidden. He put the box on the table and took out a camera. There were also several blank identity cards, passports and other official-looking papers. Her heart gave an extra beat as she was reminded of the danger everyone was in, but also with gratitude and pride that the people of Paris were willing to risk their lives to help others.

'Right. Let's be quick,' said the man, whose manner still hadn't improved.

Less than thirty minutes later, he was hustling them all back up the stairs and out of the premises.

In the same way they had made their way to the photographer, they began their trek back. Manu went on ahead, stopping at each corner to make sure the coast was clear, before signalling to the women and children to follow.

'I'm tired,' groaned Daniel as they reached the end of the third road.

'We still have a way to go,' said Manu, eyeing the lad.

'I don't want to go back to the school. I want Mama.' A tear tracked its way down Daniel's cheek.

'Don't cry,' said Adele, putting a comforting arm around his shoulders. 'Be brave.'

'You're a boy. You need to be like a man tonight,' said Manu, crouching down and talking quietly. 'You have to be brave and not show the girls you're crying. Otherwise they will get scared and upset. Your mother and father would want you to be strong now. You can do that, can't you? Besides, I can't look after the women and girls on my own.'

Daniel looked earnestly at Manu. 'Mama and Papa would be proud?'

'*Oui. Absolutement.*' Manu lifted his chin. 'Hold you head high. That's it. Good.'

Adele exchanged a smile with Manu as he stood up. '*Merci*,' she said softly.

The tell-tale rumble of a lorry engine, broke through the still night air. 'Quick. Hide,' ordered Manu.

Adele looked around frantically for cover. They were in a residential street, with just a few shadowy doorways to shelter them. Panic rose in her throat as she grabbed Daniel's hand. 'Where?'

'Back that way. There's a park in the next street. We can cut through,' Manu said. 'Hurry.'

They began to run back down the street. The sound of the engine grew louder by the second. Adele dragged Daniel along with her. She and Jacqueline had worn jazz shoes so their normal heeled shoes didn't clatter on the pavements and give them away, but it did nothing to improve their speed. Daniel was fast on his feet and Adele thanked God she had always kept fit. She glanced back over her shoulder. Jacqueline and the girls were beginning to trail behind. Adele slowed down, to wait for them, but Manu pushed her on. 'Don't wait. Go!'

He dropped back and, as Adele turned the corner, she took another look and could see Manu had scooped Blanche up and was carrying her as he ran.

Jacqueline was struggling and she let go of Eva's hand, urging her to keep up with Manu. Adele turned the corner. She could see the gates to the park were only about fifty metres away. She had to make it. She just had to. She let go of Daniel's hand. 'Run to the park!' The little boy was faster on his own and, not having to hold his hand, Adele could fall into her own pace as she stretched out her stride. She was right behind Daniel as they hurtled through the gates.

She could hear Manu's footsteps pounding the pavement, no longer worrying about being heard.

Adele continued running, just behind Daniel. 'Through the park,' she gasped. 'Keep going.'

The sound of the lorry coming to a halt and voices shouting spurred Adele on. She had no idea if they were shouting at her but adrenaline gave her energy she didn't know she possessed. She looked over her shoulder for a third time. Manu's dark figure was tearing down the path. But there was no sign of Jacqueline or the girls.

Chapter 22

Fleur

Paris, August 2015

After the emotion of the previous day, Lydia insisted on doing something more upbeat, suggesting some sightseeing and taking an open-top bus ride around the city, hopping on and off at various tourist attractions.

Fleur forced thoughts of Didier and what Lydia had told her happened back in 1942 at the park from her mind. She wanted to take on board what her grandmother had said about remembering people for the love they brought rather than the pain that love caused, but she wasn't sure she could apply it so easily to her own past. Fleur wanted to focus on the present and how she could preserve what she had now with her grandmother. She was well aware that this may be the only opportunity she had of spending quality time with her. She might not be able to control how she felt about losing her mother, but she could at least try to make it different with her grandmother when the time came. She gave a shudder at the thought and batted it away.

They arrived back at the hotel by mid-afternoon and as was Lydia's habit, she liked to take a nap. 'I'm not as young as I used to be,' she said. 'I need my beauty sleep.'

Fleur laughed. 'You certainly don't need beauty sleep.' She gave Lydia a kiss on the cheek. 'Enjoy your rest. I'm meeting Didier at six-thirty. Shall I see you before? I could bring you in a cup of tea.'

'No, don't be fussing about me,' said Lydia. 'I'll see how I feel. I might have my evening meal in my room tonight.'

'OK, but I'll check in with you at some point, just to make sure you're all right.'

Lydia gave a good-humoured roll of her eyes. 'If I'd known you'd be fussing this much, I'd never have invited you.' She winked at Fleur. 'Go on, off you go. And try to enjoy yourself.'

When Fleur went down to the foyer at just before six-thirty, Didier was already waiting for her. He was sitting on one of the brown leather sofas, looking at his phone. He looked rather more casual today in his denim jeans, a black T-shirt and a white pair of trainers. The casual clothes looked every bit as good on him as his suit had. Sensing her gaze, he looked up and smiled warmly as he got to his feet.

'Thank you for agreeing to meet me again,' said Didier.

Fleur smiled warmly. 'Thank you for coming.'

'I was more than happy to do so,' he replied. They stood for an awkward moment just looking at each other. Didier broke the deadlock. 'Erm, would you like to have a drink at the bar here? Or perhaps we could go somewhere else?' He frowned. 'But then you wouldn't have your minder to watch over you.' There was a mischievous look in his eyes and Fleur found herself laughing.

'Let's live dangerously and go somewhere else.' Fleur wasn't one for taking risks usually, but she had an unexpected desire to be impulsive.

Didier picked up his jacket. 'I know a bar not far from here. It's in walking distance, if that is all right with you.'

'That would be lovely. It's so warm this evening – warmer than yesterday anyway – it will be nice to take a walk.'

They strolled along the street, Didier guiding her across the road, his hand briefly making contact with her back as he ushered her in the right direction. 'Here we are,' he said after a few minutes of walking.

As Didier led Fleur inside, she took in the small bar with a black awning opening out over several tables set up on the pavement. If the innocuous appearance of the outside of the bar was understated sophistication, the interior was at the other end of the scale. Black and white diamond tiles inlaid with gold stars stretched across the floor. The bar was highly polished gold mirror with black and gold bar stools lined up at it. Black tables with gold leaf filled the rest of the space. It was like walking back in time to the art deco age of the 1920s where glitz and glamour sparkled, illuminating the City of Lights.

They settled themselves at a table by the window and Didier ordered them both a drink. 'I feel like I should be sipping a cocktail and smoking a cigarette whilst wearing my flapper girl dress,' said Fleur as she gazed at their elegant surroundings.

'I thought you might like it here,' said Didier.

Fleur raised an eyebrow. 'You did?'

Didier shrugged. 'Most people do.'

Fleur momentarily wondered if by most people, Didier actually meant most women. She could imagine him bringing a succession of female companions here to woo them with the surroundings. She realised Didier was studying her and she dropped her gaze to her glass, swirling the straw around.

'What are you thinking?' he asked.

'Nothing,' she replied, rather too quickly, and felt herself blush. She was sure he knew exactly what her thoughts had been.

'I thought you would like it here, as you were admiring the photographs on the wall of the café the other day and you said how exciting Paris must have been before the war.'

Fleur's blush increased, feeling embarrassed at her ridiculous assumption. 'You're very observant.'

'I did use to be a gendarme. It was my job to be observant.'

Fleur took a sip of her drink. 'That kind of brings us on to the subject of what I found out on the internet.'

Didier nodded, pressing his full lips together. His eyes grew darker. 'You are talking about the arson attack at my business premises and probably also the reward for the missing Valois.'

'Yes, I am,' said Fleur, welcoming his honesty. It wasn't quite how she'd expected the conversation to go.

'I realise the articles don't show me in the best light. You probably think I am some sort of con man who cannot be trusted. Or worse, part of some organised crime syndicate.'

'I wasn't thinking on the scale of *The Godfather* and Al Pacino,' said Fleur. 'But I won't pretend it hasn't made me cautious. Maybe a little concerned.'

'And you are right to question me about these things,' said Didier. 'I apologise for not telling you before you found out for yourself. I was afraid you would not want anything to do with me.'

'I'd like to hear your side of the story. I'd like you to convince me that I was wrong to jump to conclusions.'

His face softened. 'Thank you. I appreciate that. So, where to begin? After the robbery and the fire at my antique shop, I practically lost everything. My insurance company didn't want to pay out. I'm sure insurance companies are the same the world over.'

Fleur nodded. 'I'm sure they are.'

'The day of the robbery, I had an emergency phone call. My mother had been taken ill. A heart attack.'

'Oh, I'm sorry.'

Didier shook his head. 'It's all right. It wasn't fatal but it did mean I spent the evening at the hospital with her. I left my business partner to lock up. Unfortunately, he forgot to lock the door at the back of the premises. You see, I was usually the last one there and I would go and make my checks. The policeman in me wouldn't let me leave without at least double-checking all doors and windows were secure.'

'But your partner, I'm guessing wasn't so security-minded.'

'No. And so by a great misfortune, the premises were burgled that night. I can't even call it a break-in. The back door was left unlocked. They started the fire out of sheer vandalism.' He closed his eyes briefly. 'I can't tell you how painful it is to think of all those paintings, furniture, pieces of art gone – forever.'

'I'm really sorry to hear that,' said Fleur, seeing the obvious pain on the Frenchman's face as he recalled events.

'My partnership broke up and I was left having to start again from nothing.'

'And that's why you want to find the missing Valois. The reward will help you start up again?'

'Partly but not solely and perhaps not primarily,' replied Didier. He took a long sip of his drink. 'I confess my motivation for finding the painting is, in part, the reward. However, I am a lover of art and artefacts. There is so much history attached to antiques. Sure, everything can be reproduced, but you cannot replicate the history. I am a particular fan of Valois, as you know, and to find the missing painting would make the collection complete again. It will be as it was before the war. To bring that missing painting home is my way of paying respect to my country and all those who suffered because of the war and the occupation by the Germans.' He gave a laugh. 'It all sounds very pompous, but it means a lot to me.'

Fleur shook her head. 'No. It doesn't sound pompous at all. It sounds like someone who genuinely cares about art and history. And, I guess it kind of goes with once being a policeman. You want to put right a wrong.'

'I'm not here just for the money. I won't lie as the reward will help, but I started my business from nothing before and I have done it again, although on a smaller scale.'

'I suppose if you're passionate about something, it gives you that drive and determination.'

'Exactly.'

'You don't miss being in the police force, then?' Fleur was trying to imagine Didier the gendarme and Didier the antiques dealer, but she couldn't quite line up the two.

'No. I did my time. It was hard work. Stressful and demanding. It took over my life.'

'It must be hard to switch off sometimes.'

'Yes, especially if you are working on a difficult case. You have to make a lot of sacrifices,' said Didier. 'I enjoyed being in the Gendarmerie but it brought its own problems.'

'Such as?'

'It was not good for relationships.' Didier looked out of the window and then back to Fleur. 'I was married but the long and unsocial hours, together with dangerous situations, took its toll. My wife left me. Fortunately, we didn't have children so it made the split easier. She found someone who worked a more conventional job. It also helped that he earned a lot of money. A company director. Basically, all the things I was not.'

'And you haven't found anyone since you left the police?'

'No but I am a patient man. I will know when I have found that someone.'

'I hope you don't have to wait too long.' Fleur wasn't quite sure how their conversation had taken this direction. She could feel Didier's gaze upon her but she couldn't for the life of her think of anything to say. Didier, however, had no such trouble.

'What about you?'

'Me?'

'*Oui*. Is this not how a conversation works? You ask a question. I answer. Now it's my turn to ask the question.'

There was a hint of amusement in his voice and Fleur found herself smiling ruefully. 'I guess I owe you at least one.'

'At least one.' He was smiling now.

'OK, I broke up with my boyfriend recently. He said I was an emotional wasteland so he found comfort in a work colleague.'

Didier gave a knowing look. 'A work colleague.' He tutted. 'So clichéd.'

Fleur laughed out loud. 'I know. And she's younger than me.'

'Even more clichéd.'

They both laughed together and Fleur felt the tension she hadn't realised the mention of her ex had stirred up release from her. 'He said I'm incapable of loving anyone.'

'And are you?' The laughter disappearing from his voice.

Fleur considered the question. 'I've wondered that several times, to be honest.' The smile slipped from her face. 'Love's dangerous.'

'How so?'

Whether it was the cocktail, the tiredness from the last few days or the pressure of trying to help Lydia, Fleur didn't know, but a ball of emotion lodged itself in her throat, and she felt the tears spring to her eyes. 'Love breaks your heart sooner or later,' she said quietly, spinning the amber stem of the wine glass between her finger and thumb.

'But surely the happiness you have before then is worth it?' suggested Didier. He leaned forwards, resting his forearms on the table, his hands flat on the surface. 'Who broke your heart?' His voice was no more than a murmur.

Fleur gave a shrug. 'I told you, my boyfriend.' She tried to avoid meeting this gaze but it was as if he'd cast a spell. She looked up and raised her head, defying him to challenge her.

'I thought we were going to be honest with each other,' said Didier. There was no malice or accusation in his voice, just warmth and openness.

Fleur blinked. She couldn't deal with kindness or pity; it meant she was weak and vulnerable. She shook her head and blinked back the tears threatening to tip over the brim of her eyes. 'It's painful. It's complicated.' She took a long gulp of her drink. That all got very deep far too quickly. 'Anyway, never mind all that; we're here to talk about Lydia and the painting.'

Didier nodded and sat back in his seat, rubbing his forefinger across his bottom lip. 'OK, so I have some news. I only found this out yesterday.' He reached into the pocket of his jeans and produced a piece of paper. Unfolding it, he flattened it out on the table and turned it around for Fleur to read.'

It was a photocopy of some sort of register of names. French names, Fleur realised as she scanned the page. 'What is this?'

'I have a friend who works in administration for education. They have been able to access some historic records for me.' He tapped the paper. 'It's a list of the children at the school where your grandmother attended.'

Fleur looked at the paper again, taking time to look at each name, trying to find Lydia's name. 'What year was this?'

'1942,' replied Didier.

Fleur looked up. 'But my nan's name isn't here. Have you got the right school?'

'My source is one hundred per cent certain this is the correct school and the correct year.'

'I don't understand why Nan's name isn't here.' She picked up the paper. 'And why do some of the names have a star by them?'

'Why do you think some children would be singled out?' asked Didier.

And then it dawned on Fleur. 'They were Jewish children.' Didier nodded. 'Yes.'

'Wait, Nan told me the names of the children she was in the attic with. Daniel, Thomas and Blanche.' Fleur studied the list again. Her breath caught in her throat. 'Daniel Charon, Thomas Kampe, Blanche Rashal, Eva Rashal.' She read out several more. 'They all have a star beside their names.'

'The school would no doubt have had to supply a list of Jewish children. There was a big round-up in 1942; maybe this is related somehow.'

'It's awful. Seeing something like this somehow makes it more real. Of course, I know it's real and it happened, but it is such a big world event that we talk about and are taught about. It can desensitise you to it, but when you hear the personal stories, the experiences of an individual or a small group, then it makes it so very real and not just a history lesson.'

'And Lydia's story is one of those,' said Didier.

'I've often wondered about Nan's childhood but she's always been very vague about the war and Paris.' She looked up at Didier. 'My nan's Jewish.'

Didier didn't look fazed by this information. 'And she avoided the round-up?'

'She's always maintained she moved to Brittany and was able to go unnoticed,' replied Fleur. 'She's never spoken in detail. That's why this trip was so surprising when she asked me to come with her. For the first time, she wants to share this part of her life.'

'Are you Jewish?'

'I'm Jewish in ancestry but not in religion. My grandfather was Church of England. My mother was christened C of E, as was I. Lydia converted for the sake of my grandfather but she's always considered herself Jewish in ancestry,' explained Fleur. 'But again, it's a conversation that was never encouraged.'

'Because it would throw up too many questions?'

'Possibly.'

They sat in silence for a short time, each contemplating the list. The bar was filling up with people out for an early evening drink, meeting friends and family. Fleur wondered how many of them had grandparents and great-grandparents who had lived through the war and whether they had passed their stories and experiences down to their children and grandchildren. Or had those stories remained locked away, too awful and upsetting to revisit? Would those personal stories just die along with the holder of those secrets?

A group of people bundled in through the door, laughing and chatting amongst themselves, their enjoyment of the evening broke into Fleur's thoughts. 'I really should be getting back,' she said. 'I might ask Nan about the list of names. Can I take a photo of it?'

'*Bien sûr*,' said Didier. 'Of course. Maybe she will know some of them. There's no Bridget but, of course, she could have changed her name or have been known differently as a child.'

'And no Lydia either. I wonder if there's an updated list anywhere.'

'It's possible.'

'I'll see what Nan says. Maybe there was another class.'

'I think this is the whole school. On the right-hand side are their ages.'

Fleur took a picture with her phone and slid the paper back to Didier. 'I feel we are missing several chunks of information.'

The walk back to the hotel was a little slower than when they had left earlier, as if they both wanted to stretch the evening out as much as possible. Didier was easy company and despite only having just met him, Fleur liked him already.

'Shall I meet you here again tomorrow?' he asked.

'I'll call you once I've spoken with Lydia.' They were outside the hotel now. 'Thank you for coming over. I've had a nice evening.'

'It's been a lovely evening made all the better by the lovely company.'

Fleur couldn't suppress the grin his compliment elicited. She suddenly felt very self-conscious. She held out her hand. '*Merci*, Didier.'

He took her hand and grinned, before lifting it and kissing her knuckles. 'Goodnight, Fleur.'

She waved as Didier climbed into a taxi that had pulled up from the taxi rank across the road. As she went into the hotel, she thought back to how nice the couple of hours she'd spent with Didier had been. He was very charming. He was probably like that with all the women he met. She really shouldn't read anything into it.

When she got back to her room, she tapped on Lydia's door and went in.

'Ah, there you are?' Lydia greeted her. 'Did you have a nice evening?'

'Yes, it was very nice. We went to a bar for a drink.'

'Oh good. Better than being stuck in here with an OAP for the night.'

'I don't mind,' said Fleur. 'I love your company.' She gave her grandmother a hug.

Lydia gave a chuckle. 'And I love your company too but someone your own age is much more preferable. Especially, someone like that young man.'

'Anyone would think you were trying to matchmake.'

Lydia gave a mock innocent look. 'What, me? Not at all.'

Fleur shook her head and gave a roll of her eyes. 'No, of course not.' She paused, wondering whether this was a good time or not to broach the subject of the names to her grandmother. She took her phone from her pocket and opened up the photos.

'Didier has a contact who has been helping find information about the painting,' she said. 'The contact gave Didier a list of names of children at the school, the school you went to. Some of the names have a star beside them. We think it's because they were Jewish children.' She handed the phone to Lydia. 'There's Daniel, Thomas and Blanche on there. The names you remembered of the children who were in the attic with you.'

Lydia took the phone and popped her reading glasses on to look at the screen. Her hand shook a little and her expression grew serious. Was serious the right word? Sad, Fleur decided. Her grandmother looked sad.

'Didier is very resourceful,' Lydia said eventually, passing the phone back. She held Fleur's hand in her own. 'There's something I haven't told you because I didn't know when the time would be right. I probably should have told you when we were at the park, but it was all a bit too much.'

'Do you feel up to telling me now?' asked Fleur, curiosity and concern competing for top spot.

'Tomorrow. It's easier if I show you, rather than tell you.' Her voice wobbled and she hooked out her handkerchief from her sleeve, before dabbing her nose. 'It's probably a good idea if you invite Didier too. It's something he should know. Perhaps you can ask him if he's free tomorrow afternoon.'

'If that's what you want me to do,' said Fleur, wondering what was so significant that Didier needed to know at the same time.

'Yes. It is. Now, I'm very tired and need to sleep. Forgive me for all the secrecy.'

'It's OK, Nan. Whatever it is has kept this long, I'm sure another night won't hurt.' Of course it was far easier to say than to put into practice but there was no point guessing. Fleur would just have to wait until the next day.

She went into her room and sitting on the edge of the bed, sent a text message to Didier.

Fleur: Hi. Sorry for the late text. Have spoken to my nan about the list. She wants to tell me something about it tomorrow. She wants you there too. Can you come to the hotel tomorrow afternoon at 2pm?

She put the phone on the bedside table and was deciding whether to shower then or in the morning when her phone pinged back a reply.

Didier: No need to apologise. Please thank your grandmother for inviting me. I shall be there as asked.

This was immediately followed by another text.

Didier: I will look forward to seeing you tomorrow.

And then another.

Didier: Goodnight. And I promise this is my last text.

Fleur smiled, probably more than necessary, but she couldn't help it. She quickly tapped out a reply before she had time to change her mind.

Fleur: That's great you can come. I had a nice time too. See you tomorrow. *Bonne nuit.*

Despite feeling tired when she had come back to her room, she now felt wide awake and decided to have her shower before bed. It would give her some thinking time too as she tried to make sense of everything that was happening on this trip.

Chapter 23

Adele

Paris, July 1942

'Stop! Daniel, stop!' Adele called to the boy. He stopped running and turned back to her. Adele beckoned him to her.

'What are you doing?' Manu had caught up with them. He had Blanche in his arms. 'You have to keep going.'

'Jacqueline and Eva,' she gasped between breaths. Her eyes scanned the path beyond him. 'Where are they?' She couldn't keep the desperation from her voice.

Manu looked silently at her.

'I want Mama,' whispered Blanche. She tried to struggle from Manu's arms, but he held her tight.

'I had to get her to safety,' said Manu. 'There are Germans everywhere, Adele. I waited at the corner for as long as I could.'

Adele shook her head. 'No. We can't leave them. Tell me we haven't abandoned them. We have to go back.'

'We can't. It's too dangerous.' He motioned with his eyes to Blanche and Daniel. The little girl was still struggling to free herself. Her protests becoming louder.

Adele stepped forwards and took Blanche and placed her on the ground. The six-year-old clung to Adele's legs. 'Shh, now, Blanche. Don't cry.' She looked up at Manu. 'I have to go back.'

'No, I will go back,' corrected Manu. 'The children need

to be with you. You need to be safe. I want you to be safe.' He reached out and touched her cheek with his fingertips. 'I'll go and see if I can find them. You go back to the school. Now hurry – don't argue. We haven't got much time. This park will be swarming with Germans soon.'

Adele hesitated. She knew he was right but she hated the idea of deserting Jacqueline and Eva. She threw her arms around him and whispered into his neck. 'Please be careful, Manu.'

He wrapped his arms around her and lowered his head. Adele found herself lifting her head towards his and their lips met for a brief kiss. He hugged her again. 'I'm always careful. Now go. Stay in the shadows. Take your time rather than rush. Just get back to the school safely. Promise me.'

'I promise.'

With that he turned and ran off into the darkness. Adele took both children by the hand and broke into a run as they too scurried off into the shadows of the night.

With two young children in tow, both tired and frightened, it took Adele nearly an hour to get back to the school. She was relieved to lock the side door behind them and somehow found the strength to carry Blanche up the stairs, and the little girl then sat down in an exhausted heap in the hallway.

'You did very well tonight,' reassured Adele. 'I'm very proud of you both.'

'You're back!' greeted Cecile as they came into the dance room. Cecile and Thomas were playing hoopla with some of the school toys Adele had brought up from the games cupboard. Cecile's face changed from relief to concern. Her eyes darted across the faces of Adele and the children. 'Where's . . .'

Adele cut her off with a discreet but sharp shake of the head. 'Blanche is very tired. Daniel has been such a brave boy tonight. They both deserve a hot chocolate. I'm sure, Thomas, you'd like one too.' Adele sat Blanche down on the floor and took off her coat, while Cecile helped Daniel out of his. 'Now, sit there nicely and I'll bring you your drinks. Here's a biscuit each to keep you going. I brought them especially for you.'

The prospect of a sweet snack perked the children up but Adele was sure they were hurting underneath.

Cecile came down to the staff kitchen with Adele. 'What's going on? Where are the others?'

'We were spotted by a German patrol just as we were leaving,' explained Adele. She leaned back against the countertop and rubbed her face with her hands. 'I managed to escape with Daniel. Manu caught me up with Blanche but we don't know what happened to Jacqueline and Eva. Manu has gone back to try to find them.' She swallowed down a lump of anxiety in her throat and clasped her hands together in a bid to stop them shaking. 'I didn't want to leave them but I couldn't stay with the children. It was too dangerous.'

Cecile muttered a prayer quietly to herself. 'We can only trust in God now,' she said.

Adele wasn't particularly reassured by this but who was she to question Cecile's faith? Even if a prayer did no good, it certainly didn't do any harm. Besides, they had no other powers open to them than hope. Not for the first time Fleur wondered if hope and God were just the same thing.

She made the hot chocolate for the children. 'We'll take these upstairs and then I'm going to come back down to wait by the door for Manu. I think you should stay up in the attic this evening. I'm worried in case . . . in case they catch Jacqueline or Manu and find out where we are. Or suspect we're here.' She hated to think that they would give them up easily but it was a distinct possibility, not something she could rule out. If not tonight, then tomorrow or the day after, but sooner or later the Gestapo would find a way to break Jacqueline. If they had caught Eva too, then they would no doubt use her as a bargaining chip and what sort of choice would Jacqueline have to make? Save one child and give up another? Choose a child to save and a child to die? It was an impossible situation and sent a shudder down

Adele's spine just thinking about it. Maybe she should pray? Maybe Cecile was right?

Adele and Cecile took the drinks up to the children and once they were settled in the attic and the toys put away, Adele went back downstairs. She took the chair from the reception area with the intention of sitting by the door but her anxiety was increasing by the second and she couldn't relax. She paced back and forth along the hallway, then would sit for a few minutes before she was up on her feet again. Listening all the time for the sound of the gate opening and closing, light footsteps down the side of the school and Manu's coded knock on the door.

When she heard a vehicle drawing near, her heart pounded violently, only for the car to continue on past the school, and for her heart to take several minutes to calm to a steady beat. Every sound was amplified in the night and every nightmare vivid as she thought of what might have happened to her friends.

Her mind was momentarily distracted from her dreadful thoughts when she remembered the embrace and kiss she'd shared with Manu. The way he had looked at her and the way she had been so drawn to him. He must have more than brotherly or friendly feelings towards her. But what about Edith? Was there anything to be read into the kisses they'd exchanged or was it just in the moment because, of course, he did have Edith?

At some point in the night, Cecile came down with a cup of coffee for Adele.

'Why don't you try to get some sleep. You still have to teach tomorrow.'

'I can't. Even if I tried, I know I wouldn't be able to relax enough. Not when I can only fear the worst.' She took the coffee gratefully. 'Are the children all right?'

Cecile nodded. 'A little subdued but I suppose that's to be expected. Blanche has been asking for Jacqueline and Eva.'

'What have you said?'

'That Manu has gone to get them. I didn't know what else to say and that's not a lie.'

'Good thinking. There's no point upsetting them unnecessarily.'

Cecile stayed for a few more minutes before returning to the children. Adele forced herself to sit still on the chair at least while she drank her coffee. Despite thinking she couldn't rest, at some point, Adele must have drifted to that strange point somewhere between sleep and wakefulness. She sat upright with a start at the faint sound of the school gate clanking. She jumped to her feet, almost spilling the remains of her coffee in her lap. Standing right behind the door, she hardly dared to breathe as she listened intently.

Knock. Knock. Knock-knock.

Adele let out a sigh of relief. She unlocked the door and yanked it open.

Manu was standing in front of her with Eva at his side.

'Oh, thank goodness,' cried Adele. She threw her arms first around Manu and then around Eva. She looked up, expecting to see Jacqueline behind them. She looked in alarm at Manu.

'Why don't you go upstairs to see Cecile,' said Manu ushering Eva towards the stairs.

'Yes, go up, Eva. I'll be there in a minute; I just need to speak to Manu.' She ran her hand over the girl's head as with her head bowed and her shoulders dropped, Eva scuffed by. Once Adele was sure the girl had gone upstairs, she spun round to Manu. 'What happened? Where's Jacqueline?' She was asking the questions but feared the worst. There was no way Jacqueline would leave her daughter. No way. Not unless it was the last resort.

Manu took Adele to the chair and sat her down. He crouched in front of her, his hands holding hers. 'I'm sorry, Adele, but Jacqueline didn't make it.'

'Didn't make it?'

He grazed his thumbs over her knuckles. 'I got back to them. We hid in an alleyway but the soldiers had seen us. We didn't have time to discuss it. Jacqueline pushed Eva towards me and said, "Don't let them get her." With that she stepped out of the alleyway and ran across the road. They started chasing her. Shouting for her to stop. She acted as a decoy. I was able to run from my hiding place with Eva and we escaped.'

Adele pulled her hands away from his. 'You let her do that?' She jumped to her feet. 'What happened to her?'

Manu rose. He went to hold her but she moved away. 'She didn't give me a choice. I tried to grab her arm, I told her not to do it, but she said she'd sacrifice herself for the life of her own daughter. She pulled away and was gone.'

'What happened to her?'

Manu looked to the ground. 'I heard gunshots. Me and Eva had stopped in a doorway. Eva was upset at leaving her mother. Then the door opened and this old woman hissed at us to get inside and hide. If only we'd stopped at that doorway with Jacqueline.'

'That's where you've been?'

'Yes. The old woman gave us some water and a slice of bread. I watched from a small slit in the blackout blind upstairs.' Again he looked down.

'Manu, what did you see?' whispered Adele, so scared of what he was going to tell her, but she had to know.

'They had Jacqueline. She was still alive but they were dragging her between two soldiers. She couldn't walk properly. I think she had been shot in the leg.'

'Where did they take her?'

Manu's gaze met hers. 'I'm so sorry, Adele. They executed her in the street.'

Adele's legs gave way and somehow Manu caught her. Holding her tightly to his chest. She cried. She cried so much. Huge sobs erupted from the pit of her stomach, making her whole body convulse.

She finally managed to stop and Adele took a steadying breath. She could smell the cold outdoors of the night on Manu's clothing. 'What will happen to her now?'

'Leave it with me. I'll make sure her body is recovered.' He kissed her on top of her head, but this time there was no move to her mouth. 'You look tired.'

'I couldn't sleep. Not properly. I've been so worried. Do you think it was just by chance the patrol found us? Or did someone report us?'

'It could only come from one of us or the photographer and I hardly think any one of us would put ourselves and the children's lives in danger.'

'But can you trust the photographer?'

'As much as you can trust anyone.'

'Did Edith know we were going there tonight?'

'No. It wasn't her.'

'What if she followed us?'

'Adele, she didn't follow us. No one followed us. I was checking the whole time. And besides, why would Edith betray us?'

'She doesn't like me.'

Manu gave a small laugh. 'She doesn't like you?' he repeated with amusement in his voice.

'It's true.'

'It's not true and why wouldn't she like you?'

'Because we're friends.' There she'd said it, even though she hadn't wanted to, but her emotions were high and Adele didn't care anymore. When was the right time to say anything about her and Manu? What if he'd been killed tonight and she'd never told him how she really felt? 'Because she knows I care about you.'

Manu gave her an appraising look and his face softened. 'This isn't the right time for this discussion.'

'Probably not but what if you hadn't made it back tonight? Then there'd never be the chance. I know you're in love with Edith, but I can't help the way I feel and I just wanted you to know. It doesn't have to change anything between us.' She could feel the tears swarming her eyes. 'We can just carry on and save these children and then once they're safe, we don't even have to see each other again or talk to each other. You can carry on doing what you're doing and marry Edith and have children and . . . and live happily ever after. That's fine. I would be happy to know you're happy, but it doesn't mean I can't tell you how I feel.' She paused and took another breath. 'I just wanted you to know; that's all.'

'Adele. My dear sweet Adele,' said Manu with such tenderness in his voice, Adele thought her heart was going to break. She'd made an idiot of herself but she really didn't care. Her feelings for Manu had burdened her enough and telling him was cathartic. Also painful. She looked up at him and went to speak but he pressed his finger to her mouth. 'We will talk about this, just not tonight. I need to go and sort things out.' He cupped her face with the palm of his hand. 'Make sure you lock the door after me.'

With that he was gone.

Chapter 24

Fleur

Paris, August 2015

Fleur hadn't slept well the previous night. She had woken several times and although she couldn't pinpoint what was troubling her, she had felt unsettled. Waking early, she had come out for an early morning walk and had found herself along the edge of the River Seine. She'd left Lydia sleeping in her room with a note propped up on the bedside table to say she was getting some fresh air and would be back after breakfast.

It was another warm August morning in the city and Fleur was glad she'd remembered to pick up her sunglasses. She wandered a little further along the riverbank where the pavement sellers were setting up for the day, ready to encourage tourists to part with their euros in exchange for a plastic Eiffel Tower or a comic sketch of themselves or a print of one of the sights of the city. She passed a barge, which was a floating bookshop, where the proprietor bade her a jolly *bonjour*. Under different circumstances, Fleur might have hung around to browse at the books, but today her mind was preoccupied with thoughts of Lydia.

The city was coming to life all around her and the roads and paths were filling with commuters, early morning joggers and dog walkers.

Her phone buzzed in her pocket.

Didier: *Salut. Ça-va?*

She smiled at the informality of the greeting. She'd only known Didier a matter of days but she was already feeling at ease in his company. She took a selfie with the river in the background over one shoulder and book boat over the other. She pinged it back to Didier. She got a reply almost instantly.

Didier: That picture makes me very sad.

Fleur frowned at the message. Then tapped a reply.

Fleur: Why?

Didier: Because you are alone in the most romantic city in the world and having to take selfies.

Fleur: There was no one to accompany me. ☹

Didier: That is where you are wrong. I would have been more than happy to join you.

Fleur: I'll keep that in mind for next time.

Didier: Can you do something for me?

Fleur: Like what?

Didier: Stay where you are.

Fleur smiled at the text message in bemusement. She looked around and spotting a bench went and sat on it. So far, the exchange of messages had taken up twenty minutes, with longer time lapses between each of Didier's replies. Although it was nice sitting here by the river, she wasn't quite sure what was going on. She sent another message.

Fleur: Why am I doing this?

Didier: Just humour me. And be patient.

Another ten minutes passed and with no more messages from Didier and no reply to her last one saying she had limited patience, Fleur decided to go back to the hotel. She was just about to get to her feet when suddenly someone sat down beside her. A paper bag and a takeaway coffee cup were thrust in front of her.

'Coffee and croissant.' Didier was grinning at her.

Fleur burst out laughing. 'What?!'

'Breakfast by the river,' said Didier.

'Well, thank you,' said Fleur, taking the offerings.

Didier was easy company as they sat in a comfortable silence enjoying the croissants and coffee. There was no pressure to fill the gaps in the conversation and he was sitting just close enough that he wasn't intruding on her space, but not so far away that she couldn't breathe in the fragrance of his aftershave mixed with whatever product he'd applied to his skin. She could sit there all day and be surrounded by the coconut and jojoba scents.

A riverboat cruised along in front of them, already full of tourists. 'They're keen,' remarked Fleur. 'Not sure I could stomach being on the water this early.'

'Ah, the *bateaux mouches*,' said Didier. 'I used to work on them when I was in my late teens.'

'You did? Before you were a police officer?'

'*Oui*. I needed some money. I wasn't sure at that point what I wanted to do. I loved art and history so working on the riverboats seemed like a good idea, but it didn't pay well.'

'So what made you decide to become a police officer?' Fleur brushed the crumbs from her lap and folded up the paper bag.

'One day there was a pickpocket hanging around the boat. That in itself wasn't unusual; we always had to keep a lookout for them. This one day though they decided to snatch the handbag from an elderly lady and push her to the ground.'

'Bastard,' muttered Fleur. 'Oh, sorry. I instantly thought of my nan then.'

'*Bien sûr*. It's bad enough the thieves steal but preying on elderly people is cowardly,' agreed Didier. 'It made me so angry, I jumped off the boat and chased the thief. Took him down with a rugby tackle and sat on him until the police arrived. And that's what led me to wanting to be a gendarme.'

'Well done, you,' said Fleur.

Didier took her empty bag and cup. 'Do you want to walk? Have you got time?' He got to his feet, dropping the rubbish into the nearby bin.

'That would be nice.' Fleur couldn't think of anything else she'd rather do right now.

As they walked, Didier recounted a few highlights from his days as a gendarme. 'But I don't miss it,' he concluded. 'I'm much happier these days with my antiques. What about you? What do you do?'

'Nothing as interesting as all that,' confessed Fleur and then corrected herself. 'Well, I don't find it boring, although some people have other ideas. I work at a university in a science lab. I'm a lab technician.'

'That doesn't sound boring at all,' said Didier.

'Some days it is a little repetitive,' confessed Fleur, 'but on the whole, I love it. I work in the research department. Stem cells, which are amazing, by the way. They have the ability to self-renew unlike other cells. They haven't yet become specialist cells.' She looked up and Didier was smiling at her. 'Sorry, I got carried away then.'

'Oh, do not apologise. I can see and hear your enthusiasm for your work.'

Fleur grinned, appreciating his reply, which was the polar opposite to anything her ex-boyfriend had ever said about her work.

They walked on a little further, reaching the Jardin du Carrousel and continued walking along the shingle path towards the fountain and glass pyramid outside the Musée du Louvre.

'This is where I'd like the Valois collection to end up,' said Didier. 'In the Louvre.'

'Is that where it was originally?'

'No. It was in the museum next door to the school, but obviously that is going to be closed and developed, so the Louvre is the next best place.'

Fleur smiled at Didier's idea that the Louvre was second best. 'It would just be nice to reunite them,' she said. 'I spoke to my nan last night and she said there was something she wanted to show me today. I don't know what. I showed her the list of names you'd been given. It made her sad.'

'I'm sorry your grandmother is finding this difficult,' said Didier.

'I've told her she doesn't have to do any of this,' said Fleur. 'But she's adamant I need to know about her past.' Fleur dropped her gaze to her feet and couldn't help acknowledging that her own feelings about her past were also driving Lydia on.

'What's wrong?' They had stopped walking and Didier turned Fleur to face him. 'There's something else?'

Fleur shook her head, suddenly finding it hard to form a sentence. 'I just . . . I don't know . . . feel guilty. She's not just doing it for herself, she's doing it for me too.'

'For you?'

Fleur didn't want to answer, but this time the silence between them was charged and she felt compelled to explain. 'My nan wants me not to be scared to think about my mother. She died when I was eight.' Unexpected tears gathered in her eyes and she couldn't stop them from falling.

'I'm so sorry,' said Didier. '*Je suis vraiment désolé.*'

Next, his arms were around her and pulling Fleur into his chest, as a sob caught in her throat. Fleur wasn't sure how long they stood like that, but his reassuring hold, firm yet tender, his chin resting against the top of her head and his murmuring in French, which Fleur didn't need to understand to know that they were words of comfort, made her forget everything and everyone around them.

Eventually, she pulled away, but only a fraction, enough to grab a tissue from her handbag and dry her tears. 'I'm sorry,' she said.

His hands were still resting on her upper arms, as if he was afraid she might fall over without his support. 'Do not apologise. It is good to let the emotion out. It's much more French than British.' He smiled and the gentle humour broke the tension.

'When in Rome,' said Fleur. 'Or Paris.'

'*Exactement*.' He looked serious again. 'Are you sure you're all right?'

Fleur nodded. 'Yes. And thank you.' She looked at her watch. 'I'd better get back to the hotel. Nan will be awake by now.'

'I'll walk you back,' said Didier. As they turned and began to walk back the way they'd come, he slipped his arm around her shoulder and squeezed her towards him for a moment.

Fleur allowed herself to take comfort from the gesture. It felt good to be in such close contact with him. It felt safe. A new concept for her. As he released his hold a fraction, Fleur didn't move away and they walked all the way back to the hotel with his arm around her.

Now standing outside the hotel, Didier finally took his arm from her shoulders as they stood facing each other.

'Thank you,' said Fleur.

'It was my pleasure.' Didier held her gaze and took her hand in his. 'Are you sure you are all right now?'

His touch was as reassuring as his hold and Fleur tightened her grip a fraction. 'Much better.'

'*C'est bon*. That's good.' He dipped his head to catch

her gaze. 'It is OK to be scared sometimes but don't let it paralyse you.' He dropped a kiss on her head. 'Now, I must go and do some work before I have to be back here again.'

Fleur stood on the path and watched Didier jog across the road. He turned and waved at her when he reached the safety of the pavement before striding off in the rough direction of where she thought his shop was.

She wasn't quite sure how she felt about him. On the one hand she had felt comfortable in his company, liked his company – liked it a lot. And yet, on the other hand, she was wary of him. He had made her feel safe enough to open up about herself and that was crazy, seeing as she'd only known him for a few days. He made her feel safe and scared all at the same time.

Chapter 25

Adele

Paris, July 1942

Adele couldn't face telling the children about their mother straight away. She needed time to process it herself and accept it, so she could be strong for them. She dreaded to think how they would react. Of course, though, she needed to tell Cecile.

Adele checked her watch. It was nearly six o'clock in the morning and soon Cecile would be bringing the children down to wash and use the bathroom before the school day began. She went up to the attic. Her grief and pain must have been etched clearly on her face, for Cecile took one look at her and got to her feet, telling the children to wait there.

The two women went down to the dance room, careful to close the doors behind them so their voices didn't travel upstairs.

'What's happened?' asked Cecile urgently. 'What is it?'

Adele pressed her lips together to steel herself. 'It's Jacqueline. It's not good news,' she began, trying to prepare her friend. 'She was captured and shot in the night.'

Cecile let out a gasp and began to cry. Adele held her friend just as Manu had held her earlier. No words could ease the pain, but just having the comfort of another caring human's touch was powerful. After a few minutes, Cecile composed herself and Adele explained in more detail what had happened.

'This is terrifying for us all. No one is safe,' said Cecile. 'What about the girls? Do you want me to tell them?'

'I think I should tell them,' replied Adele. 'But they might need your help to get through the day while I'm teaching.'

'Let's do it now, while there's no one in the school.'

They went back upstairs and Cecile took the boys down to the bathroom, leaving Adele alone with the Rashal sisters.

It was the worst thing Adele had ever had to do in her life. Tell two young girls that their mother had been killed and wouldn't be coming back. There had been tears – lots of tears, especially from Eva who understood the concept far more than her little sister Blanche. Adele had stayed with them for over an hour, just holding them in her arms and promising that she would do everything in her power to keep them safe. She told them stories of their mother and how as young girls she and Jacqueline played together and some of the little adventures they got up to. It was a lifetime ago but Adele found it strangely comforting and hoped the girls got the same from it.

All too soon, it was time to open up the school and, after making sure everyone had everything they needed for the day, Adele left the attic with a deep sadness in her heart.

It was lunchtime when Manu came to the school gates as Adele was supervising the playground. He held up his hand and she walked over to him. She thought of what she'd said to him just before he'd left and although she felt a little embarrassed about it now, in the cold light of day, she had no regrets. She was glad she'd told him even if was unreciprocated. She could live with that. Today, he looked tired and drawn. His chin was grazed with stubble and his hair pushed back under a flat cap. He rubbed at his shoulder and moved it in circular motions.

'Jacqueline's body is with the undertaker. A Catholic priest has been to say a prayer. Obviously, all the rabbis have been rounded up or are in hiding. She will be buried tomorrow morning.'

'Thank you for dealing with all of that,' said Adele. 'You look shattered. You must go and get some rest.'

'I have to be at the museum this afternoon. How are the children?'

'I've told them. Eva understands but she's very contained. I'm not sure Blanche fully comprehends.'

'I wish I could have stopped her,' said Manu. He took off his cap and rubbed at his forehead.

'She didn't want to be stopped,' replied Adele. 'She loved the girls more than anything in the world. We just have to do her memory proud and keep those children safe.' She surveyed the playground as the pupils milled around, running, laughing and playing. She wished she could bring the other children down from the attic to play. Apart from the last two nights, they'd not been out in the fresh air for days.

'I'd better go before someone wonders what we are talking about,' said Manu.

'I'll just tell them we were talking about the exhibition, which is totally plausible seeing as we are both involved, one way or another.'

'We need to find out how they are going to transport the artefacts,' said Manu. 'If it's by train, it will be easier. By lorry and it could be more difficult.'

'I'm sure we will travel by train. That's what Lucille told me the other night.'

'Does she know about the plan?'

'No. I don't want to tell her until the last possible moment.'

'You don't trust her?'

'It's not that, it's just she's madly in love with Müller,' explained Adele but, as she spoke, she realised it was because there was an element of mistrust. She hated the thought that she didn't trust her sister.

The feeling of deep of sadness stayed with Adele throughout the day and by the time Lucille arrived for their rehearsal, she felt utterly despondent.

'We can't be too late tonight,' Lucille said. 'Peter is coming for supper.'

'Again? Why does he always come to us? Can't you go out with him?' Adele found herself snapping.

'I do go out with him but as we are to be married, he wants to get to know you and Papa properly, and the only way to do that is to socialise with him.' Lucille put her hands on her hips. 'I thought you liked him now.'

'It's not that,' replied Adele. She couldn't understand why Lucille still entertained the idea that they would get married when it was not something the German authorities approved of, but she kept her thoughts to herself. 'I just don't feel comfortable and I'm very tired this evening. I'm not in the mood for entertaining.'

'Are you ill? I must admit, you do look tired,' said Lucille. 'Where were you last night?'

'What do you mean?'

'You didn't come home. Papa went to bed early and I stayed up. I went to bed at midnight and you weren't home then.'

'It's not really any of your business, but if you must know I stayed here at the school. I stayed late and the time ran away from me. I didn't want to risk trying to get home and getting caught after curfew.'

Lucille looked sceptically at her. 'You do know if that happens you only have to mention Peter's name. He'll make sure you're all right.'

'That's very good of him. I'll bear that in mind.' She had absolutely no intention of bearing that in mind. She felt treacherous at just the notion.

They danced for forty minutes before setting off home. Adele wanted to go and see the Rashal girls this evening but she didn't dare, not with Lucille about.

When they arrived home, Müller was already there, sitting in the living room, talking to their father.

Lucille nudged her and whispered, 'Isn't it great to see them together?'

Adele smiled fondly at her sister. 'As men, Papa and Peter have a lot in common, I imagine,' she chose to reply.

'Ah, there you are, my darling.' Peter rose to his feet and slipped his arm around Lucille's waist, kissing her on the cheek. 'I was just talking to your father about the exhibition and the trip to Lyon. I wanted to reassure him that you would both be looked after very well.'

'So, do you have an itinerary yet?' asked Adele.

'As a matter of fact, I do.' Peter produced a piece of paper from his pocket and held it out to her. 'You will see all the details there. The exhibits will be moved by train.'

Adele looked at the itinerary and scanned the details. It was perfect, just what they needed to put their plan into action. It was then she noticed the date. 'The date, it's wrong,' she said.

'Ah, yes, I was going to tell you. The exhibition has been brought forward, so it will be in two weeks' time, not the four weeks as originally planned,' replied Müller. 'Is that a problem?'

'Err, I don't know if we will be ready.'

'Of course we will,' said Lucille. 'We just need to practise a little more, but we will definitely be ready.'

'But the children? They will need more time. I've only rehearsed seriously with them a few times after school so far.'

'I am sure you just need to give them a few more hours' practice each week,' said Müller, with a less affable tone than before. 'They need to be perfect for the exhibition. I don't want to be embarrassed.'

'Oh, you won't, darling. I promise,' gushed Lucille, putting a placating hand on Müller's arm as she ushered him back into the living room. She looked over her shoulder at Adele and raised her eyebrows. 'Isn't that right, Adele?'

'I will do my best,' said Adele with a confidence she didn't feel. The children were never going to be step perfect. They danced for fun, for freedom and for themselves. She'd just have to make the dance as easy as possible so there was little or no chance of them missing their steps. She watched as her sister sat down next to Müller, almost lapping up the attention he was giving her. Adele couldn't bring herself to be in the same room as them. 'I'll make supper tonight.' Anything to get out of sitting in there with those two.

When she finally sat down to eat, Lucille brought up the subject of the exhibition again. 'Peter was saying we will be staying in a hotel that night as he wants us to attend the after-party.'

'Stay the night?' queried Adele. 'But what about the children? Their parents will be expecting them home.'

'They can travel back the same evening. I will arrange for a chaperone to take them,' said Müller.

'I can go back with them,' said Adele. 'I would feel responsible for them. Their parents are trusting them in my care. I wouldn't like to send them all the way back on their own.'

'But you'll miss the after-party,' said Lucille.

'That's all right, I don't mind. No offence, Peter,' she said quickly. 'But I'd sooner ensure the children return home safely.'

'That's not what I have arranged,' came the terse reply from Müller. 'I have made arrangements and plans already. The children will travel back that same evening. You and Lucille will attend the after-party.' There was a sharpness to his voice and Adele could see even Lucille was taken aback by his tone.

'I'm sure the children will be taken care of,' said her father. Ever the peacemaker. 'If you want me to travel as chaperone and return with the children, I'm more than happy to. They know me very well and it may be reassuring to their parents.'

Müller raised one eyebrow. 'They don't have a choice.'

'Peter, darling,' began Lucille. 'The children love Papa and they will be very respectful to him. Just let him travel with them. Besides, I'd love Papa to see us perform. You'd like that, wouldn't you, Papa?'

Gérard Basset looked from one daughter to the other. 'Nothing would make me happier than to see my beautiful daughters dance, just the way their mother taught them. It would be my dearest wish.'

Adele was sure Lucille gave Müller a little nudge with her elbow. 'Papa would be very happy if you made his dream come true.'

Müller appeared to consider the request for a moment and the implied favour it would win with Lucille's father. Adele guessed Müller wasn't used to having to impress many people. He was more used to them trying to impress him. He smiled. 'It will be an honour to make your dream come true and it will reassure Adele that the children are being well cared for.'

'And the parents,' added Adele. 'It will reassure them too.'

'Yes and the parents,' said Müller, though it clearly pained him to admit he had to consider them. 'Speaking of children, has anyone spoken to you about a missing child? A girl. She went missing last night.'

Adele paused with her glass midway to her mouth. She coaxed her face into an inquisitive expression. 'A girl missing last night? No, I haven't heard of anything. None of the parents mentioned it this morning in the playground. And they're usually always the first to hear of these things.'

'She and her mother were stopped by a patrol last night. They were breaking curfew. They ran off but the patrol only managed to find the mother. No sign of the child anywhere.' He looked at Adele. 'When questioned she denied ever having a child with her. She didn't have any papers on her either. I can only assume she was a Jew.'

'What happened to her?' asked Adele, taking a large gulp of her wine. Maybe it was the alcohol making her bolder, but she wanted to hear it from Müller himself so that Lucille could see how callous he was. 'Was she arrested?'

'No. She was shot.' Müller didn't miss a beat as he replied.

Adele gave a small gasp and looked at her sister. Lucille's eyes widened a fraction but her face remained impassive. Adele's anger bubbled in her stomach. 'Shot? Just like that? Why?'

Müller placed his glass down and folded his arms on the table. 'Because she tried to escape.'

'But you said you'd already caught her?' pressed Adele.

'And she tried to escape,' Müller replied, not trying to hide his impatience.

'Were you there yourself?' asked Adele.

'Why do you ask?'

'Did you shoot her?'

'No, I wasn't there,' replied Müller coolly. 'So, no, I didn't shoot her.'

'But would you have done? Or if you'd been there, would you have been more compassionate?'

'It's not my job to be compassionate. Compassion doesn't win wars,' said Müller.

'But it's what makes us human. Why didn't they just catch her again and arrest her?'

'I'm sure if Peter had been there it would have been very different,' interjected Lucille. The uncertainty in her voice betrayed her words.

'You seem very sympathetic to a Jewish woman. Someone you don't even know.' Müller's eyes narrowed. 'Are you sympathetic to the Jews?'

'I'm sympathetic to people. To other human beings. And you've only assumed she was Jewish due to her lack of papers; she might have simply forgotten them,' replied Adele. Her breathing was heavy. She knew she was antagonising Müller but she couldn't help herself.

'Let's not talk about it. It's upsetting,' said Lucille.

'Upsetting because a woman was killed even though she had a child with her?' Adele rounded on her sister. 'Upsetting because we are having to face the ugly truth of what is going on in the streets of our beloved city? Upsetting because it makes our wine unpalatable?' She got to her feet, knocking her chair over as she did. 'I can't sit here and talk about Parisian women being murdered as if we are talking about cattle going to the abattoir. That woman was another human being. A mother. Someone's daughter. A sister. A friend. She was a person who didn't deserve to be slaughtered in cold blood.'

'Adele, that's enough,' warned her father.

'Do none of you feel anything for that woman? That mother?' Adele looked accusingly from one person to the other. A strained silence hung in the air.

Müller rose to his feet. 'Adele, I apologise that this has upset you. I should not have brought the matter up.' He turned to Gérard. 'My apologies, Monsieur Basset.'

'Please, sit down,' urged Lucille. Her eyes beseeched her sister's.

'I don't feel very well,' said Adele. It was the truth. She felt sick to her stomach at the way Jacqueline's death was dismissed.

'Please sit down,' said Müller. 'Lucille, fetch your sister a glass of water.'

'I need to lie down,' said Adele. She couldn't bring herself to sit at the same table as him. She righted her chair. 'If you'll all excuse me.'

'Certainly,' said Müller with a curt nod of his head.

As Adele left the room, she could hear Lucille apologising for her. 'She's not been sleeping very well. She's been working so hard and rehearsing for the exhibition and organising the children. I think the dancing has made her think of Maman a lot, and it's upsetting for her. She doesn't mean to be so feisty. She just needs a rest.'

'Of course,' Müller replied. 'I understand perfectly.'

Adele closed her bedroom door on the conversation and flopped down onto her bed. She was too angry to cry. She balled her hands into fists as she thought of what she'd like to do to those soldiers who had murdered Jacqueline. What she'd liked to do to Müller. How she'd like to shake sense into her sister.

But as she heard laughter coming from the dining room, she knew she had a battle on her hands. She could hear Müller's dominating voice. 'A toast is in order. To the exhibition and the wonderful evening ahead.'

Glasses clinked as Lucille and her father echoed the toast.

In her mind, Adele toasted Cecile and the children and their safe passage out of this country to freedom. It was the best revenge she could get for Jacqueline's death. And it would be made all the sweeter for it happening right under Müller's nose.

Chapter 26

Adele

The following evening after school had finished and Adele had said goodbye to Madame Allard and Michelle Joffre, she locked the door at the main entrance and was crossing the hall to go up to the attic, when the sound of the bell at the side door made her jump. She hurried across the hallway.

'Who is it?' she called, her ear pressed to the oak.

'It's me, Manu.'

Adele unlocked the door and let him in. 'Is everything all right? I wasn't expecting you.' He looked tired.

'Don't worry. Nothing is wrong. I have something for the children.' He tapped the leather satchel he had across his chest.

Adele raised her eyebrows in question. 'I'm sure they don't need any work.' She attempted a joke and was rewarded with a wry smile from Manu, which was far more gratifying than it should be.

'Let's go upstairs and I'll explain to everyone.'

The children were excited to see Manu and Adele was encouraged to see Daniel slip his hand into Manu's. The boy obviously felt more comfortable in Manu's company than before and perhaps the other children's enthusiasm had reassured him. Manu ruffled the lad's hair. 'That is a nice welcome. Come, now, I have something for you all.' He beckoned the other children and Cecile to gather around.

Cecile glanced at Adele, who gave a shrug. She was as

intrigued as the rest of them. Adele sat down on the wooden floor and Eva snuggled up against her. She stroked the blonde hair, which was dry and dusty. It could do with a good wash. In fact, looking around at all the children and Cecile, they could all do with having a hair wash. The last thing she wanted was any head or body lice to start spreading amongst them, not that anyone was infected, but it might be the last wash they all got for a while once they left the attic.

'So, in here, I have something for each of you,' Manu was saying to the children as he unfastened the buckles on the satchel. 'It is something for each of you to keep with you. It's worth a lot of money. Now, you must only use it in an emergency.'

Adele had no idea what Manu was talking about and was surprised when he withdrew several sheets of paper, each only about ten-centimetre square in size. He turned them over and spread them out before him.

Cecile picked up one of the paintings. 'The detail is amazing for such a small painting.'

'He was an expert in this style,' said Manu. 'But his observation is incredible and the patience it must have taken him to recreate these is astounding.'

'Why have you brought them here?' asked Adele, her thoughts turning back to their current critical situation.

'These are your currency for safe passage out of France,' said Manu looking at Cecile. 'I don't know what situation you will find yourselves in where you feel the need to use them, but to the right person, they are a priceless bargaining chip. Well, maybe not priceless but they are worth a lot of money and anyone who knows their art will be aware of this.'

'Won't the Germans know they are missing?' asked Adele, thinking of Manu's safety as much as the children and Cecile's.

Manu shook his head. 'No. I have been planning this. I've been keeping them back for such an occasion.' He picked up the first painting where the little Breton cottage with its red door and shutters was covered in a gentle blanket of snow. Manu took two pieces of muslin from his bag and sandwiched the artwork between the two before tightly rolling up the miniature. 'In the bag is some thread. Break off a piece for me, please.'

Adele reached over and retrieved the wooden spool from his bag and broke off a length. Manu placed the art between two sheets of muslin and then very carefully rolled it up into a tight tube. 'Wrap the cotton around it. A piece at each end and one in the middle,' he instructed.

It was fiddly but Adele managed to secure the thread. 'What now?' she asked, still unsure what Manu had planned.

From his bag Manu pulled out a pair of scissors and a needle. 'All you have to do now, is sew one of these into each of the hems of your coats. I'm afraid sewing isn't my thing.'

'Sew it into the coat hems?' Cecile repeated for clarification.

'*Oui. C'est ça*. Yes. That's it. I can give you all some money, but it's not much and won't last long. The paintings, however, are worth so much more. They may save your lives.' He was serious when he spoke and looked at each one in the room in turn.

Adele winced at the thought of the children understanding their lives might be in danger. She knew she was at the point where she couldn't pretend this was just a big adventure anymore. When they all left the safety of the attic, they would be in real danger. Much as it broke her heart to add to their burden, she knew they had to know the truth as it might indeed save their lives.

Adele cleared her throat. 'So, children, what Manu is saying, is that when you leave here, these paintings will be hidden inside your coats. You mustn't tell anyone about them. They are a secret.' She paused, making sure the children understood what she was saying. They nodded obediently. 'The only time you can tell someone is when Cecile says you can or, if you are on your own, when you are desperate for help. When you need someone to hide you from the Germans and take you to safety.'

'Don't use it for food,' said Manu. 'Someone will always give you food or you can find food in the forests. You can only give it to someone in exchange for taking you to Switzerland.'

Adele wasn't entirely sure the children understood. It was all beyond their imaginations and experiences, but what else could they do? She could only hope and pray that they would all reach Switzerland together and the children wouldn't have to make any lifesaving decisions of their own.

They rolled and secured the remaining paintings. 'What will happen after the war, to the paintings? If they still have them, what should they do with them?' asked Adele as she fastened the last miniature.

'If they still have them, then maybe one day the collection will be reunited back here in the museum,' said Manu. He let out a sigh. 'I think a lot of art will be lost forever once it gets into Nazi hands. Much as it pains me to break up this Valois collection, it's the only thing I can think of to help Cecile and the children.'

The look he gave her reflected her own horror at the thought of what might happen to the children and her own sadness at the artworks being lost forever. She could live with that, but she knew she could never live with letting the children down. Adele slid her hand to cover Manu's and she gave a reassuring squeeze. In that moment, the expression on his face softened a fraction and whether it was a trick of the shadows, Adele couldn't tell, but the colour of his eyes deepened, drawing her in, while her grip on his hand tightened.

It was only the sound of Daniel and Thomas arguing that snapped Adele's attention.

'Boys! Boys! Stop. Remember what you've been told about not shouting.' She shuffled around Eva and placed herself between Daniel and Thomas. 'Now, what's the matter?' She purposely softened her voice and spoke quietly. Gentle, calming discipline was what they needed. Adele put an arm around each of their shoulders. 'Why are you arguing?'

'I want this one in my coat,' said Daniel, waving one of the rolled-up paintings as if it were a wand. 'It's got snow on it.'

'I want it,' said Thomas, making a grab for it.

Adele caught Thomas's hand. 'No snatching. Now, you both can't have it.'

'What about this one?' suggested Manu, holding another rolled-up painting towards Thomas. 'This is October when all the ghosts and lost souls come out.' He gave a ghost like 'whoooo' noise and pretended to grab Thomas. The boy gave a yelp and burst out laughing before copying Manu, which led to Daniel joining in too.

'You shouldn't encourage them,' said Adele, but it was heart-warming to hear the children laughing. It was a small respite to the seriousness of their situation, one she wasn't going to deny them. Goodness knows it had been difficult enough already and their immediate future was going to be even harder.

Manu stayed and entertained the children with ghost stories while Adele and Cecile sewed the paintings into the hems of the coats. Adele watched fondly, and not without a sense of pride, how Manu interacted with the children.

She caught Cecile looking at her, a knowing smile on the woman's face.

'What?' asked Adele, conscious she'd been caught gazing at Manu.

'You know what,' teased Cecile, looking back down at the hem she was sewing up on Thomas's coat. 'It's all right. Your secret is safe with me.'

Adele went to deny there was a secret but at the same time, wondered what the point of such denial would be. 'I've known Manu a long time,' she settled for saying.

'It's about time you did something about it, then,' replied Cecile, snipping the end of the thread and smoothing out the woollen fabric to admire her handiwork. 'Why wait? Not with the war going on. You might not get the opportunity otherwise.'

At that moment, Manu glanced over his shoulder towards them. He grinned. 'I am worn out from the children. I don't know how you do it all day as a teacher.' Before Adele could reply, his attention was grabbed by Thomas who wanted one more story. 'And then I must go home,' said Manu.

'The feeling is clearly mutual,' said Cecile.

'Haven't you got another coat you need to sew?' asked Adele, avoiding looking at her friend, for she could feel the blush of red creeping up her neck. It was a good job Cecile couldn't see the internal butterflies that were cavorting in Adele's stomach as, not for the first time, she recalled her kiss with Manu.

Chapter 27

Fleur

Paris, August 2015

Lydia had remained resolutely tight-lipped for the rest of the morning about what she wanted to show Fleur and Didier, despite Fleur gently trying to coax it from her. In the end, Fleur had given up and accepted she had to wait until Lydia was ready. So here she was, waiting outside the hotel for Didier while Lydia waited in the foyer.

Thoughts of Didier and the morning were now preoccupying Fleur's mind, but she was no further forward with understanding how she felt about him than she had been earlier. There was a connection between them – she couldn't deny that – but she hardly knew him and couldn't help feeling there was far more to him than met the eye. Not that it really mattered; she was only in Paris for just over another week.

Didier's black Mercedes pulled up outside the hotel. He buzzed down the window and leaned over so he could speak to her. '*Bonjour.*'

Fleur leaned down and rested her arm on the open window. '*Bonjour* to you too,' she said with a smile. 'I still don't know what we're doing or where we're going. Once you've parked, I'll arrange a taxi.'

Didier frowned. 'A taxi? No need. I will drive.'

'Honestly, you don't have to . . .' began Fleur but Didier

nodded towards the hotel and when Fleur turned around, her grandmother was coming down the steps, holding on to the doorman's arm.

'I'd like to drive,' insisted Didier when Fleur looked back at him apologetically. 'Besides the Paris taxi drivers will charge double and take the long way to wherever we are going.'

Fleur stepped aside as the doorman opened the car door for Lydia. Fleur went around the other side and, on impulse, opened the passenger door so she was sitting next to Didier rather than in the back with Lydia. She didn't want Didier to feel like he was their driver.

'I don't mind if you want to sit in the back with your grandmother,' said Didier as if reading her mind.

'No, I'm quite happy here.'

Didier gave a nod of his head in approval. 'Where to, madame?' he asked looking in the rear-view mirror at Lydia.

'*Cimetière du Père Lachaise*,' replied Lydia.

Didier twisted around in his seat. 'The cemetery?'

'Yes. That's right. Boulevard de Ménilmontant. The twentieth arrondissement.'

'*Oui, je sais où est le cimetière.* I know where the cemetery is.'

'*Alors*, let's go,' said Lydia.

Didier looked at Fleur as if she could offer some explanation but she was as bemused as he was. 'Better just do as she says.'

As they drove along, Fleur tapped it into her phone and read the information that came up. 'Wow. There are some famous residents at the cemetery. Frédéric Chopin, Edith Piaf, Oscar Wilde, Jim Morrison.'

'It is over one hundred acres and one of the most, if not *the* most, visited cemetery in the world,' said Didier.

Fleur looked back at Lydia who was now gazing out of the window with a distant expression on her face. The earlier upbeat demeanour had now been replaced by a rather more sombre one. Fleur sat back in her seat and exchanged a glance with Didier who gave a questioning, *is she all right?* look. Fleur nodded but frowned at the same time.

She'd rather not be going to the cemetery. OK, it wasn't back in West Sussex where her mother was buried but it equalled the same thing: loss.

The city was busy and Didier expertly navigated the traffic-heavy streets before finally turning onto Boulevard De Ménilmontant. 'I will drop you both off near the main entrance and then find somewhere to park.'

'I want to buy some flowers from the shop across the road,' said Lydia.

Fleur accompanied her grandmother into the florist's with the sense that this was not the first time Lydia had done this. They emerged a few minutes later, armed with two bunches of white chrysanthemums. 'They're pretty,' she commented as they waited outside the huge double wooden doors to the cemetery.

Lydia touched the white petals with her fingertips. 'They represent immortality,' she said. 'Chrysanthemums can survive the hard frosts of winter. They are a symbol of life. Our loved ones are immortal because we always remember them in our hearts.'

Fleur looked up the road and could see Didier making his way towards them, under the intermittent shadows of the plane trees that lined the pavement. He was back in his suit today, with a white shirt but no tie. He'd shaved and a light stubble grazed his jaw and chin, accentuating his well-defined cheekbones. He seemed oblivious to the two women who passed him, looked back and checked him out.

The cemetery was indeed vast. It was like walking into another world. Fleur supposed in a way it was; it was a dead world but, at the same time, it felt full of life. She couldn't quite explain it. A brick-paved path, with steep cambers either side giving it an almost dome-like feel, filtered through the grounds of the towering monuments, elaborate mini chapels and simple headstones, while the greenery of the many trees – maple, cherry, walnut and willow – broke up the hard and somewhat monotone landscape of stone, marble and concrete. Fleur moved to walk beside Lydia, slipping her arm into her grandmother's. The path was uneven and she was concerned Lydia might stumble.

'There are many monuments here,' said Didier. 'There is one for the Holocaust, another for the Second World War, another for the First World War.' They were walking along a path lined by mini chapels, which looked like stone beach huts. 'These chapels usually belong to one family and all the members are buried here. Some are cremated and have their ashes buried in the tombs.'

'It's like a town but with no roadmap,' said Fleur. Although it didn't appear Lydia had any trouble navigating her way around.

They continued to follow Lydia as she made her way deeper into the cemetery, walking with purpose and direction. The path they were walking down now was pea-shingle, which crunched underfoot.

After a while they rounded the corner and Lydia came to a stop at a double-sized plot, rectangular in shape, edged with stone to keep the white pebbles in place, which disguised the concrete slab. A large concrete cross marked the head of the grave. The names engraved on the stone were hard to make out, having been discoloured over the years by the elements. Lydia walked around to the headstone and placed one of the bunches of flowers into the vase set in the ground. From her bag she brought out a small plastic bag and a toothbrush and began scrubbing at the thin layer of moss and dirt that had gathered in the grooves.

Fleur went around to her grandmother's side and took the toothbrush from her. 'Let me do that, Nan.'

Lydia hesitated but after a moment, let go of the brush. '*Merci*.'

It was several minutes of scrubbing before the names were cleaned and more easily read.

Marianne Basset 1893–1930
Gérard Basset 1888–1943

Parents de Adele Basset 1917–1982
Lucille Basset 1921–1942
La vie est faites des petit bonheur.
Danser pour toujours dans le ciel avec les anges
Emanuel Lafon 1912–1977
Amour, honneur et courage

Fleur worked out the translation. 'Life is made of little happiness. Forever dancing in the sky with the angels.' The last line being, 'Love, honour and courage.' She watched as Lydia knelt down at the edge of the grave. Any thoughts or prayers, she didn't voice but after a minute or two, she got to her feet.

'This was my teacher and her family,' said Lydia. 'There is one more grave to visit.'

Fleur took a deep breath. As much as this cemetery was very different to the one back home, she wasn't enjoying the experience. She wouldn't have come for anyone else other than her grandmother, who somehow seemed to be taking comfort from her visit here, just like she did in England. Fleur's jaw clenched as they trailed Lydia along the pathway. She felt Didier's hand on the small of her back and then he took her hand in his.

'It is OK,' he whispered leaning into her.

Fleur gripped his hand in response and some of the tension leached away.

Lydia came to a stop, this time at an unremarkable, single grave with a simple unadorned headstone. In a less shaded spot, the headstone wasn't covered in moss like the Basset family one had been, just a little discoloured from the weather. Fleur was able to read the name clearly and translate this one more easily.

Jacqueline Rashal
16 July 1942
Much loved wife and mother

Lydia laid her second bunch of flowers at the grave and took a moment to stand silently with her head bowed. Didier had stood back and from the corner of her eye, Fleur could see him tapping away at his phone screen. Her mind now refocused on their reason for being here, Fleur wondered if he had realised the same thing as her when they'd seen the name of this second grave. Jacqueline Rashal, wife and mother. There were two girls on the register with the same surname, Eva and Blanche. Were they related to Jacqueline? If so, what was the connection to Lydia?

After a few minutes, Lydia got to her feet and moved to stand beside Fleur. 'You are no doubt wondering why I have brought you both here,' she said at last. Didier stepped closer, standing next to Fleur as Lydia continued to speak. 'You see, Jacqueline Rashal was my mother.'

Fleur frowned at the revelation. It didn't make sense. She was sure the name Rashal had never been mentioned and what was the connection with Eva and Blanche? Were they related or was it pure coincidence? 'This was your mother?' repeated Fleur for clarification. 'I thought you said your mother was called Adele?' She stopped as she spoke. The dance teacher, Mademoiselle Basset . . . the first grave . . . Adele Basset. Fleur was so confused. She couldn't make sense of all the information. 'I don't understand.'

'I was fortunate to have two mothers,' explained Lydia. 'Jacqueline was my real mother, the woman who gave birth to me. Tragically, as you can see, she died in 1942. I was only ten years old. She was such a brave woman. I loved her very much.' Lydia continued to gaze at the grave.

'And your dance teacher looked after you? Is that what you're saying?' asked Fleur.

Lydia nodded. 'She and Manu Lafon. He was the curator of the museum next door to the school.'

'What happened to your real father?' Fleur was slowly making some sort of sense out of it all.

'He was killed in the war. He was captured by the Germans and died in a labour camp.'

At least that bit was the truth that Fleur had been told. She reached for Lydia's hand. 'Why have you not told me that before?' There was no judgement in Fleur's tone. She just genuinely didn't understand. She felt Didier give a small nudge and he handed her his mobile phone. She looked at the screen. It was a black and white class photograph, taken in a classroom with a young woman teacher standing at one side and an older male teacher the other side of the group. Didier reached over and zoomed in on the blackboard behind the group to the date: 28 mai 1942. He then expanded the screen and zoomed back in on the faces of the children, to one girl in particular.

Fleur did a double take, peering closely at the child. Although it was a photo of a photograph and the image was grainy, there was no doubt about it– the blonde child, with the heart-shaped mouth and large doe-like eyes, was Lydia. There was a younger girl standing in front of Lydia who looked very similar, so much so they could be sisters.

Lydia turned and looked at the photograph. 'As I said, you are very resourceful. I didn't know that photo still existed.'

'A friend of mine found it in the archives of the school,' said Didier. 'He just sent it to me.'

'The timing is impeccable,' replied Lydia.

'I don't understand,' said Fleur. 'If you're in the photograph in May 1942, your name should be on the list Didier has. There are two Rashal children . . .' Her voice tailed off as she suddenly joined up the dots.

'That's right,' said Lydia. 'That child is Eva Rashal, sister to Blanche Rashal and daughter to Jacqueline Rashal. My name is not Lydia. My real name is Eva Rashal.'

Chapter 28

Adele

Paris, July 1942

When Adele arrived at the school the next day, Manu was waiting at the gates for her.

'*Bonjour. Ça-va?*' asked Adele. 'Is everything all right?'

'Yes. The paperwork for the exhibition is all in order,' replied Manu. 'I will come and see you this evening with everything you need for a safe journey to Lyon.'

A German patrol car turned into the street and slowed as it passed by Adele and Manu, the two soldiers giving them long hard stares.

'What are they doing here?' muttered Manu as the car sped down the road. 'We need to be more careful.' He stroked the side of her face, as he had done the other night. Adele loved to feel his touch but at the same time, wished he wouldn't. It was torture.

She shied away from his hand and instantly regretted it as she saw the confusion and hurt in Manu's eyes. 'I'd better go,' she said. 'I'll see you this evening.'

As she unlocked the schoolhouse door, she glanced back over her shoulder. Manu was standing at the gate, his hands in his pockets, watching her, his face impassive. Adele wasn't quite sure what unspoken communication had passed between them or even if they were interpreting it correctly, but he wasn't hers. He belonged to another

242

woman and as much as she had feelings for Manu, she wasn't going to betray her morals.

The next two weeks passed by quickly. Adele's time was completely occupied with teaching, dancing and making sure the guests in the attic were all right. On the face of it, the Rashal girls appeared to be dealing with the death of their mother quite well, but Adele understood only too well the trauma and internal pain of losing a parent at a young age. Those girls would be aching inside, confused by their feelings and experiencing a raft of emotions that they were inadequately skilled to deal with. The sooner they could escape to safety, the better.

Since the argument with Müller and the more frequent German patrols by the school, Adele had not seen very much of Manu. He had been over only twice. Once to give her the papers for Cecile and the children, and the previous night to go over the plans for smuggling them out of the city.

The children danced well that evening after school. First of all they did some ballet but they seemed restless and less enthusiastic as the class went on. They had learnt about half of the routine for the performance and, rather than take them through it again, Adele decided it was time for something more fun and liberating.

'*Alors*, I think it's time to swap those ballet slippers for tap shoes,' she said, taking the basket of shoes from the cupboard. It was the right decision. The children instantly perked up and eagerly changed their footwear. 'That's better. Let's have some fun now!

'Tap, step, ball change, brush hop, toe, hop!' Adele called the steps out above the clatter of shoes, joining in at the front of the class. Maybe she should have got them to perform a tap routine for the exhibition, rather than ballet. It was too late to change it now; the show was only three days away. She had spoken with the parents two weeks ago and given them the letter from Müller which, although disguised as an invitation, left no doubt that it was, in fact, an order that the children perform in Lyon. Not everyone had been happy but they had no choice but to agree.

They were just coming to the end of the routine when from her peripheral vision, Adele saw someone come into the dance room. To her horror it was Müller with Lucille, who mouthed a sorry to her older sister from behind Müller's back. 'Keep dancing!' called Adele above the rhythmic and sometimes not so rhythmic tapping of the shoes. 'Well done, everyone.' Adele clapped in appreciation, as did Müller and Lucille.

'That sounds excellent,' said Müller. He clearly didn't know very much about dancing but Adele appreciated his apparent enthusiasm, if only it was for the children. 'Please, could you show me the whole routine?'

'Of course. Right children, we have our first audience. This is Hauptmann Müller. He will be accompanying us to the exhibition in Lyon where we will be performing.' She smiled reassuringly at the children, some of whom offered hesitant smiles.

'*Alors*. I will play the piano and you can show Hauptmann Müller how you can do it on your own.' She went over to the piano and just as she placed her fingers on the keys, there was the sound of the creaky floorboard from up above. Adele slammed her fingers down on the keys of the piano as hard as she could and began playing the music with far more gusto than was necessary. She could see from the look on the children's faces, they knew the music was being played differently but nevertheless, they began their routine.

Adele glanced over at Müller, who was watching the children but whispering to Lucille. Her sister looked up and held her gaze for a moment, before looking back at Müller with a smile. Adele knew her sister well and despite the outward expression, she could see concern and tension in her sister's face. Adele carried on playing as fiercely as possible and faster than she should. The children somehow managed to keep in time and it came to an end all too quickly. Adele hoped that Cecile would be able to make the children upstairs just sit still.

'Very good. You all danced perfectly. I am very impressed,' said Müller. 'Although I did think they were going to do a ballet dance.'

Adele's nerves were on a knife edge. 'Yes. They're doing both but it's getting quite late and their parents will be here to collect them soon.' She got up from the piano and without trying to look as if she was rushing them out, Adele instructed the children to change into their normal outdoor shoes. 'Do you want to wait downstairs?' she asked Müller and Lucille. She widened her eyes in encouragement at her sister, willing them to leave.

'Yes, let's go down and talk to the parents, while the children change their shoes,' said Lucille, slipping her arm through Müller's.

He pursed his lips together and stood very still, his gaze travelling to the ceiling.

Adele sat back at the piano and played her *Dépêche-toi* music – the one she used when she wanted the children to do something quickly. Anything to cover up any potential noise from the attic. The children scrambled to get their feet into their shoes, urged on by the tempo of the music, which got faster and faster.

'Oh no, it's the hurry-up music,' said Lucille, pulling Müller from the room. 'We'll get caught in the stampede any second now. Quick, let's go!'

Adele had never been so relieved as she was then to see Müller being led from the room. She continued to play and moments later the children were rushing out of the door and down the stairs. Adele closed the dance room door behind her and hurried after them.

Once the children had all left with their parents, Müller turned to Adele. 'It is always that chaotic? I hope they will be more under control for the exhibition.'

'They just needed to let off a bit of energy today,' said Adele. 'It does them good now and again.'

'We should go,' said Lucille. 'Peter and I are dining out this evening.'

'Would you like a ride home?' asked Müller.

'Thank you but no. I need to tidy up the dance studio. I don't want to hold you up,' replied Adele. She hadn't had time to go up to the attic today. She liked to see the Rashal girls and Daniel who were all without their mothers now. Sitting with them for an hour, reading them a story or playing a game with them or sometimes just having a cuddle was a routine Adele had come to look forward to as much as the children did themselves.

'It's no trouble,' said Müller. 'We can wait for you.'

Adele wanted to insist but she had the feeling Müller was deliberately hanging around the school. She couldn't risk him being here when Cecile and the children left the attic, assuming everyone had gone home now the music had ceased. Adele looked at Müller who gave a raise of the eyebrows.

'That's very kind of you,' she replied, keeping the tone of her voice even. 'I'll just tidy away the registers and then we can go.'

'Is that all you need to do?' asked Müller. 'You made it sound you had lots of things to do.'

'Oh, they can wait. I just didn't want to intrude or put you to any trouble.' Adele breezed past into the office and faffed around with a few papers, pretending she was tidying up. In fact, there was nothing to do; everything had been done by the school receptionist. She reappeared from the office. 'There, that's done.'

They left the building and, as she locked the door, she saw Müller looking up at the rooftop. He squinted his eyes against the late afternoon sun. 'Is there a room at the top?'

'Just the attic,' replied Lucille. She tugged at his arm. 'Let's hurry. I'm very hungry.'

'What's in the attic?' pressed Müller.

'Nothing,' said Adele walking across the playground. 'Just storage.'

Müller followed on with Lucille holding on to his arm. He paused once again at the school gates and took another look up to the roof. 'Storage? Have you been up there lately?'

'No but it was searched by some soldiers recently,' said Adele. 'I don't have any cause to go up there.'

'Interesting.' Müller rubbed his chin with his fingers before turning his attention back to Lucille and Adele. He smiled broadly. 'Let's not keep you waiting then, my darling. If you're hungry, that needs to be resolved.'

They got into the back of the car and it pulled away from the roadside. Adele looked up at the top of the school and to her horror, she saw the little face of Eva looking out of the window at them.

Chapter 29

Adele

'Is everything all right, Adele?' asked Müller as the car made its way down the street and away from the school.

Adele snapped her gaze to his. 'Yes. Everything is fine,' she said, trying not to let the anxiety in her stomach come through in her voice.

'The school is old, is it not?' he asked.

'Erm, yes, I'm not sure but about two hundred years,' she said, confused and at the same time nervous.

'A lot of children have been through those doors,' continued Müller, his gaze never leaving Adele's.

She nodded. 'Yes. A great many.'

He paused as if considering something before speaking again. 'Tell me, Adele, do you believe in ghosts?'

'Ghosts? No. Not really.' She exchanged a perplexed look with Lucille.

'So you don't think the school is haunted?'

'No. I don't.' Adele shifted her seat. She felt she was walking into a trap that she couldn't quite see.

'You've never seen or heard anything inexplicable, then?'

Now she knew what his game was and she quelled down the nauseous sensation in her stomach. 'No. Old buildings make noises; they creak and groan all the time.'

'So you think sometimes the eye can play tricks on the mind?' he asked, looking at her again. 'Do you think you can imagine you see things or people, children even?'

'Like you say, the mind plays tricks. If you want something enough, you can convince yourself it's there,' replied Adele. 'When really, it was just the way the light was shining or a shadow being cast and, yet, you would swear you saw something when really, it was nothing. Probably make yourself look quite foolish.' She added the last bit to play to his vanity. No way would Müller want to come across as fanciful and given to imagining things. 'It would be rather embarrassing to say you saw a ghost and it turns out it was a shadow.' She gave a laugh, but this time it was she who held his gaze. 'Anyway, you might find out some strange noise was only the house creaking or vermin.' She used the term Edith had used.

'I suppose it could be vermin,' mused Müller. 'Very likely to be, actually.' He gave her a smug-looking smile. He was referring to Eva in the window. Adele just knew it. Fear gripped at her throat, constricting her airways. She looked out of the window, trying to steady her rapidly increasing heart rate.

'Are you all right, Adele? You've come over very pale,' said Müller.

'I'm perfectly fine,' replied Adele. She caught a glimpse of her sister's bemused expression. She really had no idea what they were talking about, but Adele knew she had to get those children out of there as soon as possible. They were no longer safe.

'I've been thinking,' said Müller, breaking her thoughts, 'I don't think the children are going to be ready to perform in front of the Führer. I think it would be embarrassing. I'm sorry, I know how much it means to you but I would rather the performance was just you two.'

'Oh, but they just need a little more practice,' said Adele. 'I promise they will be ready.'

'No. I saw enough earlier. I don't want the humiliation.'

'Please . . .' began Adele. She was prepared to beg Müller, if she had to. Her escape plan for the children depended on them being smuggled down to Lyon with the children who were performing.

'Enough. I don't want to talk about it. My mind is made up.' Müller fixed Adele with a hard look and she knew it was pointless to argue.

The car drove on and the occupants sat in silence. Adele knew as soon as she was dropped off at the apartment and the car with Müller and Lucille was out of the way, she was going to go straight back to the school to warn Cecile. Where had Cecile been when Eva was at the window? Everyone was in danger now because for some reason Cecile hadn't kept an eye on the children. Adele had to quell her anger. It was in danger of surfacing for Müller to see.

As they pulled up outside the apartment, Müller placed his hand on the door handle to prevent Adele from hopping out. 'I was thinking, I'd like you to join us for this dinner this evening.'

'Oh, I . . . err . . . I'm tired. But thank you for the kind invitation,' said Adele, taken aback by Müller's suggestion.

'I'm sure you're not too tired to have dinner,' replied Müller undeterred. 'In fact, I'm meeting a friend of mine who I'd like you to meet. Why don't you run along and get changed.' He removed his hand from the door and checked his wristwatch. 'Be back in ten minutes.'

'Why don't we plan this for another night?' suggested Lucille, her concerned look belying the casualness of her voice. 'Adele's been working all day.'

'It is not a request,' snapped Müller.

Adele didn't miss the flame of anger in Müller's voice aimed at her sister. 'It's all right. I'll be as quick as I can.'

'I'll come with you,' said Lucille, hopping out after her sister.

Adele grasped Lucille's hand and together they rush up to their apartment. 'Did you know about this?' asked Adele, as she opened the front door.

'No. I promise. I knew nothing,' puffed Lucille. 'He never mentioned it to me.'

'What's going on, girls?' Their father came out into the hall.

'I've got to go to dinner with Müller and Lucille. He's arranged for a friend to meet us there. Like I'm some sort of offering,' blurted out Adele. 'I don't want to go.'

'Did you decline his offer?'

'I didn't have any choice.' Adele stormed into her bedroom, slamming the door behind her. She opened her wardrobe door and took out one of her evening dresses. She hadn't had cause to wear it for a long time and hoped it still fitted. She needn't have worried; if anything it was a little big and a sure sign, despite the food Müller gave them, she had lost weight over the past couple of years. Adele fixed her hair, applied a small amount of make-up and slipped into her dress. It was plain black with thin straps and a small slit in the side. She took a shawl from her drawer and draped it around her shoulders before exiting her room.

'We should hurry,' said Lucille when Adele came back into the living room. 'Peter said ten minutes.'

'If he wants me to come with him, then he'll have to wait for me.'

'He doesn't like being kept waiting.'

Adele looked at the fearful expression on her sister's face, which was so out of character, and felt a wave of sympathy for her. 'He's very controlling. I don't like it. He thinks he can have everything he wants, when he wants it and how he wants it.'

Lucille looked down at the ground. 'The thing is, he can. It's a fact.'

'It's not a basis for a relationship.' Adele looked at her father for moral support. 'Papa was never like that with Maman. It was always mutual respect and love. That's how a relationship should be.' She looked back at her father. He had retrieved his handkerchief from his pocket and removed his glasses, before dabbing at his eyes. 'Oh,

Papa, I'm sorry. I didn't mean to upset you.' She rushed over and hugged him.

'*C'est bon. C'est bon,*' said her father. He looked over at Lucille. 'Your sister is right.'

Lucille blinked back tears from her eyes. 'We need to go. Peter will be getting impatient.'

Adele tutted but followed her sister down the hallway. 'Mustn't keep Peter waiting.'

A short time later, they arrived at the restaurant and Müller's friend and comrade was already there. When Adele saw him, she had to stop herself letting out a small gasp of shock. Müller's friend was the officer who had ordered the search of the school recently. She recognised the scar that travelled from his lower lip and curved under his chin, which looked even more pronounced tonight, giving him an air of danger. Müller made the introductions. 'This is Hauptmann Michael Weld. And this is Adele Basset, Lucille's sister. I do believe you've met before.'

'We have indeed.' Weld shook Adele's hand. 'Although it is much nicer this evening to meet under different circumstances, far more social.'

'Pleased to meet you,' replied Adele, resisting the urge to wipe her hand on her dress after touching his.

'And, please, call me Michael.'

Adele forced a smile. The evening was going to be nothing short of a nightmare. She wondered if she could feign sickness, but she thought of Müller's need to control. It would probably be Lucille who suffered ultimately. As she glanced around the restaurant, rather than have to look at Weld, she had to do a double take at the couple sitting at a table on the far side of the restaurant. It couldn't be? It was!

There sitting with a German officer was Edith.

Adele purposely looked away, not wanting to draw attention to who she'd seen. She politely made out she was listening to the conversation between Müller and Weld about the upcoming exhibition and after a few minutes, looked back at the unexpected diner. Edith was smiling and laughing with her companion, obviously very comfortable in the German's company.

Once again Adele felt conflicted. Should she tell Manu about this? Was it her place to interfere? Could she not tell him?

The conversation at her table had turned to Paris and the attractions, with Weld enthusing how much he had enjoyed coming to the city. In any other circumstances, Adele would have been flattered by how much he was taken by Paris but not today. 'There is more to the city than the bright lights of the Moulin Rouge or the architectural feat of the Tour de Eiffel or the beauty of Notre-Dame,' said Adele. 'There is much you don't see, like the suffering of the people, the bread queues, the hungry children – those are not the sort of photographs anyone takes home to show their family.' To this she received a kick in the shin from her sister. Adele winced and glanced at Lucille, who scowled back at her.

'Please excuse Adele,' said Müller. 'She's very passionate about her city. As a teacher she has a heightened sense of compassion towards the children.'

'Rightly so,' agreed Weld. 'But when the war is over, there will be much better things to come for France. Then everyone will be thankful.'

Adele went to speak but Lucille interrupted her by spluttering on her wine. 'Are you all right, darling,' said Müller. He clicked his fingers at the waiter and asked for some water.

'Thank you,' said Lucille taking a sip. 'I just need to go to the bathroom. Adele, could you come with me?'

'With pleasure.' Adele rose from her seat and escorted her sister to the bathroom. She glanced over towards Edith and for a moment the two women made eye contact, but Edith looked away without offering any form of recognition or acknowledgement. She didn't look the slightest bit shocked to see Adele there.

'For goodness' sake, Adele. Stop being so confrontational all the time,' said Lucille as soon as they were in the safety of the bathroom. 'Peter is trying to impress Weld and whether you like it or not, we are here as their guests.'

'I don't care. I'd sooner starve than enjoy being here tonight. I hate them. They are all the same. Arrogant. Heartless.'

'Can we discuss this another time?' snapped Lucille. 'Let's just get through the evening without any more snippy remarks.'

Adele knew she was tense but she couldn't share the reason with Lucille. That would be admitting that she was harbouring Cecile and the children in the school. If Lucille knew that for certain, then she might inadvertently, out of some misjudged loyalty, feel compelled to share the information with Müller.

Adele took a deep breath. 'All right. I promise I'll be on my best behaviour but once this meal is over, I want to go home. I certainly don't want to spend any more time than absolutely necessary in their company.'

The rest of the meal passed without further confrontation, although Adele had to bite her tongue not to have little digs at the two German officers. At one point, Weld had rested his hand on the back of her chair and she'd excused herself to the bathroom once again, just so she could push the chair and his arm back. When she emerged, she was surprised to see Müller waiting for her. She could see he was making a pretence to keep up his mask of friendship towards her.

'Ah, Adele. We need a word,' he said. He gripped her upper arm and applied just enough pressure so she knew it was there without making her squeal in pain. 'Through here.' He led her across the small lobby and around the back of a staircase. 'Now, I won't mince my words. I'll make this crystal clear for both of us. I know you don't approve of my relationship with your sister. You have your reasons which, I must admit, are incomprehensible to me, but I do not have the time nor the inclination to challenge those reasons or try to make you see differently.'

He cleared his throat and released his grip on her arm. 'As for embarrassing me in front of my comrade, that I cannot leave unchallenged. Weld is a good friend of mine and a respected officer in the German army. Please ensure you don't make things difficult for me. He's a very charming man. You could do a lot worse.'

'He's a very married man,' Adele replied. 'I am not interested in a relationship with an adulterer.' She looked him straight in the eyes. 'Lucille and I are very different in that respect.' She thought for a moment he was going to slap her as his hand flinched at his side. She didn't care. She'd take the assault for her pride if she had to.

'I know Lucille has explained my situation and although I have no need whatsoever to justify myself to you, please be assured that my marriage is over.'

Adele stood a little taller. She knew she should be quiet now, but she couldn't help herself. 'Is that why you were having dinner with another woman who wasn't my sister the other week?'

Müller hadn't been expecting that. A fleeting look of alarm shot across his face and he breathed in heavily through his nostrils, causing them to flare. Adele's feeling of victory was short-lived. 'You know, Adele, you could have made this much easier.' He tapped his lip with his forefinger. 'Now I'm going to have to do something I really didn't want to do.'

'Which is?' She sounded far braver than she felt but guessed she wasn't fooling Müller.

'We need to make a deal, me and you,' he began. 'We both have things we would like to keep to ourselves. That woman you saw me with is my wife. She was coming to Paris to see me one final time.'

'You still get on well with your wife, I noticed,' said Adele. 'I suspect you'd prefer neither your wife nor my sister to know about each other.'

'We are still very good friends. Having said that, as you rightly point out, I have no desire for them to know about each other. So, I am prepared to overlook the matter of the missing child who I may or may not have seen at the school today.'

'This sounds remarkably like blackmail,' said Adele.

'Call it what you like, but it's just an agreement.'

'How do I know I can trust you?'

Müller gave an impatient sigh. 'I may be many things and, yes, you probably have a very low opinion of me, but I am not completely cold-hearted. Besides, if you mention what you saw to your sister, she'll wonder why you didn't tell her sooner. Why you kept it from her for so long. I don't think she will be very happy, do you?'

'I don't think I have any option but to agree.' Adele felt cornered. She didn't like it one bit, but she couldn't give up Cecile and the children. As far as she knew, Müller didn't know about the others. He'd only seen Eva. She'd tell Lucille once the children were safely away.

'You seem hesitant,' said Müller when Adele didn't reply. 'Why would you want to inflict such misery on not just your sister but anyone else you may possibly care about?'

Adele knew she had to swallow her pride. This wasn't about her. This wasn't about Lucille. It was about those defenceless children and saving them from a truly harrowing fate. 'I agree,' she said firmly. 'Now we'd better return to Lucille and Weld.'

'Good. Just one thing – Weld won't like to be disappointed tonight. You're an attractive woman and Weld is very taken with you. Of course, the choice is yours. Just remember, he's not quite so . . . how shall I say . . . not quite so empathetic as I am towards missing children. He doesn't like to think he's been outwitted.'

Chapter 30

Fleur

Paris, August 2015

Fleur was lost for words at Lydia's revelation. Of all the things she thought Lydia might tell her on this trip, her real name being Eva wasn't one of them. They were now sitting in a small café opposite the cemetery with a hot drink each.

'Why did you change your name?' Fleur asked once they were settled with their drinks.

'It was safer. We were all given new identities, false papers so if we were ever stopped and questioned, we wouldn't be seen as Jews. It was the only way to save our lives. I had to become someone new and leave Eva Rashal behind in the school attic.'

'I'm so sorry, Nan,' said Fleur. 'I can't imagine what you must have gone through.'

'Do you know what happened to your sister?' asked Didier gently.

Lydia shook her head. 'I've always believed I was the only one who survived. That is what Adele and Manu said.' Lydia retrieved the ballet shoe from her bag and placed it on the table in front of them. 'At least that's what I have always thought,' she said. 'Until I saw this.'

Fleur exchanged a glance with Didier before turning back to Lydia. 'What's significant about the shoe?' Her voice was soft as she watched for Lydia's reaction.

Lydia was gazing at the shoe with a strange distant expression on her face. When she spoke, it was not much more than a whisper. 'This is Blanche's shoe. This is my sister's shoe. I recognise the repair to the toe – my mother stitched it as we couldn't afford a new pair. Blanche has left it for me as a sign.'

Again Fleur and Didier looked at one another. She could see the thoughts racing through his mind as he considered the significance of the shoe. Fleur was sure they arrived at the same conclusion simultaneously as her wide eyes were mirrored by Didier's. He gave a nod, a wordless communication that Fleur should take the lead.

Fleur shifted in her seat. 'Nan, if this is Blanche's shoe and she left it for you, that means she has been here in Paris. It only appeared this month. She must have known you were coming.' She paused, unsure if Lydia was taking in what she was saying. Another encouraging nod from Didier and she continued with her train of thought. 'Do you remember Didier talking about the woman who brought the painting back to the museum? She was the same woman who the curator said was fascinated by the school and by the fact that you returned every year.'

'Bridget Sutter,' said Lydia, showing she was paying attention to Fleur and that her mind was still as sharp as ever. 'That's the name of the woman who had the picture. The Valois.'

'That's right,' said Fleur. 'Don't you think it would be strange for two people to visit the museum and the school?'

Lydia's eyes shot up to Fleur. 'You do not need to spell it out. I have made the connection.'

Fleur withheld a small smile she reserved for when her grandmother was being particularly French. It surfaced most when she was cross or indignant about something. Like now. 'Your sister is looking for you, Nan. Are you all right with that?'

Lydia didn't answer immediately and she looked up, blinking away some tears. 'I am. It's just so hard to believe after all this time. My darling little sister, Blanche. She was just six years old the last time I saw her.'

'And she would have had false papers too?' asked Fleur.

'We all did. Manu organised it. That was the night my mother was killed,' replied Lydia. 'Caught and shot by the Germans. Adele and Manu didn't know I'd heard them telling Thomas's mother what happened. She was in the attic with us. She was hiding too. After that awful night, she had to look after all of us.'

'Wasn't there another boy? Daniel? Where were his mother or father?' Fleur tried to imagine how dreadful it must have been. She'd lost her mother in a car accident, and that was bad enough, but to lose your mother to murder by the Germans just because of your faith was incomprehensible.

'I didn't know at the time, but Adele told me later. Daniel's mother had left him with her, begged Adele to look after him. She found out after the war that his mother had been captured and sent to one of the concentration camps. We can only assume she died there. She never came back to look for him, which was probably a blessing. I can only imagine the guilt and grief she would have felt finding out her son hadn't survived.'

Up until this point, Didier had remained silent, allowing Lydia to unburden herself from the secrets she'd kept all those years and for Fleur to share this private moment with her grandmother. Fleur appreciated his thoughtfulness. He cleared his throat. 'Would you like me to contact Bridget Sutter – your potential sister?'

Lydia pressed her lips together as if trying to hold back her emotions. She nodded. 'I would but I'm frightened. I haven't been frightened of anything since what happened during the war, but I suddenly find myself fearful. What if she is not Blanche? What if she is and she rejects me? She was just six years old; she might not even remember me.'

'But what if she does?' suggested Fleur. 'I'm sure she does – she left a ballet shoe for you. She knew you'd recognise it straight away.' She tried a different tack. 'Didier could make contact. He could find out for certain and then arrange for you both to meet. If you don't let him, you'll never really know for certain.'

Lydia sat a little straighter and swallowed. 'Yes. Of course, you're right. I said I was coming here to tell the truth and to find out the truth.' She looked at Didier and placed her pale age-spotted hand over his. 'If you could make contact with Bridget Sutter, I'd be very grateful.'

Didier bowed his head a fraction. 'I'd be more than happy to do so.'

'Thank you. That's very kind,' said Lydia. 'There is something else too.' She rummaged in her handbag again and brought out a business card from the inside pocket. 'We need to visit this gentleman. He was Adele and Manu's solicitor. He has in safekeeping some papers that may be of interest to you.' She looked at Didier as she spoke. 'Can you call the office and ask if we can see them today?'

Didier took the business card and went outside to call the solicitors.

'Is everything all right between you two?' asked Lydia.

Her grandmother was proving as astute as ever. Despite everything, Lydia was still paying close attention to her. 'Yes. Why?' Fleur replied hoping she could at least buy some time until Didier came back and then she wouldn't have to answer any more questions about them. Them? Was there even a them to ask questions about?

'I don't know. Call it my sixth sense, but I detect a change between you both.'

'There's nothing to worry about, Nan,' Fleur said. 'He's a nice guy.'

'He is indeed. And he likes you.'

Fleur gave her grandmother an old-fashioned look. 'We get on,' she said simply.

'When I said he likes you, I meant he likes you a lot.' Lydia wasn't going to give up. 'And I know you well enough to tell you like him too. Like him a lot.'

Fleur shook her head. Did Lydia miss anything? She gave a shrug. 'OK, I admit. We like each other but that is all. I mean, he's here in France. I live in England. We barely know each other. Don't get any ideas about anything happening between us.'

Lydia sipped her drink, eyeing Fleur over the rim of her cup. 'You should allow yourself the pleasure of love.'

'Love is painful.' She wished she was more gung-ho in her approach to relationships but she just couldn't bring herself to be so vulnerable.

'Love is the most beautiful thing in the world to experience,' corrected Lydia. 'And with that passion, comes the risk of heartache – granted. However, you are missing out on so much. Denying yourself the feeling of loving someone, the unconditional emotion of loving and being loved. You shouldn't shackle yourself and deny yourself that experience. You are not living life to the full otherwise.'

'It's scary.'

'But the reward is magnificent – when you find the right person; but you won't do that unless you give yourself permission to try.' Lydia squeezed Fleur's hand. 'So many people have been denied that opportunity.'

Fleur knew Lydia was referring to the children who didn't survive the war. 'I know,' she said softly.

'Love without expectation or demand. Love fiercely and fearlessly.' Lydia put both hands over Fleur's own. 'And with the right person, you too will be loved in the same way.'

If Fleur could have thought of a response to Lydia's words, she would not have had the chance to share it. Didier appeared back at the table.

'Is everything all right?' he asked, his gaze flicking between the two women, before resting on Fleur.

She pulled her hands away from Lydia's. 'Everything is fine.' She avoided looking at Didier, just in case her eyes somehow revealed all her inner thoughts and the conversation she'd just had with her grandmother.

He made some sort of Gallic grunt, as if he didn't believe her, but then continued to report on his conversation. '*Alors*, I have spoken with the solicitor and he will see us now. Or as long as it takes for us to get there.'

'Oh, that's excellent,' said Lydia. 'Let's go. The more I think about this, the more I want to do it. I can't pretend I'm not a little nervous, scared even, but my mind has been made up for a long time now.'

'It is OK to be scared,' said Didier. 'It comes with being brave.'

'Indeed. They are bedfellows,' said Lydia.

Fleur rose from her seat and couldn't help wondering if both Lydia and Didier were aiming their coded observations her way. Well, they weren't being very subtle if they were.

They arrived outside the solicitor's office some twenty minutes later.

'I'll go in on my own,' said Lydia. 'You two can wait here. I won't be long.'

Didier escorted her to the door of the office and returned to the car. 'So, we are alone,' he said, as he sat back in his seat.

'I can't help thinking my grandmother has orchestrated it that way.'

'I think you are right.'

Fleur fiddled with the strap of her handbag. 'She's on a mission to save me.'

'From what?'

'From myself.'

'Ah. Yes. It seems that might be a task too far even for your grandmother.' Didier looked ahead as he spoke.

'If I'm honest, I don't know if I want saving. It's easier not to be saved.'

Didier turned in his seat to face her and reached over for her hand. 'Not easier, just safer. In your eyes anyway.' He leaned towards her so his face was only inches from her own. 'Sometimes you have to take a leap of faith.'

Fleur's breathing quickened. She only had to move a fraction and she would be kissing him. The idea was appealing. In fact it was more than appealing. She wasn't sure who moved first but the next thing she knew Didier's mouth was on hers. Her free hand cupped the side of his face, his stubble tickling her palm. The passion of their kiss intensified and Fleur closed her eyes as his hand slid underneath her hair to the nape of her neck.

Suddenly, she was very aware of what she was doing and pulled away.

Didier gave her a questioning look. '*Ça-va?*' he asked slowly.

Fleur nodded. 'Yes.'

Didier's concerned look intensified. 'Am I missing something?'

Fleur sat back in her seat with a sigh. 'What are we doing?'

'Enjoying each other's company? No?'

'Yes. But to what end?' She needed to get this clear for herself just as much as for Didier.

'*Alors*, if we're talking marriage,' began Didier and then burst out laughing at Fleur's shocked expression. 'I am joking, of course.'

She was glad of the light relief breaking the tension that was swirling around in the compact space of his car. 'What I mean is, are we about to have some sort of fling? A holiday romance?'

'A holiday romance,' echoed Didier. 'It is not exactly my style.'

'Let's be honest, we can't ever be any more than that and I don't know if I could handle just breaking it off after two weeks. I think it would be even more painful then. If we just leave things now, there's less chance of either of us getting hurt.'

'But don't you want to enjoy life while you can? Being scared is . . . is paralysing. How can you enjoy life if you are always scared?' He gave a sigh. 'I am not in the business of coercing anyone to have a relationship with me. If you don't want to, then I respect your wishes.'

'It's not that I don't want to,' blurted out Fleur. 'But I'm not very good at relationships. I'm cold and aloof. And distant. And . . .' She stopped speaking as Didier put his finger gently to her lips.

'I don't think you're any of those things,' he said. 'You're just scared. You're not completely broken, just a little fractured; that is all.'

His kindness was overwhelming. 'It's not the relationship that scares me, it's the loss that follows. It hurts too much.' Fleur brushed a runaway tear with her fingertips.

'Loss and pain remind us how much we cared, but it should also serve as a reminder of how much we enjoyed loving. Life would be boring if every day was the same and we didn't allow ourselves to feel any emotion.'

'You still believe in love despite being divorced, don't you?'

'Absolutely. I loved my ex-wife, just not enough, and it was the same for her. I believe there is an even greater love out there. I just need to find it. How can I do that if I stop looking? I'm willing to take the risk.'

'But what if you never find love?'

'That is not the question you should be asking,' said Didier. 'You should ask yourself, not if you never find love, but what if you do. At least that's what you told Lydia. What if you don't try? You will never know.'

'I don't see how we can be anything other than a fling. Not with us living in different countries,' said Fleur. 'We could just try to enjoy the time together while I'm here, but know from the start that is all it will be.'

'And after your stay here is over what happens then?'

'Well, I guess I go back to England and you stay here in France. We get on with our lives. It's going to be hard to do anything else.'

'*Non.*' Didier said the word fiercely.

Fleur looked at him questioningly. 'What do you mean no?'

'No, I do not want a two-week . . .' He waved his hand around in the air as if searching for the word.

'A fling?' offered Fleur.

'Yes. A fling. I don't like that. It is meaningless. A waste of time.'

'Honestly, I can't win!' exclaimed Fleur. 'Everyone is telling me to be brave but when I am, I'm shot down.'

'You are missing the point,' said Didier. 'If you want a fling, you need to have it with someone else. I don't want a throwaway relationship.'

'But how can it be anything else? We don't know each other properly, we live in different countries. What's so wrong with a fling?'

'I told you. It is not my style.'

Up until yesterday it hadn't been Fleur's thing either but it seemed she'd got it all wrong. She sat back in her seat. 'I told you I was rubbish at relationships.'

'A fling is not a relationship,' said Didier. 'You need to have a rethink.' He twisted in his seat to look at her. 'Fleur, you're right when you say we barely know each other, that we live in different countries. I know all that but I don't want you for two weeks and then walk away from you. It is not the sort of thing I do.' He leaned over and kissed the side of her head. 'Please don't be scared.'

A sharp rap at the car window from Lydia brought a stop to their conversation. She was back in the car before Didier had time to open the door for her.

'Glad to see you two have been talking,' she said, pulling the seatbelt across her. She placed a brown manila envelope on the seat. 'Can we go back to the hotel now? I think we should open this in private.'

'Of course,' replied Didier, starting the engine. He pulled out into the Parisian traffic, whisking them through the city streets and back to the hotel.

'This is what Manu left for me after his death in 1977,' said Lydia placing the envelope on the writing desk in Fleur's room. Fleur had suggested they look at it there, rather than down in reception or the lobby. She'd ordered tea and coffee for them to the room and had brought in a chair from Lydia's bedroom so they could all sit around the coffee table together. Lydia continued speaking. 'He told me he'd kept a secret record of the artwork the Germans had taken from the museum. After the war, he spent all his free time trying to track down the pieces of art and reunite them with the museum. It wasn't easy as a lot of the pieces went to private collectors, were destroyed or still to this day remain missing.'

'Like Valois's painting,' said Fleur.

'Precisely,' confirmed Lydia.

'And you've always known about this?' asked Didier.

'I've never seen the paperwork but I did know. As I said, Manu talked about it often.'

'Why did you not retrieve it before now? Someone else could have continued the search,' pressed Didier.

Fleur knew this information was like gold for Didier. It would be his dream to try to track down missing pieces of artwork, especially the Valois paintings, which originated from Manu's museum. She couldn't help feeling sorry for Didier.

'Sorry, I should have explained properly,' said Lydia. 'This is the original list that Manu made. He also made a duplicate, which he gave to the museum after the war so they could track down and claim stolen art through official channels.'

'Ah, that makes sense. I understand,' said Didier.

'After the war Manu worked for the museum for several more years but in the early 1950s he took another position at Musée du Louvre. Promotion.' There was a look of pride on Lydia's face as she spoke of Manu. 'You remind me of him,' she said to Didier.

'Thank you. I am very flattered. He sounds like he was a very brave and honourable man,' replied Didier.

'He was, indeed. He and Adele were so good to me. Sadly, they never had children of their own so I was like their daughter. They loved me very much and I loved them dearly too.' Lydia pressed a hand to her forehead.

Fleur moved to the side of her nan's chair. 'Are you OK, Nan? We can take a break from all this if you need it.'

'I'm all right,' insisted Lydia. She reached a shaky hand out for her glass of water and Fleur passed it to her. Lydia took several sips before placing it back on the table. 'We should open this envelope. I didn't know whether I would ever collect this from the solicitors. I never wanted to talk about that time, to share and explain my real name, but lately I've felt that if I take my secret to my grave, then the suffering and sacrifice was all for nothing as no one would know and there'd be no one to remember. It would be as if they never existed. I've known about the envelope since before Manu died but now you know my real name and I feel confident that you, Didier, are genuine and not some kind of con man, it feels right to show it to you.' She held the envelope out to Fleur. 'Perhaps you could open it.'

Fleur's hands shook a little themselves as she broke the seal. 'So no one has ever opened this,' she said. 'The last person to see the contents was Manu himself.'

'It somehow makes me feel closer to him,' said Lydia softly.

'You should be the first to look inside, Nan,' said Fleur. It felt right that her grandmother should see and touch the contents before anyone else. It was, after all, what Manu had intended.

Lydia slipped her hand inside the now opened envelope and removed an A4-sized leather-bound book. She untied the ribbon, opened the book and placed it on the table.

'May I?' asked Didier. Lydia nodded and the Frenchman picked up the book and began turning the pages. Fleur moved to sit next to him to see over his shoulder. As she did so, her foot touched something. She looked down and saw it was Didier's wallet lying open on the carpet. It must have fallen out of his trouser pocket. She reached down to pick it up and stopped. Where it had landed, the inside leaf had flipped over and the photograph was not the one of Didier as a gendarme that he had shown her when they first met, but of a baby. A little boy with big eyes and a dimple, just like Didier's.

'What is it, Fleur?' asked Lydia.

At the same moment, Didier noticed it and he scooped up his wallet. 'It must have fallen out of my pocket when I sat down.' He gave Fleur a sideways look and shoved it into the inside of his jacket, before returning his attention to the book in his hands.

For a moment Fleur wondered if she had imagined seeing a photograph of a child; but no, she definitely hadn't been seeing things. Why would he have a photo of a baby in his wallet? Was it his? He'd said he didn't have children, though. She realised Didier was talking to her and she forced her attention back to the book.

'This is amazing,' Didier was saying. 'Look, Fleur, it has the name of paintings and sculptures, the artist and where each one went. Germany. Berlin. Lyon.'

Fleur took a closer look, side-lining her thoughts on the photo in Didier's wallet for the time being. She noticed the red pen ticks next to many of the items. 'The ticks beside some of them – does that mean they've been found, do you think?'

'It might be. I'd have to check but it seems possible,' replied Didier. 'He was able to find lots of pieces by the look of it.'

'Are the Valois paintings there?' asked Lydia.

'I can't see them.' Didier continued to flick through the book. He stopped about two thirds of the way through. 'Wait. Here. The Valois collection is listed here.'

'And look. Their code is different. D. T. B. E. C,' Fleur read the letters out.

'Daniel. Thomas. Blanche. Eva and Cecile, Thomas's mother,' said Lydia. 'It was insurance. Manu gave each of us a painting. We were to use it as currency for safe passage. To bribe officials. To save our lives, if necessary. The miniatures were rolled up and sewn into the hems of our clothing.'

'When the paintings were recovered, was Manu able to find out about the children?' asked Didier, as he continued to look through the book.

Lydia nodded. 'The paintings were returned by a private collector. One with a conscience. He had inherited them from his father who was a German officer in the war. He had been awarded them for his efforts in breaking up a circuit. By that I mean a resistance group who were running pipelines. Routes of safety out of France.'

Didier blew out a long breath. 'And probably the escape route for the children?'

'*Oui. C'est ça.*'

'But Bridget Sutter aka Blanche must have escaped with her painting,' concluded Fleur. 'She must have avoided being caught somehow.'

'It is the only explanation,' agreed Lydia. 'Of course we did not know that then.'

'All the more reason to try to speak to her again,' said Fleur.

'This brings such a mix of emotion,' said Lydia. 'I am so sad for the other children – talking about it after all these years has brought the pain and fear back. Yet, I am beyond excited to think my sister might still be alive. But the happiness the thought brings also brings guilt. Whatever the other children went through, whatever Bridget Sutter or Blanche has endured, must be far worse than what I have gone through.'

'Sorry, Lydia.' It was Didier. 'Can I just clear something up? You were all given a Valois and according to Manu's book, you were given *Août*.'

'That's right,' replied Lydia.

'So, where is it? What happened to the painting?'

'I don't know,' she replied. 'In the end, I didn't need it. I just assumed Manu had it or it had got lost. You have to remember I was only ten years old. I didn't appreciate the value of the painting. So much happened, it was far from my mind.'

Fleur could see the disappointment in Didier's face. He was so close to finding out what happened to the watercolour and yet no closer than he was before.

'How come you didn't escape with the other children?' asked Fleur. 'How did you end up separated from your sister and yet stay with Adele and Manu? What happened to you?'

Lydia sat back in her chair and closed her eyes, taking deep breaths. Fleur exchanged a worried look with Didier and when she looked back at her grandmother, she was alarmed to see tears running down her face. Her head lolled from one side to the other and she let out a small groan. Fleur was horrified.

Didier reacted first, thrusting the book into Fleur's hands, he leapt to his feet and was at Lydia's side in a second. He was speaking French. Fleur didn't know what he was saying but his voice was low, calming yet assertive. He was sitting Lydia forwards and gently easing her head forwards. 'I think she was about to faint,' he said. 'She's OK. Don't panic.'

Somehow Fleur wasn't scared. She knew Didier had it all under control. She moved to her grandmother's other side. 'Nan? You OK? Are you feeling all right?'

The colour was returning to Lydia's face and she looked up at Fleur and then Didier. 'I'm so sorry,' she said.

'Please do not apologise,' instructed Didier.

Fleur handed her grandmother a glass of water. 'I think it's all been a bit too much for you the last few days,' she said. 'I'm sorry if I upset you by asking too many questions.'

'It's not you asking questions, *ma petite puce*,' said Lydia sitting up again and looking much better than she had a moment ago. 'It's me remembering things I have tried to suppress.'

'It is enough for today,' said Didier. 'You must rest and try not to upset yourself any more this evening.'

'I agree,' said Fleur.

'So do I,' said Lydia, offering a weak smile. She exhaled a long breath. 'I think I would like to retire for the evening. Fleur, would you mind helping me?'

'Of course.' Fleur got to her feet.

Didier rose too. 'I will leave you ladies for the evening. If you feel unwell, please call me or if it's urgent . . . *alors*, you know what to do.' At that moment, Didier's phone rang out. It vibrated across the table and Fleur couldn't help glance at it to see who was calling. She thought of the photograph and wondered if it was the child's mother who could well be Didier's partner. He picked up his phone. 'I should take this. Goodnight, Lydia. Fleur.'

Fleur watched as he left the room, the phone still ringing. As he closed the door behind him, she heard him answer. '*Salut*' was all she heard or even understood as his voice trailed off into the distance.

Lydia's voice broke her thoughts. 'What is it about him that's bothering you?'

'You're supposed to be unwell,' scolded Fleur with a mock-stern voice. 'Come on, let's get you to bed.'

'You didn't answer my question,' said Lydia as Fleur helped her to her feet.

'That's because I don't know the answer.' Fleur walked her grandmother through to her room. She might not know the answer now, but she was going to find out and sooner rather than later. In fact, the very next morning she'd do just that.

Chapter 31

Adele

Paris, July 1942

Adele made her way back to the table in something of a daze. She'd done a deal with the devil and now she was going to have to pay with her soul. In that short walk back across the restaurant floor, she made the most monumental decision she'd ever had to make in her life.

This time when she sat down next to Weld and he put his hand on the back of her chair, she didn't move away. And when his thumb strobed her bare shoulder blade, she sat exactly where she was. She even looked over and gave something resembling a smile. Adele caught her sister's gaze from across the table and recognised the small but not insignificant look Lucille threw her way. Lucille hadn't missed the change in Adele's body language.

The rest of the evening was even more painful for Adele than she imagined. However, she reminded herself that having to pretend she was attracted to Weld was a small price to pay for the safety of Cecile and the children.

Adele hadn't noticed Edith leaving, but when she next looked across at the table, it was empty. She wondered if Edith would tell Manu she'd seen her with Weld tonight. She'd have to explain to Manu what had happened, how she had been blackmailed into all this. Whether or not she'd say she'd seen Edith she didn't know, but Manu's opinion of her mattered.

'So, are we going to party at the bar this evening?' asked Weld, slightly slurring his words. His hand moved across her back and slipped down to her waist. Adele had to fight the urge to squirm away. There was no point being all prim about Weld at this point, not if she was going to have to have sex with him. She inwardly cringed at the thought. It wasn't that she hadn't had sex but it had been a couple of years now and at least she had actually liked the person.

'We shall go to the bar at the hotel,' said Müller, referring to the hotel he and several other officers had commandeered since their arrival in the city.

Lucille linked her arm through Adele's as they walked out to the awaiting car. 'What is going on?' she whispered.

'It's best if you don't ask,' said Adele.

'Come along, ladies,' encouraged Müller as he and Weld stood by the open car door.

From out of nowhere a motorbike came tearing down the road, screeching to a stop adjacent to Müller's car. Adele wasn't sure what happened next but there was a shout, followed by the sound of breaking glass and then an explosion from within Müller's car.

Adele and Lucille screamed simultaneously as the vehicle became engulfed in flames. They turned away, shielding their faces from the heat of the explosion. When Adele looked back, she could see Weld lying on the pavement, his face peppered with shards of glass. He was groaning as he rolled from his back and onto his belly like a walrus.

'Peter!' It was Lucille. She ran towards Müller who was on the ground too but not moving. Lucille threw herself down next to him. 'Peter! Peter!'

Adele held her breath. Was it wrong to wish him seriously injured, unconscious or even worse? The thought shook her. Why was she even thinking like that? It made her no better than Müller or any one of the Nazis whose value of another's life was so low it was practically non-existent.

She wasn't like them. Wishing death on Müller, or anyone for that matter, stripped Adele of the empathy for a fellow human and perhaps the most important value that prevented her from being no better than those she despised. She refused to allow herself to fall to that level of wickedness, no matter whose life was at stake. She was better than them.

Adele looked down the road to where the motorbike was disappearing out of sight.

People were rushing out onto the street from the restaurant to try to help or to escape from the commotion in fear of another attack. Adele said a silent prayer of thanks to whoever was on the motorbike and had chosen that moment to sabotage the rest of the evening for her.

She looked back at Weld who was now receiving medical attention from the waiting staff as he staggered to his feet, pushing them away. He was barking orders in German but Adele didn't know what he was saying. She looked back over at Müller, who had yet to move. Lucille was crouched over him and several other officers were attending to him. Within minutes an ambulance pulled up at speed, followed by several patrol cars. Officers were shouting orders, sending patrols off in all directions to look for the bombers, the fire was being put out in the car and Müller was being transferred onto a stretcher and then loaded into the back of the ambulance. Lucille was left stranded on the pavement, not able to go with him. She watched wordlessly as the ambulance sped away.

Adele went over to her and pulled her in for a hug.

'He's breathing,' sniffed Lucille. 'But he's not conscious. He must have taken the brunt of the explosion.'

A German officer came over to Lucille. 'Mademoiselle Basset?'

'*Oui*,' said both Adele and Lucille in unison.

The officer looked confused for a moment but addressed Lucille. 'I will let you know as soon as we have news of Hauptmann Müller.'

'Can I go to the hospital?' asked Lucille.

'I don't think that would be a good idea,' replied the officer.

'But I need to be there when he regains consciousness,' protested Lucille.

The officer looked between the two women and Adele registered his unease, knowing exactly what he didn't want to admit to Lucille. 'Let's go home tonight,' she said to her sister. 'There's nothing we can do.'

'No. I want to be at the hospital,' insisted Lucille.

'That is not possible,' said the officer.

Lucille straightened her back and lifted her chin defiantly. 'Hauptmann Müller will be very angry when he finds out I've not been allowed to be at his bedside.'

'As I said, that's not possible,' persisted the officer.

'Why?' Lucille shrugged Adele's hand away. 'Why can't I?'

'Because Madame Müller will be there,' said the exasperated officer.

'His mother?' Lucille looked confused.

'No. His wife. I will arrange for a car to take you ladies home,' said the officer and went to speak to a soldier.

Lucille opened her mouth and closed it without saying a word.

'Lucille,' began Adele.

Lucille was in no mood for listening. 'You knew, didn't you? You're not shocked or surprised at all! You knew Peter's wife was here. How dare you not tell me?!'

'Lucille, it's not like that,' began Adele.

'When did you know?'

'Let's not talk about it here.'

'Just tell me.'

'Lucille, please. This is not the time nor the place,' insisted Adele.

Before Lucille could argue further, the officer returned to them. 'My driver will take you both home now. Goodnight, ladies.'

As Adele and her sister made their way over to the waiting car, Adele looked over at the crowd of onlookers now gathered to watch the commotion. A figure a couple of rows back in the crowd caught her attention. It was Edith, standing at the side, half hidden in the shadows. She was looking at the car, which was now fully engulfed in flames despite the valiant attempts at it being extinguished. Then seemingly satisfied with what she'd seen, Edith pulled the brim of her hat lower over her face, turned and disappeared into the night.

Adele and Lucille were hurried into the waiting car, which sped away, whisking them to the safety of their apartment.

Their father was waiting up for them and was initially concerned but then relieved they had made it home safely. 'So it was a direct attack on Peter?' he asked, accepting the coffee Adele had made for them all. She sat down next to her sister, who was biting her lip and fretting over Peter.

'I don't know. Why would anyone want to do that to him?' she asked. She got to her feet, wringing her hands together. 'They wouldn't let me go to the hospital. His wife is here. Can you believe that? His wife? The wife that my dear sister didn't tell me about.' She paced across the chenille rug and then back again. 'Why is she here?'

Adele exchanged a look with her father, but neither voiced their thoughts. 'Maybe the other officer was their target,' suggested Gérard, obviously wanting to divert Lucille's attention from the topic of Müller's wife.

'Weld? Again, why?' Lucille rubbed her eyes with her fingertips. 'None of it makes sense.'

'It might have been a random attack and thank goodness for the timing. A moment later and we would have been in the car,' said Adele.

Lucille spun around to face her sister. 'You don't think whoever it was, was actually trying to get us?'

'Why would they do that?' asked Gérard.

There was a small pause in the room as everyone realised why they would be targeted. It was Adele who voiced it though. 'Because we are seen as collaborators. You because of your relationship with Peter and me because it looked like I was with Weld.'

'But how would they know we were there? No, it can't be an attack on us,' said Lucille.

'That is true,' said Adele. 'Unless someone tipped off the Resistance, or whoever threw the bomb. Someone who saw us in the restaurant.' She cast her mind back to the restaurant and Edith sitting on the far side and then again standing in the crowd. Did she somehow get word to the culprits that Adele and Lucille were there with two German officers? Was she then hanging around afterwards to make sure things had been done properly – to make sure Adele and her sister were either killed or seriously injured? Adele shuddered at the thought that someone might actually want them dead.

She got up from the sofa and hurried out to her room, ignoring the questioning calls from her sister and father. In her room, she quickly stripped off the dress and put on her everyday clothes, then she left her room, slipping her jacket on as she went.

'What are you doing?' asked her father.

'I have to go out. I won't be long.'

'But it's nearly curfew,' he protested.

'Don't worry. I'll be back in time.' With that Adele hurried out of the apartment and down the stairs.

Whether it was her imagination or heightened anxiety, Adele noticed far more patrols as she made her way through the streets. She didn't want to appear in a hurry but nor did she want to take her time. She'd heard about what happened to some women when they were stopped alone in the evenings.

Fortunately, her destination was just a ten-minute walk and she arrived safely outside the building.

The main door was open and she stepped into the foyer and made her way up the stairs, coming to a halt outside one of the apartment doors.

She rapped her knuckles on the door.

Knock. Knock. Knock-knock.

Adele was aware her breathing had sped up and that wasn't from the walk to get here, but from the nerves she was tamping down inside her. Suddenly, she doubted her wisdom in coming here but it was too late now.

A door opened further down the hallway.

Adele kept her gaze trained on the door, not wanting to look around in case she appeared guilty. Neighbours would snitch on each other out of desperation for extra food rations these days.

'Adele.' The voice from the open door made her jump. She looked around and was surprised to see Manu standing there. He hurried down the hall to her. 'What are you doing here?'

Adele looked from the door she was standing in front of to the one Manu had appeared from. She'd somehow got the wrong apartment. Manu took her arm and hurried her down the hallway and into the other door. He asked her again, 'What are you doing here?'

Adele looked around her. 'I thought you lived next door.'

Manu gave a ghost of a smile. 'I do. I have this apartment too so I can see if I want to open the door or not to unexpected visitors.' Now he raised his eyebrows in question at her. 'Please, tell me, what's the matter?' He held her at arm's length and looked her up and down. 'Are you all right? You're not hurt?'

'Hurt? Why would I be hurt?'

He gave a shrug. 'I don't know. What's brought you here at this time of the evening? I thought you were out.'

Adele narrowed her eyes. 'Out? How do you know I was out?'

If she hadn't been studying him carefully, she may have missed the fleeting glimmer of guilt dart across his face, swiftly replaced by one of innocence. 'I guessed you were. Edith saw you getting into a car with Müller outside the school.'

So Edith had been spying on her. Did Edith confess to being with another man? Adele bet she hadn't but she wasn't here for that. There was far more at stake. 'That's another story,' said Adele. 'It's the children. Müller knows they are in the school attic. Or at least he knows Eva is there. And he changed his mind about having the other children perform at the exhibition. I don't know how we're going to smuggle the others out now.'

'Wait a minute. One thing at a time,' said Manu. 'How does he know about the children at the school?'

'He was suspicious. I don't know if someone told him or he suspected but he came to the school and one of the children in the attic made a noise. I know he heard it. When he was leaving, he looked up at the attic window. When I looked up, Eva was standing there. He must have seen her. There was no way he couldn't have.'

Manu pinched the bridge of his nose. 'The exhibition. It doesn't matter if the other children don't perform with you. We can still smuggle out those in the attic.' Manu exhaled a long breath. 'I'm more worried about what happens to them now. Has Müller ordered a search of the school?'

'No. That's just it. He didn't do anything. He was supposed to be taking Lucille for dinner and he said I should go with him, that he had a friend he wanted me to meet.'

A tiny pulse throbbed in the side of Manu's cheek. 'The friend. Another German officer,' he said.

'Yes. Müller wants me to be . . . how shall I say? He wants me to be accommodating to Weld – that's his friend. In exchange for his silence about the children.'

Manu's face hardened. 'And what did you say?'

'What could I say? I had to agree.'

He shook his head. 'No. Adele. You didn't have to.'

'Actually, I did. If it keeps the children safe, then I don't care. I'm prepared to do that. It's a small sacrifice.'

Manu clenched his fists and kicked out at the table beside him. 'NO!' And then in a calmer voice. 'No, Adele. You must not do that. I won't let you.'

Adele was shocked by the outburst from Manu; she didn't

ever remember him showing his temper like that before. 'You can't stop me!'

'Adele, please. It would break my heart if you did.'

She gave a laugh. 'Break your heart? How can you say that when you are in love with Edith?'

A door behind Adele opened and she spun around to see Edith walking into the room from the adjoining door to Manu's apartment. 'You should tell her,' said Edith to Manu, taking a cigarette from the packet in her hand and lighting it. She walked across the room and stood by the window, casually inhaling and exhaling the smoke. 'She should know the truth.' And then to Adele: 'Ask him why he had to get rid of his jacket this evening? He should tell you that he spilt petrol on it.'

Chapter 32

Adele

'Tell me what?' demanded Adele. Fear churned in her stomach. Had Edith betrayed her? Did Manu already know?

Manu took a deep breath, exchanged a glance with Edith before finally speaking. 'I have not been honest with you,' he said. 'I have deceived you and, for that, I am truly sorry.'

Adele had to force herself to concentrate on his words. He had deceived her. Oh God, he'd betrayed her to the Germans. He'd told Müller or Weld or someone about Cecile and the children. How could he do that? 'What have you done?' she whispered, needing to hear it from him.

Again there was an uncomfortable look between Manu and Edith. 'I've allowed you to believe that Edith and I are a couple. That she was my girlfriend,' began Manu. 'That is not true.'

Adele frowned. She hadn't been expecting that. 'You're not?'

'No,' it was Edith. 'It's a front. A cover. We are both working for the Resistance. Sometimes it's easier for us to go unnoticed when appearing as a couple.'

'We've had to keep the charade up all the time,' said Manu. 'The fewer people who know the truth, the easier it is to keep the lie and not draw others into it.'

'Even me?'

'Even you. You most of all. I did not want you to be involved in any way and if you were ever questioned, how could you knowingly lie if you didn't know the truth? I thought it was a way to keep you safe.' Manu sat down on the sofa.

'That was until you took the Jews in,' said Edith. 'That's complicated matters because now all Manu can do is worry about you.'

'He doesn't need to,' retorted Adele, having the distinct impression she was being told off by the other woman.

'He can't help it.' Edith let out a sigh and drew on her cigarette. She walked across the room back towards the internal door. 'He's in love with you.' She closed the door behind her, leaving Adele staring at Manu.

'What does she mean?' She finally managed to force the words from her mouth.

Manu got to his feet and, for the first time, looked uneasy, almost nervous. This wasn't the Manu Adele was used to seeing. He rubbed at his jaw with his hand and let out a long breath. 'She means that I'm in love with you,' he said slowly.

'I ... What ... But ...' Putting a sentence together – that was proving impossible for Adele.

Manu walked over to her. 'It's true. Everything Edith said. My romantic relationship with her is just a front.' He took Adele's hands and lifted them to his lips, kissing her knuckles. 'I love you.'

'I don't understand,' began Adele. 'How? How are you in love with me?' Her heart was jumping with joy but her mind was urging caution. It wasn't possible that Manu loved her. It would be beyond her dreams if he was. It was something she had dreamt about over the years but he was always out of her reach because he only thought of her in a kid sister way.

'I've known you for so many years and, yes, at first, it was a brotherly type of love but after I returned from working in Europe, you weren't that young girl anymore. You were a young woman.' His gaze never left her as he spoke. 'It was like I was seeing you anew, with fresh eyes.'

'Why didn't you ever tell me?' Adele was having a hard time taking all this in.

'I didn't know how. I didn't want to frighten you off, especially if you didn't feel the same way about me. I had so many doubts. What if you thought of me only as a friend? If I told you and you rejected me, how would we ever come back from that? I'd sooner have you as a friend, who I could love from afar and watch over, than never be able to speak to you again. That would be too painful.'

'So why are you telling me now?' She wanted to fall into his arms, to embrace him, to kiss him but she had to understand him and be certain of his feelings.

'I wanted to tell you before the war broke out and I was foolishly taking too much time, because I didn't want to scare you off. Then the Germans came and I became involved with the Resistance, I didn't think it was fair to drag you into it. What could I promise you? If I was killed, you'd be left with the deepest of grief, and I didn't want that for you.'

Adele gave a small smile. 'Just because we haven't declared our love to each other, doesn't mean I wouldn't feel bereft if I were to lose you. The loss would be greater as I would regret never having told you how I feel. Never letting you know that I love you too.'

'You do?' His face lit up in a way she hadn't seen in a long time.

'Yes! I do! I tried to tell you this the other night, but you wouldn't let me.' Adele threw her arms around Manu's neck and he pulled her to his chest and then tilted her chin up to him and kissed her.

The sound of the door opening again had Adele and Manu pulling apart.

'I hate to break up the party, but now we've got Manu's love life sorted, can we get back to why you are here?' said Edith.

Buoyed by the kiss from Manu and the knowledge that he loved her, Adele found a forthrightness she hadn't been expecting. 'Actually, I came to warn Manu about you,' she said.

'Me!' Edith gave a snort.

283

'Adele.' Manu's tone was filled with caution.

'Did Edith tell you she was at the restaurant having dinner with a German officer?' Adele asked.

'Yes. She did actually.'

There was a faint look of amusement on Manu's face, which made Adele cross. 'Did she tell you what happened there?'

'Of course I did,' said Edith with a sigh. 'Manu was there too.'

'What?' Adele was confused now.

'Let me explain,' said Manu. 'Edith has a close relationship with a German officer who is sympathetic to our cause. She was having dinner with him and saw you. When you went to the bathroom, her friend went over and spoken to Weld, who was only too happy to brag about his new companion, meaning you.'

'Weld was looking forward to taking you back to his hotel room,' said Edith.

Adele felt a small flush of embarrassment to her face but she stood a little straighter. 'So, as I said, I was prepared to do whatever was needed to keep the children safe.'

'I had already got a message to Manu to say you were in the restaurant,' said Edith. 'I knew he would want to know.'

'I'm glad she did. I got there just in time to cause a little distraction,' said Manu. He reached out for Adele's hand. 'I'm so relieved you weren't injured in any way and I'm sorry to frighten you, but I could not let you go back with Weld.'

Adele didn't know what to say. She was both flattered and annoyed at the same time. 'Whilst I appreciate it, you put yourself at great risk,' she said eventually. 'What if you had been caught? Anyway, it is only putting off the inevitable. You can't throw car bombs at Weld every time he turns up for me.'

'That is not happening!' Manu almost shouted, making Adele jump. He took a deep breath. 'You do not have to do that. I have a plan.'

Adele listened intently as Manu explained to her what he wanted them to do. 'Tomorrow morning, I will leave some packing crates outside by the wall. You go to school like you usually do, nice and early, and take Cecile and the children out through the side door, help them climb over the wall and hide in the crates. I'll bring the crates into the museum and hide them in a room in the cellar until all the items from the museum are ready to be packed for the exhibition and transported to Lyon. Cecile and the children will be hidden in those packing crates.'

The hedonistic moment of Manu declaring his feelings for her left Adele as the thought of what lay ahead for Cecile and the children sobered her. 'What happens when we get to Lyon?'

'There will be someone there to help us. Some of the pieces are not being used for the exhibition but going on to Germany. So not everything will be unpacked. The boxes for Cecile and the children will be marked with an "x" in the top left corner. Once the exhibition is in full swing, my associates will be there to release them and take them out through the underground sewers.'

'So, I won't see them?' asked Adele thinking how the Rashal girls, Daniel, Cecile and Thomas were going to disappear into the night and she'd never know what happened to them.

'No, I'm sorry. We must carry on as if we know nothing,' said Manu.

'That way if something goes wrong, you won't be connected,' put in Edith.

'There's just one thing that's bothering me,' said Adele. There was a loose end, which hadn't been accounted for.

'Go on,' urged Manu.

'Edith went into a building. We saw her. You followed and said it was nothing. Is that true or is there something you're still not telling me?'

'Ah, yes, that.' Manu grimaced. 'I'm sorry but I couldn't tell you the truth then. Edith went there to meet her German officer. The one who isn't very good at keeping secrets when faced with someone like Edith.'

Adele was both relieved and annoyed, although she tried

to hide the latter. She didn't like to think Manu had lied to her. It made her wonder if he had lied about anything else, but there was no point in going over everything he'd ever told her. 'I see,' she said. 'I understand but please don't ever keep anything from me again. No lies.'

'No lies,' repeated Manu.

Edith gave an exaggerated yawn. 'Can we get back to business? The reason why we are all skulking around?'

'Of course,' said Manu. 'Now, the guests in the attic. We need to concentrate on getting them to safety. As soon as they are over the wall, you must go up to the attic and clear every last scrap of evidence that could show they were there. And then you are to refuse Weld.' Manu looked her straight in the eye. '*Oui?*'

Adele nodded. '*Oui.*'

'Müller and Weld will be furious, of course, so be prepared for them to ransack the school, especially if Müller has seen Eva.' He paused and concern filled his eyes.

'What's wrong?' asked Adele.

'I don't want to scare you, but you could be in danger from Müller or Weld.'

'Müller won't hurt me,' said Adele with rather more confidence than she felt. She didn't want Manu to have to start worrying about her. 'I have something on him that he won't want me to divulge. It's my security.'

'What's that?' Manu frowned.

'His wife is in Paris and I'm sure he won't want her to hear about his affair with my sister.'

'I thought his marriage was over,' said Manu.

'That's what he told Lucille, but I saw him in the restaurant kissing his wife. At least I assume it's his wife, but whether it's another lover or not, the fact remains, he won't want her finding out about Lucille.'

'Have you told Lucille what you saw?' asked Manu.

'No. I didn't want to hurt her and as it happens, it's come in useful as a bargaining chip.'

'*Bravo.*' Edith clapped her hands slowly. 'So the little sparrow is actually a sparrow hawk.'

Adele took a deep breath. She'd like to tell Edith to shut up and that her less than enthusiastic applause wasn't appreciated, but she didn't want to cause tension between the three of them. They still had to get Cecile and the children out of Paris. Whatever happened, that was her priority. Now she knew that Edith wasn't actually Manu's girlfriend, she suddenly didn't care about the woman.

'Let me take you home now,' said Manu. 'It's getting late and you'll be caught after curfew.'

'And you will be caught coming back home,' said Adele. 'I'll be fine. I'll go on my own.'

Edith gave a sigh. 'Why don't you just stay? Honestly, you two . . .' She tutted and returned once again to the other apartment. 'I am a heavy sleeper.' She closed the door behind her and Adele heard the key turn in the lock.

Manu took her hands in his. 'You don't have to stay, if you don't want to, but I'm not letting you walk home on your own.'

'And I'm not letting you walk back on your own. Not tonight.' She swallowed and looked around the apartment and the open door leading to the bedroom beyond. There was a double bed and a small table next to it with a lamp.

Manu turned to follow her gaze. 'If you prefer, you can sleep in the bedroom and I'll sleep on the sofa.'

Adele couldn't help the smile that caught her mouth. 'Why would I want you to sleep on the sofa when you've just told me you love me?'

Manu's grin stretched across his face. 'I was being a gentleman.'

'You need to stop that,' said Adele. She gave a squeal as Manu picked her up and carried her through into the bedroom, back-heeling the door behind him.

Chapter 33

Fleur

Paris, August 2015

It was spying. No two ways about it, but Fleur didn't care. Besides, she liked to think of it as safeguarding herself. She needed to know more about Didier before she could trust him further. The photograph in his wallet had niggled her, probably more than it should. It had also stirred up the suspicions she had been trying to ignore since first meeting him. He'd been hiding something, she was sure, but whether this was connected with her grandmother's story and the shoe, Fleur didn't know. However, finding out whether Didier was lying to them was a good mark of the man. Fleur ignored the fact that she was wanting to find out for her own benefit as much as for her grandmother.

Fleur had checked the location of Didier's antique shop earlier that morning using the app on her phone and was pleased to see it was the same arrondissement as the hotel. In fact, a little research had told her the road where it was situated, rue de Saints Pères, was the hotspot for antique shops in the city. It was only a twenty-five-minute walk from their hotel on rue de Pont Neuf. The walk would do Fleur good. She needed to get out of the hotel as sitting around reading her book, although a lovely pastime, wasn't her priority right now.

'Are you sure you'll be OK?' she asked Lydia, after

escorting her grandmother to one of the sitting rooms that overlooked the courtyard garden at the rear of the hotel.

'Absolutely certain,' replied Lydia. 'I'm rather more tired than I expected to be. I'd like a little bit of time to myself, to sit and reflect.' She reached for Fleur's hand. 'You're not offended, are you, *ma petite puce*?'

'Of course I'm not, Nan.' Fleur perched on the chair next to her grandmother. 'You do know if at any time all this gets too much for you we can stop. We can tell Didier we don't want to pursue whatever it is we're doing anymore. We can just go back to our original plan of visiting some of the places that are special to you and quietly remember what happened in the past. You don't even have to talk about it to me, if you don't want to. If it's all too painful, it's really all right not to.'

Much as Fleur wanted to know more about her grandmother's past and for her to have some sense of closure, she didn't want it to come at the price of Lydia's health, mental or physical.

Lydia gave a diluted smile and nodded gently. 'Thank you. You're very thoughtful. Just like your mother.' She looked out of the window at the gardens beyond.

Fleur followed her gaze, admiring the glorious riot of colours from the dahlias, hydrangeas and roses all in full bloom planted around the edge of the courtyard, shaded slightly from the hot Parisian sun by the four plane trees in the centre.

'Your mother loved gardening. Not vegetables. She liked beautiful, colourful flowers,' said Lydia wistfully. 'That's why she named you Fleur.'

It wasn't the first time Fleur had heard that from her grandmother and she knew it was supposed to be some sort of comfort for her, but it never quite had that effect. It just made Fleur sad and with that came the anger that her mother wasn't here. That she'd had to grow up without a mother and that Lydia had to live without a daughter. Fleur's heart contracted a fraction as she looked at her grandmother, seemingly small and vulnerable in the deep-seated chair.

Fleur wasn't sure this trip had been a good idea at all. She wondered if it always made her grandmother melancholy. She moved the side table with the teapot, cup and saucer closer to Lydia and poured her a cup. 'I can stay and just sit quietly here,' she said. 'You don't have to talk. I can just be here.'

Lydia smiled at Fleur. 'I'm perfectly fine. You don't have to worry about me.' She settled herself in her chair. 'I'm very happy here with my own company.' She leaned her head back and closed her eyes, an unspoken signal that the conversation was over.

Fleur kissed her nan on the cheek, knowing it would be pointless to argue, and headed out of the hotel.

Of course, Didier's shop had to be almost at the other end of the road to where Fleur found herself some thirty minutes later. She had taken the more scenic route alongside the river and passing the rear of the Musée du Louvre, where through the three archways she could see the famous glass pyramid. Another time, she would have been tempted to take a closer look, but sightseeing wasn't her priority that morning.

She walked southwards along the street, passing several antique shops, restaurants and cafés, keeping an eye out for Didier's green double-front shop, which she had seen on his website.

Fleur was just beginning to think she had somehow walked too far and missed it, when she spotted the shop across the road. The door was flanked by two full-sized windows, both with a half-circle window fanning out like peacock feathers. The gold lettering above the door and on the glass declared it was *Maison Dacourt Antiquités*.

A red velvet chair took centre stage in one of the windows, alongside a small mahogany table, a globe, a lamp and other props all set up to represent a formal sitting room. The other window was dedicated to several watercolours, where a landscape of the French countryside and a chateau dominated the space.

From her position across the road, she could see figures moving around inside the building, but couldn't make out who they were. To try to make herself less conspicuous, Fleur took out her phone and pretended to be taking a call as she surveyed the shopfront. The door opened and a man, probably a customer, left the premises.

Fleur really needed to get closer to try to see who was inside and whether it was Didier. She crossed the road, passing Didier's car, which was parked a couple of spaces down from the shop, and came to a stop at the window displaying the furniture. A woman was standing in the shop with her back to Fleur. Her long dark hair was tightly braded in a beautifully intricate weave over her scalp and then drawn up onto her head where it was secured like a ponytail with more braids.

The woman was wearing a fuchsia pink trouser suit and as she turned to look at something that had caught her attention, Fleur appreciated the beauty of the woman's side profile. She was possibly a little younger than Fleur but oozed sophistication and style. Very chic, indeed.

Fleur was surprised when the woman bent down and picked up a young child, probably around eighteen months old. It was a little boy with a mass of gorgeous black curls and huge brown eyes. The woman sat him on her hip as she appeared to talk to someone else in the shop. Fleur couldn't see who the woman was talking to and moved further along the window to get a clearer view.

A figure moved out into the shop to stand in front of the woman and it was then Fleur could see it was Didier. He smiled at the child and then with the ease of someone who'd done it a hundred times before, lifted the boy from the mother's arms and into his own. He said something to the child, before kissing the top of his head and passed him back to his mother.

Fleur's stomach tightened at the scene and then as Didier exchanged a kiss with the woman, albeit it on her cheek, her stomach tightened some more.

An unexpected and unwelcome feeling of jealousy made itself known to Fleur. She pushed it away, telling herself she didn't do jealousy and it was really indignation in disguise, which she promoted to anger. The latter she was much more versed in where her heart was concerned.

She realised then that Didier was walking towards the door, preparing to leave. He had his phone in his hand and was tapping at the screen. Almost instantly Fleur's phone burst into life from within the depths of her bag, making her jump. She fumbled in her bag for her phone and dived into the doorway of the shop next door before Didier spotted her.

Didier's name appeared on her screen and she switched it to silent, waiting for the voicemail to cut in. Fleur could hear Didier's shop door open and close. With her back still turned to the street, she could hear Didier's voice as he walked past her.

'*Salut, Fleur. Ça-va?* I was wondering . . .'

There was a pause. She still didn't dare move. Then she heard his voice again. This time right behind her.

'I was wondering why you were hiding in the doorway of the shop next to mine.'

Fleur closed her eyes, wishing this was just a bad dream. How embarrassing to be caught snooping. She took a deep breath, reminding herself why she was snooping and what she had witnessed just now in the shop. In fact, she had no reason to be embarrassed. If anyone should feel sheepish, it should be Didier. She turned and faced him without smiling, standing a little taller and lifting her chin up defiantly.

'If you must know, I came to check you out,' she said. 'To see if you were genuine or not.'

Didier's brown eyes studied her for several long moments. He cut the call and slipped his phone into his pocket. 'And what did you decide?'

Fleur raised her eyebrows to underline how ridiculous the question was. 'Judging by what I just saw through the window, I'd say not.' She was daring him to challenge her. In fact, she was up for a fight. With every second, her indignation at being duped and the embarrassment of allowing herself to kiss him and not only kiss him but bloody enjoy it too, morphed into anger. She'd made a complete fool of herself and she should know better than to let herself get drawn in by him.

'And what exactly did you see through the window?' he asked casually. He wasn't showing the slightest bit of remorse or embarrassment. He slid his hands into the pockets of his trousers. 'I'm interested to know.'

Fleur blew out an irritated breath. He was just being bloody arrogant now. 'I'll tell you what I saw,' she said, taking a step closer to him so she didn't have to bellow across the pavement at him. 'I saw you with your partner and child. Kissing them both. Now it may be a very French thing for a man to have a wife or a partner plus a bit on the side, but it's not a thing I'm OK with.'

He frowned. 'A bit on the side?'

'A mistress. A lover. A secret girlfriend.' Fleur threw her hands outwards. 'I don't plan to be any of those so that kiss we had – you can just forget about it. That is going nowhere. Not even a fling! Understood?'

He looked like he was trying to hold back a smile, which just served to infuriate Fleur even further. 'Just to make myself clear, I don't want any involvement with you whatsoever. Not on the personal side anyway. If my grandmother still wants to work with you to find out about the shoe, then that's up to her, but I don't want anything to do with you.'

Didier reached out and gently placed a hand on Fleur's shoulder and moved her a little closer to him so a passing couple could get by. 'This is not really the time or place to have this discussion,' he said quietly. 'I have a meeting I cannot be late for. Perhaps we can discuss this properly later.'

Fleur shrugged his hand from her. 'There isn't anything to discuss.'

'I disagree but I don't have the time to explain.' He glanced at his watch as if to emphasise his point. 'Can I call you later?'

'That will be a no.' With that Fleur turned and strode off down the street. He hadn't even tried to deny it. What an idiot she'd been to believe him. And that, sadly, was the mark of the man – he couldn't be trusted.

Chapter 34

Adele

Paris, July 1942

Adele awoke the next morning and, for a moment, couldn't work out where she was. She knew she wasn't in her own bed. Then she remembered. How could she forget? She stretched out a hand across the bed, but Manu wasn't there.

'*Bonjour*,' came his voice.

She opened her eyes and rolled onto her back. Manu was coming into the room with a cup of coffee. He placed it on the bedside table, before sitting down on the edge of the bed next to her. He brushed her hair from her face and trailed a finger down her bare arm.

'*Bonjour*,' she replied, with a smile. She looked towards the window but the curtains were drawn. 'What time is it?'

Manu leaned forward and kissed her. 'I'm sorry. It's very early. We need to leave soon.'

Adele suddenly remembered Cecile and the children at the school. She sat upright, feeling guilty she had been luxuriating in thoughts of Manu and the night before when other people's lives were in danger. 'Oh, we must hurry,' she said, pushing the bed sheet and blanket from her and then, remembering she was naked, hurriedly pulling them back over her.

Manu gave a laugh. 'I think it's a bit late to be shy and modest.' He kissed her again and Adele was sure he would only have to slip back between the sheets and she would not turn him away. 'I love you, Adele,' Manu said earnestly as he broke from the kiss.

'I know,' she replied. 'I love you too.'

'Why did we wait this long?'

She shook her head. 'I've no idea but I'm glad we didn't wait any longer.' This time when she got up from the bed, she did try to hide her body but picked her clothes up from the floor where they had been abandoned the previous evening and took them through to the bathroom where she washed and dressed.

At precisely six o'clock when the curfew was lifted, they made their way to the school. Adele wondered if her father would be worried about her, and not telling him she was safe was her only regret from the night before. She'd see him soon enough though when he came into school in a few hours' time.

They reached the school some thirty minutes later and parted company at the gates. 'See you around the back as soon as possible.'

Adele hurried into the school, making sure no one was watching her, and locked the door behind her. She ran up the stairs through the dance hall and moved the bookcase door open.

'Cecile! Cecile!' she called as she hurried up the narrow wooden staircase.

'What's wrong?' Cecile was on her feet, a panic-stricken look on her face. The children were sitting on a blanket eating some bread.

'We have got to move you,' explained Adele as she began gathering up the various toys and clothes and bedding that were scattered around the attic room. 'We haven't got much time.'

Cecile grabbed Adele's arm. 'Adele, calm down. You're frightening the children.' She looked over at the apprehensive faces, all now staring at the two women.

'Sorry,' said Adele. She took a steadying breath. She spoke

in a low voice, with her back turned to the children. 'Müller saw Eva at the window last night.'

'What?!' Cecile's hand flew to her chest. 'How?'

'He was suspicious. He heard movement from the attic when he came to watch Lucille and I practising. On his way out, he happened to look up at the rooftop. He didn't say anything but later that evening, he made it perfectly clear he had seen her.' Adele went on to quickly explain about the car bomb. She omitted to tell Cecile about the deal she'd done with Müller and that she'd spent the night with Manu – it wasn't relevant. What was important right now was moving them to the museum. 'So, we need to go as quickly as possible. I don't know if he's regained consciousness and told anyone what he saw but I'm not willing to take any chances. Besides, it's only a matter of time before they are discovered. No one can stay hidden forever,' she said once she relayed the condensed version of events. 'But we can't take any chances.'

Cecile nodded. 'I'm so sorry, Adele. That was my fault. I should have been watching her. It's just hard to look after them all, keep them quiet and know what they are doing all the time when it's just me.'

Adele gave her friend a hug. 'It's all right. It's a horrid situation. Let's get everything packed up as quickly as possible. I'm scared they will come early to search the school. Or just after it's opened, just to let everyone know what they are doing and scare everyone.'

The two women gathered the belongings of the children in a more orderly manner, with Adele making it into a game, encouraging the children to help collect up their toys. Putting what little possessions they had and few changes of clothes into one bag. Adele gave Cecile the papers for her and the children.

'We'd better go,' said Adele, giving the attic one final look around.

'Where are we going?' asked Blanche.

297

Adele crouched down in front of Blanche and fastened the buttons on her coat. 'We're going on a little adventure. You've all been so good here in the school attic that we thought it was about time we took you somewhere different.' She injected as much enthusiasm in her voice as she could muster. 'You're going to spend the night in the museum. How does that sound?'

'The museum?' Daniel stepped closer. 'Is it scary in there at night-time?'

Adele reached out and took his hand, drawing him in towards her. 'No, not at all. Besides, you won't be there on your own. Cecile will be with you.'

'Will Mama know where I am?' he asked.

Adele exchanged a glance with Cecile before answering. 'I'll make sure she knows.' She hated lying to the child. '*Allez, allez, allez,*' she called out. 'Follow me!'

She led the party out of the attic and down the stairs to the ground floor, where she unlocked the side door. Adele peered out. The dawn was just leaving and it was growing light outside. They needed to hurry before any early birds saw them. She went over to the wall and arranged the boxes so they formed steps.

'Ah, there you are.' Manu appeared on the other side of the wall. 'We need to hurry.'

One by one, Adele ferried the children from the doorway, across the alleyway and up over the wall to Manu, with Cecile the last one over.

'Thank you,' she whispered to Manu as she rearranged the boxes so it wasn't obvious they had been used as steps.

'Go inside now. I will try to see you later,' said Manu. 'And, Adele, try not to worry. Act as normal as possible.'

Adele's father was relieved to see her when he arrived at the school that morning. 'I'm glad you're all right,' he said. 'I was worried.'

'I'm sorry, Papa. I didn't mean to worry you but it was late and I got caught up with the curfew.'

'As long as you are safe.' He eyed her steadily. 'And you are safe, aren't you?'

Adele offered a lukewarm smile. 'As safe as anyone can be.'

It wasn't long after the children had been called in to class, that a German search party arrived at the school.

Adele was surprised to see Müller striding across the playground. There was a small graze on his forehead and a few minor cuts and lacerations on his right cheek, but apart from that he appeared unharmed.

He came to a stop in front of Adele's father. 'I apologise, Monsieur Basset,' he said, ignoring Adele as she stood in the hallway alongside Madame Allard and Michelle, the other schoolteacher. 'But we are carrying out routine searches in the area as we've had reports of Jews being hidden. I'm just carrying out my orders.'

Gérard didn't look at Adele and remained poker-faced. 'I understand you have a job to do. My concern is for the safety and wellbeing of my pupils. I don't want them frightened by your men storming through the building,' he replied. 'Would you allow them to gather in the dance studio where we can play games and distract them?'

Müller appeared to consider the schoolmaster's request for a moment before agreeing. 'Very well. Take them now. One of my men will accompany each member of staff.' He turned to Adele. 'Please wait here. I would like to speak to you.' Adele did as requested and waited patiently for the foyer to empty as the soldiers accompanied her father and Michelle Joffre to gather the pupils in the dance studio.

'I wanted to speak to you about last night,' began Müller. 'I hope you are feeling all right this morning, after yesterday evening's trouble.'

'Yes, I'm very well, thank you,' replied Adele. 'As I hope you and Weld are too.' She didn't hope at all but she had to keep this charade of concern up.

'Yes. Unfortunate what happened and we still can't find the culprits. Anyway, Weld is recovering from a few minor injuries but he will be looking forward to your company very soon. In fact, he is going to accompany us to Lyon for the exhibition. It was the least I could do to make up for last night, don't you think?'

Adele swallowed the ball of disgust that lodged in her throat before forcing out a cordial reply. 'That is good news.'

'I thought you'd be pleased.' Müller gave a smile that was devoid of any warmth. 'Now, we'd better get on with this search.'

Within a few minutes Adele had taken her class up to the dance studio under the supervision of a soldier. Adele sat at the piano and played some traditional French songs, which the children joined in with. She was tempted to play the French National Anthem but decided that wouldn't go down too well and she didn't want to anger Müller.

After about fifteen minutes, Müller came marching into the dance room. Adele stopped playing and the singing faded away. Müller came to a halt at the piano. 'My men have checked every room,' he announced. 'And we have found no one.'

Adele remained silent. The atmosphere in the room was tense and she knew Müller hadn't finished yet. There was something else. He continued. 'They even searched the attic. It's strange, I went up to the attic myself and I noticed there are two windows. Do you agree, Adele?'

Adele nodded. 'Yes, that's right.' Her stomach was churning over. She knew where the conversation was going.

'And yet, when I looked from the roadside, I could see three windows.' He tapped his chin with his forefinger as if in thought. 'Why would that be?'

Adele got to her feet and smiled. 'That's because we have another attic room,' she said. 'Would you like me to show it to you?'

For a split second there was a look of surprise on Müller's face, which he quickly masked with a smile. 'Yes.' He signalled to his men who followed him and Adele.

Adele opened the cupboard door and walked through to the door that until an hour earlier had been disguised as a bookshelf. After she had led Cecile and the children out of the school and over to the museum, she'd had the foresight to go back to the room and move the bookcase away from the door. It had been held in place by several screws which, fortunately – with a bit of brute force – Adele had been able to remove. 'It's this way. For a time we had a caretaker and he lived in the attic room. The space was partitioned off for privacy.'

She glanced back at Müller who was clearly trying to quell his anger. 'Was this searched before?'

'I assume so,' replied Adele, as she ascended the narrow staircase. 'Your men, or rather, Weld's men, searched the whole school. Of course, I didn't accompany them.'

Müller snapped at his men in German. Adele had a good guess what he was asking them and the puzzled expressions on their faces as she watched them reply told her all she needed to know.

Müller stalked around the room and over to the window, looking out across the playground. He spun around to Adele. 'Everything appears to be in order,' he said begrudgingly. He dismissed his men who trampled back down the stairs. Adele turned to follow them. 'Not you,' he said.

Adele hesitated, her hand on the door handle. She took a deep breath to compose herself before turning back to Müller. 'Yes, Peter,' she replied with a smile.

He walked slowly over to her, each step deliberate and firm. He stopped right in front of her. 'I don't like being made a fool of,' he said. 'Not here. Not in front of Weld. Not anywhere. I could have you arrested on just my word and version of events if I was to even think you might be collaborating or conspiring against the German regime. Am I making myself clear?'

'Yes. Perfectly,' replied Adele.

'Good. I'm pleased to hear that. So, at the end of the week

we leave for Lyon, I have invited Weld to join us and I expect you to make him welcome.'

'I'm sorry but that won't be possible,' replied Adele. 'I don't think my sister would approve or be very happy if I speak to her about this notion and how it came about.' To her own ears, she sounded much braver than she felt, but she was not going to become Weld's plaything, not now she had the upper hand – and she couldn't risk Manu being angered at the thought. She didn't want him to do something to defend her honour. What he'd done at the restaurant was dangerous enough and she wasn't going to let him feel he had to defend her again. 'Similarly, my sister would be horrified if I was arrested.'

'Don't play games with me,' hissed Müller.

'This is no game, Peter. This is deadly serious.' She went to turn to go down the stairs but he grabbed her arm.

'Now listen to me, I can have you arrested and make you disappear. No one will ever find you or know what happened to you. Do you want your sister to worry about you? Is that what you want?'

His grip tightened on her arm and she wanted to cry out in pain, but she had this overwhelming feeling of inner strength that she'd never experienced before. She just needed to keep herself safe and alive until Cecile and the children had escaped. 'I don't think taking me away now will be wise, Peter. There's a certain Adolf Hitler who is expecting to see me dance. I don't know how he will feel if you let him down now and I know my sister will be in no state to perform if I have disappeared. She will know you've been here.'

Müller's nostrils flared in and out as he contemplated her words. 'I can always get another dancer. Neither of you are irreplaceable,' he warned.

Adele had one last card to play. 'Do you want your wife to know about my sister? It would be an interesting conversation they would have, backed up by some photographs.' Adele didn't have any photos at all. She just hoped Müller didn't call her bluff. She thought for a moment he was going to strike her but she stood firm, forcing herself not to flinch at the jerk of his hand; but if he had been going to hit her, he managed to stop himself almost straight away.

They stood there, facing each other for several seconds. Müller blinked first. A smile crept across his face. This unnerved Adele more than the anger in his eyes. She could read that but she couldn't read this. 'It seems I have made an error and misjudged you as a quiet, demure and compliant schoolteacher. You have my congratulations at outmanoeuvring me . . . this time. And I emphasise, this time. I promise you, there won't be another time.'

He brushed past her and down the stairs. 'I will see you tomorrow for our trip to Lyon.' He paused at the foot of the stairs. 'Enjoy your victory while you can.'

Chapter 35

Adele

Adele wanted to shrug off Müller's threat but couldn't quite manage it. Couldn't quite enjoy the victory for now. Whatever revenge he had planned she just hoped it would be after the trip to Lyon, once the children were safe. She didn't care what he did then. Well, that wasn't strictly true but her priority was Cecile and the children.

At morning break, she hopped over the wall to the museum where Manu was waiting for her. 'How are they?' she whispered after he had kissed her for what seemed like forever but also far too quick.

Manu put his arm around her as they walked back into the museum. 'They're all right. Come. We'll go and see them.'

They went through to the kitchens at the back of the building and through a rear door that opened onto a set of concrete steps to the cellar. As they went, he hummed a tune that Adele assumed was to let Cecile know it was safe. Manu pulled a cord and the cellar was illuminated in a soft yellow glow from the light bulb. The space was far bigger than Adele had imagined. It stretched the width of the building and was stacked with different-sized wooden crates, each labelled with their contents.

'What are these?'

'For Lyon,' replied Manu. He pointed to the far corner of the room. 'There's a cargo lift there to take the crates up to ground level. These marked with a blue cross are all destined for Lyon.' Ahead of them was the opening to a long tunnel. Manu began walking down the tunnel. On each side there were sectioned-off areas, all labelled differently: Egypt, Asia, Europe.

'These used to be full of exhibits,' said Manu, 'but now so many items have been stolen by the Nazis.' He resumed the humming of 'Alouette' and pulled another cord from the ceiling, which lit the way.

From deep within the tunnel Adele heard the movement of boxes and then in front of her appeared Cecile with the children. Daniel and Eva ran towards her as soon as they saw her. Adele opened her arms and gathered them in a warm embrace. Thomas bundled in to join the reunion. She looked up and saw Blanche standing there, next to Cecile. Adele smiled warmly and held out a hand to her. 'Blanche?' The little six-year-old looked uncertain for a moment but after a word of encouragement from Cecile, she launched herself into the group hug.

Manu didn't waste any time as he started explaining to Cecile what was going to happen. 'I've brought enough food to last you all through the night and day. Enough to get you to Lyon. You have to be very quiet in the crates. No crying by anyone.' He went on to say they would be unloaded from the transportation lorry and moved into the hall at Lyon. He would make sure their crates were kept together. 'They will be marked with a green cross,' he explained. 'The itinerary will show those ones are the less important pieces that are going to remain in the Lyon museum. Now you must all stay in the crates until someone comes to let you out. No calling out. No talking. You don't know who will be around.

'Cecile, you will have Thomas with you in your crate. Daniel, you will be on your own. Do you think you are brave enough to do that?'

Daniel looked uncertain. 'I think so.'

'Remember what I said to you about being a man?' Manu crouched in front of the boy. 'You and Thomas need to set a good example and look out for the girls. Do you think you can do that?'

'Of course we can,' said Thomas with confidence.

'Good,' said Manu and shook Thomas's hand. 'Daniel?'

Encouraged by the bravado of Manu and naive confidence of Thomas, Daniel stood a little taller. 'Of course, I am brave.'

'That's what I want to hear. I know you can do this.' Manu solemnly shook Daniel's hand. 'Now, girls. Eva, Blanche, come here. You two must be very brave also. You will hide in a crate each. It's only for the journey.'

Adele watched on as Manu took his time to explain to the children what was going to happen and how they mustn't be scared. He almost managed to convince Adele that it wasn't dangerous and much more fun than it really was.

For the rest of the day Adele tried hard to calm her nerves– so much so, the children in her class sensed her unease with Juliette asking her if she needed a glass of water when Adele tried to pick up the box of chalks and ended up dropping them all over the floor. She crouched down to pick them up, muttering to herself about keeping calm.

'I'm fine, honestly,' she told Juliette. 'As you know I am performing tomorrow and I'm a bit nervous. It's a long time since I danced in public.' It was partly the truth of course, but not the whole truth. In the end she had taken the children up to the dance studio for the afternoon where they had danced, did some gymnastics and played some games. It was good to see the children relaxed when dancing, unlike when they had been rehearsing for the show. They, and their parents, had all seemed relieved when they found out they would no longer be performing. Adele felt much better afterwards for burning off some of her nervous energy.

Once the school day was over, Adele locked up and hurried over to the museum.

Manu greeted her with a kiss. 'Everything all right?' she asked, the nerves once again stirring up within her.

'Yes, I've just given them their supper and prepared the

food bags for the journey. We need to get them in the packing crates by four o'clock in the morning. That will give us two hours to make sure no one is going to have a panic attack. The guards are coming at six o'clock to begin loading the exhibits onto the lorry.'

Adele spent the evening with the children and Cecile. She had brought some reading books from the school and sat with Eva at her side, Blanche on her lap and the boys sprawled out on an old piece of sacking Manu had acquired from one of the other exhibit storerooms.

'I need to get home,' said Adele eventually. 'I need to make sure I'm ready for tomorrow too.' She kissed each child on the head before leaving. '*Bonne chance, ma petite puce*,' she whispered. 'May God be with you.' She felt her heart wrench. She didn't know if she'd see them again. In all probability not. Would she ever know what their fate would be? If they made it across the border, would she ever know if they were safe and were able to live freely?

She turned to Cecile and hugged her friend fiercely. They didn't say anything to each other. There was nothing to say; they both knew how dangerous the next part of the journey was going to be.

'We will be all right,' said Cecile eventually.

'Find me. After the war, come and find me,' urged Adele. 'You will all be in my heart and I will not rest until I know you are all safe.'

Manu put a hand on Adele's shoulder and she reluctantly pulled away from Cecile. 'Come on,' said Manu, 'I'll walk you home.'

'You don't have to.'

'I want to.'

It was reassuring having Manu at her side, but frustrating at the same time. They couldn't show any displays of affection for fear of blowing Manu's cover that he was in a relationship with Edith. 'How much longer do you have to be with Edith?' asked Adele, not trying to hide the fact that it bothered her.

'You're not jealous, are you?' teased Manu.

'I think I'm allowed to be.' She nudged him with her shoulder as they walked.

'Not for much longer.' Manu said quietly leaning into her. 'We have to pose as a couple one last time next week.'

'I do worry about you,' confessed Adele. 'I know you can't tell me what it is you're doing, but I know it must be dangerous.'

'Everything is dangerous,' said Manu, taking on a serious tone. 'Do not worry. One more time and that's it.'

They walked on in silence for a while, Adele's thoughts turning to the next day. 'Do you think this is going to work? Smuggling the children down to Lyon and then on to Switzerland? I mean, do you really believe it has a chance?'

'I have to believe it can work,' replied Manu. 'We all have to. If you have hope, you can then start to believe and then you can believe that the love of decent humans will win this war. Always have hope, Adele. Always.'

It was hard saying goodbye to Manu that evening. He had stepped inside the entrance door of the apartment and kissed her, before holding her in his arms for a while. Adele didn't want to admit it to Manu and add to his worries, but she was scared that now they'd finally found each other, there was a real possibility they were going to lose each other if things went wrong with the trip to Lyon. She then felt immediately wretched and guilty for even thinking such selfish thoughts when Cecile and the children were in such danger.

After Manu had gone, Adele trudged up the stairs to the apartment. As she entered, Lucille almost pounced on her.

'Where have you been?! I was getting worried. You do know we have to leave early in the morning. Peter has arranged for a car to collect us at seven-thirty. You still need to get ready, pack your bags and get a good night's sleep.'

Adele gave her sister a long look. 'Are you not concerned about Peter's wife being in Paris?' she asked at last.

Lucille shrugged. 'Why should I be?'

'Why should you be? Honestly, do I need to spell it out?'

'I've spoken to Peter today. His wife was here to try to change his mind about divorcing her.'

'Is that what he said?'

'Yes.'

'Lucille, please don't tell me you believe him.'

Lucille didn't immediately reply. She let out a sigh. 'I don't know if I believe him or not,' she confessed. 'But for now, I'm going along with it all because I don't want to cause any problems. I don't know what you're doing, but I know you're doing something.'

Adele met her sister's gaze. 'Thank you, Lucille.'

After finally preparing everything for the trip the following morning, Adele had gone to bed and spent a good hour tossing and turning, staring up at the ceiling as she fretted about what was happening at the museum and what would happen in Lyon. Manu had intentionally not told her any of the details of the onward journey Cecile and the children would take, on the basis that the less she knew, the safer she would be if it all went wrong. She hated that thought but understood it was a real possibility. It worried her that Manu knew all the details, which would make him a prime contender for interrogation and torture should the Gestapo find out their plans.

By five o'clock the following morning, Adele was up and trying not to pace the apartment as she envisaged the packing crates being moved from the cellar. For a moment, Adele regretted their decision to move the children out this way, but at the same time she knew it was their only hope.

The car Müller had sent for Adele and Lucille turned up exactly on time. Gérard carried their bags down to the car, his attendance no longer needed now the children weren't performing. He kissed Lucille goodbye as she climbed into the vehicle, but when it came to Adele, he also hugged her, whispering in her ear, 'Take great care, my darling. Your mother would be very proud of you, as am I.'

Adele gave her father a questioning look but he was all smiles as he encouraged her into the car.

She turned in her seat to look at him through the back window as the car pulled away. His eyes fixed on hers and he gave the faintest of nods. Adele continued to look at him until the car turned the corner and he was out of sight. His parting words had seemed poignant and meaningful. Or perhaps she was just on edge and reading far too much into every nuance.

They arrived at the train station, where Müller was waiting to greet them.

'*Bonjour*, ladies,' he said. 'I was just checking our cargo.' He waved vaguely behind him and Adele looked on where further down the platform several porters with sack trolleys were wheeling the museum crates down towards the train and loading them up. She could see Manu standing there with a clipboard, stopping the porters now and again to check the numbers stamped on each crate against his list.

'Come on, Adele,' said Lucille, slipping her arm through her sister's. 'Peter is going to take us to our carriage. We have our own compartment.'

They followed Müller as he strode down the platform, the sea of people milling around parting to offer him a clear passage. As they neared Manu, Adele looked over at him. He glanced up and pushed the cap from his face a fraction, giving a small nod as he did so. His eyes then flicked towards the train.

Adele followed his gaze and to her horror saw Weld standing at the door of the carriage. '*Mademoiselle*,' he gushed as Adele approached. He took her hand, not waiting for her to offer it, and kissed her knuckles. Adele was glad she'd worn gloves. The thought of his lips on her skin made her feel sick.

'*Bonjour, monsieur*,' she replied, without injecting an atom of enthusiasm. This earned her a nudge from her sister but Adele ignored her and, pulling her hand away, took hold of the rail and stepped onto the train. She gave a quick look over her shoulder, smiled at her sister then took another glance at Manu who managed to shoot both a warning look and one of reassurance.

As the last of the crates was loaded, the train finally began to make its way out of the station, the air thick with steam as the whistle tooted the train's departure. Phase one of the plan successfully completed.

Chapter 36

Fleur

Paris, August 2015

After confronting Didier at his shop and then marching off down the road, Fleur slowed her pace when she was sure she was out of the Frenchman's sight. She let out a long sigh, surprised at how upset she actually felt about discovering the secret Didier had been hiding: a baby and partner.

She crossed the bridge onto Île de la Cité; the small island in the middle of the Seine, home to the magnificent Notre-Dame. Another time she may have at least visited the outside of the historic cathedral or wandered down the side streets to window-shop in the little boutiques that were popular with Parisians, but today none of that was appealing.

Fleur felt a heaviness in her heart that she wasn't accustomed to and as she walked over the second part of the bridge, she tried to analyse the sensation. She paused at one of the viewing points dotted along the bridge.

Two lantern-style streetlights, probably once gas but now powered by electricity, shouldered the viewing point. Fleur rested her arms on the stone bridge and looked along the river where various houseboats lined one side and the Musée du Louvre occupied the other bank, her thoughts conjuring up images of the other day when she'd walked there with Didier and he'd held her in his arms, reassuring her and making her feel safe. An unexpected ball of emotion stuck in her throat as she recalled the sensation of security and trust. Yes, trust. She had trusted him and now he'd broken that trust, and with that, her naivety that safety could be a good thing.

Fleur closed her eyes and took in a deep breath. It didn't make sense. She didn't make sense. She should be relieved and happy she'd had a narrow escape, even if she had only been contemplating a fling, a holiday romance. A little voice in the back of her head piped up. Was she only wanting a fling because she couldn't have what she really wanted: a relationship? She countered this thought with the reminder that she wasn't good at relationships.

Didier was wrong when he said she was just fractured. Fleur knew she was totally broken. And in that moment, she realised she hated being so damaged. Tears filled her eyes at the realisation.

The walk back to the hotel had not only been with a heavy heart but also with a heavy step. Fleur's emotions weighed her down and she was physically tired from just trying to make sense of herself. However, she didn't want her grandmother to see her so despondent. Lydia had enough to deal with, without worrying about Fleur.

She tapped on the connecting door and called out to her grandmother.

'Come on in!' Lydia's voice floated back.

She was sitting on the balcony of her room with a pot of coffee and a croissant on the table in front of her. The table was set for two. 'I don't think I've seen anything more Parisian than this,' said Fleur greeting her grandmother with a kiss on the cheek. She noted the ballet shoe in Lydia's lap, which had become a constant – never out of touching distance. Fleur had even seen Lydia pop it into her handbag when they got ready to go out the day before.

Lydia smiled warmly at her. 'I was hoping you'd show up before the tea went cold. Ordered it especially for you.' She pointed to the bone china teapot.

'Perfect.' Fleur poured herself a cup, surreptitiously eyeing her grandmother to gauge her composure. On the face of it, Lydia appeared in good spirits following the upset of the previous evening.

'You can just ask,' said Lydia, taking a sip of her coffee. 'I can see you trying to work out if I'm about to go to pieces again or not.'

'I take it from your fighting talk you're feeling a lot better,' replied Fleur, relieved Lydia seemed back on her usual form.

Lydia put down her cup. 'I'm much better this morning. I'm sorry about last night. It caught me out. And before you say don't apologise, I want to. I feel better for saying sorry. I've already phoned Didier and apologised to him.'

Fleur tried not to splutter on her tea. 'You have?'

'Of course. He needs to know what happened as well. It's only right seeing as he's helping me with contacting my sister. Your great-aunt.'

Fleur was side-tracked by the thought she might have another relation. Her family unit had been small from the start – just her, her mum and Lydia. There was now the distinct possibility she could have cousins, albeit second cousins. 'It's a nice thought,' she said, allowing her mind to fantasise about meeting up with relations, visiting them, having them come to stay, dining out together and forming new friendships. It was a heart-warming notion.

'I've asked Didier to come over after lunch,' said Lydia, interrupting Fleur's thoughts. 'He was busy this morning.' She looked across the table at Fleur. 'Are you going to tell me what's wrong? You don't seem very pleased he's coming over. I thought you two were getting on well.'

Fleur screwed up her face as she looked out across the cityscape, before schooling her expression into one of nonchalance. 'Nothing's wrong.'

'I know you well enough to know when you're not being honest,' said Lydia. She put her cup down onto the saucer, the china clinking as she did so.

Fleur knew it was pointless trying to pull the wool over her grandmother's eyes. 'I did like him,' she said. 'Before I found out he had a child and a partner. He said he was single and didn't have children.' Fleur went on to explain, briefly, that she'd seen Didier that morning.

Lydia sat patiently, her hands folded in her lap over the top of the ballet shoe. 'I see. You're an intelligent woman, Fleur. Has it occurred to you that they might not be his partner and child?'

'A bit,' confessed Fleur, feeling sheepish. She hadn't really given it full and proper consideration, but all the evidence backed her theory. 'I can't see what else it would be. And last night when his phone rang, a picture of a woman flashed up on the screen. I couldn't be sure, but it looked like the woman in the shop with the baby. And he didn't want to take the call in front of us.'

'That's true but I still think you should listen to what he has to say.' Lydia picked up the ballet shoe and placed it on the table. 'Assumptions can be crippling and the truth can be liberating.'

Fleur was silent for a few moments as she considered her grandmother's words. She couldn't argue with them but at the same time it was an intimidating hypothesis to experiment with. 'I'll think about it,' she said at last when she realised an answer was expected.

'Don't waste any time thinking,' said Lydia. 'That's Didier now.'

Fleur looked out on the street below and it was indeed Didier standing by his car, adjusting his buttons on his jacket. He blipped the central locking on his car with the remote and crossed the street. His beauty and elegance was enough to stop even the most determined of Parisian traffic.

'He's coming up here?' asked Fleur, suddenly aware that her hair needed a brush and she could do with a freshen-up. She then scolded herself for worrying about what Didier thought of her.

'He's going to wait in the lobby. You've got ten minutes to get yourself ready.'

Fleur looked incredulously at her grandmother. 'You've set this up?'

'You're wasting time. *Dépêche-toi*. Hurry up.'

Fleur wasn't sure why she was going along with this ambush, but ten minutes later she was exiting the lift having fluffed her hair and applied some fresh make-up.

Didier rose from the chair he was sitting in as she approached. Fleur couldn't deny how attractive he looked but reminded herself of the woman and child.

'I'm only here because my nan wants me to be,' she said, ignoring the smile he gave her.

'*Bien sûr*. Of course. I do not doubt it,' he replied. 'Shall we take a walk?'

She shrugged. 'OK.' To be honest it was preferable to sitting inside the busy foyer of the hotel.

They walked down the rue du Pont Neuf towards the river, where Didier guided her down some steps that brought them out onto the cobbled path that ran alongside the Seine. Fleur moved out of the path of a jogger and sidestepped a dog who was trotting on ahead of its owner. The noise of the traffic wasn't so apparent down by the river and Fleur wondered what it had been like during the war when her grandmother was a child living under the occupation.

Fleur knew her grandmother's story wasn't unique, but it was obviously more personal to her and she admired her grandmother's strength and attitude. Lydia had met her English husband when, as a musician, he'd come to Paris in 1951 to play in the Orchestra de la Société Philharmonique de Paris. Adele, Manu and Lydia had all been invited to an after-show party and as Lydia had often told Fleur, it was love at first sight. A year later and ten weeks pregnant, Lydia had married Fleur's grandfather and moved to England to start a new life.

Fleur wasn't so sure she'd cope so well. In fact, if she was honest, she hadn't coped nearly as well with losing her mother. Lydia had lost so much more and still managed to find love, comfort and courage.

She realised Didier was talking to her. 'Sorry, I didn't hear what you said.'

'You looked deep in thought.'

'I was thinking about my grandmother and her resilience,' replied Fleur. 'I was comparing it to mine, or my lack of it.'

'Maybe you underestimate yourself,' suggested Didier.

Fleur gave a self-depreciating laugh. 'Maybe I know myself far too well.' She had the sudden desire to feel his hand in hers or to have some form of physical contact but then reminded herself why she was actually here. 'Anyway, we're not supposed to be talking about me.'

Didier blew out a long breath. '*Alors*, so you came to the shop this morning and saw Zenya with Cedric?'

Fleur bristled. She didn't particularly need to know their names; it made it more personal somehow. 'If you mean the woman and child you kissed in the shop, then yes.'

'Ah, yes, the kiss.'

'Not just that,' retorted Fleur feeling on the defensive already when she really shouldn't be. 'You have a photo of the boy in your wallet. You took a phone call last night from . . . from . . .'

'From Zenya, yes, that's right.'

'And you never told me about them. In fact, you specifically told me you had no children and I got the distinct impression you were single. You told me about your wife but you never once mentioned Zenya or Cedric.'

'I'm sorry. I should have told you about them,' replied Didier. He looked so sincere when he spoke to her.

Fleur could feel the anger boiling inside her. 'Look, I don't know what your expectations are with a relationship. I know you said you didn't want a holiday romance, but do you seriously think I'd consider any sort of relationship when

317

you have a partner and son. If you're looking for a mistress, then you're looking in the wrong place.'

'But I thought you did not want commitment. You told me you were rubbish at it,' he said, quoting her exact words back to her.

'But it doesn't mean I want someone who is in a relationship with another woman. And besides, why would I do that to her?' She couldn't quite bring herself to use the woman's name. 'I do have some integrity.'

They walked along in silence for a few moments, before Didier spoke again. 'So, tell me, Fleur, what do you want? Do you want to spend the rest of your life having meaningless flings where you do not value yourself or someone else? Where love means nothing and you are just there for the sex? Because that is all it could be if you do not want an emotional attachment.'

Fleur wasn't quite sure she liked the impression he was painting of her. 'You make it sound cheap.'

Didier shrugged. 'Maybe because it is pointless and worthless.'

Fleur stopped walking and turned to face the river, her gaze following a sightseeing boat as it cut through the grey-green water, leaving a white frothy wake behind it. 'Maybe it's because the alternative is too high a price,' she said. 'And maybe because I don't want to pay that price.'

She began walking back the way they'd come. She shouldn't have met Didier; it had achieved nothing and only highlighted her inadequacies.

Didier fell into step alongside her. She could feel the closeness of his arm to hers and once again the desire to reach out and touch him was almost too much to bear. Now they would have to go back to Lydia and act normal when all she really wanted to do was to be as far away from Didier as possible. She couldn't cope with the conflict she felt towards him – wanting him and yet wanting nothing from him.

'Just so you know,' said Didier as they reached the bottom

of the steps that led to street level. 'I love Zenya and Cedric very much.'

Fleur cut him off. 'I really don't want to hear this.'

Didier ignored her. 'I love them both because Zenya is my sister and Cedric is my nephew.'

Fleur spun around to face Didier. 'What?'

'Zenya is staying with me until her visa comes through, then she will be joining her husband in America, along with their son.'

'Wait, you just let me believe . . .' She flung her hand in the air, not bothering to finish the sentence, her anger getting the better of her. 'Why didn't you say? Actually, don't bother answering. I'm not interested in mind games or anything like that.' She stormed up the steps, wishing she could take them two at a time to get to the top quicker.

Didier's long stride was far more accomplished and he kept pace with her effortlessly. 'I didn't tell you because you didn't ask and because I was trying to get to the bottom of what your problem is. Trying to make you see it for yourself.'

Fleur stopped in her tracks. 'My problem? Well, my only problem right now is you. I don't need you to psychoanalyse me. I don't need any sort of therapy. Counselling. CBT. Or anything like that. I'm happy as I am.'

'Why? Why are you happy with having nothing?' demanded Didier.

Fleur glared at him for a moment and was sure if it was humanly possible, she'd have steam coming out of her ears. She ground the words out, as she fought to control the urge to yell at the top of her lungs. 'Because it's safer.'

'You will never find love if you are too afraid to fall,' called Didier after her as she broke into a run up the steps.

She wanted to shout some clever retort but her words jammed in her throat as tears sprang to her eyes. She wasn't going to let Didier see her pain and was grateful he didn't chase after her as she sprinted across the road and carried on running all the way back to the hotel.

Obviously, Didier would be coming to the hotel now to see Lydia, and Fleur needed time to compose herself. Splash some water on her face and calm down before having to sit there with Didier.

She waited until the last possible moment when she heard a knock on the interconnecting door.

'I'm coming,' she said, pulling the door open. She sucked in a breath to see Didier standing there.

'Your grandmother asked me to knock. She's sitting out on the balcony.'

Fleur nodded. 'OK. Well, I'm ready.'

'Fleur . . .' began Didier.

She shook her head. 'Not now.' She had no idea what he was going to say, but she needed to put thoughts of Didier out of her mind and think about her grandmother.

Didier stepped to one side, allowing her through, and they settled themselves out on the balcony with Lydia to listen to what happened that night in Lyon.

Chapter 37

Adele

The journey from Paris to Lyon was long and the steam train didn't pull up at its destination until four o'clock in the afternoon. Adele had been subjected to making polite conversation with Müller and Weld for most of the journey, although both men did retire to another compartment of their own after they'd all eaten in the dining carriage.

Adele had been painfully aware of Manu further down the dining carriage, feigning nonchalance, but she knew him well enough to realise that behind that blank expression there was far more going on. He despised seeing her having to be polite and laugh in all the right places with the enemy, but Adele also knew that Manu was aware it was just a charade. Something she had to do, just like he had to pretend to be in love with Edith.

Finally, the engine slowed and the train pulled in to Lyon station. As she stepped down onto the platform, she cast a casual glance down the train and could see already the crates were being unloaded with Manu supervising.

Adele and Lucille were bustled away down the platform and into an awaiting car where fortunately Müller said his goodbyes. 'I have certain matters to attend to in advance of the exhibition. Make sure you're ready at seven o'clock.'

Their bags were collected by the porter who escorted them up to their room.

'This is lovely,' gushed Lucille, once the porter had left them. She went over to the window and looked out at the square beyond them.

Adele joined her at the window. There was a plaza in a quadrant of buildings with a circular fountain in the centre. On the ground floor of the buildings were various cafés and restaurants, with seating outside as well as inside. 'Do you know where the exhibition is being held?'

Lucille gave a laugh. 'It's here. In this hotel. Peter was telling me the hotel has been commandeered for the next three days while the exhibition is on. Of course, we're only here for tonight but even so, it's exciting, isn't it?'

Adele smiled at her sister. In any other circumstances it would be exciting, but she couldn't think of anything worse than having to perform for Hitler himself. 'Yes, I suppose so.'

'Maman would be so proud of us.' Lucille sighed, a smile resting on her face.

Adele hoped their mother would be proud, but not for the same reasons as Lucille. Adele hoped her mother was looking down on her, praising her for doing the right thing, for fighting back against the regime, for trying to help those persecuted by the Nazis, those who had no voice of their own and could not stand against the tyranny.

'I think she will be proud,' she said quietly. 'But she would expect no less.' Adele was aware her sister had thrown her a quizzical look and hurriedly changed the subject. 'So, are you nervous?'

'A little but only because Peter hasn't seen me perform before, and I know he is anxious to impress the Führer. So, it's second-hand nerves, if you like.'

'Why would anyone want to impress that man?' Adele couldn't disguise the disgust in her voice.

Lucille turned to face Adele. 'What's got into you? One

minute you're telling me how nervous you are, how proud Maman would be and the next you're criticising my fiancé.'

'Fiancé? When did that happen?' Adele looked at her sister's hand. Her ring finger was bare.

'It's not official, but it will be,' said Lucille.

'Until it's official perhaps you shouldn't go around saying it,' said Adele.

Her sister stopped and looked at her. 'What?'

Adele shrugged. 'What?'

'What aren't you telling me? I can tell by your face. Just say it. Whatever it is, say it.'

'There's nothing to say.'

'You're jealous. I know I've said it before and it's true.' Lucille sat down on the bed, a frown creasing her forehead.

'I am not jealous,' snapped Adele.

'Yes you are. Jealous I have someone who loves me and Manu barely even knows you exist half the time.'

Adele let out a sigh. Sometimes her sister sounded like a spoilt brat. 'And you think Peter loves you? You're the one who doesn't know what love is.'

Lucille jumped back to her feet. 'Of course he loves me. Again, you're just jealous!'

'How can he love you if he still loves his wife?'

'What are you talking about? He doesn't love his wife at all.'

'If that's the case, why was he having dinner with her when he told you he was working?' As soon as the words left her mouth, Adele regretted them. She could see the hurt on her sister's face.

'What do you mean?'

'It's nothing. Ignore me. I was just angry,' said Adele, looking away and unlocking her case.

Lucille grabbed her arm and spun her around. 'What do you mean?' she repeated, her voice tense and the words harsh. 'Who did you see him with?'

'Lucille, let's not do this now. I'm sorry. I shouldn't have said anything.'

'What? So, you're lying? Is that it? You're just causing trouble, aren't you? You want to hurt me because you're hurt. You can't bear to see me happy.'

'It's not that at all,' said Adele.

'You're going to live your days a lonely spinster. Everyone will talk about the old schoolteacher who never married, never had children of her own because she was infatuated with the museum curator. The old schoolteacher of Paris who died sad and lonely.'

Adele wanted to strike her sister for the cruel taunts. She could feel the tears burn in her eyes. 'You're forgetting part of that story,' she retorted. 'The part where the old spinster schoolteacher's sister ran off with a German officer only to find he was still married and very much in love with his wife. So the people of Paris decided she was a collaborator and she was spurned for the rest of her days and she too died sad and lonely.'

In the end the slap came from Lucille. She struck Adele's face with the palm of her hand. Adele winced. She glared at her sister who glared back, equally hard. Adele took a deep breath. How had it come to this? She and Lucille fighting about men? 'I need some fresh air,' she said with as much dignity as she could summon.

In reality, fresh air wasn't an option. They had already been briefed that they weren't to leave the hotel unaccompanied, but Adele just needed to put some space between herself and her sister. They'd already said hurtful things to each other in the heat of the moment. The only difference was, Adele had told the truth whereas Lucille didn't know the truth.

In an unconscious decision, she found herself taking the lift to the ground floor and walking towards the exhibition hall. She pushed open the double doors to the room. It wasn't as big as she imagined or maybe it seemed smaller because there were so many boxes, soldiers and hotel staff in the room. She searched the throng but couldn't see Manu. Walking with a sense of purpose, to avoid anyone stopping her, Adele strode across the room. She could see the doors at the rear where people were coming in and out of with the crates.

She stepped back out of the way as the double doors burst open and a trolley was whooshed through by two porters and a German solider. Adele nipped through the doors and walked down a corridor, again moving out of the way for exhibits and people bustling back and forth. Another set of doors and she felt the cool gust of fresh air as she walked out into the loading bay. There was Manu, inspecting the wooden boxes. He looked worried and Adele felt an immediate sense of foreboding. She could see four crates separated from the others and assumed they must be the ones marked with a green cross. Of course, there should be five.

Her heart caught and she forced herself to breathe evenly. She looked back at Manu who at the same time looked up and met her gaze. Gone was the cool poker face of the unflappable man she knew.

Adele walked over to him, trying to appear calm. 'What's wrong?'

'One of the crates is missing,' whispered Manu. He looked at his clipboard and showed it to Adele. 'Just act like nothing's wrong,' he instructed.

Adele nodded as if he was explaining something to her whilst she cast her gaze around the boxes. 'Did it get loaded?' she asked.

'Yes. I checked all five on myself.'

'It must be here.'

'But I can't find it.'

'If it's not here, where can it be?' Adele proceeded to answer her own question as the realisation dawned on her. She looked back towards the doors. 'Oh, God, if it's been taken through there, someone is going to unpack it.'

'Go back to the hall,' said Manu. 'Take this clipboard and pretend you're marking the numbered crates off against the list here. If you find the missing one, you have to stop them unpacking it. I'll continue to search through here.'

As Adele took the clipboard a voice from behind them made her jump.

It was Müller. 'Is there something wrong?' His tone of voice suggested he already knew the answer.

'We are just checking all the crates are where they should be,' replied Manu.

'And are they?' asked Müller. 'If my men have made a mistake, I will make sure they are dealt with. I don't want anything going wrong this evening. Not with the Führer coming.'

Before either Manu or Adele could reply, Müller was called away, much to everyone's relief.

'Be careful,' said Manu, as Adele went to leave. 'I don't trust him and he doesn't trust us.'

Adele made her way back to the exhibition hall. The only way to do this was methodically. Again, with confidence so as she wasn't questioned, she walked over to the first unopened crate and with a nod to the porter who replied in kind, she took a closer look, checking the number against her list or at least pretending to, while making sure there wasn't a green cross on the side. Then she made her way over to the next one. Her heart was thumping with nerves. She couldn't imagine what it must be like for one of the children trapped inside.

After inspecting the last possible crate with no joy, Adele went back to find Manu. She was conscious of the time and should really be getting ready for her performance.

As soon as she saw Manu, she could tell from the expression on his face he also hadn't located it.

'Where can it be? If it's not here or out there, I don't understand,' said Adele in an urgent whisper.

Manu ran his hand down his face. 'I don't either. I need to find a porter to make sure every crate came off the train.' He looked at his watch. 'Shouldn't you be getting ready? Aren't you having dinner with Müller beforehand?'

'Yes but I really don't want to go.'

Manu cupped her face with the palm of his hand. 'You have to continue as if nothing is wrong.' He kissed her forehead. 'Please, Adele. Go and get ready. Go to dinner and give the performance of a lifetime.'

When Adele arrived back in her hotel room, she was surprised to find it empty. She had expected Lucille to be there, but judging by the out-turned suitcase and Lucille's travelling clothes slung on the end of her bed, her evening dress gone, Adele guessed her sister had got ready and left early to avoid speaking to her. Lucille didn't cave easily after an argument whereas Adele tended to make peace sooner.

Adele opened her bag to get ready. They had a small bathroom attached to their room so that was at least something. She needed to wash away the grime of the day travelling. If only it was as easy to wash away her worries.

Adele was somewhat surprised when Lucille appeared back at the room just before she was about to leave for dinner. She could see her sister had been crying. 'Lucille, I'm sorry we argued,' began Adele. 'I didn't mean to upset you. I shouldn't have told you about Peter and his wife like that.'

Lucille shook her head. 'It's me who should be sorry,' she said, her voice trembling as she spoke. 'I'm so sorry, Adele.' She began to cry.

Adele pulled her sister into a hug. 'It's all right. I promise. You don't have to be sorry. We both said hurtful things to each other.' She patted her sister gently on the back, like she would a small child. Lucille was so upset, unnecessarily so. 'Don't be crying now, Lucille,' she coaxed. 'Dry your eyes – you're going to ruin your make-up.'

Lucille pulled away. 'You don't understand,' she said.

'I do. Honestly. We're sisters; we say things because we know we can. Things we wouldn't ordinarily say to someone else.' Adele smiled encouragingly. It was unlike Lucille to be so . . . so contrite and apologetic, not to mention upset. As she looked at her younger sister, a feeling of dread crawled across her, turning in her stomach and clenching at her heart. There was such desperate sorrow in Lucille's eyes, Adele knew whatever it was, it went beyond their argument. She dropped her hands, taking a physical step back. 'What is it, Lucille? What have you done?'

Her sister shook her head and the tears plummeted from her eyes. 'I didn't mean to. I was angry. I'm so sorry, Adele. Please forgive me.'

Adele grabbed Lucille's arms. 'What have you done? TELL ME!'

'Peter wanted to know what we were arguing about. I told him,' sobbed Lucille. 'I said horrible things about you. I told him about the children.'

'You did what?'

Lucille was crying uncontrollably. 'I told Peter about the papers for the children. I saw them in your bag last week. I was looking for a lipstick.'

'What have you done, Lucille?'

'I'm sorry. I'm sorry.' Lucille held her face in her hands.

'Lucille! What did he say?' Adele forced the words out in a measured way. 'What did Peter say?'

'He was upset because Hitler isn't coming anymore and when I told him about the papers, he . . . he just stared at me. I've never seen such . . . such anger.'

'The children. They're here,' whispered Adele in disbelief at the betrayal from her own sister.

'What?' It was Lucille's turn to look incredulous.

'The children are here. They're using the exhibition as cover to escape. Oh my God, Lucille. What have you done?'

Chapter 38

Adele

There was no time to try to warn Manu before the pre-drinks party. Adele somehow managed to compose herself and calm her sister down. 'We have to carry on as if nothing has happened,' she instructed. 'No histrionics. No crying. Nothing to draw attention to ourselves, do you understand?'

Lucille had nodded and sniffed forlornly.

She went to apologise for the umpteenth time, but Adele stopped her. 'No more apologising. What's done is done. We just have to hope to God that Cecile and the children can escape, not to mention Manu finding the missing crate.'

Adele was relieved Hitler wasn't going to be there, despite it putting Müller in a bad mood. Although he did a good job of hiding it to his guests. He smiled at the sisters and Adele stole a look at Lucille. She returned the smile but there was a nervousness to it. Müller put his hand across Lucille's back and drew her in to the other German officers and local dignitaries, introducing her. Adele held back. She couldn't care less if she wasn't introduced. Her eyes were scanning the guests, looking for Manu. She didn't realise straight away that Müller was talking to her.

'Adele,' he said in a loud voice.

Adele jumped. 'Sorry, I was just admiring the room.' It was a ridiculous thing to say but she made a point of looking up at the cornices and mural painting on the ceiling.

Müller beckoned her to them. 'This is Adele, Lucille's sister.'

'Ah, the other dancer,' said one of the officers and gave a small bow. 'Very pleased to meet you. Can I get you a drink, mademoiselle?'

Before Adele could reply, Müller cut in. 'You're wasting your time,' he said. 'Weld has already staked his claim.'

The officer grimaced. 'Weld?' He sighed. 'That is a shame.'

Adele wanted to scream at them all. She despised the way they spoke as if she wasn't there. Thinking of her as some sort of commodity they could claim if someone hadn't already done so. She was glad she didn't have a drink in her hand; she wasn't sure she'd be able to resist the urge to throw it in their faces.

She was relieved to see Manu appear in the room. From looking at him, she couldn't tell whether it was good or bad news.

'Manu! There you are,' called Müller. He clicked his fingers at a passing waiter who was carrying a silver tray laden with several champagne flutes. 'A drink for the man.' The waiter hurried over and dipped his head as he offered the tray towards Manu.

'*Merci*,' said Manu, taking two glasses from the tray. He joined the group and pointedly passed one to Adele.

Adele again tried to read his expression but it was impossible.

'Are we all prepared for the exhibition?' asked Müller.

'Yes, everything is in order,' replied Manu.

'Good. Good. No unexpected surprises?' Müller continued.

Adele felt her heart skip a beat but Manu didn't falter. 'No. Nothing. Everything is as it should be.'

Müller gave a tight smile. 'Nothing missing? All the crates arrived without a problem?'

Adele was sure Müller was taunting them. He must know. She exchanged a look with Lucille, whose eyes were filled with horror. Adele looked back at Müller. The smile was sadistic.

'Nothing missing. As I say, everything is how it should be.' Manu took a sip of his drink, his gaze locked with the German's.

Müller gave a laugh and slapped Manu on the back. 'That's good to hear. We don't want any more bad news today.'

Adele was just about to tell Lucille it was time for them to leave to get changed for their performance when Müller was called away to speak to a guest. She took her chance. 'Gentlemen, I'm afraid my sister and I need to leave.' They nodded and bade their goodbyes. Adele paused. 'Manu, would you mind just accompanying me out into the courtyard. I feel a bit stuffy and need some fresh air.'

'Of course,' replied Manu, placing his glass down on the nearby table.

'Lucille, I'll be up in a minute. Don't wait,' Adele instructed her sister.

As soon as Adele was outside and alone with Manu, she slipped her hand into his arm and walked away from the building.

'Müller knows about the papers for Cecile and the children.' She kept her voice low and tried to stay calm in case anyone was watching them.

'What? How?'

'Lucille saw them. We argued. She was so angry with me, she told Müller.' Adele felt both ashamed and guilty, as if she had betrayed Cecile and the children herself.

Manu muttered a curse under his breath. 'There's nothing we can do now,' he said. 'We have to continue with the plan. Whatever happens, we will just have to deal with it at the time.'

'I'm so sorry,' said Adele.

'Don't be. It is not your fault,' said Manu.

Adele wished she felt comforted by his words.

The evening air was fresh and Adele inhaled a deep breath. 'My lungs are contaminated from being in there breathing the same air as those pigs,' she said. 'Please tell me you've found the crate.'

Manu rested his hand between her shoulder blades and guided her away from the door. 'Not yet. Keep walking.'

Somehow Adele managed not to falter in her footsteps

but her heart missed a beat. 'I don't understand how it can be missing.'

'Neither do I.'

'What are you going to do?'

'Have another look when I go to take the others to the meeting point.'

This time Adele did stop walking. 'You can't leave one behind.'

Manu turned to face her. 'But I can't sacrifice the others for whoever is missing.'

'Do you even know who it is?'

'Not yet but it's not Cecile. Her crate is there. It's bigger than the others.'

'Are they all right though? Is there any way of telling?'

'I gave the prearranged knock on Cecile's crate and she responded the same. She's all right.'

'And the children?'

'I've whispered to them to stay very quiet. That they are all right and it won't be long now.'

'Did any of them say anything?' Adele couldn't imagine the fear and confusion the children must be going through. They were being so brave.

'No. I told them not to say anything. So, I'm afraid I still don't know who is missing. Now you must go and get ready.'

He took her back indoors, coming to a halt at the foot of the stairs and with no other reason to stand talking without drawing attention to themselves, Manu gave Adele a small kiss on the cheek and made his way back to the reception.

Adele could barely concentrate as she got ready for the performance. She was glad Hitler wasn't there as that would mean there was less security and, therefore, safer for Cecile and the children to make their escape. She couldn't stop thinking about the missing crate though.

'Adele! Adele.' It was Lucille's voice breaking her thoughts. 'We need to go and you still haven't got your shoes on.'

Adele hurried to tie the ribbons on her ballet shoes and

together with her sister went back down to the reception room, waiting outside the door until they received their cue to enter the room.

From years of dancing, Adele relied on muscle memory for much of the performance. Her mind wasn't focused at all. She could only think about Cecile and the children. The plan was that while she danced, Manu would slip out and free the stowaways from the crates. There was a rarely used staircase that ran from the storeroom where the exhibits had been delivered, down into the basement of the hotel where an underground network of passages allowed staff to move laundry through the hotel without the guests seeing it. The underground corridors were also where the piping, heating and electrical systems were relayed around the building. There would be a small goods van waiting in the back alley to the hotel and Cecile and the children would be smuggled out into it and driven away. That was all Adele knew.

The music of *The Nutcracker* was playing loudly and the audience were enthralled by the performance of the Basset sisters. As Adele swayed and moved her body around the floor, she tried to catch a glimpse of Müller. He should be in the front row, watching them, but she hadn't spotted him yet.

By the time the final bars of their dance had played, Adele was a bag of nerves and grateful she didn't have to perform again. It was now Lucille's solo performance. Surely, Müller would be about to see that. Adele stood in the doorway on the pretence of watching Lucille dance, but her eyes were scanning the audience. A movement at the back of the room caught her attention and she saw the figure of a German officer slip through the double doors. It was Müller. Adele's heart hammered in her chest. She grabbed the robe she had worn to come from her bedroom to the reception room and quickly untied her ballet shoes so she didn't have to try to walk with the cumbersome blocks in the toes. She skirted the edges of the room until she was at the double doors where Müller had exited.

No one challenged her as she pushed the door open and hurried down the hallway to the storeroom.

When she stepped into the storeroom, she could hear someone moving around, tapping on boxes, lids being lifted. 'Manu! Is that you?' she called. The cellar was cold and the walls damp even though it was summertime. She pulled the dressing robe tighter around her body.

'Adele?' Manu appeared in the passageway, stepping out from one of the holding cages. 'Come. Quickly.'

'Have you found them?' Adele hurried down to the end of the cellar.

'I've found the missing box,' said Manu. 'It had been left outside and the guards have only just brought it in. I managed to convince them to leave while I sorted it out. Said I wouldn't tell they'd neglected their duties.' He began crowbarring the lid from the case.

'Who's in the box?' asked Adele.

'Eva,' grunted Manu.

Adele looked around the enclosure. 'Where are the others?'

'They've gone,' said Manu, grunting as the lid proved difficult to move.

'What do you mean?'

'I couldn't risk leaving them here. They are waiting for five minutes and that's all. We can't let them all be captured when they are so close to freedom.'

'Oh, Manu. Hurry. Please.'

Manu gave Adele an unimpressed look. 'What do you think I'm doing?'

'Sorry, I just . . .' She stopped talking and instead clasped her hands together, willing the lid from the crate.

With one final yank on the crowbar, the lid was off.

Adele dove her hands into the box, pulling at the straw until she saw Eva's blonde hair.

'Eva,' cried Adele with relief. '*Oh, ma petite puce. Viens ici.* Come here.' She held out her arms to the child as Manu lifted her from the box.

Eva began to cry. 'I thought I was lost and going to be stuck in there forever. I didn't think you were coming for me.'

'*C'est bon. C'est bon.* It's all right,' reassured Adele, holding the child close and kissing the top of her head. 'Everything is going to be all right now.'

A sadistic laugh broke through the air.

Adele looked up and let out a gasp.

Müller was standing at the entrance to the enclosure. A mirthless smile played on his lips. 'This is all very nice, isn't it? The ballet dancer, the curator and the Jew. How kind of you to make my life so much easier.'

Adele got to her feet, moving Eva behind her. Manu stood stock-still, the crowbar still in his hand. Müller tut-tutted at Manu. 'Why don't you put that down. Dangerous thing. It could cause quite an injury.'

Adele watched as Manu paused for a moment, letting the crowbar swing gently on the end of his finger. As he dropped it, he went to make a move for his pocket but Müller was too smart. He pulled his revolver from its holster and aimed it at Manu. 'Stop! If you want to live, that is.'

'Don't get yourself killed for me,' said Adele frantically. 'Not for me.' Her gaze was glued on Manu. She didn't care if she died, but Manu wasn't to get himself killed trying to save her. He needed to stay alive to keep Eva from harm. She looked at Manu's jacket pocket and could see the handle of a gun. He certainly hadn't been carrying a gun earlier and she assumed he'd smuggled it in somehow.

'Put the gun on the floor. That's it. Nice and slow. Now kick it away,' instructed Müller.

Manu kicked the weapon towards Müller, who in turn back-heeled it out of the enclosure into the passageway.

'Adele knew nothing about this,' said Manu. 'She didn't know I had smuggled the child here.'

Adele wanted to shout at Manu and tell him not to try to save her. She wasn't the one who needed saving.

'But she knew about the child in the attic of the school,' said Müller simply. He wasn't going to be fooled so easily.

'She didn't,' continued Manu. 'She knew nothing. I told the child to hide up there. I have a spare key for the school. I was given one when I brought some displays to them some time ago. I never gave it back so I was able to hide the child without anyone knowing.'

'Stop. This is a ludicrous story. You're insulting me if you think I believe that,' snapped Müller. 'Let's not keep the pretence up any longer. We all know that Adele was hiding the child. I heard her up there myself when I visited the other day. And then I saw her. Adele, you know that, don't you?'

From somewhere in the distance, Adele was aware of the rumble of a vehicle engine as it was started. The truck that was taking the others to safety. She had to get Eva on it somehow. But how?

'I'm thinking I could just shoot the three of you right here,' said Müller. 'I'd be totally within my rights to do so. Especially if any one of you were trying to escape or endanger my life.' He moved further into the enclosure. 'But I'm not sure how your sister would feel about that.'

A movement in the shadows of the corridor caught Adele's eye. She forced herself to concentrate on Müller. 'I don't think she'd be very happy if her soon-to-be husband killed his soon-to-be sister-in-law.'

Müller gave a theatrical sigh. 'No. She wouldn't. But, then again, I'm not planning on marrying her. So what does it matter?'

'I thought you loved her,' said Adele. She couldn't believe Müller was finally saying out loud what she suspected all along.

'I'm fond of her, of course. She's good for fucking,' said Müller. He looked at Eva. 'I would normally apologise for the coarseness of my language, but manners don't apply in present company. Now, as I was saying . . . Lucille is an attractive young woman. I'd be a fool not to want to have sex with her but I am, of course, a married man and I have absolutely no intention of leaving my wife who is graced with much more sophistication and higher breeding than your dear sister will ever have. I also have two beautiful children who I would never dream of abandoning for a Paris whore.'

Adele looked beyond Müller.

From the shadows stepped Lucille. In her hand she held Manu's gun, which Müller had kicked out into the passageway. She had it pointed at Müller's back. 'I wish you'd never said those things.' Lucille's shaky voice cut through the silence.

Müller spun around and then stepped to the side, so Lucille was on his left and Adele, Manu and Eva on his right. 'Lucille! What are you doing? Put the gun down,' he stuttered and for the first time sounded unsure of himself.

'Why would I want to do that?' asked Lucille. She was still dressed in her ballet dress and, like Adele, had a robe tied around her.

'Because, my darling, you might hurt someone,' said Müller. He went to take a step forward but Lucille cocked the gun.

'Don't move,' she said, her voice ice cold. The calmness was chilling. 'And don't call me darling.'

'Please, Lucille, I didn't mean what I said,' began Müller. His gun was still trained on Adele and Eva. 'I was just saying it to be cruel to your sister; that's all.'

'Liar,' said Lucille. 'You meant every word of it.' She moved closer but stayed out of touching distance from her prey. 'Now, you put the gun down,' she said.

This time Müller didn't sound so confident when he spoke. 'Lucille, please. Let me talk to you.'

Lucille shook her head, spilling the tears from her eyes. 'You will just tell me more lies. You never told me you had children. You said your wife didn't want any and . . .' she pulled back a sob '. . . and we were going to have children. You and me.' The gun was shaking in her hand. She clasped it with two hands.

337

Adele was more frightened than before. Lucille had that defiant look in her eyes. The sort she got when she was angry and determined. Adele moved forwards. 'Lucille,' she said softly. 'Think very carefully about what you're doing.'

'Stay back!' Lucille ordered Adele, momentarily, taking her eyes off Müller.

The German seized his chance and before anyone realised, he had grabbed Adele, pulling her in front of him with his gun aimed at her temple. 'Now, I think it's time you put the gun down,' he snarled.

'Don't,' said Adele. 'Shoot him! Shoot him through me!' She was shouting now. Desperate for Lucille to act. 'SHOOT ME!' She could see the indecision on Lucille's face. 'I love you, Lucille. It will be all right. I'll be with Maman.' Her voice was steady. She would willingly sacrifice herself so that the three people she loved in this room could live. She locked eyes with her sister. 'Lucille, shoot me.' Lucille was crying and the firearm wavered in her hands. She gave a small nod at her sister and Adele could see her fingers begin to squeeze the trigger. 'Do it, Lucille. Do it.'

'NO! STOP!' It was Manu. He went to move but Müller swung around, making Adele face him.

'Do you want to see her face blown off?'

Manu stopped in his tracks. Eva was cowering behind a packing crate, whimpering at everything she was witnessing. Manu held out his hands, palms up. 'Everyone, just calm down a moment. No one do anything stupid.'

Müller spun back around to Lucille who was a sobbing wreck. She dropped to her knees. Her arms went limp and slowly she lowered the gun to the ground, letting go of it. Müller pushed Adele to the floor and made a grab for the gun but he had sorely underestimated his lover.

Sprawled out on the hard stone floor, Adele watched in horror as Lucille snatched the gun back up and fired it straight at the advancing Müller.

Chapter 39

Fleur

Paris, August 2015

'Was he dead?' asked Fleur. She wasn't sure she'd breathed properly through the whole time Lydia told her how the events unfolded.

'Very much so,' replied Lydia. 'Of course, as soon as that happened it was chaos. I remember Lucille and Adele crying, holding on to each other. They were in shock. Manu was urging the two sisters on. Saying they didn't have time and that the truck was about to leave and I needed to be on it.'

'And did you make it?' asked Didier.

Lydia shook her head. 'I don't remember everything. It was frightening. I was very scared. I remember Adele begging Lucille to come with them and Lucille insisting she must stay. In the end, I think Adele only left because she wanted to save me. She grabbed my hand and we ran out of the building. I don't remember how. I just remember bursting out into the fresh air and Adele calling out. She dropped to her knees and began to cry. The truck was pulling out of the gates. It didn't stop. Manu tried to run after it, but we were too late.' Lydia stopped speaking and took a tissue from her bag. She dabbed at her eyes. 'That was the last time I saw my sister.'

'Oh, Nan, I'm so sorry,' said Fleur. She felt awful for her grandmother, having to relive that moment. It had clearly had a profound effect on her, still reducing her to tears after more than seventy years.

'After that, Manu hurried us back into the building and I had to hide in a Bergen – one of those big army rucksacks.'

'A rucksack?' asked Fleur for clarification.

'You mean like a big kitbag, heavy-duty canvas?' said Didier.

'Yes, that's it. It was a good job I was small and light. Manu was strong. He carried that holdall with me hiding in it back on the train the following day. I travelled all the way back to Paris in it. Throughout the journey, Manu would drop in pieces of food and water. It was hot and stuffy and the smell wasn't very pleasant either. When we arrived back in Paris, I had a new identity. I was sent to live with Manu's cousin in Brittany for the rest of the war.'

'I never knew that,' said Fleur, amazed at Lydia's story. She thought of the photograph of Lydia standing outside a farmhouse with that haunted look in her eyes. It must have been after the escape.

'I stayed with them for three more years and finally, when Paris was liberated, Manu and Adele came for me. They brought me back to Paris and I lived with them. I learned that my father had died whilst being held in a prisoner of war camp. So, Manu and Adele brought me up. That is why they were like parents to me. I had a good life with them and I grew to love them like they were my own parents. They lived a happy and peaceful life after the war.'

'Did you stay in touch with them after you moved to England?' asked Fleur. She couldn't remember Lydia talking about them.

'I did. We wrote regularly and I saw them every year when I returned to Paris,' replied Lydia. 'They never married. They didn't feel it was important. Adele believed you should love without fear, for you never knew when that love would be taken away. Manu died in 1977 and Adele in 1982.'

'Before I was born,' mused Fleur. 'And when did you find out about Blanche and the others?'

'I wasn't told what happened to them until I was older. When I came back to Paris. Manu and Adele sat me down and told me that the truck had been stopped at a roadblock and there had been some sort of disagreement. All I was told was that everyone was killed that night.' Tears fell down Lydia's face. 'I can still feel how utterly devastated I was by the news. I had always hoped they'd escaped. The thought that I'd see Blanche again kept me going while I was in Brittany, the belief that my sister was in Switzerland and free. So to be told they had all been killed, I found it hard to deal with. It should have been me. I always thought that. How could an innocent child be killed by the soldiers? Who would do that?'

'But now, it seems that Blanche escaped somehow,' said Didier.

'I can hardly dare believe it,' said Lydia.

'Let Didier check first,' said Fleur. She was anxious Lydia didn't get her hopes up. What if this Bridget Sutter wasn't Blanche and the painting had just somehow come into her possession? After all, she was refusing to divulge any information about how she got it.

'What happened to Adele's sister?' asked Didier.

'Again, I didn't learn this until later, but she admitted to killing the German officer. She was arrested and executed that night. She gave her life so Adele, Manu and I could live.'

'Oh my goodness. That must have been so hard for Adele. For all of you,' said Fleur, trying to imagine the desperation they must have all felt.

'It was especially hard for Adele. And their father also. He died the following year. Adele said she was sure he died of a broken heart, and if it had not been for Manu, then she would not have survived herself.'

Fleur was speechless for a few minutes. She reached over and hugged Lydia. 'Thank you for sharing your story with us,' she said. 'I'm so sorry for everything you went through.'

Lydia patted Fleur's hand. 'Don't be sorry for me. I was the lucky one.'

Fleur sat back. 'Are you sure you'd like Didier to contact Bridget?'

Lydia nodded. 'I need to know the final part of the story. I need to know if my darling little Blanche survived or not.'

Once again, recalling events of what happened during the war took their toll on Lydia. She looked pale and drawn. Fleur could see the strain it was taking on her grandmother. 'Would you like me to order you some fresh coffee?' she asked.

Lydia shook her head. 'I think I'd just like to sit here awhile.'

'I should leave now,' said Didier, rising to his feet. He rested his hand gently on Lydia's shoulder. 'Thank you for sharing your story, Lydia. I will do my best to contact Bridget Sutter.'

Lydia reached up and covered his hand with hers. 'Thank you, Didier. You're a good man.'

Fleur avoided eye contact with Didier as she walked to the door with him. She wanted to say something to him but didn't know what. Didn't know where to start. She wanted to apologise for jumping to conclusions and misjudging him, but she was still frustrated he hadn't told her about Zenya or Cedric earlier.

So when Didier said a polite goodbye and left, she felt nothing but frustration. She had wanted him to say something. Ask her if she was all right, maybe. She gave a big sigh. She didn't know what she wanted anymore, but she did know she hadn't wanted Didier to leave.

Chapter 40

Fleur

Fleur was woken early the next morning to her hotel phone ringing. She knew before she answered that it would be Didier. Who else would ring her? And to call so early must mean good news. She silently acknowledged that she wanted to hear his voice for no other reason than she had missed him. Which, of course, didn't make sense or at least shouldn't make sense. She snatched her phone from the bedside table. 'Hello,' she said, trying to disguise the sleepiness from her voice.

'It is me – Didier,' he said needlessly.

'I know.' She hoped the smile came through in her voice.

'Sorry if I woke you.'

'It's fine. I'm hoping the early morning call is because you have news from Switzerland.'

'*Alors*, I have heard from Bridget Sutter's daughter. Bridget wants to meet Lydia.'

'Oh my God! That's fantastic! Oh, thank you. Thank you so much.' Fleur planted her feet on the floor, ready to rush to tell Lydia. 'How did Bridget react to the news?'

'According to the daughter, Bridget was shocked but not entirely surprised. Bridget has not said anything else only that she wants Lydia to be the first to hear what happened that night.'

'This is amazing. I could cry,' said Fleur, feeling the tears well up in her eyes. 'Did she say how they were going to meet? Does Lydia need to go there? Will Bridget come to England?'

'No. Bridget is coming to Paris. She will be getting a flight in today and wants to meet Lydia tomorrow.'

'I can hardly believe this. It's like a dream. I can't wait to tell Lydia.'

'I have offered to meet them at the airport and then drive them over to you tomorrow. If that is all right with you and Lydia?'

'Of course it is. Thank you so much, Didier. I really appreciate everything you've done.' She suddenly felt unsure of herself. She wanted to say she was glad she had met him. The realisation that her contact with him was drawing to a close was a sobering thought. And there was the reinforcement that underpinned her whole belief system about love; leaving or losing someone you cared about hurt.

'I have to go,' he said abruptly. 'If I have any more news, I'll be in touch. Let me know if there are any problems or Lydia does not feel up to it. Otherwise, I'll see you tomorrow when I bring them over at eleven o'clock.'

Fleur felt a little deflated at his business-like approach but she was too excited about telling Lydia to dwell on it. It was her own fault Didier had cooled off. She had no one else to blame.

Lydia was stunned when Fleur told her the news. 'I can't believe this,' she said several times. 'Tomorrow – after all this time, more than seventy years – I will see my sister again. She wants to see me. I am so very thankful.'

'We should do something to celebrate today,' said Fleur. 'Is there anything you'd like to do?'

'I think actually I would like a quiet day, not doing anything very much,' said Lydia. 'I need to have my strength for tomorrow. Today, I'd like to just sit and be.'

'That's fine. You can do whatever you want,' said Fleur. She hoped her grandmother was all right and wasn't asking for a quiet day because she didn't feel well. Lydia wasn't one to complain. Fleur decided to stay close and just keep an eye on her. 'I'll have a quiet day too, I think.'

'You're not seeing Didier?'

'No.' Fleur got up and walked over to the window. 'We like each other but we're not compatible.'

'You make it sound like one of your work experiments at the lab,' complained Lydia. 'You came to that conclusion quickly.'

'I don't want a long-distance relationship,' said Fleur, turning to look at Lydia. 'And that's what it would be.'

Lydia tutted. 'Paris is hardly long-distance these days.'

Fleur still wasn't convinced. 'I think I'll go for a walk,' she said.

'So you don't have to listen to me.' There was a twinkle in Lydia's eyes. 'And don't deny it.'

Fleur went over and gave Lydia a kiss and a hug. 'No comment. See you later, Nan.'

The day had dragged on endlessly and Fleur had been glad to go to bed that night. She hadn't heard from Didier and she found herself rather more disappointed than she deserved to be.

Now, she was sitting in the hotel's coffee lounge with Lydia, watching the hands of the clock limp their way towards eleven. Lydia had nursed a cup of tea for the past twenty minutes and Fleur could tell she was becoming more anxious as they neared the allotted time.

Fleur had received one text message from Didier to say they were on their way over. Her phone pinged again.

'They're here,' said Fleur. 'Didier has just texted me.'

Lydia put down her cup and tapped at her hair. 'Do I look all right?'

'You look perfect.' She reached over and held Lydia's hands. 'This is it, Nan. Any second now, you're going to see Blanche.' Fleur realised she had subconsciously switched to calling her that. She hoped it was a good omen for the reunion.

Lydia nodded. 'I hope my heart can take this.'

And then she was gripping Fleur's hands tightly, looking beyond her. Tears filled Lydia's eyes and she got to her feet. Fleur turned and saw Didier ushering in two women: Blanche and her daughter.

Lydia moved towards them, stopping in the middle of the coffee lounge. Blanche's hair was the exact shade of white as her sister's and shaped in a neat bob. She was slightly built and had the same elegant way about her as Lydia did.

Blanche gave a small gasp. 'Eva? It's you. Please tell me it's you.'

Lydia raced towards Blanche. 'My darling little sister. Blanche.' And then they were hugging each other, both of them crying as they spoke rapidly in French to each other. They stood back, so they could see each other's faces clearly and then they were embracing again.

Fleur realised she too was crying. Such an emotional reunion. She looked over and could see Blanche's daughter wiping tears away. Didier looked up at her, giving her a questioning look.

Fleur nodded. 'Thank you,' she said. She went over to him. 'Thank you so much, Didier.' She wanted to hug him but stopped herself.

Several minutes later, they were all sitting down with fresh tea and coffee. The excitement and emotion of the meeting under more control.

'Tell me, Blanche. What happened to you?' said Lydia. 'I was told everyone was killed.'

Blanche nodded. 'That is true,' she said speaking in English with a Swiss accent. Her voice, however, sounded just like Lydia's. 'I have only been able to piece together my story in the last eighteen months or so. I was only six when all this happened and I don't remember very much. All I knew at the time was that we had been smuggled out of Paris in boxes. When they got us out, I remember I couldn't find you. I didn't know where you were. I thought perhaps you had gone on ahead.'

'Didier has kindly told us what happened,' said Anna, Blanche's daughter. 'We've been able to put most of the pieces together.'

Blanche resumed her account. 'I just remember the truck we were travelling in being stopped. There was shouting and arguing. Thomas's mother made us climb out of the truck. She told us to run away and hide. To stay very quiet and she would find us,' said Blanche. 'I was first out and I remember running across the road and into a field. When I looked around, no one was with me. I could hear more shouting and then there were shots fired. After that, everything was quiet. I was so scared. I just kept running. I didn't know where I was going. I don't know how long I ran for, but eventually I collapsed in the middle of a forest.'

'Did you have anything with you?' asked Fleur. 'Any papers? A bag? Food?'

'Nothing at all,' recalled Blanche. 'I had left it all in the truck when I ran. I was found the next day by a farmer. He thought I was dead at first, he told me. He carried me back to his house where his wife looked after me. I was too scared to tell them anything. Not even my name. I knew I had a new name but I couldn't remember it.' She looked down and breathed deeply.

'My mother suffered with shock from it all,' said Anna taking up the story. 'The couple who found her had connections with the Resistance and they were able to get her over the border to Geneva. She was taken in by a young couple who eventually adopted her.'

'Didn't they ever try to find your family?' asked Fleur.

'I did tell them about my sister, Eva,' said Blanche. 'My parents did try to find her.'

'But of course, I wasn't called Eva Rashal anymore,' said Lydia. 'They would never have been able to find me.'

'And I was no longer Blanche Rashal. I was Bridget Keller. Later when I married, I became Bridget Sutter.'

'If it wasn't for the painting, we wouldn't be here,' said Anna. 'It had been sewn into the hem of my mother's coat.'

Blanche looked at Lydia. 'The man from the museum did that, didn't he?'

Lydia nodded. 'Yes. Manu.'

'Manu,' repeated Blanche. 'I was younger than you. I didn't remember his name, but I do remember him coming to the attic with the paintings and our teacher and Thomas's mother sewed them into our clothes.'

Fleur looked across at Didier. This was what he was here for. 'My grandmother said you were all given a picture as insurance.'

'That's right. I kept mine, never understanding the importance,' replied Blanche. 'My adoptive parents weren't educated people; they didn't know what it was. They thought it was more of a keepsake. I used to keep the picture on my wall. It was a reminder of my previous life. My only connection to my family who I thought had all perished.'

'Yes, it wasn't until my own daughter saw an article online while she was researching her arts degree that we realised what it was,' explained Anna. 'That's how we ended up here, returning it to the museum.'

'When the curator told me about the lady with the white hair who came every year to the school, I knew it had to be you,' said Blanche, gripping Lydia's hands. 'I couldn't think who else it could be. I made Anna bring me back a few weeks ago and I tied the shoe on the gate.'

'You kept that shoe all that time?' asked Fleur.

Blanche nodded. 'When we were in the attic, Adele would let us dance when no one else was in the school. I kept my ballet shoes with me. Maman had tucked them in my bag when she first took us there,' explained Blanche. 'I kept them with me all the time. I took them in the pocket of my coat when we went from the attic to the museum and were then hidden in the crates.'

'Maman had repaired the toe,' said Lydia running her finger over the faded thread. 'You knew I'd recognise it.'

'Yes. I did.' Blanche's voice broke and she dabbed at her eyes with a tissue her daughter proffered.

Fleur had brought down the book Manu had compiled and showed it to Blanche and Anna. 'He kept a record of where all the artwork went,' explained Fleur. She turned to the page where the Valois collection was recorded.

'And there is still one painting missing?' asked Anna.

'Yes, sadly,' said Lydia. 'It happens to be the one Manu gave me. I've always assumed he took it back. It was in the hem of my coat, just like yours. As a young child, I didn't give it much thought and neither Manu nor Adele spoke about it.'

'That does seem strange,' said Anna.

'Yes,' agreed Didier. 'Manu had been reuniting all the lost and stolen artwork so I do not understand why the August miniature, which Lydia had, remains missing.'

The conversation moved on and Fleur was happy to sit and listen to their stories of their lives since that night in Lyon. Lydia and Blanche held hands a lot, laughed a lot and cried together. It was both joyous and desperately sad all at the same time.

The time passed so quickly, but after several hours, both women had tired themselves out. 'We shall talk more tomorrow,' said Lydia as she hugged her sister. 'I'm so happy, Blanche. I feel a huge weight has been lifted from my shoulders.'

'It is the same for me too, Eva.'

As Fleur went to reach for her glass of water, she somehow managed to knock it over. To her horror it spilled over Manu's notebook. 'Oh no! I'm so sorry!' Fleur grabbed a napkin and started patting at the book. In those short few seconds, the book had managed to absorb much of the water. 'The edges are soaked,' said Fleur. 'I'm really sorry.'

'Don't worry. It was an accident,' said Anna.

'Here, let me,' said Didier arriving back with some more napkins he'd grabbed from the bar. He proceeded to wipe the notebook's cover and inspect for any long-lasting damage. 'I think the pages themselves are all right.'

Fleur saw him peer at the inside cover of the book and then pick at the backing paper. 'What's that?' Fleur looked over his shoulder and watched him carefully peel the backing sheet away from the hard cover. 'Oh. My. God,' was all Fleur could say.

Didier looked up at her in amazement as he slid a piece of paper out from behind the back sheet. '*Merde*,' he whispered several times to himself. He held the single sheet of paper up.

'*Août*,' gasped Lydia. 'It's the missing painting.'

It took several minutes for everyone to get over the find. 'Is it genuine?' asked Fleur.

'As far as I can tell,' said Didier. 'It has to be, surely. Why would it be hidden in the back of Manu's book?'

'Why is the big question,' said Fleur.

'He wanted me to find it,' said Lydia. Everyone turned to look at her. 'It was my insurance. My proof of who I am. My proof of what happened. He was keeping it safe for me.'

'He hid it there on purpose?' asked Fleur.

'He must have done. He left the book in safekeeping for me.'

'He probably thought you'd find it sooner,' said Didier.

'But it's found now and it can be reunited with the collection,' said Lydia with a smile. 'I don't want the reward. What do I want with fifty thousand euros?'

'Maybe you could give it to Fleur?' suggested Anna.

Fleur shook her head. 'I don't want it. It's never been about the picture. It's always been about my nan and her story.' She looked over at Didier who had barely been able to tear his eyes away from the watercolour.

He met her gaze. 'I don't want it either. I might have done before but not now. Happiness at having the Valois collection complete has no price. Money can't buy that sort of happiness.'

'Technically, you found it so it is rightfully yours,' said Lydia.

'That is very kind of you but I will graciously decline,' said Didier.

'You could do a lot with that kind of money,' continued Lydia.

'True but I think it should go to a better cause than my bank balance.'

There was a small silence as everyone once again gazed at the painting. It was Lydia who spoke. 'I think I'd like to use the money to sponsor a place at a dance school. I think Adele and Manu would approve of that.'

'I think they would too,' agreed Blanche. 'That's a very good idea.'

Chapter 41

Fleur

It had been a long day and Fleur couldn't have been happier with the way the reunion between Lydia and Bridget had gone, or rather Eva and Blanche. Blanche was staying for another day, along with her daughter, and the two sisters were already planning on Lydia going to Geneva before Christmas and Blanche making a trip to England the following spring. It was the perfect ending and Fleur couldn't be happier for her grandmother. Finally, she had closure.

Fleur showered and sat on the bed in her towel, still mulling it all over. So much had happened in the last few days, it was hard to take everything in. She picked up her phone, pretending to herself she was checking social media, but really she was looking to see if Didier had messaged her. He hadn't and the disappointment was undeniable.

Another hour of pacing her room passed by with Fleur trying to occupy herself by drying her hair and styling it, attempting to concentrate on a TV programme and scrolling aimlessly through social media. Fleur gave up and went down to the bar, ordering herself a wine. She sat down in one of the armchairs. What had her life come to? Sitting drinking alone in a hotel bar.

She had just ordered her second glass of wine when her phone pinged through a message.

Didier: I hope you are OK. I have been thinking about you.

She couldn't deny the wave of both relief and excitement at his message.

Fleur: I'm OK. Sitting in the hotel bar. Been thinking about you too.

She took a discreet selfie of her holding up her wine glass and sent it to him.

Didier: I hope Jean-Paul is looking after you.

Fleur: Just checked. Must be his night off.

When no more messages came through, Fleur ordered herself another glass of wine. She'd just have this and then go to bed. It was at that point, a man who she'd spied sitting at the bar earlier, came over.

'Do you mind?' he said indicating to the seat opposite her. He put his whisky down on the table before Fleur even answered. 'Sorry, just need to send a text,' he said, his English accent clear. He sat down and made a big display of getting out his phone and texting a message. He glanced up at Fleur. 'Just texting my mother. She's not been well.'

Fleur smiled, wishing she hadn't ordered that third glass of wine. 'I'll leave you to it,' she said, reaching for the glass.

'Oh, don't go on my behalf. I'm done now,' said the man. 'My name's Brett. Sorry this probably sounds like a cheesy chat-up. Honestly, it's not.' He gave a laugh.

It did indeed sound like a cheesy chat-up, but Fleur kept the thought to herself. 'I'm Fleur,' she found herself saying.

'Can I get you another drink?' asked Brett.

Fleur hesitated. If she said yes, she was practically agreeing to being picked up. A one-night stand with a stranger, who probably wasn't called Brett, and was on a work trip. Was this what she wanted? No, it wasn't. She thought of Didier. That's who she wanted and she wanted more than a one-night stand or a holiday fling with him. She realised that now.

'I'm here for the rest of the week,' Brett was saying. 'What about you? Might be nice to hook up for a few days, you know for R&R. Downtime.' He winked at her. 'Did you want that drink?'

'No, I don't, thank you,' she said with confidence.

'Ah, that's too bad,' said Brett, making a sad face. 'You sure I can't tempt you? No strings and all that.'

'No. Sorry,' said Fleur. 'But thank you, you've really helped me.'

Brett looked confused. 'I have?'

'Yeah. Goodnight, Brett, or whatever your name is.' She got up, leaving her unfinished wine on the table.

Brett called after her. 'Thanks for the drink.' He picked up her glass and downed it.

Fleur carried on walking across the room towards the door. She looked up and stopped in her tracks. Didier was leaning against the end of the bar watching her. There was a Scotch and a glass of wine in front of him. He nudged the wine glass a couple of inches in her direction.

Fleur sat herself down on the bar stool. 'Just so you know,' she said. 'I'm not into one-night stands or holiday romances.'

Didier took the bar stool next to hers. 'Is that right?' He sipped his drink, looking at her reflection in the mirror behind the bar.

'Yes, that's right. I'm an all-or-nothing sort of girl.'

She looked at his reflection and a slow smile spread across his face. 'That's my kind of girl,' said Didier, raising his glass to her.

'I'd like to be,' said Fleur. The nerves in her stomach were working overtime. If she had any doubt that she wasn't ready to be brave and at least try to make things work with Didier, then they were evaporating with every word.

Didier turned his bar stool to face her and twisted Fleur's seat around to him. 'All or nothing?'

She nodded. 'Yes. I'm scared to fall in love with you, but I'm even more scared of walking away.'

Didier leaned over and kissed her. 'Don't be scared of love. Be scared of never knowing how good love is.' He kissed her again, this time a little longer, before pulling away to look at her. 'Are sure you do not want to take up your other offer?'

Fleur glanced over at Brett who was watching open-mouthed. 'Definitely not.'

Didier got up from his seat and took Fleur's hand. 'There's a bottle of champagne on ice in my room.'

'Your room?'

'I booked a room as soon as I got here. Just in case.'

'I admire your foresight.' Fleur laughed out loud, then grew serious. 'I don't want to break the party atmosphere,' she said. They were walking over to the elevator hand in hand.

'But what?' Didier's expression looked serious and he jabbed the button to summon the lift.

Fleur squeezed his hand, drawing on that feeling of safety she somehow got from him. 'I can't make any promises and I have no idea how we're going to work this, but I really want to try. I'm just a little nervous, that's all.'

Didier's face relaxed and he slipped his arm around her shoulder, pulling her in towards him. 'It is OK to be nervous, just do not be scared. I promise you can trust me.'

They stepped into the empty lift and the doors closed behind them. 'You just might have to be a bit patient,' said Fleur, fiddling with the lapel of his jacket. 'All this is a new approach for me. I mean, I'm used to putting up barriers, not breaking them down, and I haven't felt like this before.'

Didier put his finger to her lips. 'Stop talking for a moment.' He kissed her and Fleur was sure one of her barriers was already disintegrating.

Chapter 42

Adele

Paris, July 1952

'How do I look?' asked Lydia, coming into the living room.

Adele put down the book she was reading and rose from the sofa, going to stand in front of the young woman who'd come to their home as a child. 'You look beautiful.'

'And so grown-up,' said Manu, standing in the doorway.

'I should hope I do look grown-up,' said Lydia. 'I'm twenty years old and about to leave for England to start married life.' Her hand went to her stomach, which was only just beginning to show the beginning of the new life she carried.

'I'm going to miss you so much,' said Adele, making every effort to keep her emotions on an even keel.

'I'm going to miss you too,' replied Lydia. She looked over at Manu. 'I owe you both so much and to stand here and thank you both for what you have done for me feels so inadequate.'

Manu pushed himself away from the doorframe and came over to her and Adele. 'And we should thank you for bringing so much love and light into our lives at a time of despair and darkness. I wish it had been under different circumstances, but you saved us as much as we saved you.'

'That's true,' agreed Adele. 'After losing my own family, Manu was all I had and we may not have been blessed with children of our own, but we were given you instead. You

have been everything to us. I hope we have been enough.'
Tears gathered in her eyes. She had never tried to take the
place of Jacqueline, Lydia's mother, but she had hoped she
might fill just a little of the gap her friend had left behind.

'You've been so much more than anyone could ever have
expected you to be,' replied Lydia. She hugged Adele fiercely.
'If I were to have to choose anyone to look after me, then I
would choose you and Manu every single time.' She pulled
away and hugged Manu. 'You saved my life.'

After a few moments, Manu stepped back. 'I have something
for you,' he said. 'It's for your new home in England.' He
went over to the bureau and from the drawer, took out a
small parcel wrapped in brown paper. He handed it to Lydia.

She unwrapped the gift and gasped at the watercolour
before her. It was a miniature painting of a ballerina standing
at the ballet barre. 'It's beautiful,' she said.

'It's a Valois,' said Manu.

Lydia looked up at him. 'Valois? As in the Valois collection
you are trying to track down from the war?'

Manu nodded. 'The very same. But, of course, this isn't
one of them. This is one I bought many years ago when I
first discovered Valois's works. It reminded me of Adele.'

'Shouldn't you have it?' asked Lydia looking at Adele.

'No, not at all. We want you to have it. We want it to go
to someone who loves ballet just as I do and that person
can only be you.'

Lydia looked at the painting. 'Thank you so much. I shall
treasure it for the rest of my life. It will have pride of place
in my new home.'

Manu cleared his throat and checked his wristwatch. '*Alors*,
it's time we should be going. Your train leaves in an hour.'

'Have you got everything you need?' asked Adele suddenly
panicking they might have forgotten to pack something.
'You've got your train ticket safe, haven't you? And your
ticket for the boat? And Robert is meeting you at Portsmouth,
isn't he?'

'Yes, yes and yes,' said Lydia with a smile. 'Please don't worry. Everything is sorted. I've done this journey before on my own.'

'I know but I'm allowed to worry,' protested Adele.

Adele held Lydia's hand all the way to the train station. She wanted to soak up every last moment she had with this wonderful young woman. She knew she'd see her again. She and Manu already had plans to visit Lydia in England, but Adele knew it would be different then. Lydia was a married woman, with her own child on the way. For now Adele wanted to hold on to the young woman who'd first come into her life as Eva Rashal on her first day at school.

So much had happened since then and much as they tried not to dwell on the awful events, they couldn't and shouldn't be forgotten. They were the events that had shaped them, brought them together and allowed them to live without fear or regret.

The journey to the station went far too quickly for Adele's liking, and it was only a matter of minutes before they were at the ticket barrier saying their goodbyes.

'I'll see you again soon,' Lydia said. 'I'll write every week and phone you when I can.'

Adele hugged Lydia for the umpteenth time, just as the guard made the last call for passengers to board the train. Adele held Lydia at arm's length. 'Your mother would be so proud of you, *ma petite puce*.'

'And she would be proud of you too,' replied Lydia.

Adele didn't try to hide her tears as Manu helped Lydia aboard and then, with Manu at her side, his arm around her shoulder, Adele watched as the train disappeared out of the station.

Acknowledgements

As always with writing a book, it is never a lone venture and there are many, many people behind the scenes to thank for their hard work and wonderful support. So, to all my family and friends at home, to my writer friends and colleagues, my agent, my editors, the teams at both the agency and the publishers and my wonderful readers – thank you so much for being there. I couldn't do this without you all.

About the Author

Suzanne Fortin writes women's fiction dual timeline, often against the backdrop of France, and in particular Southern Brittany, which inspires the settings of her books. Despite having a home in the region for over 20 years, Suzanne still wrestles with fluency in the Breton dialogue!

Suzanne also writes mystery and suspense as Sue Fortin where she is a *USA Today* bestseller and Amazon UK #1 and Amazon US #3 bestseller. She has sold over a million copies of her books and been translated into multiple languages.

About Embla Books

Embla Books is a digital-first publisher of standout commercial adult fiction. Passionate about storytelling, the team at Embla publish books that will make you 'laugh, love, look over your shoulder and lose sleep'. Launched by Bonnier Books UK in 2021, the imprint is named after the first woman from the creation myth in Norse mythology, who was carved by the gods from a tree trunk found on the seashore – an image of the kind of creative work and crafting that writers do, and a symbol of how stories shape our lives.

Find out about some of our other books and stay in touch:

Twitter, Facebook, Instagram: @emblabooks
Newsletter: https://bit.ly/emblanewsletter